SHOT ON LOCATION

ALSO BY STAN CUTLER

Best Performance by a Patsy
The Face on the Cutting Room Floor

S H O T
O N
L O C A T I O N

Stan Cutler

A DUTTON BOOK

DUTTON
Published by the Penguin Group
Penguin Books USA Inc., 375 Hudson Street,
New York, New York 10014, U.S.A.
Penguin Books Ltd, 27 Wrights Lane,
London W8 5TZ, England
Penguin Books Australia Ltd, Ringwood,
Victoria, Australia
Penguin Books Canada Ltd, 10 Alcorn Avenue,
Toronto, Ontario, Canada M4V 3B2
Penguin Books (N.Z.) Ltd, 182–190 Wairau Road,
Auckland 10, New Zealand

Penguin Books Ltd, Registered Offices:
Harmondsworth, Middlesex, England

First published by Dutton, an imprint of New American Library,
a division of Penguin Books USA Inc.
Distributed in Canada by McClelland & Stewart Inc.

First Printing, February, 1993
10 9 8 7 6 5 4 3 2 1

REGISTERED TRADEMARK—MARCA REGISTRADA

LIBRARY OF CONGRESS CATALOGING-IN-PUBLICATION DATA:
    Cutler, Stan.
        Shot on location / Stan Cutler.
            p.   cm.
        ISBN 0-525-93576-2
        I. Title.
        PS3553.U84S47   1992   92-31209
813'.54—dc20   CIP

Printed in the United States of America
Set in Garamond Light

For Victoria
without whose support and constant presence
this book would have been completed
six months earlier ...
... but without whose love, not at all.

ACKNOWLEDGMENTS

Special, heartfelt thanks to Jane Gelfman, my peerless literary representative, who persevered and continued to believe when even I despaired.

I am grateful as well to Laurie Bernstein, my astute and sensitive editor, who puts her finger on all the right places.

To Hal Miles, for his musicological research, which he pursued past all reason or value—other than a manifestation of friendship, which is not the worst of motives.

And finally, I am indebted to Stanley Silverman for reading the manuscript and fastening his nitpicking, compulsively uncompromising eye on certain areas of fact and syntax—a quality that's useful, if not particularly endearing.

Prologue

The house was, at best, a gigantic mistake. A melange of disparate elements, it might have been the mutant offspring of an architectural misalliance between a South Pacific potentate and an Iranian lottery winner.

Situated between Malibu and Point Dume on a bluff overlooking its own private beach, it had been built in a defilade created to protect its privacy (and coincidentally the sensibilities of others with better taste) and afford added structural integrity against the ocean's vagaries and occasional hurricanic violence.

Thus, it was mercifully invisible both from the Pacific Coast Highway to the east and its neighbors to the north and south.

It was huge, yet because of its design and geography possessed less a look of solitary splendor than that of a building shunned. The original intent to render an earth-clinging refuge, hunkered down against the forces of nature and space, had instead, on execution, produced an effect more closely resembling an enormous wreck disgorged from the sea, cringing on the beach in embarrassment.

At three-forty a.m. a figure detached itself from the shadow of the main house and was vaguely silhouetted in the waning moonlight silently padding toward the guest house. It was that of the Outsider, a name self-designated, but for good and sufficient reason.

The main building was loosely connected to the guest

1

house by a pathway of scattered flat stones. These were assidu-
ously avoided, as each foot instead was carefully and sound-
lessly placed on the sand between.

None of the various security appliances had been tripped;
none of the dogs barked. Had anyone chanced to observe,
such movement would not have been considered remarkable,
the traffic to and from the guest cottage adhering to no particular pattern or time frame. In fact, the blare of rock music,
even now alternately audible with the sound of waves crashing
on the beach, was unexceptional, at this or any hour. (In fairness, it could as easily have been jazz, or even classical—being
a house of eclectic tastes.)

Though no conversation could be heard, that, too, indicated little. Besides the likelihood of being overwhelmed by
the music and the ocean's noises, the absence of conversation
could as easily signify the occupants were asleep (inured by
aural conditioning to ignore such sound), awash in sexual
activity, or simply zonked out. In any event, prudence dictated
caution, to avoid prompting the attention of a potential witness. Or alerting one's prey.

The Outsider, of course, knew the workings of the compound intimately. (And most especially the location of all its
occupants this night.) One could possess intimate knowledge
without being an intimate. This was an establishment where
one could even reside and remain an Outsider. For there was,
despite all the people living here and their varying degrees
of acceptance, only one significant, indisputable Insider—and
that was the house's owner and master: three-time Oscar winner, actor Stacy Jaeger.

Given the hour and custom, the Star was undoubtedly
asleep in his huge master suite atop the main building, also
undoubtedly alone, since his interests in things carnal had
long since yielded to things gastronomic.

In any event, he had also long since distanced himself from
any interest in what went on in the guest cottage, or in the
lives of its occupants.

In fairness, his disinterest extended beyond this immediate
circle to embrace most of the world, its works, woes, and

functions. Though in all, he maintained a contrary *appearance* of avid interest. Women, politics—even the more than casual observer would consider him an advocate—he *was* an actor (and did have public relations people).

But at the gut level, figuratively and literally, food, food, food was his monomaniacal preoccupation. The hardest addiction.

He no longer made movies, he made meals. Indeed, it was only in their contemplation and consumption that Jaeger these days became fully alive. Not since the time of the late Orson Welles had such a giant allowed his accomplishments to be eclipsed by such a singular failing.

And as Jaeger presumably slept in sated exhaustion, the Outsider proceeded on cautious feet toward the guest house. Its occupants of record being Stacy, Jr., the Star's first son, though namesake alone was no guarantee of preference, the Outsider would know in intimate detail; Carey—second born, with good and sufficient complaints of his own; and Iris, third child and most apparent beloved—though at such an emotional remove as to derive little benefit from the fact.

To the official company could be found, at various times, girlfriends for the boys—boyfriends for the girl. None of which, save one, was the shadowy wraith expecting to find in attendance, having with considerable effort established as much.

So now it was that the Outsider stopped, with heightened senses sniffing the wind for any lingering hint of danger, nourishing courage with air, and with each breath gathering rage to transmute into energy, the better to prepare for what lay just ahead.

Outsider, Insider—irrelevant terms of remote interest only to the individuals concerned. Only one real relationship obtained—that of servant to master. Service to the Star remained always at the core. It was what the compound, its occupants, the entire direction of its personnel and accoutrements thereto were designed to provide.

And now, the Outsider, personal feelings, resentment, neglect aside, would render another, most outstanding service, even though it had not been sought. But, indeed, wasn't it part of the job to anticipate the needs, whether he knew it or not, of Him From Whom All Goodness Flowed?

But it was remarkable, nonetheless, that the Star somehow tolerated all the unremitting abuse visited upon his favorite child; that he so little protected her from immediate dangers. It was as if he had determined that somehow her madness had caused it to happen, and that it was enough she visit serially the most costly—and often mercifully remote—sanitoria of the world for protracted periods of time. That he was thus discharging his paternal responsibility, but that any quotidian intervention was too personal and painful to be involved in. This, while her current victimization was so apparent to everyone else.

Well, he was a Star, whose eyes dwelt mostly on his own image, and even when turned outwardly, saw only what he wanted to see. And there was little doubt he would never appreciate in any significant or even conscious way the favor he was about to receive. But of course, that's what made the doing so wonderful—it would be without overt compensation. At least from him. But it *would* be in the Star's interest, no question of that. A surcease from the pain, or minimally, distraction. A setting of priorities with the family put in its proper perspective, and he free to pursue his calling—indeed, *forced* to render obeisance to that genius with further accomplishment.

Three forty-seven.

The Outsider crossed the remaining distance, eased open the always unlocked door, and entered the building. Crossing the living room, silencer-equipped pistol in hand, and momentarily pausing at the bedroom door of the Favored Child. Oh, how one yearned to enter that door and lie on that bed.

The world would soon enough be told that Iris, poor misbegotten child, and the sole potential witness, having taken her customary two Halcions, had slept through it all—no doubt attired in a pair of her trademark-color purple pj's.

The door was open. A nightlight on. The target was elsewhere—as reconnaissance had indicated.

With a cautious tread, breath withheld—no time to blow it now—the Outsider tiptoed over to the kitchen.

And there, as planned and expected, sprawled asleep with his head on the table (by arrangement, design, and chemical aid), was Wesley Crewe—bringer of bruises, causer of contusions—the Favored Child's lover.

All the pieces were in place, all the players on their figurative marks. Just beyond Crewe's outstretched hand was an overflowing ashtray, full of cigarette butts and marijuana roaches. An overturned glass was mired in sticky amber fluid, over which several flies hovered stuporously, sharing an interest in its potent remains.

The Outsider took three deep yoga breaths to clear the lungs and concentrate necessary energy. Then, focusing on the predesignated target area, calmly pumped three silencer bullets into Crewe's head.

Which, incidentally, the Outsider couldn't help noticing, sounded exactly like someone spitting out cherry pits.

Three fifty-two.

1

Rayford Goodman

It was a dumb case of neglect. Which is surprising for me. I come from a generation takes care of business. I get a ticket, I pay it; no getting stopped for a broken taillight and busted for outstanding warrants. I don't lose my keys. Forget my wallet. I don't need a bank card to get money nights or weekends. I'm almost always reliable because it's logical and makes life easier. Still, every great once in a while I do manage the dumb thing and end up paying dues.

I'd been entertaining—or vice versa—this semi-professional friend of mind, Julie by name. Julie was of a somewhat younger generation—which put her in a lot of company. Most people are younger when your main war was three or four back (no charge for Panama).

Also no big surprise she put a sort of more modern spin to what we cleverly used to call the world's oldest profession. The girl (lady, woman, independent contractor) had become a very gadget-positive, high-tech, cost-effective entreprenette.

Which tended to cut into the spontaneousness of the thing just a smidge. Like being beeper-paged to her call-waiting cellular phone during the hands-on part of the user-friendly operation. Another client wasn't too hard a guess. ("Just stepping into the tub, can I get back to you in, say, twenty minutes?")

I'd called Julie in from the bullpen for short-term relief following a wipeout in the meaningful-relationship playoffs with my amateur girlfriend, Francine by name. Since my sexual

7

batting average had been sort of on injured reserve after an earlier heart attack, and Francie had raised it into the all-star category, I wasn't about to risk another slump—I think maybe that's enough with the baseball metaphors—when the very same girlfriend (ladyfriend, personfriend?) saw fit to dump upon me. Which she did for reasons known mostly and making sense only to herself. But you had to feel were related to a leaving-me-out-of-it, self-made decision not to have our love child. My educated guess because her age and evil ways. What's these days cutely called "substance abuse."

At any rate, Julie had been up to the job, and pleased to say, so was I. Nevertheless, habits dying hard, I couldn't resist making a halfhearted stab at a favored-nations discount which she turned down pretty stone cold.

"Maybe when you're a senior citizen—not too long, right?"

You can imagine, that didn't do a whole lot for me finance-*or* ego-wise. And about wound up the transaction.

We were sitting in my bedroom, the radio tuned to KHIP, d.j. Steve Sommer doing his thing, where the station offered a thousand dollars if they couldn't find any jazz record you named in thirty minutes (this time "King Oliver, Gennett Records, 1923, 'Big Mama's Cooking Up Some Blues,' on callback beating Alan Frank of La Mesa, at one-twenty-three in the a.m."). I knew the feeling. Bartender . . .

I walked Julie out to her car (twelve minutes on the clock since a certain high-tech, cost-effective call), where I planted a no-hard-feelings kiss on her cute little interface, and she was off on her merry networking way.

I caught myself giving off one of those little sighs people tend to do when they get older. I'd have to watch it. If I wasn't careful, next thing I'd be making funny little smacking noises with my lips. And growing longer ears.

I stopped by the box to pick up the mail I'd forgot, and headed into the garage. That was so I'd be right next to the garbage cans while I sorted it. Any envelope with "Confidential," "For Immediate Action," or "Rayford Goodman has just won eighty-seven quadrillion dollars" got tossed unopened.

I was just sifting through the junk when I heard the nasty complaint of the cat sort of lived there.

He was a big guy, with a permanent snarly expression, my guess when he learned about biting somebody's electric cord. He'd moved away from wherever that was and settled on the roof of my car, deciding it would be OK for me to feed him long as I didn't make any emotional demands. Like wanting to touch or coochy-coo. Fat chance.

I called him the Phantom of the Garage, and we left each other pretty much alone. Except to remind me to feed him. Which he was now doing with a very whiney yowl I didn't like any more in a cat than a person.

"Just a damn minute, I'll get to it," I whined back.

But first I quickly finished running through the junk. This included a one-time-only chance to own an exact miniature replica of Lindbergh's *Spirit of St. Louis* in a rare and precious alloy; some kind of pitch for what looked like the pampas puppies of Patagonia (actually Doris Day), and a somehow too official-looking envelope to just toss. What it turned out—a summons to jury duty. Which gets us back to the neglect I was talking about earlier.

I vaguely remembered a questionnaire some weeks before.

I think at the time I opened it—during Happy Hour (or hour three of Happy Hour)—the idea of being on a jury seemed fall-down funny. (Just because I said I'm responsible doesn't mean I'm not into good times.) And either for laughs, or a free drink, I somehow sent it back without copping out.

Well, of course I could still get out of it. But it would of been a lot easier they first sent the notice. What it boiled down to now was a pain-in-the-ass drive down L.A. Civic Center and explaining to them no thanks, another time perhaps. At which point the feline freeloader took a swipe at my ankle, backed quickly out of range, and gave off another surly yowl. "All right, Phantom—a fucking minute," I said, realizing I'd turned into one of those people talked to animals. I don't know why he thought he was entitled to instant gratification.

Speaking of which, thinking back to Julie, mine had been a bit more instant than I'd of preferred.

*　　*　　*

Superior Court sat at and in the Criminal Courts Building, 210 West Temple Street, in the liver of L.A.

There is something basically downbeat about any downtown. While downtown keeps getting reborn more often than a Tennessee Christian, no matter what they do it still keeps turning out Scranton or Newark. Definitely not something belongs in California.

But I wouldn't be there that long anyway. I'd just pop on in, give 'em my medical history, and get myself excused because of my delicate condition. No way they'd want me anyhow. Once I cleared up I was really a private detective and not basically a writer, like I'd playfully said on the questionnaire.

As I got near the front of the building, I could see it was going to take a little longer than I thought, since there were about two or three hundred people in line to get through security. We live in troubled times.

It took about forty-five minutes just to get to the metal detector. I had to admire how on the ball they were. The machine was so fine-tuned I beeped it out even after twice emptying my pockets. And only got a pass when it turned out it was the metal band on my Hong Kong imitation Ebel watch kept setting things off. (At least it wasn't plastic.)

They were so busy checking me out they totally missed the guy behind me setting off the buzzer. (Being a professional, *I* took note he was about five-foot-seven, maybe a hundred thirty to forty pounds, dark hair on a low forehead, one continuous eyebrow on a face with a five o'clock shadow at nine forty-five in the morning. The only thing missing was a checkered kaffiyeh and a T-shirt saying, "Yasser, That's My Baby.")

There being enormous numbers of crooks and lawyers (some no doubt both), and potential juries, and hangers-on, and workers, and families and friends and enemies and finks and cops, it took almost ten minutes to get an elevator. I could see this was going to be the Ventura Freeway of courts. I finally got my floor, then spent another seven or eight minutes following various dumb signs and dopey instructions to find the room I'd been commanded to appear at. Then figure out the notice which more or less said if you want out of it, you need a sworn written medical excuse. And this is the wrong building to take it to.

By that time I was late for assembly and had to put off getting out of it till after the orientation lecture.

This was given by a gum-chewing, monstrously overweight lady who explained the history of the Anglo-American judicial system, the meaning of the Magna Carta, and which part of the room was for smoking.

She then went into great lengths how we qualified for our five dollars a day, plus mileage one way (weren't we supposed to go home?), and how if we didn't check in and follow approved procedures we might just not get our five dollars. For those of us looking to cash in this bonanza.

During the question-and-answer period I asked how, since I was willing to give up this wonderful employment, could I get out of it besides medical, and preferably in this very building (figuring my profession alone would do it).

I was told by the same fat lady with a chip on her stomach my question was inappropriate and I would have to follow approved procedures.

When I asked what were the procedures, the lady told me for about four minutes how she'd only answer one question per person because it wasn't fair to take up all the time of the other people merely to satisfy one person. As she took up all the time of the other people.

When I said I agreed to the terms and repeated my question, she said I'd already had one question.

The jury assembly room was like a theater without a stage, row after row of attached seats, practically no leg room, and hundreds of people jammed together trying to hog the armrest.

After the educational speech by the lady I'd come most to hate outside of marriage, we sat for hour after hour, each one longer than the last. The others waiting to be called for duty, me to be called to explain why I shouldn't be called. It felt sort of like flying charter to Korea. But of course, I'd get out of it.

*   *   *

It began to look like the easiest way would be to do the medical-excuse thing. And that would have to be tomorrow. I'd just have to tough it out here for the day, as the orientation lady had further informed us unauthorized departures, other than for routine "comfort breaks," which I had a feeling meant food in her case, could result in "serious charges." I doubted that, given the number of real crimes going unpunished, but I couldn't afford any asterisks on my report card when it came time to renew my license. I would get out of it, just not right away.

After a good seventeen years, I suddenly realized in the drone of loudspeaker announcements, my name had been called, together with a bunch others. We were a potential panel.

Maybe I'd simply get thrown out by a judge, or challenged by an attorney—as we were taken in a group (including Mr. Arafat, I noticed) to a large, impressive courtroom.

After a real long while (papers getting shuffled, people moving in and out, microphones tested, lights adjusted—at five dollars a day, we were the least of the court costs), a bailiff finally announced the judge, for which all rise.

The judge, to my surprise, turned out to be a good-looking Jewish fellow in his late thirties. I'd seen so much television it came as sort of a shock a judge could be anything but a middle-aged black lady.

He introduced himself (Judge Steinberg) and told us they were empaneling a jury in a capital case. In the event some of those who had answered they understood English didn't, he further explained a capital case was a murder. So this was the big time. And judging from the size of the courtroom, an important one besides. I found myself almost wishing I could stay and see it through. But of course I had other things to do. And now that I'd been called as an actual potential juror, I could probably deal directly with the judge and get him to excuse me.

Judge Steinberg explained that in California the judge does all the questioning of potential jury members. Lawyers for both sides submit questions in writing, which he can or not, up to him, he told us with a grin, ask. He further explained they'd put in this arrangement after Prop 13 to save time and money. I guess so it'd only take eighty-four years to have a trial instead of a hundred and ten.

Then he set about voir-diring our group, asking various questions and dismissing quite a few real quick. I began to think I'd have no trouble at all getting off right here. And not have to go through the doctor thing. Although I didn't know if that'd excuse me from hanging around for other potential juries.

Anyway, he'd set one other guy (a real white bread—crew cut, beer belly, looked like something out of a Fifties sitcom) before he came to me.

I started to tell my story why I had to be excused, but the minute I opened my mouth he explained he asked the questions and did most of the talking.

The idea was to save time, so would I be good enough just to answer his questions, preferably with a yes or no. I said if that was a question, the answer was yes.

"Let's start with the biggie," said the judge. "This being a crime with special circumstances, how do you feel about capital punishment?"

"Well, depends," I said. "If I have to answer in one word."

"That's already more than one word," the judge pointed out. "Let's really try for one. Believe in capital punishment?"

"Yes."

"OK, you got me, now I'm curious," he went on. "In as few words as you can manage without seriously wasting the time of this court or subverting the intention of the Prop 13 amendment, are you in favor of capital punishment?"

"No—because they don't actually do it. By and large. Instead everybody gets eighteen appeals cost millions of dollars and takes forever. *After* which they wind up life in prison anyway. Which they don't mean, either. So you might as well start out that way." I figured I'd give them the benefit of my opinion. Not that it mattered, since I was going to get out of it.

"Uh-huh," said the judge. "I take it that translates into

you're basically in support of it." Then, seeing I wasn't quite through, raised his eyebrows. "More on the subject?"

"Yeah," I went on. "I know the argument how it's better a hundred guilty guys go free than one innocent one gets executed. Sounds good. Doesn't exactly work, either."

"Which you are going to be kind enough to explain to us," said the judge.

"With the court's permission," I said, having seen my share of movies. "Say a hundred guilty actually went free. A whole lot of them'd kill again. Which'd mean more than one innocent person getting killed. Say, maybe forty. So, am I wrong, wouldn't it be better one innocent guy got burned than forty innocent guys got burned? Plus the satisfaction nailing the hundred?"

The judge took a moment to weigh my argument. Either that or he just liked scratching his chin.

"In sum, philosophical insight aside, to be absolutely certain we understand you," said the judge. "Are you in favor of capital punishment or against it?"

"I'm against *saying* we do it and *not* doing it."

With which the judge nodded, did his chin-scratching number again. "Gentlemen?" he said to the D.A. and the defense lawyer.

They both sort of shrugged, like somehow or other I wasn't clear. Not that it mattered. I was going to get out of it.

"Challenge for cause?" said the judge. Both slowly shook their heads.

"Preempt?" Again the double shake.

"Welcome to the jury, Mr. Goodman," said the judge.

I wasn't going to get out of it.

2

Mark Bradley

Pendragon Press, in whose vineyard I so vigorously labored (wherein I planteth and careth not of the fruit therefrom), had its corporate headquarters on Sunset Boulevard, just east of the Sunset Plaza shopping area. It was in the building that used to house the Playboy Club. This had been a prestigious move from a fly-by-night location grandiosely and delusionally called the "Crossroads of the World" farther east. Crossroads was a place where lots of potential deals failed on the "first and last month" rent provision. To give you an idea, my dope dealer used to maintain a "corporate suite" there—in the days when one still did such things. B.B.F. (Before Betty Ford).

Now, however, Pendragon had achieved respectability—or at least solvency—due in no small part to my own contribution as first semi-ghost writer ("as told to") to the near-famous, and more recently as co-biographer, due to an incredible prank of fate, with Rayford Goodman of his own "auto"-biography, and even *more* more recently the story of Claudio Fortunata. Both books achieved great popularity as Goodman and I painfully and with irreconcilable differences collaborated on the writing (theoretically—*I* did the actual writing) and the solving of incidental murders involved in the telling (in large measure, admittedly, the efforts of Goodman).

Now, however, and thank god, that was all behind me as I sat in my publisher's office, prepared to review the conditions and terms under which I was to commence my next project—*the* project, the personal novel that was the crown of our deal, that heretofore elusive reward for my wallowing in the scandal and filth which was the bread and butter of Pendragon's brunch.

At this particular moment I permitted myself a moment of pleasant anticipation that it was finally payoff time, and I admit, just the tiniest apprehension that given the chance to prove myself artistically I might conceivably prove less than totally equal to the task. But, I thought, girding my loins (something I *was* equal to—being a quick loiner), I'd sure give it my best shot ("Not So Quiet the Night" had been simmering a long time).

And at long last Dick Penny, my editor/publisher/principal tormentor, phone in hand, his back turned, revealing the always startling spectacle of the holes in his hairline from whence had come the plugs implanted in front, concluded his call (with a characteristic "Well, fuck you, too!") and swiveled around to give me his full attention.

"Well, well, well," he said. "Mark, Mark, Mark."

Oi, oi, oi, thought oi—recognizing the incipient moves of betrayal from long experience with Penny's duplicitous nature.

"Here we are again, a scribe and his benefactor."

"An independent writer and his publisher," I amended.

"Or put another way, an employee and his employer," he continued, no good sign.

"Leave us not meander midst the shrubbery," I suggested. "I am here to remind you of your contractual obligation to publish my novel following the completion of the other crap I did for you."

"Yes, yes, yes," admitted Penny, again with that thrice-spoken form that betokened nothing good. "And I must tell you, I'm really looking forward to the completion of your great novel which Pendragon will be honored to publish."

"Okey-dokey."

"Hopefully this year."

"I don't see any reason why we couldn't."

"Immediately after 'Jaeger, A House Divided.' "

"Oh no, no, no," I said.

He merely smiled, no pretty sight I can assure you, under any circumstances. (Penny smiling evoked images of Torquemada, de Sade, Michael Ovitz . . .) But made especially grotesque by the fact he was evidently in the process of replacing his caps and had, at the moment, only little fanglike stubs for teeth. There was a kind of mesmerizing symmetry in the hair plugs and tooth plugs that distracted me for just a moment before I recovered.

"Jaeger, as in Stacy Jaeger?" I finally found myself asking.

"You betcha, buddy," he said, inadvertently producing two little bubbles of spittle between the front stubs. "I've registered the title, cut a handsome deal for worldwide and ancillary, and put out feelers for movie and mini-series positions."

"For a book that hasn't even been mentioned till this minute."

"It's been mentioned. Not all of us sleep in late, doing god knows what degenerate things to god knows whom. *But*—far be it from me to criticize your filthy, perverted choice of lifestyle."

Penny's not from heaven, as you may have gleaned. Aside from his endearing physical aspects, he made it a practice to commence each of our projects by insulting and infuriating me. This was a tactic that put me so on the defensive that I was continually distracted from any rational resistance. Which, one had to admit, made him a much better businessman than I. Not that much of a compliment, the Eighties having clearly enough exposed the venality and corruption of his ilk.

"I'm assuming we're not talking authorized biography here."

"With his son sitting in jail, accused of the murder of his sister's lover, what do you think?"

"I think you're an opportunistic vulture who'd sell reprint rights to his own mother's deathbed confessional."

"Only the foreign, I'd keep U.S. and Canadian. How does it grab you?"

"It does not. Dick, I told you after Fortunata, enough already. I want to do my book; I *have* to do my book."

"And well you shall, my boy. If you knew how much I

admire a man of your persuasion even considering turning down the sort of money I'm prepared to offer, merely to write another sordid tale of twisted childhood. What is it again, 'My Days and Nights in the Public Lavatories of America'?"

"All right, that does it, you fucker!"

"Boy oh boy, touch-y! I always thought you had a sense of humor. All right, let's put personalities aside."

"I'm not going to do it, Penny."

He made a motion, as though defining a marquee. "Bradley and Goodman, Together Again!"

"You think that's an *incentive*? That just means I write and two of us get credit and split the money."

"Well, not exactly. Be fair, he does bring a few talents to the game, like solving a couple of murders."

He didn't solve them *all* by himself. I was there. I did contribute.

"Anyway," I said, choosing not to be bogged in specifics, "there's no murder to be solved here. So even if I was going to do it, which I'm not, the Jaeger kid confessed. It's a straight-ahead case. What could Goodman possibly add to the project?"

"You mean besides being on the jury that's going to try him?"

Francine Rizetti, my crack researcher—and I use the term with some apprehension, given the extent of her known chemical dissipations—met me in my office with an armload of books, a thick file, and what looked to be several reams of computer printout.

"I've done the preliminary shit on Stacy," she opened.

"How could you? How could you know I'd be doing a book on him? Even that Pendragon'd be doing a book on him?"

"What're you talking about? Pendragon does a book on anybody who makes the cover of the *Enquirer* four times in a row." So saying, she dumped the works on my desk and turned her attention to a customized stash bag. This she opened to reveal an awesome connoisseur collection of pills which resembled nothing so much as a cross between Gaudi's pavilion at Güell Park and a sack of Moroccan jewelry. She delicately selected a choice entry which she popped into her mouth and washed down with the dregs of a cold cup of coffee sitting on my desk.

"That coffee's been there since Thursday," I said, as if I really thought it would inhibit her.

"Oh sure, now criticize my caffeine habits," she mumbled, downing whatever.

"No, I'm going to *approve* your killing yourself," I said, hardly talking about coffee. "How do you get all that shit, anyway?"

"Doctors."

"You have a *doctor* that gives you all that?"

"No, I have six doctors that give me all this. Although I'm having trouble with one. He said I was 'polypharmaceutical'—don't you love it? Which he went on to add was 'contraindicated.' I think the guy's on something."

Francine was, I have to admit, pharmacological hangups notwithstanding, a genius when it came to research. And no small contributor to first my own, and lately both mine and Goodman's collaborative, efforts. Which she promptly proceeded to demonstrate.

"You've got, of course, the three Stacy marriages," she said, without even having to refer to notes. "The two South Pacific innocents who took him for seven-figure settlements, and the indigenous number who only managed child support of twenty thousand a month—what an eater *that* kid must have been. There are, again naturally, the movies he's done, the making of them, the fights, the hits, the flops."

"I'm not even sure I'm going to do the book."

"Of course you are."

"What do you mean, 'of course'?"

"With your lifestyle, the money you spend, the toyboys you spend it on."

"Ah, but I've discovered fiscal responsibility—in the guise of celibacy."

"Hey, *I'm* the one discovered celibacy."

"No, you just weren't able to get laid; there's a difference,"

I pointed out. "Except with what's-his-name," I added, referring to Goodman and their incredible erstwhile romantic
teaming.

"That was an aberration."

"Yeah, well, what're you going to do if I collaborate with
that aberration again?"

"I'm quite able to separate my personal from my professional life."

"Given you have no personal."

"I think boys in glass houses shouldn't throw brickbats."

I wasn't going to dignify that. Besides, my personal life at
the moment being nothing not to write home about, following
the failure of my last attempt at a manfully meaningful relationship with Brian, the rat.

"I'll look at the material," I said, not too thrilled with my
inner dialogue, either. "But I'm a long way from agreeing to
do the book."

"Right," she said.

And smirked. And seemed very smugly sure I would do
the book.

Penny seemed sure I would do the book.

Probably even Goodman felt sure I would do the book.

Which was when Penny entered the office and held up a
final edition of the day's *Los Angeles Times*. On the front page
it said, "Star's Son Recants Confession. D.A. to Seek Death
Penalty."

I would do the book.

3

Rayford Goodman

After a lot of highly publicized cases that ran on for years (which drives me really nuts), this one moved surprisingly fast. It was like everybody'd gotten so sick of the usual stall and delay, both sides figured getting down to business was the best approach.

In little over a week they'd settled on a jury. Which turned out to be me, the sitcom guy from the Valley with the butch haircut, two generic retirees from wherever, all solid middle-class, white establishment types.

Then there was a female executive administrative assistant with a definite workout body might bear looking into at sequester time (Sylvia Ferris, about five-nine, a hundred twenty-five, red hair, freckles, tits).

Plus, a retired black lady schoolteacher from the inner city, an Asian "dealer in antiquities" looked pretty antique himself, a badly dyed blond-helmet middle-aged lady "in advertising" (sold classified ads), and a Spanish graphic artist who kept chewing his cuticles.

And finally, a fundamentalist black minister I couldn't understand the defense lawyer letting by ("an eye for an eye" and all that), an old woman manager of a bridge club who looked like the seven of osteoporosis, and a Pakistani bank clerk with a tic.

The judge, ever fair, did ask about the Arab terrorist type. (Who I had a feeling not only believed in the death penalty, also the cutting-off-the-hands penalty.) But it turned out his name wasn't on the list, he was in the wrong room, and didn't speak English all that well. Or at all. Dismissed.

Another couple alternates, and Steinberg said he was satisfied Carey Jaeger had a jury of his peers.

A little note on that. I can't imagine some smart lawyer hasn't challenged a conviction somewhere on the grounds any jury made up of only people registered to vote is automatically *un*-peery. Being most people don't vote, and the criminal element *definitely* not—how can they say peer? Just a thought. (I myself only voted once when there was one guy I didn't hate as much as the other. Which I was plenty sorry at the moment.)

Next, the judge said not to be influenced in any way that the defendant was the son of about the most famous actor in the world and a three-time Oscar winner. (Who everybody knew got robbed of a fourth on account of his stand on too few Eskimos in executive positions in Hollywood.)

We shouldn't get sidetracked the defendant was connected to just about the most exciting and controversial actor in town.

We were also supposed to forget how in his heyday he'd boffed ("sampled the charms") just about every actress from the Pasadena Playhouse to the Old Vic (and maybe old Vic, too, who would have been young Vic at the time).

We were to put out of our minds any and all connections to the sex-symbol superstud father and who he slept with, and consider only the facts in the case. (The *main* fact, the judge seemed to forget, but I'd bet, Stacy Jaeger'd long ago totally fatted himself out of the sleeping with business.)

The point he went on so long and colorfully was base our conclusions on the facts alone without regard or consideration that the murder was screaming headlines in half the papers of the world. Right. Good luck.

In fact, like twelve heads on one neck, the whole jury then turned to snatch a look at old Stacy Jaeger himself, acting real painfully fatherly in the first row of the orchestra (house seats, no doubt), with his neat-combed blond hair and big Cary Grant glasses.

Alongside, crowded off the armrest, his titular girlfriend, Soheila Morris, who was dropdead gorgeous and obviously loved all three hundred pounds of him for himself.

The other side was his other son, Stacy, Jr., who looked not only like he came from a different mother, but a different planet. More native than Caucasian.

Plus a couple others in the entourage which might have included Security. Hard to tell with that family, some branches of which tended to run big.

When we were finally through disregarding the celebrities, there was a batch of long-shot lawyer motions, including the stock defense call for a change of venue due to prejudicial publicity.

Which the judge ruled out that the case'd had *so* much publicity there wasn't any place this side of Uzbek a jury wouldn't've heard or been influenced by all the notoriety. They'd just have to trust the common sense of us good men and women who'd been selected (trapped) for the job.

That, of course, occupied most of my days. I'd had no other cases pending anyway, so no great loss there. During the week I'd closed a deal with Penny to collaborate again with Bradley on "Jaeger—A House Divided."

Like me, Bradley was push/pull about collaborating on another book. One, we weren't crazy about working together (or even being together), and two, you couldn't beat the money.

"You sure it's legal?" he asked Penny. "For him to be on the jury and doing a book about the principals?"

"The lawyers tell me it's OK," said Penny, "I mean, he can't discuss the case with you—while it's going on."

"So we won't be writing about the case?" said Bradley.

Penny smiled his piranha smile. (I'd never noticed what funny teeth he had before.) "I said he can't discuss the case with you. He could possibly write you a note, say—or leave materials around. I think you can work it out."

I was starting to feel like an alternate juror in my own life. "Hey, you don't have to do all this 'he' and 'him' stuff. I'm right here. Talk to me."

"All right," said Bradley. "How about this. According to my

understanding, a member of the jury is expressly enjoined from doing any independent investigation, or even visiting the scene of the crime or its environs."

"I would never have anything to do with environs," I said. "Look, I know what I'm not supposed to do. We'll just have to be careful about all that. No law says we can't be working on the other parts during the trial: Stacy's background, life, all that stuff."

"You mean 'all that stuff' *I* get to do."

"Something like that."

Bradley threw up his hands, looked at the ceiling, and overacted a sigh.

"I—am—so—sick—of doing *all* the work . . ."

Which really was a crock of turdity. I, after all, was the one did the solving. And here again we had solving. Although I admit it sure looked open and shut. Even if Carey did take back his confession. The fact was he was guilty (every place but the actual courtroom). Still and all, Bradley had no call to be such a prima donno.

"He doesn't do all the work," I reminded Penny.

"No," said Bradley. "All I do is the writing. All I do is put down every line. Can you point to one single *word* in either of our books that he actually *wrote*?"

"I'll be pulling my weight, as usual, as I always do," I said to Penny. "Would you please tell that to Mr. Temperamental here, Mr. Overdramatic, Mr. Dances With Boys?"

Which seemed to stop things. Wrong, it was just taking-a-deep-breath time before Bradley counterpunched.

"And you will as usual be gay-bashing and making my life something less than paradisal."

Paradisal?

"You got me there, pal. I'm not big on making anybody's life paradisal."

"OK, guys, OK, now," said Penny. "Just calm down. You don't have to love each other. If Gilbert and Sullivan, and Laurel and Hardy, and Martin and Lewis—"

"They broke up."

"You get the idea. You don't even have to *like* each other.

Work is work, business is business. And if you want to get emotional, just think about the future—you can look *forward* to breaking up."

Which is how we got the details out of the way.

Now, in the second week, the judge finished reading the charges. In itself always kills me. The defendant is charged with murder. Murder with special circumstances. Conspiracy to commit murder. Conspiracy to commit murder and inflict grievous bodily harm. Inflicting grievous bodily harm in city limits. During off hours. While wearing a belt. And spitting on the sidewalk. There were, I swear, ninety zillion separate charges. Drives me bananas. If they can't catch you for what you *did,* you ought to be home free. It's their rules, play by them.

For the record, since we all knew he'd murdered the Crewe guy, the judge asked Carey how he pleaded. And Carey, who'd looked like a grungy wino when arrested but now sported a short haircut and dressed like an English accountant, said with a straight face, "Not guilty."

Enter, the lawyers. For the district attorney's office, they led off with an Alvis Johnson, who was technically black, but had a real civil service sense of style in a mid-range, off-the-rack suit, with a tie didn't reach the top of a too tight collar. The only thing missing was a lock of hair falling on his forehead, which his genes got in the way of. Dedicated as hell.

What he had to say was Carey Jaeger was "a man who's had every advantage, who's been spoiled rotten, never really worked a day in his life, a child of privilege who's never known responsibility for himself or others. Selfish, uncaring, we see here, ladies and gentlemen, the end product of the me, me, I, I generation without morality or self-discipline who, in a drunken or perhaps even drugged rage, callously took the life of a fine young upstanding citizen, engaged to be married, with everything in the world to live for, and every right to a long, satisfying, and productive life." (Talking here about the free-loading bozo whose only exercise was beating up on the Jaeger girl time to time.)

But back to the accused. Johnson went on to tell us the

people would demand this vicious killer be shown no more mercy than he had in callously killing one of what he went on and on to make sound like the very cream of the evolutionary dairy.

The defense team, a whole other story. They were dressed like the million bucks they were getting. Cary Grant suits, Michael Douglas haircuts, alligator-foreskin shoes. The head of the team, J. Wadsworth Nichols, was a media star in his own right. Who now entertained us with his impartial version of the events we would be reviewing.

Turned out appearances could be deceiving. While it might, superficially, seem we were looking at the picture of someone who had "without reason or cause pumped three bullets into the head of a sleeping man," reality would very definitely develop a different photo.

"In this case a dedicated, loving, caring brother, overwhelmed with anxiety and distress over the vicious mistreatment of his beloved sister, carried out over a long and protracted period of time, finally reached a breaking point, a moment of temporary insanity, when, no longer able to distinguish right from wrong, knew only that he must deliver his helpless sibling from the tormentor who threatened her very existence—even as a knight of old might come to the rescue of a damsel in distress."

Neither guy being shy about overstating his case.

And then we broke for lunch. Which was good timing, because if we'd already eaten we might not've been able keep it down.

Since of course the trial just started we weren't sequestered. So, we'd be on our own for lunch. We were told by the ever helpful Judge Steinberg to avoid heavy foods which might tend to make us sluggish and lethargic during the afternoons. Despite the fact, he added with a twinkle, "you are going to find the proceedings infinitely fascinating and endlessly engaging."

Also, of course, any alcohol was a no-no.

And then, to prove he wasn't a total original and *had* seen

a bit of TV, he laid on the cliché tag not to discuss the case
with anyone.

So I went out to lunch with Bradley, Mandarin Chinese,
ordered a double Smirnoff rocks, and discussed the case.

"I don't know why the guy recanted," I said between sips,
holding off on eating those heavy foods the judge warned
against. "My guess, they didn't like the plea-bargain."

"But he's not playing with very high cards. Suppose they
do strike his confession, they still more or less caught him at
it."

"With the proverbial smoking gun. A pretty sorry-looking
'alleged perpetrator'—don't you love that stuff? Is the other
guy 'allegedly' dead?"

"There'll be expert opinions," said Bradley. "But you know,
though, if they're going for, say, temporary insanity, or dimin-
ished capacity, or any of that, it's a hard row to hoe."

"Hard row?"

"Agricultural analogy."

"Hey, just because we're writers doesn't mean we have to
be—whatchamacallit."

"Incomprehensible?"

"Right. But they must have something in mind. The lawyers
aren't going to just wait and see what crazy bounce the ball
takes. Football analogy."

Bradley dug into some sort of fish thing didn't seem too
appetizing to me, but it was part of a number three lunch
here at the Smiling Dragon. I kept to the basics, egg roll, pork
fried rice, and kreplach. Since it struck me we didn't know
what the dragon was smiling *about*.

"And," I went on, "this Wesley Crewe guy definitely *was*
pretty regularly beating up on Carey's sister."

"Hmn," said Bradley, taking a long look at something on
his chopsticks didn't register among the known food groups.
"The interesting question in all this is where was Papa Stacy,
and how come he didn't do something about it?"

"From what I hear, Papa Stacy was probably at the dinner
barrel. And I suppose possible he didn't know."

"Living in the same house—or compound, anyway?"

"It's not that rare a movie star's not the best parent."

Bradley didn't right away answer. Instead wrinkled his nose and offered me the stuff at the end of his chopsticks.

"Smell this," he said.

"Does it smell bad?"

"I think so."

"No, thanks."

That seemed to put a damper on his appetite. Hey, I wasn't that thrilled with their drinks, either. It takes some kind of talent to hurt vodka on the rocks.

"Enough?" said Bradley.

I agreed. He took the check, paid with a credit card, marked his receipt with my name and the information: "Illegally discussed Jaeger case"—and added a twenty percent tip.

"The service wasn't that good," I reminded him.

"Yeah, but it's a company lunch. I don't want to establish a precedent of light tipping, or Penny'll start insisting on it."

We got up, left, and walked back up the hill toward 210 Temple and the Criminal Courts Building.

There was a huge crowd outside.

"Jesus Christ, they ought to do something about speeding up their security procedures," said Bradley.

But I could see it was more than that. I'm smart. The two fire engines and four police cars gave it right away.

We pushed our way through the crowd and up to what was definitely a police line.

"What's going on?" I asked the policeman holding one end of the line.

"Just keep back," he answered, protecting and serving.

Then I spotted Frank Chow, an L.A. detective I knew, and quickly ducked under the tape and headed over, Bradley right behind. The cop was torn between stopping us and losing the line altogether, by which time I'd caught up to Chow.

"Frankie. What's happening?"

"Huh? Oh, Ray. Hi. Bomb."

"Scare?"

"Boom."

"Exploding bomb?" asked Bradley, a stickler for details.

"You got it."

"Let me guess," I said. "Judge Steinberg's court?"

"That's the one."

School was out. Recess.

4

Mark Bradley

We went back to the office. Goodman phoned in to the court. For the first half hour all the lines were busy. After that a recorded message announced all lines were temporarily out of order. We called City Hall, went on endless hold. We called the *L.A. Times,* where we achieved only a very sustained hold before being given a dozen different numbers to push for various functions, each of which *then* put us on endless hold. It wasn't an auspicious preview for the way we could expect services to be maintained when the Mother of All Earthquakes we'd been repeatedly threatened with actually shook loose.

We had the TV on, naturally, but—details were "sketchy at this hour."

Goodman finally got through to the Criminal Courts Building. A breathless recorded message informed him jurors were to check back tomorrow morning at eight, when another recorded message would advise when and where the trial would be resumed.

Francine hacked into the wire services on her computer, and illegally stole the big news there'd been an explosion in the courtroom where the Carey Jaeger trial was being conducted. We were getting nowhere at an astonishing electronic pace.

And then finally after about forty minutes, the local TV burst in with a special bulletin promising full details.

Local anchorperson Carlos Herrera, working so hard on the story his jacket was off and his tie askew, came on and grimly reported the following: "During a routine lunch break, called by Judge Myron Steinberg, presiding at the trial of Carey Jaeger, indicted for the murder of Wesley Crewe, longtime lover of Jaeger's sister, daughter of movie star Stacy Jaeger— shown here at the Cannes Film Festival in 1984 when his picture, *A Piece of Eight,* won honorable mention for the Palme d'Or—an explosive device was allegedly detonated."

"Oh, that was an alleged explosion," said Goodman.

"Initial reports indicate that the explosion did extensive damage fire officials estimate at three hundred and forty thousand dollars."

"Yeah, yeah," I heard myself saying, wondering how they could employ so many words and reveal so little information.

"For a direct, on-the-scene report, we go now to the Criminal Courts Building in downtown Los Angeles, and our correspondent, Vince Martin."

The picture changed to Vince Martin, standing outside the Criminal Courts Building and behind the police lines, attired war-correspondently in a bush jacket with its belt rakishly tied.

"This is Vince Martin, just outside the Criminal Courts Building, where we understand a bomb has gone off at the Jaeger trial."

"Yes, we know that, Vince," interrupted anchorman Herrera back at the studio as the screen split to favor us with a simultaneous view of both hardworking journalists. "What have you learned?"

"Well, Carlos, it appears some sort of explosive device has been set off inside the building. We haven't been given any specific details yet, but—wait a minute, Lieutenant? I see Lieutenant Chow of the Los Angeles Police Department. Lieutenant, can we have a minute?"

"Not now, fella," said the lieutenant, moving on.

Martin then turned to a uniformed officer keeping the crowds at bay. "Officer, I wonder if you could—"

"Back there, get back," said the officer.

On the part of the screen showing anchorman Herrera, we

could see him canting his head, trying to catch these words, then forcing a small but concerned smile. On the other part, Martin was trying to find someone in authority, missing, and in desperation corralled a mini-street person, about ten.

"Hey, there, young man—were you here when the alleged explosion occurred?"

"No, no, I didn't do nothing. Leggo," said the kid, pulling sharply away, in the process tearing open Martin's bush jacket and slightly skewing his toupe.

The correspondent, disheveled and out of options, turned to face the camera and in desperate earnestness said, "Well, that's all the news we have at this moment, Carlos. To recap, there's apparently been an explosion at the Criminal Courts Building in downtown L.A. We'll stay on the scene here, and get back to you as the story breaks."

The split screen disappeared and a full shot of Herrera appeared instead. "Thank you, Vince, for that on-the-spot report. And now, more details, after these important words."

With which they went to a commercial.

"Well, that sure cleared things up," said Goodman. "I always love the way they send out remote crews so someone can stand in front of a building and say the same things they could have said back in the studio. 'Behind me, Chet, is a door, in back of which some people are talking. But we can't hear them at the moment, Chet, because the door is closed.'"

Which is when Francine came back in with a printout and a red and guilty nose, having continued her illegal invasion of the news wires and ingestion of proscribed substances.

"OK, here's what it looks like," she said, sniffingly. "The bomb went off at one-ten, at which time the only one in the room was a bailiff, brown-bagging it. Other than losing his lunch—they didn't say whether directly or indirectly—he apparently escaped, as they say, unharmed."

"Nobody hurt," I repeated, glaring at her.

"So it seems," she replied, staring down my disapproval.

"Probably timed that way—lunch. For those with *appetites*," I riposted.

"The epicenter if you're being technical, target if you're not, looks like the defense table," she went on, ignoring me.

"Uh-hah," said Goodman. "Which we all had access to before the jury was picked. So, target the defendant? Carey Jaeger?"

"Apparently."

"But was it a warning?" continued Goodman. "Or a serious attempt that, you should pardon the expression, bombed out?"

"In other words, to kill or intimidate?"

"Lunchtime," reminded Francine.

"Which puts it as likely intimidate. Which, next question, why?"

"And the envelope, please," I said.

"Could be to press Carey to recant his recanting, and get right to the sentencing. Avoid trial, and keep whatever quiet whoever wanted the whatever kept that way," explained Goodman explicitly.

But possible.

At which point Dick Penny entered.

"I heard what happened," he said.

"Yeah, they blew up the courtroom."

"I don't mean that. I mean," referring to a chit, "you put in for a full day's parking when you were only there half a day."

And got the fish eyes he deserved.

"Kidding, just kidding!" he said, inadvertently flashing his tooth nubs. "Don't you guys have any sense of humor? Although I *was* under the impression there'd be free parking for jurors."

"There is, only it's on the outskirts of Yuma and half an hour each way by shuttle," replied Goodman, who I wasn't quite sure wouldn't have gone for it if *he* were doing the paying.

"Of course," said Penny, reverting to talking with his mouth closed, which sounded like Rich Little doing William Buckley, "the bombing isn't the worst thing that ever happened. From the point of view of our project. The way I look at it. Commercial-wise."

Which, also of course, was always the way Penny looked at it.

"Keep up the good work," he concluded, simultaneously miming typing. He'd never quite got used to the idea that writing wasn't all typing, that some of it involved thinking and planning.

"You know," said Francine, "there is one other thought that occurs to me."

"Which is?" Goodman obligingly prompted.

"Jaeger might not have been the target."

"Well, who else would it be?" bit Goodman.

She smiled pleasantly. "You—for example."

I could see Goodman was crazy about the example.

"Not everybody's favorite person," she added. "Just a thought," she added to the added, leaving the room—leaving Goodman steaming. And she wasn't even a woman scorned. She was a woman scorning.

Goodman ate some air, took another breath. Let it carefully and slowly out, reminiscent of the old Forties actor Edgar Kennedy, who used to be considered master of the slow burn. "I'll never understand women," he said finally.

He'll never understand?

Since we—or more specifically, Goodman—apparently had the day off, I figured we might as well utilize it by interviewing some of the principals in the case. A frontal assault on the Jaeger enclave didn't promise much chance of success. If past experience was any indication, there'd be half a dozen TV vans parked outside the place, to say nothing of the occasional helicopter trying for the long, dramatic zoom. (That would be the *Enquirer,* looking to steal an unflattering, foreshortened, and distorted shot to go with next week's probable headline: "Broken-hearted Stacy Gains Fifty-Five Pounds." "Stuffing himself like six pigs," says Friend.) Anyway, Goodman, as a juror, wasn't supposed to go near the scene of the crime unless it was undertaken at the direction of the judge.

The whole thing had sort of come together so fast, I hadn't really made a master plan for the book. Usually in a biography I work in conjunction with the subject (especially when it's "autobiography" or "as told to"), and it becomes collaborative, at least in the organization of the work. But since this was definitely going to be unauthorized, I'd be getting all my information sideways, not only without cooperation, but probably in spite of an organized and hostile opposition.

"Well, I think the first guy you want to take a shot at, certainly the most important," said Goodman, "has to be Ken Curry."

"I can't imagine he'll cooperate."

"No, but he might at least see us, if only to tell us to get lost. And who knows, maybe something'll break."

I hate to admit it, but there were times Goodman was starting to think like a writer.

"You're right; let's go for it," I said.

Ken Curry was Jaeger's partner. Some said his Svengali. A teacher, founder of an illustrious school of acting, it was Curry who had "discovered" Jaeger. Mentor, teacher, guru—he was all these and became a lot more: Jaeger's full partner. Though still maintaining the school, Curry actually devoted most of his time and effort to managing the affairs of his star pupil.

"You have to figure he'd be in Malibu, at headquarters," I said.

"Maybe not. Somebody has to be out and about, taking care of business. Let's give his office a shot."

While "The Academy" (Curry didn't use his name to define his school or style) was located in relatively reasonable rent country (West Hollywood on Fountain), his offices, as befitted a multimedia mover and macher, were located at 2020 Avenue of the Stars, Century City, the multi-towered mini-metropolis that used to be the back lot of Twentieth Century-Fox (a company even now no doubt considering logos and name changes for the impending *fin de siècle*).

I must say I certainly considered we had a very slim chance of gaining an audience on this, of all stressful days. Given our potentially damaging, or at least adversarial stance. I was wrong.

In the office itself, neutrally identified as "Crescent Enterprises," we were ushered to his door by a dark-haired, nubile creature who intoned, "Mr. Curry will see you now," in a breathy, hesitant voice. It sounded like the one line the girl gets who's sleeping with the assistant second-unit director.

"Come in, come in," said the understated, elegantly bespoken (in terms of Savile Row) Curry, rising to greet us. "And Miss Malouf, will you turn that down?" he said, pointing in the general direction of the hidden speakers, from which Muzak appeared to be exploiting even older than usual public domain with something vaguely Dixielandish.

If either of us had any Colonel Parker-like preconceptions, they were quickly disabused. Curry looked like nothing so much as an English aristocrat (well, perhaps some Sephardic somebody back somewhere), soft-spoken, refined, polite. His office was equally elegantly, determinedly understated—if any million dollars' worth of furnishings could be called understated. (The door had *hinges* more costly than my condo.) The artwork alone had to be another seven figures, not least of which was a museum-quality Persian rug. Show business sure been good to some folks.

"What can I do for you?" he inquired in his soft yet resonant voice.

"You know who we are?" asked Goodman.

"Well, certainly—your reputations precede you."

"And you know we're going to write a book about the Jaegers?"

"So I understand. Your publisher all but took out an ad on the Fuji blimp."

"Naturally"—I thought, worth taking a chance—"we'd love to do this with the cooperation of Mr. Jaeger himself."

"Well, as you can imagine—please, please, be seated." (I never expected this.) "He's pretty much preoccupied at the moment. Would you care for a drink, coffee?"

"Nothing, thanks," I said.

"Any vodka would be OK," said Goodman, in case things were getting too classy.

"Certainly," said Curry, crossing to a discreet bar cleverly customized in an old-fashioned early model crank camera situated between two floor-to-ceiling windows facing north and west. "I do this myself because if I ask my secretary to serve drinks, she won't give me head."

"That's women's lib for you," agreed Goodman.

Curry smiled at me. He knew I knew he was kidding. And even his vulgarity was somehow elegant.

"As you can imagine, Mr. Jaeger's understandably tremendously upset at the moment. Interviews and/or biographies aren't very high on his list of priorities."

"But *you* don't object?"

"Well, officially, since the book is unauthorized, I wouldn't like to feel I contributed to anything that could cause my friend trouble—or even unpleasantness."

"Yeah?" said Goodman, crossing over to where Curry was fixing the drink, since it seemed to be taking a bit longer than he would have liked.

"But on the other hand," Curry replied, completing the exercise and handing Goodman a goblet of Murano crystal heavy enough to cause vodka elbow, and having one himself, "if in some way I can be of assistance, or cause you to look on Stace—or, for that matter, any members of the family— with a more sympathetic eye . . ." His voice trailed off. All very civilized here.

"Well, as the salesman said to the farmer's daughter, let's take a crack," said Goodman, once again revealing that aversion to refinement and sensitivity for which Hollywood is so justly famous. "How is Stacy taking all this? I mean, I know it's no thrill, but if this Crewe guy was beating up on his little girl, Iris—"

"Which he certainly was," said Curry with some heat.

"And therefore which," I couldn't help interjecting, "has to make you wonder why Stacy allowed it to continue. Why, for that matter, it somehow or other got to be Carey's problem to take care of, for want of a better term."

"That's a good question, surely," the sudden flare of temper abating. "The answer is I don't actually know what Stacy knew—or when he knew it, as recent parlance has it. It certainly is an unfortunate, tragic state of affairs."

"You were there that night?" asked Goodman.

"Well, later. They called me. I was home."

"Alone," I said.

"Yep. Sometimes you get unlucky," he said, just a touch lecherously.

"I suppose," said Goodman, who I must admit was showing signs of improving at this, "the one who'd know the most would be Iris herself. I mean, about how much she was beat up on, and how long, and say, who knew."

"Well, there's no question—can we be off the record here?"

Goodman gave me a look. I hated going off the record, ever, since that was often when you learned the most. On the other hand, being off the record you often also learned stuff you could corroborate elsewhere.

"If that's the only way to do it," I said.

"Not that earth-shattering, or surprising," said Curry. "But the salient fact, at the moment, is not who knew and who didn't act, but that Carey *did*. There's no one suggesting anyone *else* did it. So the action or lack of it in others is hardly the issue, any more, really, than his either confessing or recanting. Which is sort of just lawyerly maneuvering, I imagine."

"You don't know?"

"I do know. But cooperating with you and revealing a legal stratagem are sort of separate things, wouldn't you agree?"

"Back on the record?"

Curry nodded.

"Well, we would like to interview you in depth, if not about the murder, then just Jaeger's life prior to it. Would you agree to that?"

"I don't think I could," said Curry. "Personally, I'd like to. I'm sick and tired of those unauthorized bios that do a hatchet job. I think everybody's better off cooperating and at least that way you get to see the talent and the charm and maybe *like* the subject, instead of reacting to resistance by hostility."

"So cooperate."

"But I'm not the subject, am I? This isn't the saga of Ken Curry's rise to fame and fortune. So all I can do is try in a small way to show you the good things, help you to see this is an extraordinary, I have to say, genius of a person, and someone very rare and special on this earth."

"OK," I said. "I can see you're not what would be termed a disgruntled employee."

"I am his partner—and damn proud to be, too," said Curry.

"Then I have two questions," said Goodman.

Curry looked up.

"One, can you arrange for us to interview the daughter, Iris?"

"I'm afraid that won't be possible," said Curry. "The poor darling left this morning for the family home on Bali."

Uh-huh!

"You had another question?" said Curry.

"Yeah, can I get a refill on this?" said Goodman, holding out his empty glass.

5

Rayford Goodman

The morning paper said the target of the alleged bomb wasn't Carey Jaeger, as everyone thought, but Judge Steinberg himself. According to "reliable authorities" (the new version of "they say") the bomb was set by something called the ADA—Arabs for Democratic Action (talk about people unclear on the subject). And they were the folks claiming responsibility. Which at least beat when terrorists used to take "credit."

It seems Judge Steinberg failed to recuse himself (which sounded to me like something Amos would say to Andy, "I's goin' recuse myself, Andy") in a matter involving the ADA's previous demonstration for democracy when they spray-painted swastikas on a synagogue. (Which made for a counter-demonstration by the Jewish Defense League spray-painting Star of Davids on a mosque. Sort of a nose for a nose.)

At any rate, the judge wasn't about to be intimidated "by those who would undermine the foundations of American justice." So, Carey Jaeger's trial would go right on, and there wouldn't be a whole lot of recusing.

That from the paper. From the phone I got a recorded message jurors should report ten o'clock this morning to the new courtroom of California versus Jaeger.

Bradley not only knew all this already, but had been up two and a half hours, half of that at the gym. I might get over him being gay, but also a morning person? Asking a lot.

He was going to see could he get some info out of anybody

at the compound, since with the action back to the courtroom, there was a fair chance things might've eased up out at Malibu.

I'd stood under the shower a good ten minutes. I knew we were in the fifth year of a drought and weren't supposed to shower more than three or four minutes at a time. But we weren't supposed to drink the better part of a fifth of vodka the night before, either, and have our head feel like Gene Krupa lived there.

I popped a couple more aspirins (good for heart-attack patients), downed a couple more cups of coffee (bad for heart-attack patients), and read the sports pages cover to cover. It always took longer mornings after we won. Mornings after we lost I didn't read them at all—who wants to bum out all over again? And first thing you knew, it was time to split.

On the way out I fed the Phantom (by this time bending over to put cat food on the floor being possible). The son of a bitch came this close to my being able to touch him, then suddenly remembered he was living with Jack the Cat Killer and leaped back.

I got into the just about totally restored '64 Eldorado convertible, popped in an Erroll Garner tape for a little piano traveling music, and headed on down the hill.

I caught the freeway by the Hollywood Bowl and pointed the big old bus downtown.

No big surprise, security was extra tight, and it was a good forty-five minutes before I got through and up to the new courtroom. The uniform at the door took a quick look at my juror badge and passed me in. (Not that juror badges were that great ID, having just your name, no photo, and the word "Juror.")

I was one of the last ones in and barely took my seat before the bailiff said all rise. Then he told us where we were and what we were doing there and how those of us having business before the honorable court should now draw nigh. (I was already nigh.) And here came the judge, fast-stepping head-high steely eyed, everything but flexing his pecs. He settled in and took a moment to case the court.

At the defense table, it was a different Carey Jaeger. No

more squeaky neat victim of a misunderstanding. Instead he was definitely shook, and didn't believe for a minute the bomb'd been for anybody but number one. Behind him, Stacy looked long-suffering, but not as if he'd missed the blue plate special for breakfast. His girlfriend I guess didn't get up this early, so it was just him and Stacy, Jr., for support. The judge gave the gavel a rap.

"I don't intend to go into any great detail about the events which have transpired here," he began. I really sort of love the way public speakers public speak. They never just talk. Make a guy a mayor or a judge and he's on the record for the history books. "Other," continued the judge, "than to reassure any of those who would subvert the judicial process that their efforts will avail them nothing. No violence, or threat of violence, will influence this court. I specifically enjoin the jury to disregard those events which have no direct bearing on the case in judgment before them and to concentrate all their efforts on the duty they have assumed. Let us proceed. Mr. Johnson, are the people prepared to continue?"

Mr. Alvis Johnson, the assistant D.A., put on his tip-of-the-nose looking-over-the-top glasses—sort of a black Spencer Tracy (definitely couldn't dance)—and said the people were ready. He then called as his first witness Sheriff's Deputy Jeff Braxton, of the Malibu station.

Braxton was a tanned, blond beach-boy type a well-situated producer's wife might blow the whole deal over if he stopped her for a broken taillight one sunny Tuesday afternoon.

Yes, he'd been on duty the night in question. He'd been called by a Mr. Ken Curry toward the end of his shift, at— checking his pad—oh-five-forty-eight hours. Which I translated right away to five-forty-eight. There had been a shooting at the Jaeger compound.

He responded and was physically present by oh-six-eighteen hours, at which time he was shown the body of a Caucasian male, approximately thirty years of age, who'd been murdered by three shots to the head.

The defense, in the elegant but porky person of J. Wadsworth Nichols, rose to object in a very refined way that neither a murder nor a number of shots had been established. Judge Steinberg sustained the objections.

Johnson led Braxton through the form necessary to set up something actually happened, in all likelihood a murder— ("Objection." "Sustained.")—something out of the ordinary, and there was a dead man.... Here the defense waited, in case Nichols might contend death hadn't been established, but Nichols only smiled and waved a fat-fingered forty-dollar manicure for him to continue. Braxton placed the alleged suspect in restraints, called for backup, Homicide, Forensic—the whole shmear—and on the arrival of bigger brass was directed to take the alleged suspect into custody and book him. The time was oh-seven-fifty-five hours.

On cross, J. Wadsworth Nichols commended Deputy Braxton for a job apparently done with competence and in accordance with generally accepted practice, and not wanting "to delay you further from the resumption of your duties as knight errant and all-purpose bulwark against the hordes threatening civilization," allowed as he had no further questions at this time. I got the feeling Mr. Nichols had speechified before an audience before.

There followed some business between the attorneys and the judge we weren't let in on, during which I looked around the room. There were a gang of press, which you'd expect with such a high-profile case. There were also a very lot of cops who looked to be under the direction of Lieutenant Frank Chow. These were deployed in a formation covered the area pretty good, except the front, where only one had the whole wall with the door to the judge's chambers, and another the door the defendant and the jury used. The bailiff was carrying, too, but it looked more tradition than real security.

Plus, probably because the terrorist part made things federal, there were a lot of guys with either radio receivers in their ears or hearing-impaired.

The defendant, Carey Jaeger, sat slumped at the defense table, looking more and more tranked to the tits.

The conference at the bench ended, and the prosecution called a Mr. Ira Jelks, who was an assistant from the coroner's office. That was some sort of surprise. That we didn't get the coroner himself. Even before the limelight-loving Thomas Noguchi, California coroners weren't shy about making the most of celebrity murders. Could there be some heat avoiding going on here?

Mr. Jelks's testimony was straightforward. For that matter, most forensics testimony tended to be, you should pardon the expression, cut and dried. Mr. Crewe had died somewhere between three-thirty and four-thirty of the morning in question, a fact determined by such things as rigor mortis, rictus, and that it was the only logical time. "Objection: calls for a conclusion." "Overruled: conclusion is what is elicited from an expert witness."

Death resulted from three bullets in specific Latin locations which, if I was any indication, didn't mean diddly to the jury. Right occipital this, or cranial lunar lobe that—you get my meaning, they shot the guy. There was more stuff about tissue samples, brain slices, and eyeball slivers. I personally couldn't help wondering how anybody got into that line of work. Did you start out wanting to, or was it more like, "Well, I was gonna go to meat-cutter's school under the GI Bill, but they were all booked up"?

The most important thing, it seemed to me, was the opinion the victim had been shot mostly or totally in the back of the head.

On cross, defense tried to stick a little doubt on the obvious conclusion of cold-blooded murder.

"Mr., uh, Jelks," said Nichols. "Isn't it possible Mr. Crewe might have momentarily turned after having first launched an attack of his own?"

"What do you mean turned?" asked Mr. Jelks.

"Before being shot. You know, he say, took a swing, missed, his momentum turning him around, and *then* got shot through the back of the head?"

"Not in my opinion," said Mr. Jelks.

"But it *is* only your opinion."

Prosecution objected defense was arguing with the witness.

"Darn right I'm arguing, Your Honor," said the esteemed Mr. Nichols. "A man's life is at stake here. We cannot *assume*—"

"Sustained," said Judge Steinberg, having been there before.

"Mr. Jelks," continued Nichols. "Is it, let's be really precise, is it *possible* Mr. Crewe had simply turned away—for whatever reason—when the bullets struck him?"

"Well, if by simply turned away you mean he had his head down in his hands so he could be shot from behind and above—"

"I have no further questions, Your Honor," said Nichols, cutting off an answer everybody knew wasn't going to do his client a whole lot of good.

It was now a little after twelve. I was amazed how fast things were going. The way I understood, they always took a month and a half to establish something happened on a Monday.

So, we already knew now there'd been a crime, and that the dead guy'd been shot—and it only took one morning. Moving right along.

The lawyers were at the bench again, discussing—this time I could hear—whether they wanted to call the ballistics man before lunch or after. It seemed like that might depend whether it was going to be routine or Nichols intended to do any serious challenging. Nichols said that in consideration of the gravity of the matter before adjudication, the seriousness of the offense, the severity of the potential punishment—

"Cut the bullshit, Waddy," Steinberg said clearly. "You want to break for lunch or not?"

"Let's do, Your Honor," said the esteemed advocate.

"Lunch!" said the judge. "Court will recess for approximately one and a half hours; back at one-thirty sharp." And banged the gavel.

"All rise," said the bailiff as Steinberg made his way back toward the door just to the left of his bench. I turned to face the juror on my right, Sylvia, the administrative assistant with the executive body. I wanted to see if she might be interested in a light lunch and some heavy verbal foreplay. When I caught a glimpse of a guy in an awful robin's-egg blue sweatsuit with a brown fanny pack pushing his way toward the front. He was wearing a beard and a wig, but it was Arafat!

I looked around, quickly spotted my friend. "Chow! Frank Chow," I yelled, pointing at the guy. Chow didn't hear me, but the guy did, and immediately turned and backed off, bee-lining for the door. I tried to push and shove my way toward the guy. But the group in that instant had got totally on its feet and was a solid wall. The press was busy checking each other out. Trial buffs were buffing, and everybody was cram-ming very slowly through the one exit.

"Frank Chow!" I called again, louder. This time getting his eye.

"What?" he either said or mimed, I couldn't hear. I pointed at the departing figure of Arafat, now at the door.

"Stop that guy!" I yelled. But there was so much noise he couldn't hear, and by the time I fought my way to Chow, and him to me, it was too late and the guy was gone.

"What, what, what do you want?"

"There was a guy here. Dark, black hair, five-nine, with a wig and a beard today—I feel about ninety percent sure, your bomber."

By this time we had pushed our way out into the hall. Chow pulled out his walkie-talkie, but it was either malfunc-tioning or the batteries'd conked out, and in the crowd, with his start, there wasn't much chance we'd be able to find, or stop, him.

We pushed to the side of the corridor and leaned against the wall, letting the crowd go on by.

"You really feel strongly about this guy?" said Chow.

"Yeah, I do. I spotted him my first day."

"And you didn't think to *say* anything?" growled Chow.

"Hey, don't forget, he hadn't done anything yet," I re-minded him. "Plus he fit the profile so good I just couldn't really believe it. You free for lunch?"

"Yeah, I guess," said Chow with a sigh. Then, pointing to the men's room, "Let me wash up and take a leak."

"Or vice versa," I suggested.

"I'll only be a minute," he said, and headed across the hall.

Which was when we heard the shot, both raced through the door, and saw Arafat on the floor, one of those new plastic guns in his hand, and most of his head on the wall.

"About lunch," said Chow.

"Another time perhaps," I said.

6

Mark Bradley

The chances weren't really very good. But I'd learned long ago one had to touch all the bases, hit the goals, make contact with the ball—whatever the hell the sports metaphors were. (1) you never knew when something unexpected would turn up, and you had to be *there* for it to happen, and (B) if you didn't have an idea in the world where to start, eliminating some places, persons, or things *was* a start.

So, after setting Francine some research chores at the office—basic biography, family tree, early life, most of the Stacy pre-movie stuff—I hopped into the Beamer and pointed it to the beach.

I took Sunset out to Whittier, Whittier down to Wilshire, and Wilshire all the way out through Westwood and past the Veterans Hospital and turned right into San Vicente Boulevard. Then to 7th, right again and into West Channel Road, twist on down to Pacific Coast Highway, and another right toward the setting sun (figuratively) and the site of the Jaeger saga out past Malibu.

Well, it was a mess. TV vans were still parked out front, as well as a police car and other official vehicles. Private security and a deputy both rebuffed my efforts to ring the bell and see if there wasn't someone I could talk to. "Ha ha" and "get lost" figured prominently in their collective rejections.

There was no entry at the sides. A high chain-link fence topped by razor wire discouraged unauthorized attempts.

There was a gate for deliveries, but that, too, was manned by *polizei*.

Since to the best of my recollection, private beaches had been outlawed (or perhaps never lawed in the first place) in California, theoretically, anyway, there should be a potential entry from the rear, you should pardon the expression.

I betook myself down the road, looking for some sort of beach ingress, but found there was none for about three-quarters of a mile. And then there was.

I parked, took off my shoes and socks, and hiked down to the beach, then headed back toward the compound.

It was a lovely day, a bit on the warm side (next time I'd consider taking swimming trunks), but cool enough to be pleasant walking, and I couldn't help thinking life couldn't be too terrible if I was able to eke a living out of activities that called for being on the beach midafternoon of a working day.

On the other hand, once I reached what would be the Jaeger beach, if beaches were private, I had to admit that work and *accomplishing* something were two different things entirely.

The Jaeger place was situated high atop a bluff, and obviously unscalable (except to those frightening people who climb sheer cliffs with their fingernails). There was one of those unirail, forty-five-degree-angled open-elevator gizmos, but it, too, was enclosed in chain-link fencing, with a substantial lock on the gate and clearly defined admonitions to keep the hell out private property immediate jail if not shooting impending for violators.

I waited half an hour, in case someone ventured down, but no one did, and I had to put this into the category of places and things eliminated, or bases touched (runners stranded?).

The hike back went quicker. I'm not sure it's not inherent in the Albert Einstein area, but *I've* certainly noticed it's always less time/motion/energy to come back from somewhere than to get there.

I got back in the car, wiped the sand off my feet, put my shoes and socks back on, and headed back south on the PCH.

As I was about to repass the Jaeger compound area—which wasn't visible from the highway—I noticed an electric cart coming down the hill. I pulled over about fifty yards short of the road—on a hunch. Sure enough, the cart stopped at the entrance to the highway, and a sparklingly attractive, cheek-boney young David Bowie clone got out, crossed over to a mailbox nestled inside an artful pile of stones, unlocked it, and gathered up the mail.

Then he climbed back in the golf cart, settled his attractive person behind the controls, and drove up the hill out of sight, presumably back to the main house. Clearly he was someone who either worked or lived there, or had some official connection to the family. I decided to hang around a while and see if he came out again. Call me conscientious.

I don't know how investigators can *stand* stakeouts. It is the single most boring thing imaginable. I sat in that car for over two and a quarter hours. You can't play the radio too long, for fear of running the batteries down. You can't keep the air conditioner on (and it was getting really uncomfortably hot in there) for fear of using up your gas and irresponsibly polluting the environment. Your bladder constantly reminds you you can't sweat *all* your liquids away, at the same time you're suffering from dehydration. It is not a pleasant way to pass the time.

But, sure enough, eventually young Bowie came back out, this time in a classic Mustang convertible—of that dark green color which only looks good on some Bentleys, to my way of thinking. However, with the blond hair and the blue eyes, not exactly an unattractive picture.

I turned the ignition on, and after he got about a quarter of a mile ahead of me, eased into gear and discreetly followed.

With the near-end-of-day traffic, it wasn't difficult to stay close enough to keep him in sight and have enough cars around not to be conspicuous.

He went on through Malibu—Carbon Beach, Las Tunas, Topanga—through Santa Monica, Ocean Park, and on into Venice. Which has its chic spots, too, but that didn't seem to be the direction in which he was going.

He (we) wound up on a little side street in front of a sleazy South Seas-y bar named Kon Diki, which I assumed was a campy play on words for Kon Tiki, Thor Heyerdahl's famous raft. ("You're Thor? I'm so thor I can hardly pith!")

Experience and predilection immediately informed me this was a gay bar. I wasn't wrong.

I went up to my friend (who didn't know that, yet) at the bar, struck up a conversation, introduced myself, and asked if he'd like a drink.

I had sort of hoped he wouldn't order something with an umbrella in it.

You can't win 'em all.

I suggested Talesai, which has the best Thai food in Los Angeles, but Goodman declined ("No spicy gook").

Ditto the subtler Cafe Katsu ("Too far").

And Pazzia ("Too noisy, I hate those new restaurants with no rugs and all hard walls").

What would he like?

"Beef, someplace serves beef. Steak, chops—American food. You know, like on TV, beef's the best."

"Right, on TV. They have to keep changing spokespersons as they drop like flies from heart attacks. How about The Grill?"

"That's noisy, too." (And expensive. I think I knew my customer.)

"All right, I got it, a little exotic and very cheap—the Horto-bagy, on Ventura Boulevard. Hungarian."

"All right," said Goodman, having heard the "very cheap." "I like to think of myself as adventurous."

So, Hortobagy it was, and definitely not dietetic.

Which is where we were that night, filling our stomachs and each other up and in on the details of our action-packed day.

The food was tasty, the portions abundant, and modestly priced. My companion was only partially mollified.

"I already apologized," I repeated. "I'm sorry, I just didn't remember they don't have a liquor license."

"I don't see how you can forget something like that."

"They have wine."

"I don't drink wine; wine is a gyp."

"Did you know," I continued, to change the subject, "the word *gyp* comes from *gypsy* and it's really a derogatory term?"

"Since nobody could ever accuse the gypsies of stealing or conning anybody. I'll give you this. The food was great, and they fill your plate pretty good."

Goodman had had the Peasant Plate (a name, come to think of it, that might offer food for objection from another quarter). This consisted of a cucumber salad followed by a wooden platter of beef, liver, chicken, pork, veal, sausage, potatoes, and cabbage in a portion large enough to satisfy a Clydesdale. (I myself showed marked restraint, consuming barely enough for a Lippizaner.)

With very little encouragement I got Goodman to agree to sample the palacsinta, the wonderful Hungarian dessert crepes they served so well there. And got back to business.

"Before I go on, finish your story," I said.

"Not that much left. Definitely not that much left of the bomber guy. Chow was really pissed I hadn't alerted him. But though I really sort of did notice him that first day, I didn't *really* think anybody looked so much like a terrorist could actually *be* a terrorist. Which is pretty dumb of me in the home of typecasting."

"How'd he get by Security?"

"Well, for the bomb, the way I think he operated, he hung near the head of the line. Then when somebody set off an alarm—me, the first time—he waited till everybody was all alerted and focused on the other person—me—then slipped in behind. Looks like what happens with the people at Security—once the bells go off they keep thinking it's just more of the same for the same guy."

"But you'd think after the bomb, and tightened security, he wouldn't be able to smuggle in a gun."

"Well, I think the reason for that, the gun was made out of that new plastic stuff doesn't register. Wonderful world, right?"

"Even so, didn't they search?"

"Or, maybe he stashed it the first time, when he brought in the bomb."

"I mean the building."

"It's a big place. Whatever, he obviously got it in. And there are ways around, even if it's something dogs can sniff. They put it in Clorox or something toxic. There'd certainly be more places easier to hide than on an airplane, and lord knows they've managed that often enough."

"And the Arab guys claimed it again?"

"Right, according to Lieutenant Chow. Though they're keeping that quiet for now, in case it gives them some sort of edge."

"It's weird. A lot of crazy people."

"Especially since it's never since they started blowing things up actually achieved anything."

"Well, the Mau Maus ..."

"Different ballgame. Anyway, that's up to date with me. Far as I know, the trial is still on tomorrow, just the men's room needs a little hosing down. A lot of hosing down."

"There goes the rest of *my* appetite."

"So, get back to you. You followed this guy to this bar ... the Kon *what?*"

"Diki. Right. He settled down, and I sidled up to him ..."

"I'm afraid to ask what sidling is."

"*And,*" I continued, used to this and maybe kidding myself but almost convinced that for Goodman it wasn't really all that malicious, "I struck gold."

"I'm guessing you're talking about in terms of our investigation," said Goodman, pushing the theory to its limits.

"Naturally," I said. "His name turns out to be Gilbert Rexford, and he works for Stacy Jaeger. Confidential secretary."

"Terrific. Good work. So, what'd you worm out of this confidential secretary that was confidential?"

"Well, naturally there was considerable chaos the night Carey shot the sister's boyfriend."

"According to testimony at the trial, there was a good couple of hours between the dirty deed and the cops being called."

"Well, that's basic Hollywood, isn't it? How to handle stuff?"

"Right. Tell me again what palacsinta is? Pancakes?"

"They're delicate little crepes, filled with cheese or fruit preserves. Great."

"You think they have brandy? Brandy's a wine, technically."

"They have a palacsinta with chocolate that's a little heavier," I said, trying to distract him.

"It's true brandy's not a pure wine; it's a wine they've added more alcohol to."

"I'm sure they wouldn't, any more than a liqueur."

"Still and all, I say brandy's a wine."

Having convinced himself, he called over the waiter and argued the position long past any chance of success. And certainly long enough to annoy me.

"Listen, are you interested in this or not?"

"Of course I'm interested," he said, glaring at the retreating waiter. "So you managed to get this fellow Gilbert to spill the beans. How'd you do that?"

"I *pumped* him, what do you think?"

"You're trying to aggravate me."

"Do you mind? I'm really rather proud of the way I accomplished this. Nobody's been able to learn zilch about this thing. There've been only the sketchiest reports, no interviews, and I found out a lot."

"You're absolutely right," said Goodman. "Go on."

"Well, it's surprising. And I must say, I've learned this from you: all sorts of people say all sorts of things they have no intention of. I bought him a drink or two, allowed him to have an impure thought or two—"

"I hope you didn't sacrifice your all."

"I may be a professional, but I'm a professional *writer*. And what it was, they were pretty much paralyzed. Somebody thought they ought to call a doctor just in case—though Crewe was clearly dead. Gilbert thought they should call their lawyer. Somebody else suggested their P.R. guy.

"Ironically enough, it was Carey who, later on, anyway, thought they ought to call the police."

Goodman considered this, then said, "Even all that wouldn't take hours."

"Gilbert wasn't totally clear on exact times. But apparently what took so long was they decided to call Ken Curry and get him to handle the whole thing—or Stacy did. Curry's always been his manager, and he insisted they get him there and put everything in his hands. So, by the time they decided that and by the time they reached Curry, and by the time he got there, a couple hours had gone by."

He thought about that for a while.

And then the palacsinta was ready and our waiter approached with it. He carried both plates in one hand and they noisily rattled against each other. It gave an impression of service with a palsy, but I knew from previous experience that it was the custom to serve palacsinta in this way—or at least this guy's way. Just a little culinary show business. Sort of Hungarian Benihana.

"I thought the guy was gonna drop the stuff," said Goodman, when the waiter was still in earshot. "Maybe he needs a shot of *brandy*," he went on. "To steady his nerves."

I patiently explained the custom, found myself somehow arguing about the purpose of this—which tended to happen with Goodman.

"I don't *know* why they do it. But watch when he brings the coffee, he won't rattle the dishes. It's strictly for palacsinta. Think of it as a drum roll."

I took a break at this point, knowing also from previous experience it wasn't a good idea to vie for Goodman's attention when he was eating tasty food.

But when the dessert had been consumed, and its fine points elaborated on and praised, I reached for the kicker.

"I don't suppose you'd like to know the *really* fascinating part?"

"I would if you can tell it in mixed company."

"You remember when we talked to Ken Curry and subsequently in the papers and on TV about Iris Jaeger's leaving the country and off to Bali?"

He nodded.

"Well, it's not exactly true."

"Go on," said Goodman, pushing the empty plate away to indicate giving me his complete attention.

"According to Gilbert she had a nervous breakdown, evidently not the first, and they called in a helicopter and had her zipped off the compound and flown to some very private retreat in northern California."

"Which you got the name and address of?"

"Probably could have, but there's just so much of myself I'm willing to put into my work. I do have standards."

(And Gilbert had another date.)

7

Rayford Goodman

Court was closed. Till they could sift for clues and re-surface the bathroom. So, the deal was meanwhile work on the book.

Which was why, after the usual morning regrets, and the pains—god, what was *real* old age gonna feel like if it hurt this much already?—I was going to the office.

It wasn't that easy. The first part—getting out of bed, showering, shaving, throwing up—went more or less on schedule. Even feeding the Phantom without getting scratched or bitten. We were into total ignoring today. Off more or less without a hitch.

But the car, god damn the car. There has to be life in metal. It can't be any coincidence you bring a car home at night and not a thing's wrong, everything smooth as silk, and you go to sleep and right in your garage it breaks itself.

The auto club came, couldn't get it started. Something about compression and piston piss—maybe pitch—whatever: definitely expensive. They wouldn't tow cars low-slung or classic like mine—spite of the contract says they tow. Fucking lawyers again, I'm sure.

So, it was Tom John and the flatbed for at least sixty bucks, to take it to Orma Garage on Pico, near Hauser.

Orma was a repair outfit formerly owned by an Ethiopian who'd had some vague troubles, now passed on to a Sri Lankan named B.J. I kept counting on Third World operators to take a certain amount of time catching on and up to Beverly Hills prices. This one was learning fast.

He very cheerfully gave me the great news I needed rods and pistons. This was going to take a bit of doing and a lot of time. "First, I have to find used parts ..." (At least, he knew his customer.)

So then we had to arrange for loaner wheels. I wound up with a tinny compact made by the folks brought us World War II, which looked like it'd fought in it. It was red and rust, with a bumper sticker read, "My Other Car Is Up My Nose." I was afraid if I took it off, the car might fall apart.

Which I had to sign for, and guarantee, and leave a deposit on. And get a jump start for.

All of which is why I didn't get to the office till close to twelve noon.

I didn't have to go into any great detail. In California, car trouble is the one always acceptable excuse. I don't know how people in New York cop out of things, but out here, nothing works better than car trouble. Because it's true so much.

Bradley's office had all the warmth and cheer of a Motel 6 (which used to be the cost, not the number of minutes that bought you). He had this theory if he ever made it comfortable, he'd get trapped in it. At the moment it was a long way from comfortable, because besides Bradley, Francie was there.

In spite of what I told him, I still had trouble about breaking up with her. Especially since it wasn't my choice. The best I could say maybe there was a message in the hurt. Maybe guys like me weren't supposed to relate and commit and grow old with the best yet to come. Maybe nobody really had that and everyone just pretended when they got too lazy or it got too tough or expensive to dump each other.

Or maybe the cup really was half-empty the way I always knew.

Like tinfoil on a sore tooth, Bradley found the spot and rubbed it. "Francine was just telling me about her latest hot romance," he said, I thought for a guy supposed to be aware pretty fucking insensitive.

"Really?" I said, into my David Niven impression. "That sounds positively fascinating."

"I think so," Bradley continued. "She's been dating this guy works out at Disneyland."

"It's only temporary," Francie added. "He's an actor; just while he's waiting for a movie."

"Right, sharpening his skills, assaying the role of, what, Goofy, is it?" said Bradley.

"Don't I wish. Goofy is a star. Norbert's just a featured player."

"Featured player, lines—or barks?"

"OK, well, sort of background, actually. Atmosphere dog," she answered, I could see embarrassed, too. "Which, if it was me," she went on, seeming to get into the spirit of the thing, "I would have a sense of humor about."

"This is all beside the point. The man works at Disneyland. Now, tell Goodman what happened," said Bradley, I don't know—baiting me?

"Maybe he's not interested," said Francie, either suddenly shy or embarrassed.

Which, of course by then I was at least curious. "Now I'm going to have to *ask* you to please tell me about this wonderful, warm affair?" I heard myself saying.

"It's not what you think," she said, I can't imagine having a clue what I think.

"Seems like Mr. Goofus came home in costume, too anxious to take the time to change, since it was the night they were to consummate their union," continued Bradley bitchily.

"I don't know that I'm really interested in this," I said.

"Yes, you will," he insisted. "One thing led to another in predictable fashion, but when they got down to the nitty-gritty it turned out old Goof wasn't all that well endowed."

"So?"

"You know that wouldn't bother me," Francie said. What did she mean *I* know?

"But sometimes it's just not meant to be," said Bradley.

I must have been missing something. "It didn't work out?"

Francie explained. "I suppose it wasn't the best time for me to hum, 'It's a Small World, After All.'"

I missed her a lot at that moment. Funny girls are hard to come by.

"Well," I said, laughing on the outside, "I see your point. If you date cartoon characters, you got a right to expect a sense of humor."

The amenities out of the way, Bradley got down to business. "We've been thinking of ways to go."

OK by me.

"Well, it'd be good if we could find out where this Iris got stashed," I said.

"Yeah," Bradley said. "Although it's a long shot if she'd talk to us—or if they'd allow her to. But I agree it's worth trying."

"I can't find her so far," said Francie, with a nod at her laptop computer. Her eyes all sparkly. Maybe too sparkly. "Patients in private institutions aren't in any central file I know of. And while I suppose I could get a reading on all the institutions in California, hacking into them one by one isn't going to cut it. She might not even be registered under her own name."

"Doesn't seem promising," I agreed.

"OK," said Bradley. "I think you should go on with the research you've started, and Goodman and I'll just have to find a new way to go."

What we tried was getting an interview with just about every member of the family, including pets. We couldn't reach Stacy, of course. Didn't except to. Or Stacy, Jr. Long shot.

Using agents, connections, and phone-company contacts, we finally got numbers on Jere Jager, Stacy's brother; Cindy Jaeger, his sister; and Mary Ann Jaeger, Stacy's mother. For Soheila Morris, his girlfriend, who'd had a few couple-line "favor parts," Francie hacked into the Screen Actors Guild computer to get the number.

It took about four and a half hours to collect the information and contact the lot—which was pretty good work. It was the results weren't so hot. Jere, Cindy, and Mary Ann Stacy had all been contacted before and given the word. We got the same runaround from each and every. "Considering the circumstances at the moment, with Carey on trial, on the advice of counsel we're not making any statements to anyone."

"But we have nothing to do with the trial," insisted Bradley, only semi-accurate. "We're writing a book on Stacy and want it to be as authentic as possible. Therefore an interview with those of you who know and love him can't be anything but helpful."

"Considering the circumstances at the moment, on the advice of counsel we're not making any statements to anyone."

Soheila Morris, the girlfriend, took the call, we figured on the off chance there might be some picture work involved. But Bradley wasn't convincing enough as a producer, and she wound up on-the-advice-of-counsel-ing us, too.

You can call legwork investigative reporting or private eye-ing. But either way it sucked.

Discouraging.

Francie left the room. To snort some cocaine, I felt pretty sure. Hoped not.

I did another one of those getting-old sighs.

"Hey," said Bradley, misinterpreting what I was sighing about, "this sort of thing never stopped Kitty Kelley. If we can't talk to the people who're for Stacy, let's find the ones who're against him."

And when we got Courtney Blalock, Carey's girlfriend, and she agreed to meet us, we kind of had a feeling she'd turn out to be one of the ones against him. Weren't wrong.

Le Dome is one of those restaurants seems to fill a big need. It's classy enough to cover semi-formal occasions, and down and dirty enough to be enjoyable. Mainly, a young hot crowd with money.

Bradley and I were sitting at a little table in the room to the right of the bar at five-thirty, the time we'd agreed to meet. By five forty-five Bradley was getting a little nervous she wasn't going to show. We ordered another drink. All right, *I* ordered another drink.

"Give her a chance, she's only fifteen minutes late. Enjoy

the ambience," I said as a very pretty girl in a very short dress sashayed by. "Or whatever," I added, remembering.

By six-oh-five he was really getting antsy, and I was getting cheerfully indifferent. Actually, Bradley was downstairs on the phone checking the office for messages when Eddie brought over "your guest."

I rose and introduced myself, and Courtney Blalock sat down. I remained standing for just a second longer than necessary—because it was such a good view.

Plenty times, even here, average girls look average. But there are days when it seems everyone with any break in the genes department felt the call to come west and each girl is more gorgeous than the one before. This was one of those days and Courtney one of those girls.

What does it mean to say she was about five-ten, a hundred and thirty tops, and the tops were great? With the tiniest waist, the shiniest hair, the whitest teeth, the firmest body. It means all of a sudden my heart sang.

I gave the waiter her order—Evian with a twist. Into health and self. Which, reminding me of work, didn't fit as girlfriend of a man the D.A. described being drug- and alcohol-ridden. Maybe she was repenting.

I took another investigative look at those marvelous boobs. She wasn't repenting, she was in shape, period. In fact, she glowed. Only a nervous narrowing around the eyes showed any kind of stress.

On a personal level, I figured no chance she'd take *me* for a health nut, so I told the waiter besides the Evian come again on the vodka ("I knew it, I knew it!" Old gay joke). And Bradley was back, coincidentally.

"Ah, glad you're here," he said, shaking hands. "I was just getting worried."

"I had some second thoughts," said Courtney.

"Please don't," said Bradley. "We're not out to do a hatchet job. We simply want to tell the truth."

"As sensationally as possible?" she asked.

"No, not at—" said Bradley.

"Right on," I said. "But we'd rather get the real dirt instead of the made-up dirt. It's clear the House of Jaeger isn't exactly all in order. What with your boyfriend facing a murder trial, just for openers. But still, it's possible we could put a better face on it. Raise some sympathy? Or like that."

"I don't see how that could make any difference by the time the book came out."

"Well," said Bradley, "murder trials are notoriously long. There's a chance we might have something to say in time to say it."

Still something wasn't registering. We weren't in sync.

"You know, the book's not only about the, whattayacallit, unfortunate events out at the compound," I said. "It's a biography, basically, about Stacy."

Still not connecting, though there was a little tightening of the eyes. Question?

"Something you want to say? Talk about?"

"I don't understand," she said. "You're an investigator, right?"

"Right. Investigator/writer."

"So what're you investigating?"

"Well, at the moment I'm not investigating, I'm writing."

(I wish Bradley would stop rolling his eyes any time I say that.)

"Well, I'm not interested in the writing."

"What are you interested in?" said Bradley, getting his eyes in line again.

"Carey and I've lived together for two and a half years."

"Right," said Bradley, raising an eyebrow to encourage her.

"I don't care about the book about Stacy; I care about Carey."

"Of course," said Bradley.

"But you're not investigating that. You just want the book and to play up the scandal, and that stuff."

"No, no, we're interested in whatever—talk to us," said Bradley.

But I could see her going into the shell again. Back off.

"I don't think so," she said, rising. "I'm sorry."

"Don't go," said Bradley.

I rose, too. "Come on," I said. "Please. What did we do? What do you want?"

Lights out.

"Considering the circumstances at the moment, on the advice of counsel, I'm not making any statements to anyone." With which she started off.

I caught her arm. "Talk to us. You got something to say. We want to hear it. All right, you're not interested in the biography. You thought we were investigating? OK what?"

She took a long moment before answering. Fighting past the advice of counsel. And something else. Fear?

It seemed to need another push. "*What* did you think we'd be investigating?" I asked again.

"Why Carey would confess to a murder he didn't commit," she finally answered.

8

Mark Bradley

It wasn't difficult for her to see she'd engaged our interest. The dialogue immediately following pertained mostly to settling back down and offering earnest assurances of our discretion, character, and willingness to act in the pursuit of justice.

The drama and intensity had also drawn the notice of several nearby customers, and the aspiring actor serving as our waiter. To deflect the attention of the former, and dispatch the latter, I ordered another gin and tonic. Courtney, now also reseated, opted for a refill of Evian and lemon twist, while Goodman not surprisingly remained faithful to vodka on the rocks, although his twist was departing from "Smirny" to Tanqueray Sterling. By which time we had privacy again.

"OK," I said, "fast rewind here. You're saying Carey didn't do it. An opinion."

"A fact. I *know* Carey didn't do it."

"You were with him?" asked Goodman.

"Yes."

"All night?"

"No, just from about two in the morning to about five."

"Only the critical time of the murder. Sort of convenient," I said. "And where was this?"

"At my apartment in town. Beverly Hills."

"Forty, forty-five minutes away," noted Goodman. "And what makes you sure of the time frame?"

"Because Ken had told us he was going to be on the radio some time in there."

"Oh?"

"You know that program on KHIP, Steve Sommer? Where you win a thousand dollars if they can't find the record?"

"Happens I do," said Goodman. "One of my favorites."

"Well, Kenny's into jazz—Dixieland, actually—and he was scheduled to call in and he said he'd stump them with some old number with Wingy Malone—"

"Wingy Ma*none,* one-armed trumpet player in the Thirties and Forties," corrected Goodman.

"A one-armed trumpet player?" I couldn't help repeating.

"Better than a one-armed drummer," Goodman pointed out. Then, to Courtney: "Did he?"

"What?"

"Stump them."

"No, they're incredible."

"But he *was* on the air," I threw in. She nodded. "And this was what time?"

"Near as I remember, about three-thirty or so."

"And it was around five when Carey got the call?"

"Right."

"From Ken."

"Yes. He said there'd been an accident at the compound and to get back right away."

"So, basically, you're confident Carey's innocent because the murder seems to have gone down during the hours he was with you," I summed up.

"Plus, the word of . . . somebody else, too. Who *knew.*"

"Who?" both Goodman and I said together.

"I can't say. I really can't. But Carey didn't do it. Couldn't have."

"Yet he confessed," I reminded her.

"And recanted."

"But did confess," insisted Goodman. "Why would he do that?"

"You're a writer? You're a detective?"

"You tell me," insisted Goodman.

"Just suppose," said Courtney, first taking a sip of her Evian, "your father is one of Hollywood's most famous actors. Just suppose you've never gotten along; he's never really respected you, or shown you any kind of meaningful love." She let her voice trail off, inviting him to take over.

"You might try and *get* his respect and love," Goodman responded, connecting the dotted lines, "if you knew his favorite daughter was being abused by her boyfriend—"

"Not that she wasn't used to that," she added.

". . . by stepping in and fixing the bastard," said Goodman, completing the thought.

The waiter came with our reorder, effectively giving us time to consider the premise. Courtney took a long drink of Evian.

"That would be at least a viable premise," I agreed.

"It's one scenario," said Courtney.

I took a sip of my gin and tonic, keeping to the pacing.

"And another is . . . ?" I said.

"That when your father, the famous, powerful, all-seeing, all-knowing, all-insensitive god took matters in *his* hands and in Mr. Goodman's words, 'fixed the bastard' *himself* . . ."

"You could show your love and devotion by being the fall guy?" asked Goodman.

"Think about it. Whose freedom has a better dollar value? Who can earn more money out than in? And conversely, who would they be less likely to make an example of, and be more sympathetic to?"

I couldn't help thinking if that were true, our book ought to be called, "Stand-in for Murder." But did I believe her? "As you say," I finally commented, "it's one scenario."

"Which nobody at the trial's even suggested," added Goodman. "Including that they hired this hotshot big lawyer, J. Wadsworth Nichols. Who certainly figures to want to get his client off."

"But at the price of the one paying the million-dollar fee?" she asked.

That really didn't ring any bells for me. First, Nichols *always* got million-dollar fees. Second, with his ego he'd certainly never knowingly lose a case. Although, of course, representing someone everyone's certain is guilty and getting him partly off would be a win, too. (Clarence Darrow, Loeb/Leopold.)

We all drank some more, thought some more.

"OK," I said, "maybe so. Intriguing, anyway. Worth thinking about."

Which prompted Goodman to muse, "But if Stacy's such a rotten father like you say, would he risk his ass for the daughter?"

"Rotten as far as Carey's concerned. 'Unfeeling' was the word, actually. For Iris it's always been a different story. One, it's father-daughter—sometimes scary father-daughter."

"Let me get this straight," Goodman hopped in. "Are you saying ... ?"

"I don't want to go into that."

"Wait, wait," insisted Goodman. "We're not talking John Huston here? *Chinatown*?"

"Let's keep it that Iris has always been delicate, or had more need—this isn't her first nervous breakdown, you know. Maybe Stacy felt guilty about either too much attention *or* too little."

"And maybe the 'too little' allowed a situation to develop only he could end," I continued. "The semi-spousal abuse."

Goodman did that clicking thing that "tsk" doesn't really express.

"Or plain sexual jealousy?" Courtney continued.

Goodman sighed. "It's beginning to get a little soapy for me," he said, and swilled another swallow. "Not to mention disgusting."

"You really think Carey would do that?" I asked. "Take the rap for a father who hadn't shown him any love, if what you say is true?"

"If what she says is true, he's *lucky* his father didn't show him any love," said Goodman.

"Seriously," I went on. "You think Carey would do that?"

"It looks to me like he has," said Courtney.

"So you say," said Goodman.

"So I say," she said.

"And wouldn't I like to believe you," he went on. "On looks alone. *Your* looks, I'm talking about." With which he smiled. Rather engagingly, I thought.

But she'd given us something to consider. Goodman, characteristically, couldn't think on an empty glass. He caught the waiter's eye.

"Sir?" said the would-be actor, thereby earning a speaking part. Goodman circled the table with his hand, but Courtney shook her head. I declined, too. Whereupon he shrugged and held up his index finger. The waiter nodded and departed. One could deduce it was a pantomime Goodman had performed before.

"The press and the D.A.'s office have characterized Carey as unstable," I said. "The family has a history—Iris. Plus, with him into drugs and alcohol."

"Absolutely untrue," she said.

"Absolutely?!"

"All right, at one time," she allowed.

"But he quit?" said Goodman, a skeptical eyebrow emphasizing his confidence in that.

"Yes."

"And does what?" I asked.

"Well, he's tried his hand at a number of things."

"Right," said Goodman.

"I admit, a lot of things didn't work out. It's no picnic being a second-generation Hollywood kid. But after a while, and some failures, he got his act together, went back to school, graduated Wharton Business . . ."

That was news. Hardly the picture we'd gotten.

"And formed a partnership with Ely Appleton and Associates to produce and market specialty videos."

Ely Appleton. I made a note. Someone else to interview.

"And the 'Associates'?" I asked, an arrow into the air.

"Wesley Crewe."

Bingo, into whom the arrow falleth. The spousal abuser and murder victim. I didn't need a note to remember that.

Actually, I didn't have a chance, anyway, because that was

when Eddie—the owner—led a very distinguished gentleman to our table. None other than the estimable J. Wadsworth Nichols, attorney for the defense, whose action I'd caught before, at court.

He declined an invitation to join us, instead merely addressed Courtney.

"Young lady, haven't you been advised not to make any statements that might be prejudicial to your lover's interest?"

"Yes, I have, and I'm not."

"To your way of thinking."

"To her way of thinking," reiterated Goodman.

Nichols turned to him. "You're ...?"

"Ray Goodman."

"Don't I know you?"

"Likely. I'm sort of famous."

"You're on the jury!"

"That, too."

"Uh-uh-uh, what you're doing is a no-no."

"So fire me," said Goodman.

"You're not allowed to investigate—"

"I'm not investigating, I'm writing a book," he said. (I felt my eyes reflexively curling up again.)

"This is a serious breach," said Nichols.

"Hey, maybe so. But in the interest of justice? of maybe finding out your client is innocent?"

"I'm ... I'll have to consider whether I have to report this or not."

"That I'm having a drink with a pretty lady unconnected with the trial or jury?"

"You might get an argument over whether she's totally unconnected. At any rate, miss, I think you better adhere to the instructions we agreed on."

"I didn't agree on anything," said Courtney.

"Well, I would remind you, if anyone says anything that could cause a mistrial, or impede the judicial process—to say nothing of libel, if it comes to that—there are remedies under law. And as for you," he indicated Goodman, "I have serious reservations about what constitutes proper behavior on the part of a juror. I think you would all do well to terminate this meeting and refrain from any others."

"Is this an all-purpose threat?" said Goodman. "How about the waiter, serving booze with intent to cloud a witness's judgment? Suppose we just told you to go mind your own business, what then?"

"I guess we'd simply have to wait and find out if that business conflicts, and if it does, what penalties might ensue," said the now not-so-estimable Nichols, departing.

Leaving us to wonder whether he didn't believe Stacy was actually the guilty party and not his client, and if so, what he was doing on that side of the argument. Assuming million-dollar fees weren't a live incentive.

It was clear, there were strange forces at work here. Pressures, pushes. And, coincidentally, how did J. Wadsworth Nichols even know Courtney was talking to us? Well, OK, he might have deduced as much after reports from the others we'd contacted. When he didn't reach Courtney, he could have assumed she was next. But how did he know she'd be talking to us *here, now,* at Le Dome?

I put the question to Courtney.

"I don't know what's so mysterious," she said. "I've been followed ever since the night of the murder. All that means is now I have a hint who's behind it, or at least part of the conspiracy."

I looked at Goodman.

"Girls this pretty aren't paranoid," he said simply.

"Oh, I do know I've been followed," she reiterated, rising. "And all things considered, I guess I better be going."

"Can't hold your Evian, eh?" said Goodman, also rising, a lot less gracefully—or steadily. "We should talk again. Maybe broaden the subject."

She merely smiled. I didn't get the feeling being hit upon was that much of a novelty.

"You did say there was someone could back up your story," said Goodman softly, having presumably disarmed her.

"I'll think about it," she replied.

"And maybe we'll talk tomorrow?" he persisted.

"And maybe we won't," she said.

"Life's sure full of suspense," he concluded, taking her hand and holding it noticeably longer than necessary.

She removed the smile from her lips, her hand from his, and her presence from the room. Goodman sat back down, suddenly slumping.

By now it seemed like a good idea to get some food into him, so I ordered a couple of duck salads for openers and asked for some bread. We'd stay right there in the side room off the bar, while I tried to get him to sponge up some of the sauce.

"It's a whole 'nother picture, Carey and this Courtney— not exactly a coupla dopehead deadbeats," he mused—from somewhere near the middle of his chest.

I couldn't argue with that. This was getting weird. Or, at least, interesting. Up to now I'd never doubted Carey was guilty. I still didn't actually *believe* Courtney's pitch, but I did have a seed of doubt.

"I don't know how this really affects us," I said. "We still, I suppose, go on planning and writing the biography."

"Hey, we're only talking the ending," said Goodman sagely.

That seemed reasonable, till I considered it over the salad.

"You know," I finally had to say, "if it's possibly true that Carey *didn't* do it, it wouldn't be just the ending. I'd slant the book entirely differently."

The waiter wanted to know if we wanted wine with our appetizer. I said I didn't think so. Goodman said definitely not—he wanted something to drink, thumb and forefinger gunning his empty glass for emphasis.

"I mean, in one case it's a routine movie superstar bio— the early days, deprived and weird, no doubt. Professional beginnings, the struggle, the big break. Then love life, marriages, divorces, kids breaking cars, getting busted—bad investments, losing your looks, AA, the usual Hollywood success story."

"Golly, if you don't make it sound like the all-American dream."

"Well, isn't it true? How few are really happy? And yet, who'd turn it down?"

"Are you waxing philithophy, phillis ..."

I was losing him. "I think maybe you had enough to drink, pal."

"In the words of the philisophicker, 'I drink, therefore I am' ... whatever." With which he gave every indication of preparing to nap.

This called for some executive decisions. I paid the bill, got a hand from Eddie, and walk-carried Goodman to the parking area.

Eddie said it was all right to leave Goodman's car parked in the lot—which, fortunately, Goodman didn't seem to remember anyway. We poured him into my BMW. I took the fast right, the quick lane change left, and turned up Sunset Plaza Drive. Even with the concentration necessary to make the tricky turn against heavy traffic, I couldn't help noting we were apparently being followed by the cliché plain black sedan. (Which, in my rapidly growing experience, meant bad guys. Good guys drove cliché plain *brown* sedans.)

It's not easy twisting and turning up mountain roads while looking through a rearview mirror into headlights trailing you. At least they weren't making any effort to hide the fact.

Of course, it was always possible somebody else was just plain going our way. But it got progressively less likely as we bore left into Rising Glen, then left again on Thrasher—and past the house rumored to be Madonna's. We were being followed. (I doubt by determined fans.)

I nudged Goodman.

"I'm up, I'm awake. Just resting my eywers."

"Well, use your eywers and look behind us."

He turned, seemed really pained by the light, but got the implication immediately.

"All the way?"

"Since we left Le Dome." We were approaching his house.

"Well—we'll just find out, won't we?"

I pulled over. The black sedan, making no effort at concealment, pulled in behind us. There were two men in the car—

never a good sign (unless you were in West Hollywood). The passenger got out, crossed to our car, motioning us to stay put. The other man was on the phone.

"Hold it there, just hold it right there," said the man, whose looks and attitude did a good job of convincing me he wasn't a cop. Could have been a stunt man, if one were tremendously optimistic. We held it right there.

It was only a minute or two before we saw the lights of a second car approaching, paralleling, then pulling slightly ahead of us. It was a black Mercedes limo. The largest black Mercedes limo I'd ever seen. Which I'd seen before. Which we both recognized. It belonged to Armand (The Dancer) Cifelli.

We had crossed paths with Armand Cifelli (or, as I thought of him, Armand Robbery) in the past, never quite to our advantage. Although I had the impression there'd recently been some trafficking between Goodman and him which might have proved otherwise. I suspected I didn't want to know the details.

Mr. Cifelli was in charge of things illegal in the greater Los Angeles area. Not much of anything with a profit potential and/or a chance to die in the obtaining failed to be within his purview.

The felon who was assistant director on the shoot (one hopes not literally), and had indicated that we hold it right here, now motioned us out of the car.

"Wait," said Goodman to me. "I'll check it out."

"Both," said the hood.

"Or you could come with," added Goodman, knowing when to accede to a request.

We walked up to the Mercedes as the window slid down.

"Hello, Mr. Cifelli," said Goodman.

"Mr. Cifelli," said I.

"Hello, boys," said the ghost of George Raft. (With inflation I could just see him flipping a Krugerrand.)

"You want to come in?" said Goodman.

"Thank you, Ray," said Cifelli. "I would like to stretch my legs. Getting so sedentary in my old age." With which he actually started out before the door was open, confident someone would open it in time. Someone did.

I'd noticed this before. When he wanted to sit, he sat—and a chair magically appeared beneath his finely tailored ass. He was not a man whose wants—or even whims—ever went unsatisfied.

"Sorry," said Goodman, leading us to the garage, "the alarm's broke on the front door."

Immediately one of the elite guard popped through the garage door first, to see if there weren't some armed insurrection in there, waiting to topple the regime. As we followed there was a rustling in one of the corners, and Cifelli's man instantly drew a weapon.

"No, no," said Goodman, "that's the Phantom. My cat." Who identified himself with an ill-tempered yowl. "Always hungry. Still worries it could be his last meal." (I knew the feeling.)

Goodman turned the alarm key in its slot, then opened the back door. Before we could step into the kitchen, however, another of the "boys" had to first pop in and check for Eliot Ness—or whatever. Evidently danger lurked everywhere.

"A little melodramatic, I admit," said Cifelli in his usual eloquent style. "But complacency can lead to deposition." (Mr. Cifelli tended to talk like a politically correct professor at times.)

"That sounds like something from Cato," I ventured.

"Or from Cicero," riposted Cifelli. "Illinois."

"OK, Mr. C.," said the advance scout. And we entered the kitchen and followed Goodman out to the living room.

"Can I get you a drink?" said Goodman, who I noticed had completely sobered. Nothing like a rush of adrenaline to shape a person up.

"Has your cellar undergone any improvement since my last visit?" asked Cifelli, who I was beginning to find engaging once again now that the tension had abated.

"Absolutely. I'm now prepared to offer you nothing but single-malt scotches. Would a Glenfiddich suit your palate?"

"Excellent," said Cifelli. "Appreciate it." I couldn't help

thinking it was a little odd Cifelli's company added refinement to Goodman. But it did.

He raised an eyebrow at me—offering a drink. I declined.

"I'll just keep you company," he said, pouring one for himself, then bringing both over to the coffee table, behind which Cifelli had ensconced himself.

Once we were all comfy cozy, and they'd both taken ritual sips, Cifelli smiled and addressed us.

"I suppose you're wondering why I've asked me here."

We smiled back. Knowing we didn't have speaking lines at the moment.

"Need a little favor."

Then came the part I hated.

9

Rayford Goodman

Little favor, or *the* favor?" I said, having in mind what went down between us last time. Don't ask.

"Oh, I think it's just a little favor. We needn't escalate it into *that* one."

All right, what we were beating around the bush about, a while back I'd run into some big trouble staying alive when a couple folks had in mind I shouldn't. It was tough times and not something I was able to bail myself out of. So I'd gone to Cifelli and gotten a little help with the problem.

He helped so good no one ever saw either of them again. Which gets us to the fact I was in major debt.

"Just a little favor," he repeated.

"OK, shoot," I said, which by Bradley's expression I could see wasn't his favorite choice of words. I was agreeing in front because I early learned you were going to do a favor, decide right away and do it with a smile. So whoever you were doing it for would at least appreciate it instead of planning to get even.

"Writing a book about Stacy Jaeger," said Cifelli.

"That we are."

"For the time being, I have no problem with that, conceptually," said Cifelli in that high-class style he had always seemed a long way from regular gang-speak.

Actually, he had a sort of star quality all around. I don't

think I ever saw him without a real deep tan. So if there was lots of stuff he wasn't afraid of, skin cancer was another.

He had movie-star teeth, which he probably got at the same dentists movie stars did. Dressed like a million dollars, which it probably cost, featuring soft as baby-foreskin suits from Brioni and Battaglia. He had this real prominent Roman nose looked carved out of marble, scary hooded eyes, and bright gray hair combed straight back, Robert DeNiro/Michael Douglas/John Gotti style. Coppola would of cast him in a minute.

So, back to business. He had no problem with us writing a book. Marvy.

Now he found a piece of lint (also probably imported) on a lapel needed attention. Brushed it off. Then, since we seemed about as important as the lint, he went on in a kind of bored voice, "I've been approached by interested parties to act on their behalf about this book."

Really? Who could be "interested"? In a book didn't even exist?

"Really?" I heard myself saying, in spite my previous experience less said the safer.

"Actually, they'd prefer there be no book at all—at this time." He paused.

"Yes?" I filled in. "Yes" tending to be a good way to go with Cifelli types.

"Because of various ... pressures ... situations ... conditions obtaining."

I figured I'd try something else. I said, "Ah?"

"But I felt we didn't need to take such an arbitrarily rigid position. And you'll be pleased to know I prevailed upon my associates to permit the book to go forward."

Not my favorite thing when if someone leaves you alone it's a favor already. (I didn't say this.)

I could see Bradley starting to get real red in the face. And hoped he wouldn't do anything stupid.

"Since," Cifelli went on, "I knew I could count on you to be discreet and not do anything harmful to those interests."

"Ah-hah," I said.

"Mr. Cifelli," Bradley said, looking deliberately away from me making little head-shaking moves. "Forgetting the issue of freedom of the press, First Amendment, the Constitution, Bill of Rights ..."

"Not to mention *Godfather III,*" I threw in as a note of caution. Meanwhile I could see Cifelli sensing a little resistance, his eyes narrowing in a way wasn't a whole lot of fun to watch.

"Exactly *how,*" Bradley went on, despite a lot of gross pantomime on my part, "do you want this thing done so as not to be harmful to these 'interested parties'?"

"Well," Cifelli said, showing more patience than he had to, "you remember we had a talk like this once before, about another book? And that time you were considering writing some fairly radical things that ran contrary to *my* interests?"

"Right," said Bradley. "And we did accommodate you. But I didn't expect it was going to become a habit."

"Me neither," Cifelli allowed. "Though you have to admit, it didn't turn out half bad."

"Well, sort of half bad—we didn't exactly get everything that was promised," said Bradley, asking for it.

"True, for which I apologize. Certain things are beyond my control. But you did get a significant amount of money."

"And to go on walking without a cane," I added, going for the light touch. Which Cifelli rewarded me with a smile. A small smile. Bradley's look of contempt taking away any pleasure I might of felt in it.

"Be all that as it may, the situation here, by a wild coincidence, is much the same. We're just talking a slant. I think it would be nice if this book about Mr. Jaeger reflected what a fine, upstanding, patriotic, talented citizen he is—and how much joy and good he's brought to the world."

"Got that?" I said to Bradley.

"Right, I'm taking notes," he answered peevishly. Then, to Cifelli: "Basically, what you're talking about is our writing a piece of fluff."

"Oh, it doesn't have to be dull. I know you're far too skilled not to find some way to make it engaging and entertaining. It's just that in this time of travail for Mr. Jaeger, I wouldn't like to see anything add to his troubles."

"So that's it," said Bradley. "And I don't have to say, 'what if we don't'?"

"I wouldn't," said Cifelli, very quietly. With the deadest, coldest eyes you ever tried to avoid.

"We'll take the matter under advisement," I said, knowing Cifelli would allow me save a little face.

"That's all I ask," he said, since we understood it *wasn't* all he asked. Then, "Augie?" And he started for the door. Augie managed not only to get it open before Cifelli got to it, but snatch the bottle of Glenfiddich along the way.

After they'd gone I crossed to the bar and poured myself a nightcap of the cooking vodka.

"God fucking son of a bitch damn it!" said Bradley.

"Look," I said. "This isn't totally bad."

"Oh no? Could have fooled me."

"Up to now we've been futzing around, taking notes here, interviewing there—it was mostly your regular kind of thing."

"Whatever that means."

"It means it was, you know, could of been about any your basic Hollywood superstars. Their highs, lows, their fucks, whatever. Except for the big break, the kid killing his sister's boyfriend."

"Well, yeah?"

"But what's happening now? OK, the kid confessing and recanting—not so unusual. Or the girlfriend coming forth and swearing he didn't do it. Also not too unusual. Whether we believe her, another story. But nobody before without an ax to grind even remotely suggesting he didn't do it. Then first, no less than super lawyer J. Wadsworth Nichols steps in to shut the girlfriend, Courtney, up. Why, really? Maybe she does have someone can back her story Carey couldn't of done it."

"Go on."

"And if we accept somehow even so he was just trying to protect his client from a careless word might damage the case, we get seriously wondering by this visit from our old friend Armand Cifelli."

"Also telling us to soft-pedal whatever it is which we don't even know yet."

"Right. But what we do know now for sure, what with all this nervous activity—there's more to this than meets the eye."

"To coin a phrase. Only, if we do find out what it is, then we can't say it?"

"We worry about that when the time comes," I answered. "First we find out what the what is."

He mulled that a minute. Then said, "Do you think it's possible Carey didn't do it?"

"Or, it's possible he did but for *other* reasons. And *that's* what they don't want to come out. Have a drink?"

"Yeah," he said, enjoying the possibilities. "Don't mind if I do."

"Help yourself," I said, heading for the bathroom. "I gotta pee me."

When I came out, I put another head on my vodka and we kicked it around another few minutes till Bradley said something about food for thought and wanting to sleep on it. Since I didn't want to touch at least one of those lines, I just said good night and he left.

I finished the potato juice and went out to the garage to check the Phantom had enough costly viands get him through the night.

You couldn't tell from his cranky yowl. That was the same noise he used for everything. I dumped some dry food in his bowl. He yowled.

"Don't yowl, it's your crackers. You like your crackers, dumb beast."

He waited about fourteen inches out of reach of the dreaded human touch (not that I was all that high on touching him, either) till I turned and went back in the house.

I was just about to turn off the lights and set the alarm when I heard a car pull up outside. Looked through the peephole. The car was so dull it was either plainclothes cops or the Albanian ambassador.

There wasn't any point waiting for the detectives to ring

the bell (I didn't have any business with Albania), so I opened the door.

"Rayford Goodman?" said Phil Kogawa, who only knew me about twelve years.

"No, Phil, I'm an incredible simulation."

"Would you come with us, please?"

"Would I come with you please where why?"

"Lieutenant Ellard would like a word with you."

"Is this a please come with us where I can say no?"

"You're a free citizen in a free country."

"Then I'd be happy to go with you. Let me get my jacket and turn on the answer phone."

It wouldn't be necessary for me to take my own car. That was a fifty-fifty shot. If I was in deep doo-doo and wouldn't be returning, that was one reason. If I was a responsible citizen assisting police in their inquiries—as the limeys put it—and they'd drive me back, that would be another.

Still another reason, my car seemed to be missing. I had a vague feeling left at Le Dome.

So I got in theirs.

They took me to a little eight-unit building (octoplex?) just south of Wilshire on Crescent Drive, in Beverly Hills. It didn't take a whole lot of sleuthing to figure out something serious had gone down. Some of the clues were four cop cars out front, a yellow police tape demarking a "crime scene"—and TV vans beginning to show.

We parked and Kogawa told me to wait in the car while he went off to round up Lieutenant Ellard, and the other cop went wherever.

Sitting in the back of a Dodge compact was not my idea of restful comfort, so I showed enough independence to at least get out and stretch my legs. At that, it wasn't more than two or three minutes before Kogawa came back with Ellard.

"Lieutenant? This is Mr. Rayford Goodman."

"Thank you, Sergeant," said Ellard, which Kogawa figured out meant good-bye. "How do you do, Mr. Goodman?" continued Ellard, offering his hand. Good beginning. I took it.

Lieutenant Ellard had replaced Chief Broward (thanks

god), who'd been an enormous pain in the ass for a long, long while. Broward had also been a lot of things besides my enemy.

As head of Beverly Hills detectives, he'd been in the thick of it for close to thirty years—including those years I was at the peak of my fame and form. That part was OK.

What wasn't was he kept getting in my way and trying like hell to frame me to get even for showing him up to be a stupid asshole way back in the Sixties, when we'd bumped heads over my biggest case.

But on top of everything else, he was a thief. I knew it, and he knew I knew it. Which tended to cause hard feelings.

Anyway, long story short, he'd suddenly claimed to've got lucky in the stock market (which I also knew he would), took his ill-gotten gains, and retired to some sunny place with casual banking laws.

The new guy in charge of Beverly Hills detectives was this Lewis Ellard. Ellard was a handsome man in his early forties I sincerely hoped I'd get along with better than the other guy. The odds on that were pretty good, the other guy being the dickhead he was.

This being our first meet, we spent a moment sizing each other up. He looked more like a corporation lawyer than a cop, which may be a job description for Beverly Hills these days. I noticed he had on better clothes than he ought to be able to afford. But hey—maybe his family had money.

Another thing about Ellard, he was black. It was something of a surprise to find a black chief of detectives in Beverly Hills, inasmuch as there are only about seven black people *living* in Beverly Hills. And four of them are Temptations.

"Mr. Goodman, I'm sorry to get you out so late at night," he began, a definite improvement in front.

"That's OK, I'd only be wasting my time sleeping anyway. What's happening here?"

"If you'll bear with me, I'll get to that in a minute. I just have a few questions that might help us. Earlier tonight, I understand, you were at Le Dome?"

I nodded.

"With"—he consulted a notebook—"a Mr. Mark Bradley?"

I nodded.

"Who is a . . . friend?"

I smiled.

"I said something funny?"

"If you're looking to find out if Mr. Bradley and I have some sort of relationship, the answer's yes." He raised an eyebrow. "We're partners. Write books together."

"Oh, yeah. I thought I recognized the name. The Claudio Fortunata book."

"That's right, we wrote that. Did you read it?"

"Uh-huh."

"Like it?"

"Interesting."

"The kiss-of-death word. What didn't you like?" (Which was beginning to scare me. I never used to care if a *client* liked me.)

"It involved a lot of police procedural stuff."

"So?"

"Well, you guys have some funny ideas about how a police department works."

"You have a funny police department. Did, anyway. Before Broward retired. I'd guess some place without extradition."

"I can see you weren't exactly a fan of Chief Broward's. I hope we get along a bit better."

"I'm for that, pal."

" 'Lieutenant' works better than 'pal.' "

"Gotcha. What's up, Lieutenant?"

"OK. While you were at Le Dome with Mr. Bradley, I understand you had drinks with a third party."

"May I ask how you knew we were there?"

He thought for a moment. "As a gesture—to show you I hope we're going to have a better relationship—we knew because we were following the person who came to see you."

"Well, then, I guess you know the answer to your own question."

"You had drinks with Courtney Blalock?"

And the little hairs stood up on my arms.

"And now you're going to tell me that's why I'm here. The reason all these cops?"

"Uh-huh."

"Courtney?"

"Yep."

"Dead?"

"Afraid so."

Shit, I hadn't expected that.

10

Mark Bradley

Actually, being escorted through the lobby of my upscale condo in West L.A. by a pair of macho policemen in the middle of the night didn't exactly hurt my image. If anything, there was a certain cachet attaching to the enterprise.

Passing comments ranged from "Did they catch you breaking and entering?" to "Look who's dating the Village People!"

I took the fact that I wasn't handcuffed to be a sign it was on the level. Any of *my* friends and I would've been cuffed *and* blindfolded.

But I wasn't feeling that flippant. I don't care how poised and sophisticated you are, if you're also an ordinary citizen with minimal contact with the police, you have to feel a certain apprehension on being "invited" to have a chat. Oh, it's entirely at your pleasure, of course. You're not at all required. Until they get a court order. Should you make that necessary. I found it significantly intimidating.

The upside was there was no talk of Miranda (and I don't mean Carmen), or charges or anything actually threatening. There was no talk, period. That, frankly, I don't understand. I don't see why they can't give you some information that might set your mind at ease. But they don't. Whether it's on the advice of their legal department lest they compromise some case, psychological intimidation, or just plain insensitivity (which gets my tentative vote), it sucks. (Or works.)

At any rate, they weren't exactly underplaying things by

sending a black-and-white for me (maybe all the brown sedans were at the garage refurbishing their drab). But aside from the relatively Kafka-esque distress of finding yourself in the backseat of a screened-off vehicle with no inside handles (what if there's a fire!?), it wasn't too bad. Mostly because I was only in that situation for something less than ten minutes.

By that time whatever minimal manhandling had been involved was over when I was delivered to Crescent Drive and into the care of the officer in charge. I could see Goodman had drawn similar attention, but was at least apparently free, since he was standing alone across the street. I was about to cross to him when I was dissuaded by a firm restraining hand attached to the person I soon learned was Lieutenant Lewis Ellard.

"I'll let you join your friend in a minute," he said. "But first I'd like to question you separately, for obvious reasons."

To see if our stories jibed? About what?

I found out about what in short order. And I answered what must have been the same questions Goodman had. We'd been at Le Dome; we'd met with Courtney Blalock. She'd told us of her conviction that Carey Jaeger hadn't killed Wesley Crewe. I repeated the gist of her conversation as I recalled it. Up to and including the appearance of attorney J. Wadsworth Nichols.

"The lawyer for the Jaeger kid?" asked Ellard.

"Correct," I said, realizing for some reason Goodman evidently hadn't relayed that. Which I guess explains why a smart detective would rather interview witnesses separately.

"Why do you suppose your friend didn't tell me that?"

"I haven't the slightest idea," I answered. Privately I wouldn't have been surprised if it were no more sinister than he'd simply forgotten, being semi-drunk. A fact loyalty inhibited my reporting.

"What did Mr. Nichols want?"

"Primarily for Miss Blalock not to talk to us."

"Why do you think that was?"

"I really don't know. Maybe he thought she might say something prejudicial to his case."

But that still sounded hollow to me, inasmuch as someone supporting the claim that his client was innocent certainly seemed on the same side.

"OK," he said, hesitating a moment before putting away his notebook. "Anything else?"

I thought about our meeting with Cifelli, but could see no profit in reporting that, and a lot of potential loss.

"Nothing else," I said.

"Right, then." He put away the notebook. "Would you mind joining Mr. Goodman in identifying the body?"

"It's not high on my list of preferences."

"You don't have to. If you think you're not up to it."

Were we going to play macho chicken here? But before I could definitely demur, Goodman crossed over and tipped the scales.

"Come on, Bradley, let's go get this thing over with." And he took me by the arm, propelling us on ahead of the lieutenant.

"Why do we have to do this?" I whispered.

"We don't, but it's a chance to take a look around. Who knows, there might be something we spot could give us an inside jump on the case."

"What case? What're you talking about?"

"Our book. What do you think? Murders are happening. It's getting hot. Let's don't dodge it, man—this is the fun part!"

Who was I to dampen such enthusiasm? And his instincts weren't bad. Except for the fact we were supposedly into one of the patented Cifelli-brand whitewashes, as I reminded him.

"We'll jump off that bridge when we come to it," he reasoned.

So I found myself reluctantly led up the few stairs to the stoop at the rear of which beveled-glass double doors had been wedged open to facilitate the heavy official traffic engendered by the occasion.

The "scene of the crime" (and I couldn't help thinking how before I knew Goodman those were places I never had cause to visit) was in the first apartment to the right, not surprisingly marked "A."

Other than the address (Beverly Hills) there was very little to distinguish it from what elsewhere would be considered an ordinary, not too great apartment. It was one fair-size room, sparsely furnished. There were a couple of butterfly canvas sling chairs, a small, old-fashioned trunk with a lot of stickers of famous places and ocean liners on it which served as a coffee table (junk-shop chic), a lot of throw pillows, and a rickety set of bookshelves with a portable TV on top. Behind opened French doors on an inside wall could be seen twin pull-down Murphy beds (unpulled).

At the end of a small hallway was an old-fashioned kitchen and dinette. In the hallway itself there was a closet on one side, and on the other a small bathroom in pink and black and blood. Ellard cautioned us not to touch anything, as the coroner hadn't yet arrived. Believe me, there was nothing I'd want to touch.

What I'd most not want to touch was Courtney Blalock. She had not died of natural causes.

The body was half in the tub and half out, partially wrapped in the plastic shower curtain she'd evidently grabbed in her final throes. It was unbelievably bloody. I felt myself glad to be so close to "facilities" should the need to relieve myself of Le Dome's duck salad prove as imperative as it gave every indication of doing.

Goodman came in right behind me, took a quick look. "Well, shit," he said. "It's her."

I saw him look carefully all around the tiny bathroom, at the walls, the towel rack, the partially open medicine cabinet. I admired his ability to detach, considering I'd seen his more than usual attraction to the lady. I was being somewhat less successful.

"Would you excuse me?" I said, pushing him out as I felt my gorge rising. I lifted the toilet seat. But no, if I was going to be sick, I quickly decided between threatening spasms, I wasn't going to do it in such close proximity to the body. I'd take forever to recover if I did that. Instead I popped quickly out, and with a few semi-yoga breaths managed to quiet the quease.

Goodman and Ellard, meanwhile, had stepped into the kitchen, where I joined them.

"That's her?" said Ellard.

"That's her," said Goodman. Ellard looked at me. I nodded.

"Knife, huh?" asked Goodman. "I don't suppose prints and stuff?"

"Ongoing investigation," said Ellard, not giving away much.

"You didn't find the knife," said Goodman.

"I'm not *say*ing if I found the knife," said Ellard with just a touch of irritation. "We just got here. We're trying to put all the information together. With your cooperation, hopefully. Do either of you have anything to add that might help?"

"Only that she said she was being followed," I put in. Goodman pressed his lips together in displeasure. He had a reflexive aversion to helping the police that I felt was unwarranted. It was one thing when he had Broward to contend with, who was constantly bent on his ensnarement (or enframement). But it was a whole new game now. He ought to give Ellard the benefit of the doubt.

"You know that was police folks—you admitted it," said Goodman (showing me why he didn't). But I also knew there was the Cifelli group. How many people *were* following her?

"Did she have any idea she was in danger?" said Ellard.

"We really didn't talk all that long," said Goodman. "Nichols came by and put the kibosh on it." (Kibosh?) "And now she's deader than Kelsey." (Kelsey?)

"Ah, 'Nichols came by'—I don't remember you mentioning that," said Ellard, putting Goodman on notice.

"Whatever," said Goodman, not caring. "When'd it happen?"

"Well, it's a pretty narrow frame since we're talking probably, what, two and a half, three hours or so from the time she left you? The autopsy ought to be able to pin it down a bit closer."

"I don't think you'll have to wait that long," said Goodman, pointing to the policeman and the young man with him standing politely down the hall. The kid was in his teens, black, and had one of those trendy haircuts that look like a bellboy dipped in ink. The policeman had a hand on his shoulder, and the kid had his hands on either side of a large pizza box.

"Domino's," said Goodman.

"Yeah?" said Ellard.

"Half hour," Goodman explained. "They guarantee it."

Later, after the police had driven us back to my place, and Goodman had declined the offer to be driven to his ("The less I have to do with these guys, better I like it," he confided, I hope sotto voce enough), we compared notes.

"I thought that was pretty slick of me, to nail down the time of death," he said.

"I did, too," I replied. "If she was alive at the time the pizza was ordered."

"There's that," he allowed. "It did seem a pretty tight schedule."

"Maybe someone called in later from someplace else, and ordered the delivery, just to be sure the body got discovered."

"And give whoever a chance to establish an alibi. God damn, beautiful girl."

"You sort of liked her," I commiserated.

"Yeah. I was hoping to make a deposit in her sperm bank."

So much for sensitivity.

Because he was a detective and because it was a lead, however slim, he did go through the motions of calling Domino's and asking if they recalled who had called and ordered the pizza to Crescent Drive about an hour ago. They told him the answer was the same as when the other detective called—nobody knew, nobody remembered—it was a busy place.

At least we found out Ellard was pretty much on the ball. Since he'd already called. Big improvement over Broward, to whom it wouldn't have occurred till a week from Tuesday.

It was all moving a little too fast for me. Whatever happened to writing biographies of country-western stars whose biggest scandals were drunkenness and impregnating preteens?

"There is one plus," Goodman continued, evidently keeping his mind on the case. "You got Carey Jaeger sitting in jail. Which means at least he couldn't of done it."

I shook my head. "I guess you missed the early news. The judge reversed himself and accepted a motion for bail."

"And Carey was out?"

"Carey was out."

"Hmn."

"Frankly, I'd always been under the impression you couldn't get bail in a capital case with special circumstances."

"You can if the special circumstances are special enough."

"Meaning?"

"Meaning you're rich enough or famous enough or both. How much was it?"

"Three million."

"I guess old Stace could manage that. Didn't he get something like five million for *Earth Stranger*?"

"They say. Still, according to the report I watched, he had to put up his house to cover it."

"I'm sure Carey's the first one Lieutenant Ellard'll look into. Plus, he couldn't be that stupid," he said.

"Or have any motive *I* can see."

"We have to get hold of the coroner's report, or at least find out who her doctor was."

"Why's that?"

"I'd like to know did she have high blood pressure."

"Oh?"

"I got a peek in her medicine cabinet," he said. "There was a bottle of Vasotec, which is a medicine lowers blood pressure. The patient's name was scratched off, but I memorized the prescription number."

I smiled. The guy really was a detective. In the midst of all that carnage to notice that. And memorize the number.

"It's part of being a pro, Bradley. The little things count."

"Well, I do admire that," I said.

"You've got to keep yourself together at all times. No offense, but you can't notice things if you're busy throwing up."

Go give the man a compliment.

"You're probably right," I said. "Generally. In this case you're wrong. Twice."

"Oh, yeah?"

"I *didn't* throw up, and I *did* notice something."

"Which was?"

"The underside of the toilet seat had blood on it."

"There was a guy there—a guest! Someone long enough or casual enough to take a pee."

"Right. Before the murder."

"And then lower the seat after? Why? How come?"

"Hey," I said. "I'm good, not perfect."

And since it was late and we weren't likely to get any more done that night, I offered to take Goodman home. He said he wanted to pick up his car at Le Dome. I said I'd take him there. He said he could grab a cab. But he said it like he wanted me to insist.

I insisted.

At that hour in the morning, there was virtually no traffic and I got to Le Dome's parking lot in under ten minutes. They were already closed, so it looked like Goodman was going to beat them out of a tip. I went down the hill and pulled up beside his loaner.

We hadn't said a word. In fact, I thought he was napping. But when I reached over to open his door, I found I was wrong.

"Try this," he said. "The toilet seat was up because the guy was a casual kind of guy didn't think about things like that. Then she got murdered. And it got blood on it. And the seat got lowered, because he wasn't the kind of guy didn't think about things like that."

"Two guys?"

"You got it," said Goodman. "One guy friend, one guy murderer."

11

Rayford Goodman

For a private investigator, local TV and morning papers often give a lot more information than a civilian would realize. And it's always a big help you get other people do your legwork. Like, they placed Stacy Jaeger for us—no big surprise—home. Quoting "a spokesperson," Mr. Jaeger had taken to his bed (or kitchen, more likely) "totally distraught" over "this further tragedy which has befallen us."

I sometimes had the feeling there was good money to be had writing alleged statements for people in the news to supposedly say. (When a distraught neighbor killed his estranged wife, their five children, two dogs and an unspecified number of goldfish, Mr. Rafael Martinez, a trainee sanitation worker, commented, "All of us in the community are moved beyond measure at this most brutal and wanton attack, and infinitely saddened that there remain among us those who still find violence the sole means through which to vent their outrage over society's indifference to their needs." Freely translated from "Holy shit, the crazy fucker did *what*?!")

The media further established that Stacy, Jr., was home, too. (The same spokesperson quoted the sometime lifeguard as "at my father's side as our troubles continue to mount, seemingly without end.")

Carey, it turns out, or was alleged, as we were shown a quick clip of a car with celebrity glass you couldn't see through, was en route to the compound at the time of the crime. The news also told us he was escorted (and alibi-supported) by legal superstar J. Wadsworth Nichols. Which was supposedly confirmed by another angle of the same car with the blacked-out windows turning down Stacy's road.

Iris, a sidebar in the morning paper reminded us, was reportedly in Bali. We, of course, knew better. That she was actually (Bradley'd been told) in northern California under private lock and key.

So, scratch Stacy, Stacy, Jr., Carey, Nichols (who never was a suspect, really), and Iris. Now all we had to do was find out where Jere Jaeger, Stacy's brother, was; Cindy Jaeger, his sister; Mary Ann Jaeger, the mother; Ken Curry, the manager; Soheila Morris, Stacy's girlfriend; Ely Appleton, Carey and Wesley Crewe's partner; Kiji Malouf, his and Curry's receptionist; and Gilbert Rexford, Stacy's secretary, were.

"Hey, why limit it to just them?" Bradley asked, I figured a little sarcastic, when I read down the list.

"Because you got to start somewhere. So I'm starting with the people I know had some interest or connection with the deceaseds. Crewe and Courtney."

We were in Bradley's office, next morning. Him, me, and Francine, who was at the moment getting coffee. Not because, she made sure we understood, getting coffee had anything to do with her job or sex but because *she* wanted some coffee and wasn't so petty she wouldn't also, incidentally, along the way, get us some, too.

I love women's lib so much I think they should *all* be in the front lines. Who's better at combat?

The reason I was there and not at the trial was the trial was still in recess.

Judge Steinberg had at first "refused to permit the terrorist renegades to subvert the course of justice" (I think he wrote his own quotes, judges are used to that sort of thing) by allowing them to think they could close things down by merely blowing them up. They'd found another courtroom. Even the suicide was only a slight delay. But now with the murder of Courtney Blalock, the judge'd finally accepted a motion for postponement, based this time on compassion for the defendant having his old lady wasted. (Phrasing mine.)

So, the question was where did we start?

"*My* question still is why," said Bradley. "Why don't we just let the trial take its course, let the police do whatever they're going to about Courtney—and when the truth comes out just write it up, hopefully in a way that doesn't upset Cifelli too much?"

"Because that way you narrow your options. And you might not know what *was* the truth."

"What difference does it make, if you're going to let other people dictate whether you can tell it or not?"

I figured I'd let that slide. Bradley had what we used to call a streak of idealism in him.

Now, I don't dislike that in a person. I'm not a total sell-out. I wish the world was different. And the good guys always won. Or even often.

But the things wrong with the world aren't mostly my doing. So I don't know why he has to get pissed off at me when I can't help if someone puts the screws to us. (In fairness, he maybe didn't know I owed Cifelli for "helping" me out of some serious shit. But the cause of righteousness wouldn't of been helped the least bit I got myself killed instead.)

So that's why I let it slide.

Francie came in with the coffee. And by the cranky way she put it down, I got the feeling it wasn't a good idea to complain about the no sugar or cream. Then a bell went off in her office next door, which I knew meant something was coming through on her computer. She went to check.

"She's really beginning to annoy me," I said. "I'm trying to be patient and understanding, but she could at least have some manners."

"I know. Maybe it's just postpartum blues."

"No excuse for forgetting the cream and sugar." I took a look at the list I had drawn up of possibles and it was a little depressing. Half them you couldn't locate, most wouldn't talk to you, and the rest would cover for the rest. Good luck.

But then maybe we were about to have some at that as Francie came back in with a printout and about half a smile on her face. Both of which she gave Bradley.

He took a look at the printout, nodded.

"So? We're going to play stump the dummy here? What?"

"Remember the prescription?" said Bradley.

"At Courtney's? The blood-pressure one?"

"Well, you were also right about your hunch the name of the patient and the address of the drugstore weren't scratched out for no reason."

"Go 'head."

"With the prescription number and the name of the store," said Francie, "it was just a question of getting into their computer."

I had such mixed feelings about this computer stuff. It was wonderful how quick information could be gotten. It was awful how easy privacy could be stolen.

"And you had no trouble getting in?" I said.

"Not a lot; it wasn't Omaha."

"All right, don't tease me."

"The toilet seats," interrupted Bradley. "We assumed the up seat when it got the blood, the murderer. The down seat, after the murder, a different guy, for some reason there after but not the killer."

"And we were wrong," I put in.

"Exactly. Up seat, murderer guy—down seat, post-murder *lady*."

"Ah-hah," I said, realizing ah-hah.

"Assuming whoever lowered the seat was also the one taking the prescription."

"Don't tell me," I said. "Iris Jaeger."

"You do like to get the last word in, don't you?" said Bradley—getting the last word in.

Which, of course, wasn't all Francie had found out. Once she was into the drugstore computer and had the prescription number, she not only got the name of the patient, but where the particular pharmacy was. And once she had that, and into *their* confidential files, the doctor's name doing the prescribing and the facility.

So that's why we were in Bradley's BMW (the damn Cadillac still going through my bank account with a shovel) on our way up Pacific Coast Highway. We had just passed Santa Barbara (and the local pharmacy), on our way to Marsden's Meadow.

Marsden's Meadow, we knew in front, wasn't for grazing Guernseys. It was for locking up Hollywood loonies.

We got past the burned-out places in Santa Barbara which really broke your heart. Losing your home had to be the worst. Your place, your clothes, your things—your history.

I remember when I was still married to Luana her calling that the house next door was on fire and what should she do? I said take the photo albums and the loose-leaf book with all my business records. She took her fur coat—the most insurance-replaceable thing of all.

Maybe they shouldn't be allowed in combat. Or vote.

(They put out the fire.)

About seven miles out of town there was a woodsy sign— the kind made out of letters cut from twigs—saying, "Marsden's Meadow—Private." A narrow gravel road ran up a hill and into a grove of orange trees. (I guess the meadow part came later.) We turned in.

"I know this is a wild-goose chase," I told Bradley. "They're not going to let us in."

"Especially if she isn't there, or, rather, if she's both not there and it's their fault," he agreed. "But you've got a clever plan up your sleeve that's going to trick them into letting us see for ourselves, right?"

I gave him my Manny Lisa smile. Because I didn't have a clue in the world what I was going to do. Pretending to be a state health inspector wouldn't work with that kind of sophisticated facility. Iris was too well known they'd buy I was any kind of relative. Delivery of gifts and such wouldn't be in person because they'd legitimately have to look out for contraband—drugs or anything might be harmful to the patient. I started to wonder what I *was* doing there, besides going through the motions.

Well, it was more than that. It was instinct, hunch, go with the flow. It was also a real nice day for a drive and I hadn't any idea what else to do, either.

By which time we were through the grove and down into the meadow. At the end was a large, well-tended lawn, in the middle of which sat Manderlay, or Windsor, or some place you wouldn't be surprised to find Laurence Olivier kept a locker.

"Straight up to the door and honest?" asked Bradley.

"Straight up to the door and wing it," I said, figuring it would come to me when I needed, like it always did.

There wasn't an old butler answered the door. Not a totally muscle-bound weight lifter with a scar, either. But close enough, and definitely on the keeping-order side of the business, opposed to the pipe-smoking, "tell me about taking baths with your mother" one. He could talk, walk, and I think follow simple English.

"We're looking for facilities to place a family member with some problems," said Bradley, when my ad-libbing checked out to lunch. "Is there someone we could talk to?"

It was a little farfetched. Not the sort of place you just found yourself at. We would of phoned. But with no better plan, I didn't think I should be too critical.

The guy in the white cotton jacket with the big key ring on his belt grunted us in.

"In" was somebody's nice country home. If somebody was an earl. There was a whole lot of polished wood and an amazing amount of quiet. It looked about as busy as a Texas saving and loan. On reaching a closed oak door he knocked softly, stuck his head in.

"Men with questions," he said. Got an OK, I guess, since he stepped aside.

It was a big room furnished as you might expect. If you just kept believing you were in England. The kind of office the lord would collect his dues from the tenant farmers. The part of the lord was played by Angela Lansbury.

"Good morning, and welcome to the Meadow. How may I help you?" She was tweedy, and the shoes were sensible. But the tweeds were Chanel and the shoes sensible alligator.

"Actually, we're here about ... Mother," said Bradley. "Well, *my* mother, Mr. ... Snowcroft is a friend of the family."

Angela burst out laughing. "You do that *terribly,*" she said. Then looked at me, laughed again. "Mr. Snowcroft?!"

"Sled seemed a little on the nose," I admitted.

"Snow*croft,* not craft," said Bradley, embarrassed. "Jesus, I could have used a little help."

"Now, then, what really do you want?" asked the lady in the costly clothes. (Mrs. Wagner, said the nameplate.)

"Well, inasmuch as the pussy's out of the pouch ..." I began.

"We're writing a book," interrupted Bradley with a look seemed to suggest I might be getting off on the wrong foot again.

"I was going to say that," I answered him. Then, to her, because she'd raised an eyebrow. At the thought of *me* writing a book? "We do that. Write books together. You may have heard of us, Rayford Goodman and Mark Bradley?" She shook her head. Awful how many people don't read.

"Celebrity biographies," Bradley went on. "And *this* one is on Stacy Jaeger."

"Ah," said Angela. "Now we have it."

"Yes, well," said Bradley. "Naturally the more members of the family we interview, the more accurate the biography."

"And you would like to interview ... ?"

"Iris Jaeger," I said.

"Who, you have no real way of knowing, may or may not be a resident patient at the retreat."

"No, that part we know," I said. "For sure."

"Well, first of all," she began. "I'm not at liberty to divulge the names of any of our patients or even *if* they are patients. It falls under the category of confidentiality."

"Yeah, when it's not murder involved," I said.

"And misleading information directed at the authorities.

Hindering an officer in the course of an investigation?" said
Bradley, taking a shot.

"Ah," said Miss Lansbury-Wagner, not buying it. "It com-
mences to sound like something the lawyers might best sort
out."

"If you want it that way. If it helps business getting involved
in a public hassle over one of your inmates—"

". . . residents at the retreat," she corrected. "And now it
sounds like blackmail."

"You got it," I said.

"But let's *not* do it that way," said Bradley, good cop to
my bad cop. "All we'd like is a few words with her."

"Out of the question."

"Mostly because she's not here," I said. "Mostly because
we happen also to know for a fact she was in Beverly Hills
last night, at and in the apartment of one Courtney Blalock,
who, some coincidence, got herself brutally murdered."

"Oh, no," said Miss Lansbury. "If we had such a resident,
that resident would have been here."

"Would be here now," prompted Bradley. "Which is easy
for you to evade on confidentiality, but we believe is simple
misdirection. And since we *know* she's gone, that brings up
the question how she got out. And who's responsible? And if
she also happened to kill somebody, who gets to pay all those
millions for negligence once the lawyers get through? See how
complicated it gets?"

"Yes, indeed, I do," she said, and took a minute to think.
We let her. Then she picked up the phone, dialed an in-house
extension number. "Is Three-seventy-four in her room?" she
said. "Excellent. I'm escorting two visitors up momentarily.
Please secure the hallway." And she hung up.

"Secure the hallway?" I said. "Must be some heavy-duty
'retreating' going on."

"If you'll accompany me," said the lady, not much on small
talk. At least it wasn't "walk this way."

And we did, up a small, private, key-operated elevator, to
the third floor. Then through another oak door—a very heavy

oak door with a very heavy lock. Down a corridor, and to three-seventy-four.

There was a ten-inch-square wire-reinforced window set in the door. Angela just pointed. We looked in.

Dresser, desk, chair, open closet—purple blouse, purple skirt hanging—bed. Lady sleeping in bed.

"Through a door?" said Bradley sarcastically.

Angela snapped her fingers. Another white-coated attendant unlocked the door, opened it.

"Can we talk to her?" I asked.

"I'm skirting the edge doing this," she said. "But I think you'll find it's academic anyway."

Bradley looked at me. I shrugged. We walked in.

The lady on the bed was tranked to the tits. She would have no speaking lines in the immediate future. Real academic. Still, no matter how we looked at it, the zonked-out person in the purple sweat suit *was* Iris Jaeger.

12

Mark Bradley

No question, Wesley Crewe had been murdered. Equally true, Courtney Blalock. But considering the astonishing thousands of murders annually in this advanced civilization of ours, two murders, even two murders of people one way or another connected with each other, did not necessarily a conspiracy make.

Ergo, given that this might be a particularly abstruse subplot of God's great drama—I personally think He might consider a rewrite—certain facts were still available to the more structurally straightforward among us. Iris *was* at Marsden's Meadow, and therefore even if possibly an unindicted conspirator for murder one, unquestionably home-free on number two.

Oh, you could make the case for a split-second helicopter run down to someplace near enough to then coordinate a dash to Beverly Hills and back to Marsden's in the middle of the night. But by someone who needed a shot just to put on eyeliner? Not remotely likely.

So it might just be time to stop looking for any greater situational conflict than that which had been apparent from the outset. To wit: a sodden, self-centered, overblown movie idol had egotistically and monomaniacally neglected and mismanaged the upbringing of his children (at the minimum), and as a result, scandal and disgrace had been visited upon his household. Murder and madness, yes—but separate and apart.

Such being the case, wasn't it also time to just get on with writing the biography I had contracted for—in more or less conjunction with Rayford Goodman? Wasn't it a fact that all these speculations only fed procrastination? And that writer's block and/or laziness came in many guises? And was a precursor to penury?

Or put another way—shouldn't I get up?

Which I finally did, still reluctantly. With musings not solely confined to affairs affecting the purse.

It hadn't escaped my notice that I was rising from a very cold, very solitary bed. That since the departure of the late, increasingly albeit undeservedly, lamented Brian, it had remained pointedly only a place in which to sleep. Or, more accurately, toss and turn and watch TV.

I was, after all, a very young man, barely thirty, possessed of desires and needs, almost all of which were going unrequited and unmet. A body is a terrible thing to waste.

It was remarkable how little it mattered that it was I who terminated the relationship, and that it was his behavior and/or lack of commitment that made it necessary. The pain remained and, in fact, intensified. Talk about the unreliability of eyewitnesses, remembrances of the heart (*there's* a title) made them seem downright photographic by comparison. There is nothing quite so perfect as a departed lover.

Clearly these were not thoughts conducive to a productive day. So now up, I shaved, showered and dressed, and betook myself to the door, whence I recovered the morning paper, and thence hence to the kitchen for a spot of nourishment.

Freshly squeezed juice from Florida oranges only served to underscore the demise of the California dream. We had second-mortgaged Eden to the go-go S&L's. And now had to pay Piper Laurie.

Toasted English muffin from Mrs. Gooch's, marmalade from Harrod's, and coffee from old Juan's mountains of Colombia managed at least and at last to settle my depression onto a functional level. I would get on with the rest of my life. Ecology and economy I would leave to others (I've only got two hands).

As was my usual custom (even when *in* a relationship) I quickly perused the news, and got, in a manner of speaking, *straight* to the crossword puzzle. After such a negative preamble, it turned out to be a breeze.

I zipped through line after line—couldn't write fast enough—till all that remained was the lower right-hand corner.

It's true I've noticed that's traditionally where the puzzler turns testy, probably from fatigue, or the bitchiness characteristic of an obsessive-compulsive anal retentive (who do you think writes those things?).

But I'd had such an easy time of it, I was completely blindsided when the final two words *crossed*, in blatant contravention of any concept of fairness, *both* pertaining to accoutremental fetishes of Zulu war gods. Needless to say, I found this an indefensible stacking of the deck on the order of, say, "archaic Tagalog word for ancient Trobriander intestinal disorder. Obsolete. Variant."

In a mild rage (or a large pet) I threw the paper across the table—knocking over a filigree glass candelabrum which, obviously not up to defying the laws of physics, shattered on impact, escalating my rage from moderate to murderous. Not to belabor the fact (a little late in the game for that) my day wasn't starting out the best.

I rose from the table, went to the kitchen, got the dust pan and brush, and swept up the crystal remains. What the hell, it was old anyway. Over a hundred years.

I crossed back into the kitchen, dumped the slivers and shards into the waste basket, turned, and faced the photo wall, on which were about a hundred pictures of Brian, in various costly guises. Brian in my bought-for-him skiing togs. Brian in my bought-for-him dinner jacket. Brian in my thank god only leased-for-him Mercedes 450SL.

After I'd taken them all down, and reflected on the need to repaint the kitchen when I saw their shapes clearly outlined in sauté residue, and their afterimage still stuck in my mind,

I spent a serious few minutes wondering if it wasn't time to get going on the Prozac. (Fuck Brian!)

Francine hadn't wanted to come in at all. Absenteeism was getting up there. If she'd been working for anybody else it might have been to her advantage, because surely by now she would have been confronted by management and either fired for cause or had a stint of rehab imposed. I was really beginning to seriously worry about her.

We'd all done the drug and drink thing, more or less—it was Hollywood—but we'd got over it and moved on. She hadn't. I was very much afraid we were in for some major accounting before very much longer.

Anyway, I'd gotten her to agree to work at my place for a few hours anyway, if only to nudge us both out of our funk, so here she was and there we were.

"I've got to get this damn project organized," I was saying. "I'm all over the lot."

"It's hard to find a focus," she agreed, sniffling through a very red runny nose, which might well be why it was hard for her to focus. "But I got some good stuff for you."

"Yeah?"

"First, I thought it might be helpful if I could narrow down that huge list of suspects some way."

"I'll say it would."

"And it occurred to me one or two or even several might have been out of town during the murders."

"Great thinking. How'd you go about that?"

"There are at least two ways. Either the airline computers, which are real easy—or even easier, travel agents."

"You're a cockeyed wonder."

"That's an entirely separate matter," she said. "I opted for travel agents. First I was able to locate the agent for Stacy's company. Easy. Long story short, Mom, Sis, and Bro were all at the Stacy compound in Bali when Wesley Crewe bit the bullets."

"Wonderful, absolutely wonderful—that's a big help."

"I didn't go into when each came back, or for the second murder."

"No, that's a good enough start for now."

"More, but just a minute." And she went to the bathroom.

That was a wonderful break. Not that they were necessarily hot suspects, but with one shot she had eliminated Cindy Jaeger, Stacy's sister; Mary Ann Jaeger, his mother; and Jere Jaeger, his brother. Goodman'd be glad to hear that.

Way short of any reasonable time for a personal function, Francine was back. God.

"All right," she said with renewed enthusiasm—*quelle surprise.* "I also did some California company and corporation runs, and found, for whatever it's worth, Jaeplo—one of Stacy's companies."

"Don't you mean Jaep*ro*? Jaeger Productions?"

"Probably, but 'plo's what I got. Anyway, they own among an awful lot of things, guess what medical facility?"

"Marsden's Meadow."

"On the money."

"I guess that way, with a daughter who needs more or less constant institutionalization, you cut out the middleman."

"But you can also pretty much control who says what to whom about whoever," she pointed out.

"Yeah, I hear you," I said. "Only we *saw* Iris there."

"Hey, just giving you the news," she said. "Got any coffee?"

"Sure," I said, getting up to go to the kitchen and put a couple of cups in the microwave.

A minute and I was back. She was out of the room.

I wasn't proud of myself. I didn't even like myself. But I went to the bathroom door and listened. Sniff, sniff. Pause. Sniff, sniff. Damn.

Then she flushed the toilet. Big misdirection. Oh, god.

I went back into the living room and sat down. She returned, sat down, took a sip of coffee, put it down.

"More business things," she said, flipping through her notes.

As usual with Hollywood biggies, Stacy was into a zillion crisscross enterprises, some winners, some losers—*beaucoup de* losers. The most obvious of the latter was the usual California over-investment in real estate, in this case semi-staggering, which was certainly in the toilet and had to be costing a fortune. Not only depreciating, but in a dead market an ongoing cash-flow hemorrhage.

Still, with all the money the guy'd made acting, he should be able to stand it more than most. But maybe not.

"Good stuff, Francine," I told her. "Certainly an area we'll touch on in the book, if only peripherally."

Which seemed to be as long as she could sit still. Up, she went to the fridge, took out a diet 7. Evidently the coffee wasn't working for dry mouth. Christ, we'd have to do something—maybe organize an intervention.

Though I didn't even know if that was legal. Could friends put you away? Or only family? The irony was, it was the kind of question I'd usually ask *her*. (I couldn't just let her go down the tubes. And she wasn't going to stop.)

". . . only part of which is curious," she was continuing.

"What's that?"

"I said, all the offbeat charities he's into"—she referred to the printout as she settled back down. "A lot of which aren't even deductible—according to the check stubs. Like Studies for Viable Alternatives, names like that. Very legitimate-sounding, but then why not deductible?"

"Beats me."

"You might want to look through the stuff I got on Crescent Video, the company Carey Jaeger's involved in with Ely Appleton and the very late Wesley Crewe. Which has the feeling of a shell. Though they supposedly own a warehouse in the Valley someplace. There's another one, too, feels too light."

I took the pages she handed me. A lot of data. I'd check later whether even if it were something illegal it had anything to do with the case.

"Any luck getting addresses on our other principals?"

She took another hit of the 7-Up. "I got Stacy, Jr."

"Through the DMV?"

"Well, you know after that nut murdered Rebecca Schaeffer, California changed the law on access to driver's license addresses, because that's how he found out where she lived. Although they left enough loopholes and exceptions it's not all that hard to get around, with a little imagination."

"Yeah?" (Aren't we talkative.)

"For example, you can get an access exemption if you're a process server. And anyone can become a process server simply by buying a license for a hundred dollars."

"Which at least eliminates the creeps who don't have a hundred dollars. So you did get it through the DMV?"

"I didn't even try, because celebrities usually give business addresses anyway."

"Soooo?"

"I found him through the Video Collection."

"The one on Doheny?"

"Right. I'd heard Junior keeps an apartment in West Hollywood, so I took a shot he'd rent videos from them. Since they also deliver, I figured they had to have an address. As you can imagine, their computer wasn't exactly hard to crack, password being the store name. Not even the manager's kid's name. Or, with this kind of originality, maybe the kid's name *is* Video Collection. Anyway, Stace Jr.'s place is on Robertson, between Santa Monica and Melrose. The number's on page four. As usual, my brilliance was exceeded only by my inventiveness. Excuse me, bathroom."

Which will be exceeded only by your death, dear Francine. What the hell was I going to do?

What I was probably going to do was postpone doing anything as long as possible, just like anybody else.

But she was certainly good at her work, even with one brain tied behind her back.

OK, next stop try to beard Stacy, Jr., and see what he had to say about the night in question—since he wasn't in town but, if my information was correct, out at the compound at the time.

The phone rang, and Goodman checked in. I filled him in on what Francine had found out, and he filled me in on how much the repair on his Cadillac was going to cost. He was at the shop.

"Visiting my money. Tell you what," he went on. "Why don't you keep after the company stuff and like that, and I'll check out Junior." Sounded reasonable, so I gave him the address from page four, just as there was a big crash in the bathroom.

"Talk to you later," I said quickly and hung up.

I dashed to the door, knocked.

"Francine!"

There was the sound of some bumping around.

"OK, I'm OK."

"Open up."

" 'm OK."

"Come on!"

"I said—"

"Open the damn door!"

There was a good bit of fumbling with the lock, then I heard it click. I turned the knob and pushed.

She was kneeling on the floor, trying to pick up pieces of glass. The room was filled with the acrid smell of burnt cocaine. Freebase.

"Out. Just get the fuck out," I said.

"Hey."

"I mean it, just get out of here."

"I'll clean it up."

"Francine, you get out of here before I really belt you."

She shrugged. "Promises, promises," she said, stepping past me, picking up her purse, walking through the apartment and out the door.

I bent down and began to pick up the pieces. Which wasn't going to be that easy.

13

Rayford Goodman

Court was set to reconvene at one-thirty. I guess all the bloodstains would be bleached out by then. And everybody'd be breathing a little easier the Arab guy used the plastic gun on himself instead of Judge Steinberg. Or Carey Jaeger, I couldn't help thinking was a possibility.

So I took the opportunity to aggravate myself by visiting my sick car at the auto shop during the morning. There B.J. explained parts for cars totaled up about three times more when separate than put together. I knew this. I just couldn't live with it. Stuff in boxes costs more by itself than put together by workers with health plans, and pensions, on assembly lines, in factories, bit by bit?!

He also told me about the premium on parts for cars over twenty-five years old. I would think they'd be glad to get rid of the inventory after all that time.

Anyway, we jested each other a lot like that and I told him time was money and I needed my wheels. I also needed to stop driving the Jap clunker, which was an embarrassment and felt about as secure as rice paper.

And since I'd done all the good I was going to by then (none), I took off to follow up Francie's lead and see I couldn't learn something from Mr. Stacy Jaeger, Jr., might help save my license and keep me in moaning distance of inflation.

Junior lived on Robertson, south of Santa Monica, in an apartment looked like a converted barracks—from the Spanish–American War. First thing I noticed, it backed onto an animal hospital, as anybody with a nose or ears would of, too.

The directory—a piece of paper nailed to a post—listed "Jaeger" as 2G. I found that interesting, as there were only four apartments altogether, two down and two up. West Hollywood had a logic all its own.

The door to 2G was open, even though the window air conditioner was on, which gave me a clue it was a push which was more uncomfortable. We weren't talking luxury accommodations here.

Stacy, Jr., hadn't been all that impressive dressed in his go-to-court best, sitting next to old Dad. Looking like a sumo linebacker. His off-duty duds didn't add any tone to things. Basically, he had on torn jeans. Period. Not even fancy tattered. Torn. On Whitney Houston it just looked phony. On him it was more like something waiting for the rag bag. He was large and hard-fat. Not a star.

At the moment he was also balancing on his neck, on a couch, dirty bare feet on the coffee table, staring at the TV and sucking on a bottle of beer. On the table real appetizing by his feet was a pepperoni pizza from Domino's. Nice breakfast.

The TV set was picture only, sound off. The sound was semi-vintage Dixieland, from a cheap stereo. My guess, Muggsy Spanier—Bob Crosby and the Bobcats. (People used to make a living knowing that sort of thing.)

A joint burned in a full ashtray. Old newspapers, empty takeout cartons. Enough litter and trash it could've been the set of "Sanford and Son."

"Hi, there," I said, shuffling my way in, bent over, no threat old me.

He looked up, must have seen me, didn't seem all that interested one way or the other.

"Rayford Goodman," I said. "Like to talk to you. 'kay?"

I took another couple steps in; didn't see anybody else. One-room apartment, bathroom door closed (my lucky day).

No kitchen—hot plate in a corner. Sour garbage smell. I couldn't bring myself to say nice place you've got here.

"I was wondering if you could give me a minute."

"Rayford Goodman?" he said, eyes still on the tube.

"Yeah." I looked to see what he couldn't take his eyes off. They were showing a black-and-white flashback of Joe DiMaggio hitting in his fifty-sixth straight game in 1941. Then they cut to some old geezer they claimed was Joe now.

"Uh," I tried again, "I'm doing a book on your family."

"Oh. On the advice of the lawyers, I respectfully decline to answer—"

"No, that's different, that's the Fifth Amendment, you take when you're guilty."

"I'm not supposed to talk about the case."

"I didn't want to talk about that, necessarily. Just your family in general. Things in general." Which was when the hi-fi changed cuts, and Ray Bauduc and Bob Haggart got into "Big Noise from Winnetka." This guy with this music? So, *then* I said it. "Nice place you got here."

"You weren't expecting the son of a huge superstar to live in a shithole like this."

"Along those lines."

"Well, officially, I don't. We're all supposed to live out at the compound. He likes that. So we're still the kids and he's still the big cheese. But we all have our little getaways."

On cue, showing how great the getaway was, some poor dog getting treated across the way started to howl, and all the other scared mutts joined the chorus. With which he dragged himself up and popped out the tape. "The fuck this get in here?" he said, replacing it with some louder heavy metal to drown out the dog's pitiful howl.

"He doesn't believe in giving us a bunch of money. Might destroy our incentive," he went on.

"I was sort of under the impression you were some kind of favorite."

"If you mean I don't get picked on as much as Carey—maybe. Is ignored better? You wanna talk favorite, you're talking Iris." And he lowered his voice before confiding, "And I'm not totally sure I want to know why."

Uh-oh—really? I took the opportunity to turn the heavy metal to medium. Hate that crap.

"So what does that make me?" Junior said. "Wednesday's child?"

"I never did understand that, tell you the truth. Or God bless the child that's got its own. That's another one. What? Own what? Independent income?"

"Independent income would be nice."

I stubbed out some butts that'd started to catch fire in the ashtray. Though that was the best-smelling thing in the place. "So what do you do—actor, right?"

"Technically. I bet you think it's an advantage being the son of a star."

"I would figure it'd open some doors."

"Yeah, to people who *know* you're not *him*."

"Hasn't been going too good, I get the feeling."

"Hasn't been going at all fucking good. See, even *he* knows I'm not him." And then, to me? To himself? "Son of a bitch."

I couldn't help thinking it would be nice for your old man to help you, seeing he's so rich. But still and all, this was a grown man. What made him think he was entitled to a free ride?

But in fairness, I might think that because my father wasn't rich. Or putting a lot of pressure on me to measure up. Or even around, much past my tenth birthday.

"Hey, well, still and all—it's family," I said before we got too sentimental.

"Putting me on?"

"Yeah. How about your brother? You and him get on all right?"

"I can't talk about the case."

"Just talk about your brother. Get along?"

"My half brother. Just like in the fairy tales."

"Not your favorite person."

"Nah, really, he's all right. I'm just, I don't know—it's hot. I'm hung over." He closed his eyes, I guess in pain.

"That's the price," I said.

"I can see by the little veins in your face you might know something about that."

No need to get nasty. "Hey, I look at drinking as aerobics for the liver."

He wasn't into witty.

"Food helps," I said, looking at the mess between his dirty feet. "Eat your pizza."

"I'm a vegetarian. Never eat that shit."

I could see his body was a temple.

Just then the toilet flushed, and there was a bump against the bathroom door.

"Oh!" he said, popping up. "Hold it there, babe. Don't come out." And then to me, "You better go now."

Who was in there? Gay guy?

"Just another question or two?"

Doorknob rattling.

"Wait, babe." To me. "Goes like this—get the fuck out!"

You don't have to hit me over the head. Not that people don't from time to time. I took a deep breath. Forgot not to do that. Jesus, what a toilet. Switched to a shallow one, through my mouth. Gave him a little wave. Headed out.

On the wall by the door, I noticed for the first time a big picture of Saddam Hussein, adoring himself. This generation has some weird sense of humor.

Depressing shit. And that's a kid with all that success in back of him. Though, I suppose, a lot to be said for the reverse. It seemed like Hollywood second generation were either very successful (Liza Minelli, Alan Alda, Michael Douglas—the jury still out on Kiefer Sutherland) or total lost causes. I wondered, were there any star's kids with just plain ordinary jobs?

But—on the way downtown now—at least I didn't have to listen to that crappy rock 'n' roll heavy metal hate rap junk. As good old Tony Bennett wondered "Who Can I Turn To? (When Nobody Needs Me)." Not that that didn't make you sad. Tony Bennett did that. The man was too good. All those great old songs, calling up all those great old feelings—when the songs were new.

I always swore I wouldn't be one of those people got old and thought all the old things were better, old times, old songs. But honestly, "When one relaxes on the axis of the wheel of life, to get the feel of life ..." Compared to "Ah cain't get no—satis-fac-shun"? Give me a break.

But how could you not get sad famous people—politicians, actors, sports stars—all got old and feeble (ah, Joe). Or plain died. And your place, your time, and the people who made it, just weren't there anymore? A beat away from making you, wonderful you, no part of from now on. Thanks a lot, Bennett.

Music off, I pulled into the lot just below the Criminal Courts Building and stashed the beat-up Asian floozy. I just closed the rusty door in time to catch fellow (girl-fellow) juror, Sylvia Ferris, popping out of her snappy Miata right ahead. No law said *all* the good times were over.

I followed behind—one of your better behinds—and caught up, then flashed a very sincere smile, and said, "I've been wanting to talk to you."

"What did you want to say?" she replied, but kept walking.

"I wanted to say I honestly believe you're the prettiest girl I've seen outside a beer commercial."

"I'm overwhelmed," she said back. "Are we talking imported beer—or just Bud?"

"We could be talking fine wine," I replied in my suavest. "Real cork, first class, none of that twist-off cap stuff."

She flashed a double row of perfect white California teeth this generation seems to have as a given.

"Let me think a moment," she said, unnervingly adding a dimple. Help me, lord. "I do believe it was established during voir dire that you're unmarried?"

"I'm the most unmarried you'll ever see."

"Oh, bitterness. Your ex-wife wasn't a homebody?"

"I should have guessed when I popped my first button and she'd never heard the words sewing box."

"Didn't give a darn."

Ah, humor. Very appealing.

By which time we were through security, and in the lobby, at the elevators.

"I was wondering," I said, "maybe we could continue this at lunch."

"It's afternoon—we already had lunch."

"Well, if you're going to be conventional ..."

And we were at our floor, our door, and into the jury room. Well, almost—*she* was into the jury room. I was into having my sleeve tugged by partner Mark Bradley.

"I didn't expect to see you here."

"Well, I thought I might like to watch some of the proceedings. I was watching some of *your* proceedings."

"Oh, Sylvia Ferris, yeah. We have mutual interests. I hope. Gotta be getting in."

"Two things. Francine did a massive search of California companies and corporations, a zillion pages."

"Yeah, she's good at that."

"Which I haven't totally waded through. But one of the Jaeger production companies, entities, whatever, in conjunction with Appleton and Associates—the company Carey's involved with?—has an awful cute name. Cosa Casa Films."

I let all that register a second. "And you're going to tell me Armand Cifelli's on the board of directors?"

"No."

"Chief executive officer?"

"Uh-uh. Not even on the masthead. Just a simple 'consultant.' "

"Uh-huh."

"Who got paid three hundred and ten thousand dollars last year."

"Ah-hah."

"By a company that didn't make a movie."

"Ah-hah-hah."

"Or even actually have an office."

"Well, now, you know, to some people that could look suspicious."

"Does to me," said Bradley.

"Real interesting. Got to go."

"And another thing"—he still held my arm. We were getting physical. "We've got to do something about Francine."

"I no longer want to do something about Francine. I now want to do something about Sylvia."

"I'm serious. She's ready to crash. We may have to do an intervention, or something. I'm very, very seriously worried."

"An intervention."

"That's where everybody gangs up on someone and forces them into rehab."

"That's all it would take. She'd never talk to me again."

"She doesn't talk to you now. She's on the edge, Goodman."

The bailiff showed at the door, crooked a finger. I was holding up class.

"I'll give it some thought," I said. "Talk to you later."

And I fell in behind the last juror, the antique dealer, just entering the courtroom, determined to march right in, sit right down, and mete me out some justice. Or at least cop a little body warmth off Sylvia.

14

Mark Bradley

Frank Chow, Goodman's detective friend, had saved me a seat which, as you might well imagine, was hard to come by. We'd become a nation—a world—that cherished scandal infinitely more than achievement. And this one was juicy. Though the misdeeds of actors didn't rate in consequence with politicians—actors were *supposed* to be immoral—they were usually so much more attractive misbehaving the public still relished them most. (Though the actual defendant wasn't even an actor, it was clearly Stacy Jaeger who was on trial and getting top billing.)

The courtroom was abuzz with anticipatory excitement, an almost palpable gnashing of collective caps and rubbing of hands. The only thing missing was Madame Defarge.

The jury settled into its box. It began to look as if Goodman was trying to settle into Sylvia's box, his chair was pulled that close. With her auburn hair, fair skin, and Irish perkiness, I could see the attraction. I'd guess she was just about forty, a peak age for women in my view (skewed though it might be)—when, given today's healthful living, they still looked great and yet had enough experience and life smarts to be a total package. Evidently Goodman thought so, too, though I wouldn't be surprised if the person's prominent *poitrines* didn't factor into it (which by their placement and weight, one was pleased to report, gave evidence of being a blessing from above rather than an enhancement from Dow Corning).

119

On Goodman's other side was the classified-ad woman. She might have been no more than five or six years older than Sylvia, but with her phony bouffant wig looked a generation more. What I called the Ann Miller syndrome—people locked in a style time warp. It was amazing how many people did that, clinging to the same look they had in high school, with the same hairdo, same sort of clothes, and probably still sporting the same values.

The guy with the crew cut was another with A.M.S. (a hundred dollars says he's wearing a short-sleeve dress shirt under his plaid jacket—with pens aplenty in the pocket guard).

Of more immediate interest to me, Stacy Jaeger was in his by now accustomed seat, left row center, behind the defendant's table, dressed in a spiffy black shroud cross between Orson Welles and Johnny Cash, his always startling blond hair immaculately center-parted, his eyes clear and magnified by huge tortoiseshell glasses.

With him was the incumbent girlfriend, Soheila Morris, looking elegantly demure in what I judged to be a superior Anne Klein ensemble. (I often thought it was too bad Anne Klein didn't live long enough to realize how much better she was becoming year by year.)

Soheila was a dark, exotic beauty with an almost palpable sexuality—the Persian princess of every man's erotic fantasy. Almost.

On Stacy's other side sat his trusty major domette, Gilbert Rexford, resplendent in a sky blue cashmere blazer that had to cost more than one would expect he could afford. Not a chance it was a fat-Stacy hand-me-down.

And behind all these supporting players, the cast of extras making up the press and eager onlookers. Curtain up.

The M.C. (bailiff) entered and invoked our attention with a main-attraction intro of the Right Honorable Judge Myron Steinberg. (Who names anybody Myron these days? Hey, can "My" come out and play?) His Honor called us to order, set the stage procedure-wise, and after Rexford was invited to wait outside (I guess he was going to be a witness), the next act commenced.

Alvis Johnson, of the prosecution, led off with a complaint that the people were sore in need of testimony from Iris Jaeger, by all accounts resident within the cottage at the time of the murder.

The judge (as if he didn't read the papers) inquired as to what the difficulty might be in obtaining her compliance to a summons.

Mr. Johnson "informed" him that she had been spirited out of the country, in his view a most questionable tactic, and a veritable illegal suppression of evidence. At which point, not surprisingly, the estimable Mr. Wadsworth Nichols rose ponderously to object in the strongest terms that her absence was not to be construed, as his learned opponent seemed so readily inclined to insinuate, as any deliberate and willful avoidance of civic duty, but solely a consequence of her medical condition which, always precarious in the past, had now— due to the vicious and unprincipled hounding of the prosecution, with its calculatedly deliberate and malicious leakings to the press—worsened to such a degree that there was no alternative to her institutionalization.

The logical question which followed was why, such being the case, she hadn't been placed in a facility in this country— as one might expect, close enough for her "caring father" to be in contact? The answer was that her principal physician and longtime psychiatric counselor resided in Bali. (Goodman and I exchanged looks. Nobody'd heard of Marsden's Meadow?)

After a sparkling exchange of multisyllabic rhetorical insults between Mr. Johnson and Mr. Nichols, the judge appeared receptive to the idea that avenues be explored to impel Miss Jaeger's appearance, via extradition if need be, in order for the court to determine her competence to testify.

Mr. Nichols objected; the court so noted and suggested they move on to other matters. I imagined the court stenographer was pretty damn glad it didn't have to be recorded in longhand.

Johnson then said, "The state calls Mr. Lamar Newsome."

Mr. Lamar Newsome, it developed, was a twenty-four-year-old, none-too-bright recent arrival from South Carolina, about

whom the word *redneck* came readily to mind, employed by
Coast Residential Security, and the guard in service at Jaeger's
the night Crewe was killed.

Johnson took him through a routine establishment of the
basic facts not already placed in evidence, which included that
he was on duty at the time in question; that the premises
were secure, that no strangers had called, no devices had been
breached (suggesting an inside job—hint, hint), and that in
the routine course of his rounds he had discovered the body
of Wesley Crewe at 4:14 A.M., awakened Mr. Jaeger and so
informed him. He had remained on duty until the "regular
police" arrived at about 6:15, given them his statement, and
gone home.

On cross, Nichols was at pains to establish that Newsome
didn't exactly know who or how many people were on the
premises at the time; who or how many people had knowledge of the security codes and therefore might come and go
without his actual knowledge; and "hadn't a clue" why the
police hadn't been immediately notified. Because? He had
been instructed by Mr. Senior to go back to the security room
and wait there.

Would he know who might have come onto the grounds
during that time?

Well, he had some idea. Carey had gone and then it looked
like had second thoughts and come back.

He had seen that?

He'd seen him come back.

And go?

Not exactly.

Who else?

Mr. Curry, and Miss Morris.

And what time was that?

Not till much later, maybe five-thirty or so.

Both together?

Couldn't say.

Hadn't he logged them in?

Not exactly. In the excitement and all, he'd sort of forgot
the log part.

One got the idea that Coast Residential Security placed a willingness to work for minimum wage considerably before competence and experience. However, it seemed no particular damage had been done to either the defense or the prosecution by the testimony.

Mr. Newsome was excused.

Consulting his watch and finding it getting toward the end of the afternoon, Judge Steinberg said, "Ordinarily, I'd consider recessing now. But we've been delayed so much by the various extracurricular activities around here that with your indulgence, I'd like to press forward and at least start the next witness. If that's all right with you gentlemen," he said to the attorneys.

The gentlemen had no objections. Unlike TV, there didn't seem much arguing with the judge.

Therefore, in response, Johnson intoned, "The state now calls Gilbert Rexford."

The guard at the far door beckoned, and Rexford came in, walked confidently down the aisle, slowing to give a light touch to Stacy's shoulder in passing as he headed for the stand.

The oath was administered. Then Rexford settled into the witness chair, opening the button on his jacket and carefully easing his cocoa-colored trousers at the knee to avoid wrinkling. His person and property settled, he then directed an attentive gaze at the D.A.

"For the record, will you state your name, occupation, and residence."

"Gilbert Rexford, personal administrative assistant to Mr. Jaeger, living in the compound."

"Which is ... ?"

"Unlisted."

The defense attorney asked if he might approach the bench. This he was invited to do, in company of his counterpart, where I presume he argued for protection against invasion of privacy for his secondary client, Jaeger, and for the withholding of a public listing of his address.

The D.A. I would imagine argued it was already a matter

of record, and since his opposite number was against it, he was, per se, ipso facto, *for* it.

The judge seemed to concur, since he sent them back to their places and directed young Rexford to answer the question.

Gilbert gave the address. I was beginning to understand why trials took half a lifetime. I also noticed these less than enthralling developments had had an unintended side effect as one of the senior-citizen jurors had begun to nod off. To his credit, Steinberg noticed, too, and motioned for the bailiff to nudge the guy. Which he did. The juror bolted awake.

"Present!" he said, grabbing the biggest laugh of the day.

"And a good thing for justice that you are," said Steinberg indulgently, getting a nice judicial chuckle of his own (and reasserting charge).

And now Alvis, in a very matter-of-fact sort of way (if you overlooked the fact that he was black and this wasn't an English court), commenced examining this more promising witness. "I ask you now, Mr. Rexford, to cast your memory back to that infamous night, and see if you can't help us reconstruct the course of events leading up to and following this most heinous of crimes."

" 'kay," said Gilbert.

Nichols wanted to know was that a question.

Steinberg wanted to know was that an objection.

The learned gentlemen exchanged wry smiles and Nichols sat back down.

"Mr. Rexford," Johnson continued, "let's go back to about midnight. To your knowledge, who was in the house?"

"At midnight, me, of course—I was in the small screening room, watching a picture the studio'd sent over for Mr. Jaeger."

"You were alone?"

"Yes, I was covering it for Mr. Jaeger, as I often did when he just wanted to say no to a project and needed some sort of information why."

"So you were, in a sense, working."

"Right. You want everybody?"

"Everybody."

"Well, the day workers had left. The night cook was on duty—Mr. Jaeger always has a night cook."

Can't imagine why.

"Who would have been somewhere say around the kitchen, pantry, cook's quarters. The night guard was either in his office or making rounds."

"There was always a guard at night?"

"Always a guard, anytime."

"So, it would have been impossible for any stranger to have gained entry to the grounds—"

"Objection. Conclusion," said Nichols.

"Sustained," said Steinberg.

"The night guard was in a position to personally see, or at least monitor any security devices—"

"Objection."

"Sustained. Mr. Johnson, why didn't you ask those questions of the guard himself?"

"Not important; withdraw the question." Then, seeing he'd looked a little dumb, decided to sail a little outward. "I just felt I could really save the court's time, this being such an open-and-shut case—"

"Ob-jection!"

"*Mr.* Johnson," said Steinberg with an impatient shake. "Jury will disregard." (Like the game when someone says whatever you do, don't think of an elephant.)

"Mr. Rexford," Johnson resumed, "you have testified there was a cook on duty. We know there was a guard on duty. Were there any other employees there that night?"

"Not to my knowledge."

"Very well. Who else was there?"

"First, of course, Mr. Jaeger—upstairs in his bedroom suite."

"You saw him there?"

"No, but I saw the elevator was on the second floor, and Mr. Jaeger never used the steps."

No kidding.

"Go on."

"Stacy, Jr., was in the editing room in the basement, working on a tape."

"This is midnight."

"That's right, most of the family are sort of night people. You want me to go on?"

Johnson nodded.

" 'kay. Carey was in the kids' cottage."

"Objection," said Nichols. "The witness says he was in the basement. How could he tell who was in the cottage?"

Gilbert fielded it himself. "Because he told me earlier he was going to the cottage."

"But he could have changed his mind," insisted Nichols.

"Your Honor," said Johnson, "Mr. Nichols is arguing with my witness during my questioning."

"So you're objecting to his objection."

"Right."

"You're sustained; you're overruled," he said to Johnson and Nichols in that order.

Rexford went blithely on, "Besides, I *saw* him go. Then later I saw a light on the phone from his room when he made a call."

"Or *some*one," said Nichols.

"Mr. Nichols, you will have your chance at cross," reminded the judge. "Stop it, both of you."

" 'kay," continued Rexford, a bit surprisingly eager. "Iris was in the kids' cottage, probably in her bedroom—"

Nichols rose.

"Because she was *mostly* in her bedroom," Rexford went on. "And by that time *usually* took her pills, and would *probably*—"

"Mr. Johnson," said the judge, "I don't favor this trolling for random seafood. I would like you to start framing your questions a little tighter, so we don't get these rambling essay answers from the witness."

"Yes, sir, thank you, sir," said Alvis, I thought a bit smarmy.

"Mr. Rexford," he resumed, "who else was present either in the house or in the kids' cottage?"

"No one I haven't mentioned in the main house; in the cottage only Wesley Crewe."

"OK," said Johnson. "So we've got Mr. Jaeger upstairs in the main house, yourself and Stacy, Jr., in the basement."

"Right."

"The cook in the cookery, and the guard either making his rounds or in the security room."

"Yeah."

"Which leaves, at the scene of the crime itself, Wesley Crewe—the victim; Iris Jaeger, asleep from her medication; and *only* Carey Jaeger, the defendant."

"Right," said Rexford with no noticeable reluctance. For a friend of the family, he seemed to be pitching right in with the coffin nailing.

"Objection, Your Honor. Calls for a conclusion. Mr. Rexford can't know for a certainty that no one else was present."

"Sustained."

"But you saw no one other than those you described," continued Johnson.

"Right."

"And you heard of no one."

"Right."

"Either from the guard . . ."

"Right."

"Or any of the others."

"Right. There was no one else. Carey was the only one."

"Objection!"

"Sustained. The jury will disregard."

I looked over at Goodman. He was sighing. I looked at the others. The jury wasn't disregarding. *You* try not thinking of elephants.

15

Rayford Goodman

After court was over for the day, I made up to meet Bradley at the St. James's Club for a drink. This was not only a club, but a new hotel, actually, remade from what used to be the Sunset Towers.

The Sunset Towers had been a very famous apartment building in which very famous stars did very famous fornications—in the good old days.

After the movies (and the movie stars) fell on hard times, the building sort of went to seed, and for a while just ordinary people did ordinary fornications there.

And after a while, nobody did much of anything. For a long time.

Then it changed hands, and the town got lucky. Because instead of a seventeenth mini-mall in a mile, they decided to keep the basic gorgeous building and restore it to all its old Art Deco glory. Which was great for the eyes—and the privileged few.

But bad for us regular mortals, as they right away turned it into an exclusive members-only hotel.

So it was for looking but not touching. Unless you were Mark Bradley, and then you somehow had a lifetime complimentary membership. (Someone in the front office maybe caught his "eye"?)

Anyway, as usual when something was trendy, expensive, or otherwise outrageous, Bradley had an in.

We split up at the parking lot outside court, and he took off. I went looking for my subcompact loaner, which I seemed to have misplaced. I was beginning to think maybe it got accidentally mistaken for a mini-dumpster and hauled away, when lo and behold, I bumped into the lovely Sylvia Ferris heading for her Miata.

Since it turned out she lived relatively close by the St. James's, on Olive, and didn't have any prejudice against trendy, expensive, or otherwise outrageous places (or was maybe starting to discover my charms), she agreed to join us for a drink.

I spotted the loaner and explained I was driving the embarrassing junk because my classic real car was in the shop being restored to concours condition. She didn't seem to care much, which was unusual since in California generally you are what you drive.

But it turned out she mainly didn't care because she wasn't going to drive in it, or even be seen near it.

I think this was less car snobbery than she wasn't about to commit for the night and a possible close encounter of the basic kind without more info. At any rate, she said she'd follow in her own car.

It took a bit, freeways being freeways (god, when were we going to stop having more people?), and we got separated on the way. No sweat, though, as we arrived more or less in a tie at the entrance to the St. James's (a spelling I could live without, too).

She popped out of the Miata, got smiles and bows. I got out of the loaner clunker and thought the snob valet parker was going to put on rubber gloves.

She slipped her arm through mine and we went inside together, which I certainly hoped taught the attendant not to judge a book by its car.

In the lobby we passed a bunch of Deco art stuff from the school of MGM. One of the featured pieces was an Erté sculpture of a long, lean lady getting tugged by a couple long, lean borzoi dogs. Since I didn't recall bumping into too many borzois lately, I wondered what happened to dogs went out of style. Was there an old dogs home?

Likewise when they broke *into* style. I was a kid there were about a dozen dalmatians to a city. All in fire stations. Now they're in every commercial and a hundred and one to the block.

Anyway, the place was pretty. And it really felt like old Hollywood. Or the *Queen Mary.*

Bradley was already there, at a table in the bar. I introduced Sylvia, and he was gentleman enough to act like that'd been the plan all along.

We all sat down.

I recognized a local TV anchorman who I'd seen for years and watch go slim to pudgy and dark-haired to silver white, on a corner stool at the bar, alone. A fairly famous actress I'd had a crush on twenty or thirty years ago and now sold waterproof undies was on another stool, also looking lonely. Neither one did much to make me feel any younger. You'd think, both being celebrities, they'd be with somebody. Or at least talk to each other.

Bradley had already ordered something to suit the decor, a sidecar or a Manhattan, something out of a black-and-white movie; Sylvia decided on a champagne cocktail (not a good sign); and I went for a Tanqueray Sterling on the rocks, two onions. On second thought, never sure what happy surprises life might have in store, changed onions to olives.

We all took a breath (speaking of which), settled in, established the guy was who he was and the lady who she was, and I noticed I was the only one sighing.

Young people thought old people were *supposed* to be old. They didn't know we were really young people with something terribly wrong.

The drinks came. Thank god. We sipped—some of us. Some of us gulped. Meanwhile the news guy moved over to hit on the diaper lady. Which somehow made me feel better.

At the sound of Sylvia's voice, I turned back.

"Beg your pardon?"

"I just said, 'Some day.' "

"Oh, yeah."

"You were there, too," she said to Bradley.

"I certainly was."

"What do you think?"

"I don't think you're supposed to discuss it," said Bradley.

"*We're* not," she said, showing a dimple you could bury yourself in real comfortably. "I asked you."

"I think it was some day," said Bradley.

"Well, *I* think it was downright weird," I said.

"Oh?" she said, crinkling her nose. I'm not much on nose crinkling, being permanently put off by a haberdasher out here named Bijan who constantly features himself on billboards leaping and laughing and nose crinkling. Since he's the most expensive tailor in the world, I guess I know why he's laughing, anyway. But in her case, with the dimple, and her coloring, and the warmth of her flesh against my side, it seemed pretty damn cute.

"Don't you?"

"In what way?" she said, licking the corner of a lip. I'd be happy to do that for her.

"How this Rexford guy, next thing to a member of the family, gets on the stand and practically destroys Carey."

"I'm pretty sure you're not supposed to discuss the case," said Bradley.

"*I'm* not discussing it," said Sylvia behind just the tip of the pinkest tongue.

"She's not discussing it," I assured Bradley. "What *I* meant, if the D.A. called Rexford, he had to testify. But how come no holding back, or trying to put a good face on it? At least raise some doubt?"

"Uhm," said Sylvia.

"Not that there seemed much doubt, right?" I said.

She shrugged.

"I could see everybody felt that way, the whole jury. That there wasn't any doubt. But really, you look strictly at the evidence ..."

"Maybe Mark's right. You know, not discussing it?" she said, but smiling when she turned to me. Between the two of us. Saying not discuss it, but not really meaning it.

"There's something I don't guess you know, Sylvia. We're

writing a book on Jaeger. Bradley and me. That'll include the trial. So you can imagine how much inside dope we already have."

"Mostly things that're a matter of public record," said Bradley, for whatever reason.

"But a lot's not," I put in. What was he trying to do, undercut me? "Believe me, we know stuff, a lot of which probably won't even come up, could change a lot of minds."

"I think we ought to change the subject instead," said Bradley. What did he care I was making a big impression?

"But I could tell you things, believe me, way past reasonable doubt. Something's rotten in Rotterdam."

She just kept smiling at me, eating up the words. With hopes for more. My hopes. Than words.

"I think you're making a mistake, *Ray,*" said Bradley—who never calls me Ray. Like I'm giving away trade secrets or something. Dummy didn't know I was trying to score here?

"There just seems a lot of holes," I went on. It was *my* date, not his. "It doesn't compute. I keep getting the feeling the whole thing's been scripted and everybody's got a part."

"And do I have a part?" she asked, way more hot than innocent.

"You have many, many parts," I said. "All good."

"You really think so?" she said in a little-girl voice out of her big-girl mouth.

"No, I'm only trying to give a shy little mouse just the teensiest touch of self-confidence," I said, tongue in chick. (I wish.)

But lest things get too good, Bradley stepped in again, taking hold of my arm. "Maybe we should all have another drink," he said. "And definitely *change the subject.*"

Having another drink, anyway, wasn't something you find me arguing a lot against.

I got the waiter.

"Another all around," I said.

But to my surprise, Sylvia said, "No, not for me, thanks." And got up. "I have to be going."

"What's the hurry?" I said, struggling around the leg of the table to get up.

"I just have to. Really. Thanks for the drink, I enjoyed it. Nice meeting you," she said to Mark. And before we could so much as shake hands, took off like a shot.

I sat back down. That was confusing. "What the hell do you make of that?" I said to Bradley. Like he'd know.

"I make that you tried to impress the wrong woman in the wrong way," he said.

"What do you mean?"

"It's remotely possible she understands what being a juror's supposed to be about. And the rules. Which include not discussing the case."

"Bullshit, she *wanted* to discuss the case. You weren't facing her, she was encouraging me."

Bradley shrugged. "Just a thought."

True, she was maybe friendlier before. Nah, she was friendly during. A lot.

"Anyway, if she's got such a high moral tone," I said, "she shouldn't be ordering any champagne cocktails."

He gave me a look.

"A lady doesn't order the most expensive thing."

Meanwhile, the anchorman said something got a big throaty laugh out of the diaper lady (who seemed to be holding her liquor—far as I could see). Not everybody was striking out.

But the sparkle seemed to've gone out of the cocktail hour. So we decided call it a day. Bradley got the check, paid, and wrote on the receipt, "Illegally attempted to influence fellow juror." As if sex was against the law. A subject I wouldn't open up I was him.

We walked out, past the girl with the borzoi bow-wows, down the marble steps, and outside. Right in front was a familiar big black Mercedes limo, back door open.

"Gentlemen," said Armand (The Dancer) Cifelli, leaning forward where we could get the full force of his Sicilian charm. "Won't you join me? The boys will take care of your cars."

"The "boys" were all of a sudden on either side of us, like we were going to make a wild break for it. But when I didn't jump at this warm invitation, the "boy" on my side gave me a quick sharp jab in the biceps. Not enough I'd stumble into Mr. Cifelli. Just enough for black and blue.

There were parts of this relationship I could easy pass on. We got in the car.

"You know," I said, once the door was closed and we started moving, "I had a thought one day. Possible you weren't actually Mr. Cifelli, but just an actor hired to do threatening and showing up in the middle of the night and all that crap. While he stayed home, pigging out on junk food and watching TV."

"You have a vivid imagination," said the all too real Cifelli.

"Humor is an oblique way of expressing resentment at being constantly hassled and pushed around," said Bradley.

"I'm sorry you feel that way. I'd hate to give the impression I was hassling and pushing around. Even obliquely," said Cifelli—to the master of oblique.

"Well, I mean," Bradley went on, getting bolder—maybe too bold, "we're not here because we want to be, are we?"

"But, see—you're wrong, you'll want to," said Cifelli. "Trust me, I'm doing you a favor."

And while it's true sometimes Cifelli's favors were only letting you go on living a while longer, sometimes it did work out to mutual advantage. At any rate, we didn't say much more as the limo continued west on Sunset. Then headed down Whittier, across Wilshire, through the passway by Robinson's and the Beverly Hilton and turned right on Santa Monica. Left on Century Park East, then across Constellation, and into the underground lot before Avenue of the Stars. It stopped being any surprise we were going to 2020, Ken Curry's office.

What was a surprise, once we got to the suite and into the conference room, was who all was in the group. Besides Cifelli, Bradley and me, and of course, Curry himself, there was his secretary—the dark-eyed number we'd met last time; super lawyer J. Wadsworth Nichols; big old Stacy Jaeger (live and in person); girlfriend Soheila Morris; and definitely out of the blue, Richard Penny, our publisher!

Strange bedpersons.

Bradley and I exchanged looks, and he managed to mumble, "This, I didn't expect."

Nor me, as equally unexpected, background music was some early Hot Lips Page. (There wasn't an enormous amount of late Hot Lips Page.)

"I think we're pretty much all here now. Aren't we?" said Curry. "Before we get started, drinks?" he asked, and for some reason looked at me.

"No, thanks," I said, wondering why the words didn't come easy. Bradley just shook his head. Cifelli ordered an espresso, which he seemed to know they'd have. Nichols said regular coffee. The one went to fetch it, though, which seemed surprising, was Stacy's girl, Soheila. Looked like Curry still wasn't interfering with Ms. Malouf's lib. Or the fringe benefits, if you wanted to take him literally.

Another possibility was Soheila was pretty much at home here. Jaeger seemed to be already drinking something thick which I finally decided was soup. While Curry kept taking sips from the world's thinnest glass, which he refilled time to time from a bottle of 1947 Noellat Musigny—whatever the hell that was.

Penny, who for some reason kept his hand mostly over his mouth, mumbled, "Sit down, guys, it's good news."

"So what's going on?" said Bradley, who had yet to learn about who did openers in what company.

"We'll start in a moment," said Curry, and turned to me again. "You're sure you don't want a drink?"

"I'll have a San Pellegrino," I said.

"Soheila?"

"I'm sorry, we don't have San Pellegrino. We have Ramlossa."

"In that case I'll have a vodka rocks," I said. I was, after all, in the middle of cocktail hour.

"So," said Stacy unexpectedly, in that famous soft, high voice. "I understand you all been asking 'round about me."

And I noticed he still had traces of a southern accent. Something you never noticed in his movies.

"That's what you do when you write a book," said Bradley, a touch testy. "It's called research."

Penny lifted his hand a few inches, as if to signal caution. If I knew Bradley, it wouldn't be enough to shut him up.

"And getting goons to snatch you up on a public street is called intimidation," he continued, which I felt sure would go over big with Cifelli.

"I'd hold it a minute," suggested Penny, his hand still over his mouth.

"And out of the research, once intimidation doesn't stop one, comes reporting and writing," my partner continued, irritating just about all of us.

"And deal making, and peripheral benefits," put in Nichols. Whatever that meant.

"It jest sort of come to me that's a funny way to go about things, write somebody's life talking to evuhbody but the person," said Stacy with a nod made his big glasses slide down his nose.

"It's not the way we'd have chosen," said Bradley. "The only reason there are unauthorized biographies is because the subjects don't wish to be—"

"Biographed," I put in.

"Still an' all," said Stacy, getting southerner by the minute, pushing his glasses back up, "don't it strike you somehow wrong ev'one profit from somebody else's accomplishments except the one done the accomplishin'?"

There was a slight silence.

"You want to take that, Mr. Penny?" said Bradley.

"There are ways to answer those objections. And we're here to address them."

But before we could get a reading what those ways were, the door opened to the office, suite, whatever next door. And in strode a very tall, distinguished-looking black gentleman. With a Marvin Hagler haircut and wearing a plum-colored, wonderfully tailored double-breasted suit looked to be made out of unborn thousand-dollar bills.

"Gentlemen," said Curry, half bowing, half clearing a path, "this is Mr. Ely Appleton." Who, if memory serves, was the guy Carey was in with (according to Courtney Blalock), and partners with the late Wesley Crewe, too. But memory served more. He was also an ex-substitute forward for the Detroit Pistons named Elias X. By the looks of things, definitely first team here.

Curry underlined that when he said, "Mr. Appleton will explain the whys and wherefores that brought our various interests together in order to produce this meeting."

"I wouldn't say that, Kenny, OK?" said Appleton.

"Cancel that," said Curry. "The part that concerns you two," Curry went on, trying to recover, directing his conversation at Bradley and me, "is that for reasons Mr. Appleton may or may not wish to share, we've decided to cooperate with you on this book concept."

And as Bradley and I exchanged looks, not having the slightest idea what was actually going down, Ely/Elias Appleton/X. explained, "You get to do the book, OK? Authorized. With cooperation. Go for it." Which seemed to cover all he was about to say, since he nodded to the others and turned in a kind of military way.

Then, to Ms. Malouf, almost angry, "Kiji. Tea. My office. Now!" and stomped on out with hard, heavy steps that rattled the coffee cups.

Leaving a very big hole in the room. A thousand questions. And a large feeling of weirdness.

Which was about when Soheila came back with my drink. Just as the late Oran "Hot Lips" Page was going on about "that lucky old sun with nothing to do" (but roll around heaven all day).

16

Mark Bradley

Whoa. Hold it. Please hang up and dial again. You have reached a disconnected thought. He who opposeth now allieth?

"It's a lot like Russia," Goodman said. "Just when you've got the teams all divvied up, the other side decides to join you. I take it this means you, too, Mr. Cifelli?"

This query was met with a very cold look from the "family"-oriented gentleman.

"Not that I have any real need to know," amended Goodman reflexively.

"We are all in accord here," said Cifelli, switching to what he intended as reassuring. But coming up quite a bit short as far as my needs were concerned.

Seeing my ongoing semi-shock, Goodman leaned in and whispered, "What it boils down to, kid, the fix is in." With which I couldn't but agree, discomforting as I found it to be. Then added, compounding the distress, "And we're a fixture of the fix."

Out loud again, he still resisted. "Don't we have a slight technical problem as far as I'm concerned?"

"I'm sure there's nothing that can't be worked out," said Curry, once more apparently in control now that Appleton had left the room.

"Like, I'm on the jury. It was a close enough call working

just with Bradley, terms of legality. But to actually collaborate with the guy on trial's father . . . ?"

"I wouldn't worry about that," said Curry.

"I think he's right," I joined in, finally finding my voice. "I can't see it as anything but an obvious conflict of interest."

"Momentarily," said Nichols.

"And talk about conflict of interest," continued Goodman, turning his palms up and toward Nichols, clearly conveying his meaning.

"I wouldn't worry about that, either, if I were you. My status is not an issue," J. Wadsworth replied.

"I sincerely question that," I said. "But I'll grant you our more immediate concern is Goodman."

"That, only superficially, too, I assure you," said Nichols. "A mere detail."

"You're going to fucking turn me in, aren't you?" said Goodman. "For having a drink with Courtney Blalock."

"Not at all," assured Nichols.

"It's not something you have to concern yourselves with," said Curry. "Trust me." (Something I found just a touch hard to do.)

At which point Ms. Malouf stuck her perky Parkes nose back in the door. "Excuse me. Mr. Jaeger? Creative Artists on three. Rowland Perkins?"

"Tell him I'm in a meeting," said Jaeger. "I'll call back."

"I like that," said Goodman. "One of the most important men in Hollywood, you're in a meeting."

"I *am* in a meeting," reminded Stacy.

"And anyway," said Goodman, not so uncomfortable with the fix he couldn't be distracted by an unrelated peeve, "it's what everybody does now instead of work—take meetings. Other day I had ants, called up the exterminator. In a meeting. The guy spritzes bug juice, he's in a meeting!"

"To get sort of back to the subject, Stacy—don't you think you should take the call?" asked Curry.

"Look, I said I'll do the picture. You tell me do it, I need the money, I know I'm in a bind. So jest *arrange* the money and I will do it."

"For the lawyers, right?" said Goodman, staring at Nichols. "What was it, a million?"

"I wish," said Stacy. "That's jest retainer."

"And not strictly speaking, of general interest," said Curry, about as close as he was apt to come to the words "shut up" to Stacy.

At which point it was Mr. Nichols who decided to take some expensive umbrage. "It's all right for a baseball player hitting .238 with forty-seven runs batted in to get a million dollars, but not an attorney when a human life's at stake?"

"I'm not too thrilled about the ball players, either, you want to know the truth," said Goodman, ever the even-handed kvetch.

"Excuse me," reminded the nubile Ms. Malouf, "Mr. Appleton's waiting for his tea. What should I do?"

"Tell Mr. Perkins Mr. Jaeger will get back to him momentarily," said Curry. With which, following a somehow pointed toss of her luxuriant hair, Curry added, "Please," and she left the room. (I guess those moves work.)

"Stace—you know, it's not all just money, there are the artistic considerations. He might just have wanted to know how you and Oliver Stone hit it off," I couldn't help feeling trying to impress us with a bit of name dropping.

"Anyway," he continued, "I think we're getting a little afield here. Now that we're in bed together, so to speak ..." (Here Goodman gave me a look I could've lived very nicely without) "... the important thing is we get the project moving. The financial details, the upfront guarantees ..."

"I don't think the boys are interested in that," interjected Penny hastily.

"Sure we are," I said. "It'll be in the papers anyway, won't it?"

"Well, you know, a lot of that's publicity, the figures are greatly exaggerated. Don't think for a minute when you read Mr. Jaeger's getting two million dollars—"

Hey, what what what?! And we have to fight like hell for peanuts?

"And, of course," continued Penny, smoothly switching to

the offensive, "there will have to be some sort of renegotiating. Downward, naturally—as regards your participation—in light of the impact, developmentally, of the added increments, word-wise."

"Do the words 'go fuck yourself' word-wise impact any part of your anatomy?" said Goodman, cutting to the chase, albeit with relative elegance for him. At least he was learning the business.

"We'll talk. I'm nothing if not reasonable," said Penny, who was, ergo, nothing.

"Damn soon," I went on the record. "I don't see this development as doing anything but increasing our importance to the project."

"Boys, boys, please," said Penny. "All in good time."

With which we retired to our corners to consider to what advantage we might put a break in negotiations.

"Since my input doesn't seem to be needed anymore," said Cifelli, the silent partner through all this, "I don't suppose anybody would mind if I took a hike about now?" A picturesque metaphor, indeed, since Cifelli gave the impression he took a limo just going to the washroom.

"Actually," said Curry, "I think this ought to do it for all of us for now."

Which got the company up and inclining toward departure. Penny, anxious to postpone a reckoning with us, leaped at the chance for a free escape. "For the time being I think you fellows will want to replan your strategy on the book itself. We'll arrange an early interview with Mr. Jaeger, who might want to start reminiscing into a tape recorder himself when he gets a moment or two, and if there's nothing else, I agree with Mr. Curry, why don't we all go our separate ways?" Which he punctuated by insinuating himself into the head of the line inclining out.

Since even though there remained a lot to talk about but nobody wanted to do it in front of most of the others, there was tacit agreement. Not that Goodman could resist a parting shot. "Just out of curiosity, how does Elias X fit into all this?"

"Mr. *Appleton,* as a member of our board, and a participating partner—" began Curry.

"I'll take that," said Cifelli, stopping at the door. "Gentlemen?"

We both gave him our fullest attention.

"It's none of your business."

Which somehow didn't give me the feeling that everything was exactly on the up-and-up.

The "boys" had delivered our cars to the cavernous underground parking lot beneath the complex at Century City and were waiting at the down escalator with our keys and parking tickets.

"Do you think a gratuity is in order?" I asked Goodman facetiously as we took them.

"No, more like a tip." With which he slammed a vicious punch into the bicep of the one who'd hit him at the St. James's—Augie, I believe. "Don't do that anymore," he said (the tip). "And don't steal from me, either," he added, a reference, I suppose, to the bottle of scotch he'd swiped from the house. Neither message, however, seemed to impress the hoodlum, who instead plunged his hand toward what was undoubtedly a shoulder holster, and certainly showed a hostile intent.

With a choice between a very much unwanted involvement and loyalty to a partner, I tapped the second guy urgently, hoping to divert him. "Hey, hey, hey," I said loudly, and I hope disconcertingly, "let's not do something dumb. Talking to you!" I virtually screamed. This did distract him, for he regarded me as either an unpredictable psychopath who merited serious concern or a different kind of nut who needed cracking. Meanwhile Goodman, a plaid belt in the art of rough and tumble, quickly grabbed the first goon's lapels and pulled his jacket down over his arms, temporarily immobilizing him. At which opportune moment we were joined by Cifelli.

"Hey," he said softly, stopping all activity cold.

"This guy," started Augie.

"Quiet. I'm sure with reason. Stop it. Get my car."

The second hoodlum, whose name I wasn't privy to, departed instantly, while a glowering, red-faced Augie remained on guard.

"As for you, Rayford," said Cifelli. "While I'm sure there was a reason, in all probability justified, I still like to think of you in a more executive fashion. Try to be above it, will you?" And he headed off in the direction of his limo, Augie trailing, but not before delivering himself of a scowl that would stop a turbine. And seemed to promise if looks couldn't kill, there were other means. I quickly distanced myself as a tacit participant by averting my eyes and instead took a look at the tickets which'd been given us with the keys. "We're 14D, Green," I said.

As we made our way past the various pastels between us and green, Goodman was uncharacteristically silent. Then, just as we passed 12D Green, and were beside 13D Green, said, "Try this on. Stacy needs a lot of money, to defend Carey, right?"

"Right."

"But first, why doesn't Stacy *have* a lot of money? He's been earning the big bucks lotsa years."

"Well, Francine said he was over-invested in real estate, for one thing—if he had even most of his money in stuff bought at the peak—"

"Yeah, well, sure. But people like that, so they just borrow a couple million more. Easy enough when you're that big an earner."

"Except he hasn't been working all that much, in recent times."

"Exactly. So while, let's say a wild scenario, the murder of Wesley Crewe, supposedly by son Carey, would cost lots and lots, and leave him even more broke—leaving no one to benefit . . ."

"The murder of Wesley Crewe," I picked up, "supposedly by son Carey, would force Stacy back to work."

"To earn enough for legal fees, but along the way many more millions than even the millions the legal fees would cost."

"Which could benefit a whole host of others. Some of whom we don't even know."

"Right," said Goodman. "Which is sort of like you might call a motive. This is 14D Green."

17

Rayford Goodman

We were assembled in the jury room, fifteen minutes early like they told us. I was being my usual charming self in general, my super charming self in particular with Sylvia. I'm not sure about the rest of the folks, but I definitely wasn't impressing Sylvia. She barely said hello, and there was no mistaking her dancing totally away from my every try at small talk.

I didn't remember having a fight, though I did recall last night's get-together ending a little short of whoopee.

Anyway, I didn't figure that was going to be the most dramatic happening of the morning. So I was pretty much prepared when the bailiff told me Judge Steinberg wanted to see me in the locker room before the start of today's game. Nichols as much as said there'd be some kind of trick play. What I hadn't expected was the direction, and the depth of the bench, you might say.

The judge's chambers didn't hold a lot of surprises. I couldn't help thinking they must save a lot on wall paint since there weren't any walls, just book shelves full of law books full of old cases. (It must have been a big strain when the first judges had to go by what was right instead of what did they do last time.)

He was on the phone when I came in, held up a finger he'd be right with me. I waited by a wall, looked up to find myself facing a book said, "California—1980–1985, E–H" and couldn't help wondering whether it didn't include "*Goodman* v. *Goodman,* Divorce of." (Or would that be under "Cleaners, Taking Ray to"?)

"At this very moment," Steinberg was saying on the phone. "Though I must say I do not consider this call proper, either. And I'm going to terminate it." With which he hung up.

"I have a feeling—" I began, but again he held up his finger. There was a knock on the door, it opened, and a court attendant showed in Alvis Johnson, the D.A. guy, and J. Wadsworth Nichols, attorney for the defense.

"Gentlemen, come in, please. You may all be seated." "All" seemed to include me, so I sat, too.

"It has been brought to my attention that Mr. Goodman here has comported himself in a manner violating the rules governing juror behavior."

I glanced at Nichols, but he was too busy checking out the moon on his pinky fingernail to meet my eyes. Johnson, though, gave me an interested look.

"It appears Mr. Goodman not only discussed the case, he speculated on the guilt of the accused, did so in public, and did it with another juror, whom he had specifically invited for the purpose of influencing her vote."

"Hey, now, just a minute, Judge," I said. "That's not exactly—"

"Be quiet, Mr. Goodman," said Steinberg sternly. Or steinly. "This is not a judicial procedure. I am the sole arbiter of the information set before me. Did you, in fact, not meet with Miss Sylvia Ferris, a member of the jury, outside the court?"

"Yes, but—"

"And did you not instigate that meeting?"

"Yes, but—"

"And did you not, at that time and in that place, the"—he checked his notes—"St. James's Club, discuss the current case with Miss Ferris?"

"Judge, have you happened to take a *look* at Miss Ferris?"

"That Miss Ferris is a beautiful woman, a desirable woman, and a woman whose company you might normally seek out

are not the issues at stake here. The fact remains, Miss Ferris—
the same beautiful, desirable woman you, even possibly with
innocent intent, in the sense of ulterior motive not tied directly to these proceedings, tried to impress with both your
knowledge about the defendant and your opinion about the
case—has, in conformance with her sworn duties, brought to
the attention of this court the range and extent of your illegal
behavior."

"Now, wait a minute, Judge."

"No, you wait a minute, mister! I won't tolerate this in my
court. First, and that is why I wanted you other gentlemen
present, I am terminating Mr. Goodman's participation on this
jury. The number one alternate will be seated instead. Second,
I am considering a variety of charges under law to be pursued.
Third, since I also learn *belatedly* that Mr. Goodman is not, as
represented, primarily a writer but a private investigator,
which might well have affected his selection in the first
place—"

"Judge, you never gave me a chance!"

"Quiet! And since Mr. Goodman is *licensed* by the state as
a private investigator, said license dependent on his good
graces in the eyes of the law, I am also forwarding to the
proper authorities notice of these proceedings to determine
whether said license should not, in fact, be revoked."

To the representatives of the state and the defense he said,
"Do either of you gentlemen have any objections to these
actions?"

Neither did.

"Do you," he said to me, "have anything further to say?"

I, who hadn't been allowed any damn say in the first place,
did have one thing. "The broad could have just said no," I
said.

But I knew it was much more than that. I knew now we
hadn't just bumped into each other. She'd been laying for me
in the parking lot (you might say). I'd been set up.

She'd got me talking at the club. *Said* not to talk about the
case, but that was only for Bradley. That was the side of her

wasn't smiling, wasn't egging me on, wasn't rubbing her leg against mine.

And while I'd figured, since yesterday, a way would be found to get me off the jury, I didn't think for a minute the wheels were turning even *before* the meeting. (Nor that I'd have this kind of hassle.)

So while I was being escorted to the elevator, my juror badge stripped, drummed out of the service, I had a few other thoughts. One, with Nichols in on the deal promoting Jaeger's participation in the book, and that deal making it absolutely necessary I get off the jury, how come neither him nor Jaeger, nor any of that crew worried they were losing the one guy they could count on to find the kid innocent? How about the *case*?

So, out the building and walking downhill to the parking lot, I was now sure of three things. One, the kid definitely wasn't guilty. Two, there was something very fishy about everyone being in cahoots to get a guy off the jury was on their side (which they'd know from Sylvia). And three, I was damn well going to have to solve the case or not only be out of business, maybe even go to jail.

Oh, and four (as I crossed to the rusty clunker and pried open the squeaky door) I better take care of all the above or I'd wind up *owning* cars like this.

"The *good* news is, now I can work full-time on the book," I was telling Bradley back at the office. Once I explained all that'd gone down at court.

"I'm totally confused," said Bradley. "I just plain don't understand it."

"Who does? But one thing's clear. For whatever reason, there's a conspiracy to have Carey take the rap in the murder."

"But if it was just to get money, to make Stacy go back to work so everybody could get his piece, getting Carey indicted would achieve that. Making it necessary for Stacy to work because of the legal fees and so on. But it wouldn't be necessary to convict the kid."

"Unless the one actually did the killing was either more

valuable or essential to the plan—say Stacy himself—or whoever's pulling the strings."

"It's all very complicated. And where does the bomb thing
fit in?"

"I figure that was to pressure Carey to go along with being
the perp. And not get too fancy in his own defense."

"You mean the bomb was meant for him, not Steinberg?"

"Just a theory. Not really to kill him—it went off during
lunch—just scare him back into line. Remember, he'd recanted
his guilty plea."

"All right," said Bradley. "Suppose your whole crazy hy-
pothesis is correct, explain the bomber committing suicide."

"He wasn't let in on the real reason. They told him it was
the old jihad jive."

And at least we had a direction now. It wasn't anymore
just writing a biography. We had to solve the case. Which, of
course, would make for a better book. Also a better life, for
me. Compared to having my ticket lifted (to practice private
eyery) as well as possibly getting my aging ass tossed in the
clink for jury tampering.

To that end (no pun, as they say, etc.) it struck me we
might divide the work, Bradley concentrating on the writing
and me the solving.

"I never doubted for a minute I was going to do all the
writing," he whined (an old song).

"I didn't say 'all the writing,' I just meant for now. What
we should concentrate on."

"All right, all right. I do have to do some blocking. And I
have to talk to Stacy and get, as Penny would put it, 'his valuable input.' Meaning Penny's money's worth."

"Oh, well, I'll want to join you when you do that," I said.
"Stacy's certainly an important part of this, maybe *the* important part. One of the places we can maybe kill two birds with
one stone."

"Or one bird with two stones."

"That, too."

And as Bradley made a note to set a time, Francie came
in, looking like the last few minutes of a misspent life. Which,

according to Bradley, might not be too far from the truth. She sure looked awful. Eyes all red-rimmed, nose puffy and runny.

"Sorry I'm late, I've got the flu," she said, not too convincing. The cocaine flu, more like it. "And I feel real shitty, so don't anybody give me a hard time." Then, to Bradley specifically, "You have anything special you want me to do?"

"You mean other than take care of yourself?"

"I *said* don't start with me."

"Francie, look, I'm not starting," I said, starting. "Just asking a question. Have you *considered* rehab?"

"You mean the third thing you try that doesn't work?"

The little wench, she knew she'd nail us with that. "All right, the third thing doesn't work, and the other two are?"

"Drano and Campho Phenique."

Bradley laughed. "All right, so not every solution works for the problem it's supposed to. But there's been some good success with rehab programs."

"Yeah, almost eight percent. And even that's only from the most motivated, which I don't happen to be."

"Because you're having such a terrific time," insisted Bradley.

"Let me put it this way, before we end this fucking conversation: nobody gives up anything until they have to."

"So," I said, "we're looking for a new world's record for rock bottom?"

"OK, you guys, fuck both of you!" she said and stormed out the room.

The door slam didn't quite work because it was one of those kind with the gizmo on top *keeps* it from slamming. But we got the point.

"I thought we handled that really well," said Bradley, with both us guilty we'd screwed up. "Damn."

But to our surprise it was only a few minutes before she returned, hit the portable tape she always used, and spoke for the record.

"Before I leave for the day, to contemplate a stress-related lawsuit concerning harassment and completely fictitious allegations of wrongdoing insinuated by both Mr. Bradley and Mr.

Goodman ..." (I guess she'd had a blow) "I thought you probable defendants might be interested in some stuff I came up with." And here she tossed some pages of printout on Bradley's desk.

"The name Ely Appleton appears with surprising frequency on any number of Jaeger-financed organizations, usually in a high executive position. Which then becomes not so surprising, since it develops he's Jaeger's business manager."

"I thought that was Ken Curry," I said.

"Ken Curry is his personal manager," said Bradley. "And career-guidance maven."

"OK, so Appleton, as his business manager, is managing a lot of his businesses. So?"

"Almost none of them are money-making propositions."

"Maybe he's not good at it," I suggested.

"I mean, really almost totally none."

"I think I understand where Ms. Rizetti is headed," said Bradley, re our little potential plaintiff. "If the man has no talent for it. If he continually heads enterprises which lose money, why would anybody keep him on as head honcho?"

"In the words of Ray Charles, 'Uh-huh,' " said Francie.

"And if Jaeger, being an actor, was real casual about money matters, it's not too unusual," I said. "But why wasn't his friend and mentor Ken Curry at least looking out for his interest?"

"You got the right one, baby," said Francie, still doing Ray Charles. "And his real name's Khoury, by the way. K-h-o-u-r-y. Lebanese. Now if you gentlemen will excuse me, I shall either return to work or consult with my legal advisers," and she clicked off her tape. "Or spend about forty bucks catering lunch for my nose," she added and left.

The beat goes on.

And one of the ways it went on was a call from Lewis Ellard, the new chief of detectives for the Beverly Hills Police.

"I heard about your trouble down at Judge Steinberg's court," he began.

"I guess jury service is an honor I'll have to pass on," I said.

"Well, I also understand there might be some legal ramifications as a result."

"So they tell me." Had I traded one enemy on the force for another?

"I thought I might just give you a call and tell you I hope everything works out for you."

Too weird. "Well, thanks. I guess it'll work out."

"Also I'm a little concerned about the kind of open secret about your lady friend."

I didn't know how to field that. Neither wanting to bust Francie or deny she was my lady friend on a technicality.

"Uh, yeah?"

"I think you better try to get her straightened out, my man."

Was that going to be a wedge? All of a sudden Mr. Mainstream was Mr. Street?

"I'm not . . . exactly sure I know what you mean," I hedged. "You could be wrong," I added weakly.

"I think you do know, and I ain't. Trust me, I know all too well. Just a hint to the wise."

"OK, I guess. Thanks."

Then there was a moment he was maybe going to add something, didn't.

"Anything else?" I prompted.

"Well, on the Jaeger thing. My thought was you would probably be spending more time on the actual case, now that you're free from legal restraints." I didn't say anything. "Still with me?"

"Yes, sir."

"And, uh, I know you had some problems with my predecessor. But I didn't want you to think of me as an adversary."

"Well, thanks. That would be a novelty." He certainly seemed trying to establish that.

"And so, like if you found out anything, you'd be inclined to share it with me."

"Uh-huh."

Beat.

"Have you . . . found out anything?"

"I just got fired this morning," I said, not about to buy into this new best-pals arrangement before he gave me a gang more than I gave him. "How about you?"

"Well—again, another show of good faith—I'm sure it didn't get past you that murder one was gun and murder two was knife."

"Uh-huh," I said, real noncommittal.

"And, of course, we can't be positive they were necessarily committed by the same perp."

"Yep."

"No prints, by the way."

Figured. At least he owned up they found the knife.

"But if they were by the same perp, one of the reasons for the change in M.O. was the gun got dumped."

"Just a wild guess, being the house fronted the Pacific Ocean, some place to do with water?"

"Exactly what we figured—or, more accurately, my op number in the sheriff's department at Malibu. It didn't seem likely it would be directly in front of the house, of course . . ."

"But they took a chance, and lo and behold."

"Exactly, Mr. Goodman, lo and behold—found the weapon."

"But the serial number had been filed off."

"No, the serial number was intact."

"But it was unregistered."

"Gee, you're not too good at this, Mr. Goodman. It *was* registered, it *was* the murder weapon, and to spare you the straight line, it was owned by Mr. Ely Appleton."

Now isn't that just pat as hell? I thought.

"Very interesting," I said.

"So, if in the course of your investigations you should run across anything else interesting about Mr. Appleton . . ."

"You'd be the absolute first to know," I lied through my teeth.

18

Mark Bradley

One of the things I'd learned in my years of investigative reporting (well, celeb biography, then) was that it could be a mistake to pursue one direction from start to finish without the interaction of other components. Meaning, now that we had two aspects of intelligence strongly implicating Ely Appleton, the logical, or at least impulsive, course of action would be to pursue Mr. Appleton full-out and to the exclusion of everyone and everything else. But that would be a tactical mistake. Because we might well find out many more things about Mr. Appleton by a more oblique approach. How did he relate to other principals, for example? Who were his associates? What parts did they play? And so forth.

To that end, I was sticking to my schedule of interviews and nose-poking by following my prearranged plan to have a look at the Academy, Ken Curry's acting school.

Besides whatever remote possibility of light that might cast on current events, it served an expositional function for the biography. Since it was there, under the tutelage of Mr. Curry, that Stacy Jaeger had learned his craft and ultimately been "discovered"—that quaint euphemism equating humans with some distant shore, as if neither existed before coming into focus in the eye of the beholder. (Does an actor emoting in a theater devoid of an audience actually put on a performance? Little Zen show business there.)

Goodman, as was so often the case, pursued his own

agenda which, as near as I could tell, involved a lot of impulse and instinct. To say nothing of frequent stops at bars to "get the lay of the land" (with straight face) and "water the horses." I had some trouble relating to such an unstructured methodology, which seemed perilously close to simply lurching about. ("I sometimes reel, but I never lurch.") Nevertheless, I couldn't totally fault it, since he had met with some considerable success in the past.

So, after my "What'll you be doing?" I had reluctantly settled for his "You know. The usual. Routine. This 'n' that." Whatever.

I arrived at the Academy's location, on Franklin, and managed to find parking in back of a florist shop a block or so away. Being spotted *in fragrante* by the florist in attendance, I had little choice but to opt for the pretense that my presence was for the purpose of dispensing a small basket of spring sprigs to Francine.

This I did, together with a card saying, "Love comes in many forms—as I'd be the first to admit—but I do love you, and I'm worried. I just want to help."

On the one hand, I felt good about sending a peace offering. On the other, I was a touch embarrassed it was really motivated by my need to find a parking space. What a great Catholic I'd make—"Father, forgive me, for I've sinned on the flower thing. Oh, yeah, and the Abomination in the Sight of the Lord number."

The Academy, so I understood, had originally been a remodeled private residence built in the Thirties, with the theater part comprising the dining room/living room area, and the upstairs actually housing the semi-starving actors. But with the success of the school, and its most illustrious graduate, in whose good fortune everyone seemed to share, a new, completely modern building had been constructed. It had the last word in showcase theater, a marvelously complete state-of-the-art stage, ninety-nine comfortable seats (the maximum number to avoid paying the actors under Equity rules), rehearsal rooms, recreational areas, modern dressing rooms—everything the aspiring actor could want (barring a place to crash—

the liability lawyers and "improved" building codes having removed that option).

No one confronted me or asked me who I was as I entered and wandered about at will. In the main auditorium, a scene, or perhaps workshop, was in progress, with one fairly pretty girl, one seriously attractive boy, and a dozen remarkably less favored others about whom one could only wonder what on earth ever possessed them to get into acting?

They were doing one of those plays that seem to always take place in some desert motel in Arizona either before or just after the atom bomb has fallen. The philosophical import is usually promulgated by a totally inarticulate failed cowboy and a stupid waitress. Sometimes an inhuman, atavistically brutal representative of the law adds a secondary threat.

At the moment, the cowboy and the waitress (it didn't escape my notice they were the good-looking ones) were sharing a newfound sense of wonderment that the desert possessed so many grains of sand, and that the cactus, for all its primitive beauty, yet could hurt the unwary. I got out of there in a hurry.

There was a class in mime I peeked in at, then pretended to sightlessly grope my way out of; another where students were tutored in the art of swordplay—which struck me a bit anachronistic (how often did that come up, really, in plays set in Arizona motels?). And finally, one in makeup. This was Narcissus heaven, as a dozen students faced light-ringed mirrors and applied bits of hair and gobs of greasepaint.

I suppose it was the fact that this particular class was an exercise in changing appearance to conform to the demands of a part which first put the idea in my head. But I think I would have recognized the dark, curly-haired girl on the end in any event. She was the one who'd been in bed at Marsden's Meadow, made up as and pretending to be Iris Jaeger.

"OK," said Goodman after I'd relayed these facts over an afternoon espresso pick-me-up at Cravings. "That tells us a lot. We now know pretty sure Iris was at the apartment the night Courtney was murdered."

"Making her the murderer?"

"Definite possibility. And the other interesting part there had to be some sort of cahoots with Marsden's to've done the fake Iris number."

"Right," I said enthusiastically. Then, on reflection, "And what exactly do we gain from knowing this?"

"That it could easily involve Stacy, Senior."

"Uh-huh."

"And/or Ken Curry. Possibly Ely Appleton."

"Plus, of course, Carey."

"Yeah. And you can't rule out Soheila or the Malouf girl."

"Or, for that matter, Gilbert Rexford. Even, actually, Nichols."

"No, I think we can rule out Nichols."

"OK, great—we made a lot of progress," I said, sagging at the thought.

"Let me put it this way," said Goodman. "Waiter, a little cognac for my coffee?"

I decided not to mention it actually *added* a suspect—the girl who'd played the part of Iris. Two, if you included Sylvia. Because even depressed, I didn't really believe that in any kind of ordered universe we were supposed to be uncovering additional suspects.

"Actually," said Goodman after the long pause which followed, and he'd had time to consume his cognac and assume a more optimistic outlook, "it's good. Everything you learn is good. Even if for a while it seems more complicated. It'll serve a purpose."

"My instinct felt that way at the time, but now I can't see how or why or in what way."

"Well, it does tell us there's a conspiracy. Can't be the work of one person. Too much involvement. Plus, you catch the news today? On the trial?"

I hadn't.

"Carey's not going to take the stand. As much as threw in the towel. That's a boxing thing, when you surren—"

"I *know* what throw in the towel means." (I didn't say what it means when the towel is looped through the belt of a strolling boopsy boy in form-fitting shorts.)

At which point Goodman slapped his forehead, in the universal pantomime for *dummkopf.*

"What? What?" I said.

"Pizza. The pepperoni one delivered to Courtney's. For Iris!"

"How do you know?"

"I can't definitely, but I got a feeling," said Goodman, uncharacteristically tossing down some bills to pay the check and rising, " 'cause there was one just like it at Stacy, Junior's."

"Yes?" I said, also rising.

"Which came up he never eats pepperoni—being a vegetarian!"

"So Iris is at Junior's?"

"The whoever in the bathroom! Which at the time I figured just a date."

We were heading back behind Cravings, where I'd parked my car.

"And another thought," said Goodman. "If Iris was that tight with Courtney she stayed with her, it might have been Iris Courtney was talking about when she said there was another person knew Carey hadn't killed Wesley Crewe."

"Which would mean she *wasn't* at the compound when her boyfriend was murdered."

"Right."

"But why not? And why did she go back?"

"Your basic heterosexual hassle, old bean—they had a tiff. She stormed out in a huff. Thought it over. Cooled off. Returned to patch things up."

Like gay couples don't fight, storm off, and chill out. Well, somewhat right. We *don't* "tiff," "huff," "cool off," or do a lot of "patching up." But the fact was, both hetero or sexually otherwised, we were obviously headed back to Stacy, Jr.'s place.

The door was open. Bell Biv Devoe were dispensing "Poison" via the hi-fi in the pigsty. The place was covered with trash, and *was* trashed. All of which I took in at a glance before we got in far enough to see, on the far side of the couch, the bruised and battered and apparently unconscious Stacy, Jr. And next to him, rocking back and forth, looking very far gone, a purple-jumpsuited Iris, this time the real thing.

"He's alive," said Goodman, feeling a carotid—which I can never find on myself, much less on barely breathing assault victims.

Iris was vaguely humming to the music, hands and face stained with blood. But a forced closer look disclosed it was secondhand, not her own. Obviously Stacy, Jr.'s.

"Iris. Iris. Did you do this?" asked Goodman gently.

"La ila la ila la," semi-sang Iris, not the most responsive. To the question or the music.

"Listen, Iris, honey," said Goodman. "We have to get some help. What happened here?"

"La la la, uhl, la la la . . . ?" And a look of frustration crossed her features. "Ula la la! La?"

Ooh la la? Like we expected she'd make sense. All the while she kept compulsively rocking.

"Do you think she did it?" I asked Goodman.

He quickly looked about. "I don't see anything she could have done it with," he replied. "Iris, honey, Iris . . . Who did this?"

"La la, la la, la il la."

"I guess first an ambulance?" I said. "Then police?"

About when we heard the clump of what sounded like several pair of booted feet stomping up the steps.

Without a moment's hesitation Goodman grabbed me and pulled me out the door. We headed out to the back and around the corner, out of sight before the—what, troops?—arrived.

"What do you think?" I whispered as we halted behind the corner, stooping low.

Wisely enough, he wasn't about to discuss it. He stood up, made a quick motion with his arm, and I followed up an attached ladder and onto the roof of the building.

We heard agitated noises, guttural commands, confused stomping, all getting closer. I don't know how or why, but we both knew it wasn't police. This being one of those two-story

barracks type buildings, the staircase was outside, I guess satisfying the fire laws. I think it took Goodman by surprise,
though, when there didn't appear to be any fire escape on the
other side of the building—which in my view, too, there
should have been.

With the sound of the first feet starting to ascend the ladder
to the roof, he took me by the arm and pointed to the roof
of the animal hospital adjoining, a mere hundred yards away.
Well, it looked a hundred yards. I suppose it was, I don't
know, five or six feet? It wasn't a driveway width, just an alley.
But it was three stories high, and there's a geometric aspect
when fear is factored in. Called the Certain Death syndrome.
It looks farther and you jump farther.

We did, though on impact one of Goodman's feet went
right through the roof a few inches, momentarily immobilizing
him as we heard the shouts and alarums emanating from
across the alley. I helped him pull free, and we scampered
toward the security of the other side of the slanted roof.

Before hitting the downside, I took a peek back and saw
a couple of terrorist types in baggy, nondescript clothes. Just
as about forty thousand bullets stared chewing up the roof I
got a glimpse of one guy who was black, the same kind of
clothes, including a checkered kaffiyeh on top of which sat an
incongruous "Raiders" cap.

"Hey, that was weird," I said to Goodman as we slid down
the slanted roof, pieces of which were splintering behind us.
"Did you see that?"

"See what? The way the sun made pretty patterns through
the bullet holes?" he said as we slid farther down to the
rainspout.

"I don't see any cause for snideness," I said, following his
lead and placing my feet sideways along the gutter, testing its
strength.

"Would you think it was snide if I said let's get the fuck
out of here?" he said.

"No, that I would find perfectly reasonable," I responded
as we scurried to the fortunately available fire escape on the
animal hospital building, amid the howl and tumult of a hun-

dred dogs and critters responding to the bullets and our clatter.

I couldn't help thinking I didn't recall jumping roof to roof over a potentially fatal abyss, facing death by bullets, before I met Goodman. Was it *really* making me a better writer?

19

Rayford Goodman

Once out of the pit ...

In the old days of Hollywood when they made serials for the kids at neighborhood theaters on Saturday afternoons, they'd have really heroic heroes. And really bad bad guys. But only semi-smart writers. So what they'd do, since each episode had to end on a cliff-hanger, a seemingly impossible situation to get out of, they'd cop out.

The hero would be in an impossible situation, running through the jungle. He'd fall through a camouflaged trap into a deep hole where there'd be a hundred razor-sharp spikes, eight thousand poisonous snakes, molten lava, and an earthquake about to erupt, plus a thousand murderous Hessians closing in and another thousand poison-arrow natives with an attitude. How could he possibly escape? You couldn't imagine. And neither could the writers.

So, they'd show the end of last week's chapter (the above), then start this week's with "Once out of the pit ..." And the story would go on from there.

So, once out of the pit ...

Actually, what we did, after we got down from the animal hospital, we cut through an alley into the next street. Then to another alley leading to the back door of Koontz, a hardware store, where we browsed among the nails and designer coffee makers.

We gave it about twenty minutes for the bad guys to clear

the area. Then, still looking to be on the safe side, separated. I waited just inside Koontz while Bradley, who more fit the neighborhood, you get my drift (West Hollywood), sauntered back to get his car. Then he was going to come back and pick me up, as they say.

That was the plan. Should of taken less than ten minutes, tops. And when it went to fifteen, I started getting nervous we'd been outsmarted and Bradley was in trouble. I was just heading out the door when I ran into a different kind of trouble.

"Rayford, sweetie—how are you?" said what any red-blooded American boy with his genes in order would call a beautiful woman.

"Hi," I said in my best not-a-good-time-to-talk way.

"Don't rush off, dear. Give me a moment."

It was Luana, my ax-wife, and a moment was the only thing I hadn't given her when we divorced. Well, not totally true, I did get the house. But I had to pay her for the half I gave her in the first place. California is not perfect.

"I don't want to seem unfriendly," I said. "But I'm really in a—"

"You're *always* in a hurry. And you're always unfriendly. I just can't imagine why. I'm starting to think you don't like me."

"No, look—honest, no hard feelings."

"Well, yes, I do remember, there was a good bit of that, wasn't there?"

That was familiar. Back into the wounding and hurting. I didn't feel much like reminding her why I'd pulled up lame in the potency department after my heart attack and stopped going for the gusto. Part me, part medication, but a big part her being clearly less into someone old and sick. Shit, why did I still care?

"I'm sorry. My partner's in trouble. I got to go."

"Well, of course. You've always been responsive to the needs of your partner."

Why did *she* care—enough to keep zinging?

"But in *this* neighborhood?"

I gave up. We could've communicated we'd still maybe been married. I plain went. With just a dashing slash of my epee.

"Up yours," I said wittily.

I didn't really have a plan. What could you plan? If they had him, they'd probably be already gone. But if they were in the middle of grabbing him, maybe . . .

He was sitting on the trunk of his car, the hood raised in distress.

"Dead battery," he explained.

"Jesus," I said. "Whyn't you come around? Leave me hanging out, the potential butt of indecent overtures."

"Can't you for once? And it took you long enough to get here. I could have been in trouble."

"Well, I *was* in trouble. My ex-old lady needed some hardener for her nails, or something, and got to practice her nastiness on me."

"Sorry about that. Anyway, I guess whoever was after us also went out some way other than frontally. But the police and the ambulance are here, as you can see."

"I can see."

"So I guess everything's under control. Or will be, once the auto club comes and gives me a jump—so to speak."

We settled to wait, and after a bit saw the ambulance people taking Junior away on a stretcher. And the cop folks leading Iris to their car, wrapped in a blanket.

They all left, and I lit up the one emergency aggravation cigarette I always carried with the one match.

"I thought you'd given that up," said Bradley.

"I did. Only you need one after running into Luana."

"How did you happen to have one on you?"

"It's a small town. You never can tell when you might run into Luana."

And we waited. It was nice to smoke. Especially at moments when you didn't much care if you lived or died.

"If you don't mind my asking," said Bradley. "Why did you break up with her?"

After the jokes, and the glib bantering, I had to think.

"Partly my fault," I said finally. "I never could learn which were the fights she wasn't going to remember in the morning. And which were the ones I'd better buy flowers or forget having any conversation till Tuesday."

"That was it?"

"No, no, of course not. It was just—I couldn't be natural. She needed figuring out all the time."

"Well, we all need figuring out."

"Hey, I don't want to fight you, too."

"No offense."

"I'm not serious. I don't know. Part, too—the damn egotism of the woman. Always believing whatever she was doing, reading, thinking, watching, was more important or better than whatever I was doing. And god forbid sports."

"I'm for that. Kidding."

"She'd never leave me alone to live my own life. Always wanting me to share hers—even if what I was doing at the moment was making hers possible."

"Maybe she just wanted to be with you."

"Right."

"So, what's so terrible about that?"

"She didn't want to be with me—she wanted me to be with her."

I'd gotten unused to smoking. The cigarette burned down and scorched my finger. Fitting end to the conversation.

Also the AAA truck showed up to put a spark in Bradley's battery.

Back at the office, Francie'd left us a tape on the research she'd done on Carey.

He'd been busted several times on dope and D.U.I., currently had a suspended license. Interesting, since according to Courtney, he'd driven back to the compound. Although the sort of people got their license suspended tended to be the sort didn't obey the law about not driving anymore, either.

She'd found a couple business deals south of the line of honest, too. Payoffs Stacy'd had to make to keep him out of jail. No hint of anything on the plus side, so his involvement in a deal with Appleton was certainly no proof he'd reformed. She'd also checked on Wharton, and Carey never even went there, let alone graduate. So, either Courtney'd been lying to us, or he'd lied to her. Logical bet the latter.

"So, what do you make of that?" asked Bradley, turning off the machine.

"Well, someone used to doing deals, lying—more reasonable he could be conned or con himself into taking the rap, if the pressure was intense enough. Or the payoff. She did a good job. Where *is* Francie?"

"Went home."

"Well, she's entitled, considering all the work."

"If that's the reason," said Bradley.

Right. If that's the reason, I thought. Knowing it wasn't.

"I'm sort of losing the thread here," Bradley said after a bit.

"In what way?"

"I don't know, it's just all crazy. Are we looking for the murderer of Wesley Crewe? Are we after whoever killed Courtney? Is it the same person? And what are we to make of this business with Junior? Iris I guess *is* actually a nutcase."

"Would you rephrase your question?"

"Well, what's the *case*—or are we on a case? Or just writing a book from twenty-seven angles?"

"You're getting a little hyper. After all, you're not used to finding bloody folks beat up and crazy ladies going la la, not to mention running across roofs getting shot at."

"I think you may be right," he said. "But what really worries me, I don't know what I'm doing with somebody who considers all that the fun part."

What a kidder.

We worked on the book for a couple hours, plotting the early chapters. The stuff dealt with Stacy's parents, childhood, kid life. How hard could it be to write that? You got somebody like Francie to look up all the stuff, and then you put it down.

Although I must say, since I've now collaborated on two books myself, I do find it a little annoying when people come up and say they've got a story. And it always turns out no story, but they missed the bus and their wife thought it was the one blew up.

Or they say, "I've got this great story, and just need someone to put down the words." Even I was beginning to see putting down the words wasn't the *total* snap I'd thought. Though I wouldn't let on to Bradley I knew he did more of that than me.

Still, I gave him what to write, solving the cases. (The thought struck me that might be distantly related to: "I've got this great story, and just need someone to put down the words." Well.)

"The trouble is," Bradley said after a bit. "I can't really start writing the beginning till I know the ending."

"The big picture," I said, sharing the problem.

"Never mind," he said.

We gave up after another few minutes and he drove me to my loaner, still parked behind Cravings, and we knocked off for the day.

I went home, fed the Phantom, who punched me in the ankle, caught the news.

They announced Iris wasn't in Bali, as previously reported. But was suffering from nervous exhaustion (craziness) and had been placed in an institution to rest up. Right. That would be Marsden's Meadow. Stacy, Jr., had been found beaten and unconscious, as a result of a robbery attempt. Sure, they were after all his worldly goods. And was resting at Cedars-Sinai.

Stacy, Sr., was shown, eyes full of tears, outside the courtroom, where the case against Carey was not going well. It began to look as if this wasn't going to be one of those trials that went on till some of the witnesses died.

J. Wadsworth Nichols ran reporter interference for him. "Please, ladies and gentlemen, have a heart. Mr. Jaeger is under enormous stress, and these unfortunate recent events only add to the burden. He will not be making any comment at this time."

"No, no," said Jaeger weakly, in that reedy voice we knew

so well, taking off his glasses, and with a gesture I seemed to remember from "All the Don's Men." "You all I'm sure understand—what—oh ..." And he sort of stumbled (same picture), quickly helped by Nichols, who said, "That'll be all." And, half-supporting, led him to a Lincoln Towncar. I bet chosen over a limo to give him a little more common touch. Maybe I'm cynical.

Then the phone rang.

"Rayford?" said the voice, the voice of Luana. Who else called me Rayford?

"Ray. I told you Ray. I like to be called Ray."

"Well, yes. Listen, I'm sorry about today. That was thoughtless and reflexively cruel. You don't deserve that."

"Ah. OK."

"You do forgive me?" in that husky, promising voice.

"Whatever."

"Good. Just wanted to set things right."

"OK."

Then there was a little pause I didn't intend to fill.

"Right. Be saying goodbye, then," she said.

"OK."

More pause.

"Goodbye?" I said.

"Oh, uh, when you get a moment, Rayford? This month's check?"

I had the cigarette all ready to go.

20

Mark Bradley

My morning started out just great. With a call from Citibank asking if there was any special reason why I'd used my entire MasterCard credit line within the first two days of the month. Ditto Visa.

I quickly checked my wallet. Had my cards. Then I remembered the backups, dashed to my spare room office, checked—bye-bye. My ex-roommate, Brian, had apparently taken them when he left. It wasn't bad enough he took my self-esteem and hope for comfort in my declining years. Son of a bitch. Actual bitch.

In truth, he'd had them with my permission while we were together (god, when did I stop being the receiver of drinks and start being the sender?), but I'd just assumed he'd return them to their accustomed spot on leaving. Since we'd been apart some time, I couldn't imagine why he'd waited till now before deciding to steal me blind. But the wait was effective. My guard was down. My pain threshold, too. Rat fink.

While technically, of course, I wasn't really liable for more than fifty dollars per card, I somehow *needed* to suffer the pain to atone for my stupidity. I called Citibank back, and Visa (and, on an unhappily accurate hunch, Neiman Marcus and Saks) and told them I would honor purchases to date but to cancel all cards and issue me new ones.

But goddamn Brian.

Bad enough our relationship had soured. Bad enough I'd

found him shallow and unwilling to commit. Did he have to go prove me a total shmuck for being involved with him at all? Item one of the way not to start your day.

Item two was stepping on the scale and discovering I'd gained two and a half pounds. That was partly (mostly) Goodman's fault, the kind of meat-and-potatoes restaurants he favored and the number of meals we were forced to share in the practice of our collaboration.

So, let's see—losing a couple months' worth of wages was Brian's fault and gaining a couple months' worth of fat was Goodman's. Looked like I was really in the clear. Except for being an idiot. Although that might be genetic. Say, Mother's fault. All just evil companions and bad choice of folks. I was still perfect.

The intercom emitted a rude sound, more like a burp than a buzz, and it turned out to be Goodman announcing his arrival.

"Right with you," I hollered through what, high tech promises to the contrary, I firmly believed was really just two tin cans connected by a length of string. (The TV part *never* worked.)

I grabbed my carryall, pre-loaded with wallet, scratch pads, pens, recorder, tapes, extra batteries, and—ever the romantic hopeful—toothbrush and change of unmentionables, and headed down.

Goodman was waiting inside my garage. We'd be taking my car, but parking his in my space. Los Angeles was increasingly restricting street parking to neighborhood residents only, a tactic on which Goodman not surprisingly had an editorial position.

"They fix the lack of parking space by making it *all* no parking. Wonderful. What they really did was raise the price of 'free parking' I'm sure the Constitution guarantees from change for the meters nobody asked for to a $28 ticket. Who they think they're kidding?"

I let him take my Brian-inspired scowl for agreement. There's something to be said for consistency, and Goodman's dependable anger represented stability in an otherwise changing world.

So I pulled the Beemer out, and he put his nondescript junk loaner in my place. (Actually, I'd originally had two spaces, but since the departure of he who shall henceforth be nameless to bigger and better suckers, I'd been renting out my second slot—boy, that sounds dirty.)

He got in, and we took off for Century City.

Though we'd originally expected to work apart today, we'd both been summoned to "take a meeting" with Ely Appleton, Stacy's business manager. Inasmuch as he was one of the principals we'd wanted to interview anyway, his calling for the meeting was a plus. By letting him choose time and place and instigate it, there was a good chance his guard would be down and we might gain a psychological edge. Besides, this way I didn't have to write yet.

In the basement garage beneath 2020 Avenue of the Featured Players, we found a spot (12C Green) and proceeded up to the suite Appleton shared with Ken Curry.

We were greeted coolly by the olive-skinned administrative assistant (the aloof Ms. Malouf), who lowered the sound on the hi-fi on a shelf behind her desk (it was some Big Band-period swing thing).

"Count Basie?" I ventured.

"I really don't know," she said.

"Duke Ellington!" it occurred to me, with a sudden strong conviction. Till I saw Goodman roll his eyes in disdain.

"Count Basie? Duke Ellington?" he said, dripping sarcasm. "Not even close. Jimmy Lunceford. Obvious."

"Of course," I said. "Just kidding." Who wouldn't know that?

"You're into jazz?" Goodman asked of the stylish steno. "Unusual for someone your age."

"It's not me," she said, not at all surprisingly—which I would have bet good money on (Lunceford!)—pointing toward Curry's office. Then she rose, revealing her formidable frontal features, turned for a reverse angle that was equally choice, I imagine, for someone not a vegetarian, and said, "This way, please." And she led us past the closed door to Curry's office, and around a corner to another of the same size and architectural importance. She knocked, opened, stuck her head in.

"Mr. Goodman and Mr. Bradley," she announced, and evidently got the OK. She stepped aside and we entered.

A very impressive room prominently featuring steel, chrome, glass, and what appeared to be an original Leroy Neiman of a basketball player strongly resembling and probably representing Ely Appleton, in the act of some incredible feat of derring dunk.

At our entrance, the same Mr. Appleton, all gleaming skulled mocha macho six-foot-eight of him, uncoiled from an Eames chair of a wondrous fawn suede, and rose to greet us with apparent warmth—if presenting thirty-two predatory teeth in a feral grimace can be perceived as warmth.

He was resplendent in a cheery pumpkin-colored double breasted gabardine suit, a Sulka foulard of mixed earth tones knotted with Virgo precision in a half-Windsor (a modified version of the late Prince of Wales's singular contribution to the world, or was that taking Wallis Simpson off the market?), tastefully centered in a Turnbull and Asser pale pink shirt. As he rounded the desk and presented a huge hand—I presumed for shaking rather than low-fiving—I also got a glimpse of natty Cole-Haan two-tones gracing his surprisingly small feet.

"Welcome, gentlemen, thank you for coming. Turn that down, Kiji," he instructed Ms. Malouf, indicating his own music, which was markedly different even to the non-afficionado. I raised an eyebrow to Goodman, by way of a mild challenge.

"David Sanborn," he replied, whoever that was (on saxophone).

"Coffee?" inquired our larger than life host.

I nodded, Goodman likewise.

"Coffee, Kiji. And try to make it hot this time, will you?" he said, not enhancing employee relations, I'm sure.

But to my surprise, she not only didn't lib at him, she darn near bowed.

"I see you take a somewhat different attitude toward the

help than Mr. Curry," I said, being as good a place as any to begin.

"Ah, well," said Appleton. "Maybe that's 'cause I have different plans for them."

"Such as?"

"All I'm interested in is efficiency, OK? Typing, filing, answering the phone."

"And Mr. Curry?"

"Mr. Curry has an agenda of his own."

"Or maybe just wants us to think so," said Goodman—also, I had a feeling, floating a random trial balloon.

Appleton shrugged. "I think he likes them a lot younger."

We had an immediate confirmation of the efficacy of his method as the music was abruptly lowered. Apparently Ms. Malouf had no trouble following his instructions—hot coffee notwithstanding.

"So, what can we do for you?" I asked.

"I just wanted to clear the deck, establish lines of communication, that sort of thing, OK?"

"OK, but I don't exactly follow."

"Well, it shouldn't be necessary for you to go running off in all directions to get whatever information you need when you can access any of that stuff from us, OK?"

Oh ho, OK. Were we talking of the little trip to Junior's yesterday? Were we getting too near something we weren't supposed to?

"What stuff?" said Goodman, reading the same message.

"Whatever stuff it is you want," said Appleton. "We're here to help. Full cooperation. After all, that's what we're paid for, isn't it?"

"Um-hm," I replied. "Well, good. Because I do have some questions about *your* involvement in Mr. Jaeger's life."

"Yeah?"

"Well, I understand that many of the investments you've put Mr. Jaeger into—the preponderance is my understanding—haven't worked out."

"Win some, lose some."

"My understanding is lose practically all."

"I don't think that's exactly accurate, OK?"

"Then there's the matter of all those semi-charitable things."

"Semi-charitable is not accurate, either. Every charity or interest may not be tax-deductible, OK? That doesn't mean it's not worthwhile."

"OK, but, in the face of so many losing ventures—"

"Look, Mr. Jaeger makes a great deal of money, an enormous amount of money, OK? Maybe he's been less active for a while, but he set all kinds of records for highest-paid performer in the past."

"So you're saying he has so much money it doesn't matter whether his outside ventures succeed or fail?"

"No, I'm not saying that. You're saying that. Naturally, we want everything to succeed. It's just that there isn't all that much pressure—"

"Yet," Goodman piped up, "when he had to raise bail for Carey he needed to put the house up as collateral. I don't get that."

"It's not so hard to understand. Lots of rich people have cash-flow problems from time to time, OK? You have your money in something you can't just arbitrarily pull out of. Or if you do, you stand to lose too much."

We weren't going to get straight answers here, it was clear. But then, who wants to document his responsibility for bad decisions?

"I am interested in one thing specially," said Goodman.

"And what's that?"

"The business relationship between you, Carey, and the late Wesley Crewe." I could see it was a question that made Appleton uncomfortable.

"We had an ... association, true, OK? But you have to understand, sometimes, with someone like Stacy involved in so many many things, and, say, he wants something for his kids, OK? So, maybe you put one or another down as an officer when they actually don't function in the company all that much."

Certainly often true, but why should I take his word for it?

"Really?" I said. "I don't know, but I got the impression that, what was it, producing videos? was Carey's main job."

"Well, maybe what's a main job for somebody like Carey's not a main job for someone like you and me, OK? Say he had an involvement—which, can I ask where you got this information?"

"Not really," I said. (It was from Courtney, of course, dead, but I didn't want anybody to think the avenue was totally closed, in case it meant something.) "Reporters don't reveal sources."

"Reporters? I thought you were employees helping Mr. Jaeger write his autobiography."

"Well, that's a little cold," said Goodman. "We were writing this book before Stacy came aboard. He got to be part of the package, but that don't mean we're about to bake some puff pastry."

"But you have the same interests."

"If by that you mean making the book a success," I said.

"Well, sure we want the book to be a success."

"But you can't necessarily do that," said Goodman, "by just doing a p.r. number. People aren't interested in some sugar-coated version. Especially a guy who's led that colorful a life."

"Colorful but good," said Appleton.

"Good when it's good," I said. "And whatever when it's whatever."

"Sort of, you know—the truth," said Goodman.

Appleton took a moment to think that over. Then said, "Correct me if I'm wrong, OK? But didn't our Mr. Cifelli have a chat with you about that?"

"I don't care for the way this is going, Mr. Appleton," I said. "I have a contract. We, both Goodman and I, have a contract—to write this book."

"But with Jaeger's approval."

"Oh, no, no way," said Goodman. "Cooperation maybe. Not approval."

"I think this is where we walk out," I said.

"Wait, wait, gentlemen, let's not get all cranky here. If we have a little disagreement over details, that's just one thing.

Let's hold on. You say you have final approval; my understanding's it's Jaeger. Easy enough to find out, OK? For now, let's just get on with it. You ask me what you want to know and I'll ask you what I want to know."

"Fair enough," said Goodman. "How about this video company, what're we talking, pornos?"

Which is when Appleton got really mad.

"Absolutely not! I would not, at any time, remotely consider that kind of crap!"

And before we found out exactly which kind of crap he would consider Ms. Malouf returned, carrying a tray on which were demitasse cups and a carafe of strong coffee. I still couldn't help noticing how different she was in his presence than with Curry. Definitely more deferential.

"Coffee," she said demurely, putting the tray down.

"Well, *pour,*" Appleton said irritably, albeit quiet-voiced. She appeared immediately disturbed, in her agitation spilling a bit.

"Woman, woman!" he almost hissed. She hastily mopped the slight spill with one of the rather beautiful damask napkins on the tray. "Leave it, leave it. Out!" He waved her away, clearly not a man of great patience.

"It's all right, it's nothing," I couldn't help saying in her defense, since she was virtually cowering.

"It's not all right," said Appleton quietly. "We weren't talking brain surgery."

"You make me so nervous," she finally said in her own defense.

He glowered at her. "That will be all," he said in a voice so quietly murderous it made *me* nervous.

"Yes, sir. Sorry," she said, and hastily departed.

"Women today," he said, forcing a smile. "They get spoiled. They forget their place, neglect their duties."

"Listen," said Goodman, veering suddenly. "Tell me about being a Black Muslim. I remember when you were with the Pistons and you converted and became Elias X. Right?"

Appleton took a deep breath, I thought to compose himself, then went around back of his desk and sat down before replying, in an apparent effort to address himself to damage control.

"We all have many roads to travel before finding our place in the grand scheme of things."

"Right. But I see you're not Elias X anymore. You stopped traveling the Muslim road?"

"Freedom of religion, one of America's great principles, OK? The freedom to practice, to abandon the practice, whatever." (I sure had the feeling he hadn't abandoned the male-privilege part of it.)

"So what now?" said Goodman. "Black Republican investment broker?"

"There is something to be said for that. For the creation of work, providing workers with the opportunity to set food on their tables."

"So you're not a Muslim anymore," Goodman persisted.

"What does that concern you, Goodman?" he said, suddenly snappish. "Would that be a *Jewish* name?"

Oh?

"In the words of a Hollywood agent, according to an old joke, 'not necessarily,'" he replied, getting to what? Though in any event, gaining an upper hand in my view.

"You *are* Jewish?" Appleton persisted, a tactical mistake either way.

"Actually, I'm Presleyterian—we believe Elvis is dead and gonna stay that way. What do you care?"

"I don't, of course," he said, taking another stab at charm. "We are all Americans, aren't we?"

"So what's it going to be," I said. "We going to work together or at cross-purposes?"

"I certainly hope we're going to work together," replied Appleton.

"All right, then," said Goodman. "Just another question or two. Iris?"

"Hopeless. Bad enough before, but add the trauma of seeing her brother murder her lover—"

"She said that?"

"No, of course not. She's unresponsive. But she was there."

(We knew pretty much she wasn't.)

"With her *lover*," he repeated.

"You say that with some intensity—the lover part," I pointed out.

"I don't happen to approve of extramarital relationships."

"Oh, was one of them married?"

"Premarital, then," said Appleton.

He didn't approve of premarital relationships?

"I guess you were pretty unique in the NBA," said Goodman. "According to Wilt Chamberlain."

He didn't answer. I got the feeling he spent a lot of time suppressing anger and trying to give the impression of impassiveness.

"And Iris is where?" I persisted.

"Institutionalized," he said. Marsden's Meadow, my guess.

"And Junior's at Cedars?"

"Oh, no."

No?

"He's gone home to Bali."

Where had we heard that before?

"But now, gentlemen, I find that I'm a little pressed for time. Let me just review one thing, OK? You say your understanding is you write whatever you want, and we have nothing to say about it?"

"More or less," said Goodman.

"And you don't feel that the people paying you all this money have the right—"

"First off," I pointed out, "it's not your people who're paying the money, it's the publisher. And second, it's not the way it works."

"It's the way it works around here."

"Well," I said, "I guess that's what they call an impasse."

"There is an ancient saying in the Koran that when two people try to cross a narrow bridge from opposite sides, one must change direction."

"Or?" said Goodman.

"Go for a swim," said Appleton, reaching behind him and turning his music back up—very loud.

21

Rayford Goodman

It wasn't my all-time favorite meeting. Except you could see there were wheels within wheels and a lot of dealing off the bottom of the deck. Which was a plus to know.

Another thing, didn't look like Curry and Appleton were best buddies, the name never even came up. OK, both feeding off Stacy, natural to be competitors. Then why in such rich digs share the same secretary? Speaking of which, take no shit from Curry and *plenty* from Appleton? Same person.

And moving and manipulating Junior and Iris—what was that all about? Which gets us back to the main event—why was everybody trying to railroad Carey for Wesley Crewe's murder?

We'd wound up the meeting with a lot of dancing around and fending off, learning zilch. Well, not exactly zilch. We did learn, by the *lack* of help, they weren't really doing the deal Penny was paying them for. Or, at least, some people weren't. We'd find out more about Stacy in a bit.

About the one plus the whole morning, we had Appleton set up a lunch today out at the compound. Which is where we were heading now, sort of slow boat to China—because we had about an hour to kill yet.

"I don't understand," said Bradley, "why they would make a deal to cooperate—authorize the biography—and then hold back just about any information."

"I've been wondering that, too," I said. "And the only thing strikes me—besides the fact they're collecting a couple mil to do it (not the worse motive I ever heard)—they're afraid what we're going to find out."

"All right. I can buy that. That was where Cifelli came in, to get us to cool it. But then why become a party to the party?"

"Hey, isn't one of your Yuppie words *co-opt*? That the term? Get us on the team to control things. Steer us away from whatever they don't want found out. Or worse comes to worst, put their own spin on it if we do."

"But again we're talking 'they.' "

"No question. Got to be conspiracy, there's too many people going too many ways for it to be solo."

"But what possible reason could a whole group of people have killing a nonentity like Wesley Crewe? What possible importance to that kind of creep—the star's daughter's boyfriend? Even as nuisance value, you do it with money. Or a visit from a couple of Cifelli's boys, if it comes to that. Why murder?"

On the nose. That was the part didn't make all that much sense. I gave him the definitive answer—a shrug.

Trying to kill time, we'd taken a longer route through Pacific Palisades, but even with that, we would still be a good forty to fifty minutes early. So we decided to stop for coffee.

The town looked so familiar. They'd shot more than a few movies here. When they needed a small-town look and didn't want to go too far on location.

We found a diner. I remember when diners weren't quite respectable, which was part of the attraction. Sure wasn't the food. Which reminded me the dopey idea used to be around you could tell good places to eat if there were trucks parked outside. Like it made sense big lunkhead truck drivers would have the most discriminating taste.

Anyway, we pulled in to the parking lot between two trucks, that I still felt wasn't a good endorsement. But we were only going to have a cup of coffee. Which I'd give odds from the sign, "Best Coffee in the World," we weren't likely to find there.

Inside looked like it might have been the place Jack Nicholson did that great scene with the waitress where she wouldn't make any substitutions. *Five Easy Pieces*. Which reminded me of an interesting night I once had doing security for Phil Spitalny and his All-Girl Orchestra (after Phil went home).

They brought the coffee. (My bet was safe.) At least it gave us something to sit over for twenty minutes or so.

"Got a thought," I said after a bit. "Maybe the mistake is we're trying to tie everything in one neat bundle."

"Even one sloppy bundle," said Bradley.

"Right. But try this. Say—which we know—there's a conspiracy by the whole bunch to do something."

"That's pinning it down," said Bradley.

"Wait. But the conspiracy's only one thing. Maybe the murder's another."

"Oh?"

"Talking the original murder, not Courtney. Crewe. Suppose somebody murdered Crewe—alone. Whatever reason. Kind of guy he was, probably had it coming. *Then,* whether to cover that, or even serve another purpose, the conspiracy."

"Uh-huh," said Bradley, interested. "For the sake of argument. But what does that do for us?"

"Lets us separate the two. One thing we want to find out, what's the conspiracy. The other's who murdered Wesley Crewe."

"Real great," said Bradley. "So now we've progressed to where we don't simply have one thing we can't figure out, we have two." With which he finished the coffee, got up, and tossed a couple of bills on the table. "That's a real big help. Yich."

"Just an idea."

"I mean the coffee."

Stacy's secretary, Gilbert Rexford, let us in. He and Bradley exchanged what I'd have to say were your basic significant looks. Then they went on to say how good to see each other and when were they going to get together? I tried not to think about it.

Me he gave a cold hello. Different fraternity.

I notice the guy was wearing a lot of silk and cashmere

and suede had to cost in the neighborhood of a Stealth bomber. Unless Stacy Jaeger was awful good to the help, there was some supplementary pay happening here.

He told us we were expected and led us through a long foyer filled with a lot of South Sea Islands stuff. There were spears and shields and shell things and nets, and sponges and cork and I suppose somewhere a blowfish, though I didn't see one for sure (maybe it got ate).

And bowls and tools and knives and paddles and even an outrigger canoe sailing up by the ceiling, which was kind of shellacked thatch. The whole feeling was like you'd imagine a retirement home for a bunch of Trader Vics.

We passed through that to a dining room could have been a missionary settlement somewhere. Also, I guess, put together from genuine island antiques. I kept expecting some sultry Tondelayo to sashay out and make tiffin.

Instead, Gilbert took us through a butler's pantry beyond that, facing a bamboo door. This was on a swivel hinge (as was Gilbert).

He pulled open the door, and I could see the other side was finished in a smooth stainless steel, and led into the world's most modern kitchen. Major culture shock.

There, finally, preparing our lunch, was the great man himself, Stacy Jaeger. (With two dusky helpers which the old movies would of called half-breeds and today would be "of unspecified multi-ethnic origin." Like most, in my experience, they seemed to have only the best features of whatever races their parents were when taken with the heavy sweats.)

In the background, some vintage Nat Cole ("Smack Dab in the Middle"). God bless CD's.

"There you are," said Stacy with that famous, know-it-anywhere, whisper-intense voice made you pay extra attention even he was only clearing his throat.

"Stacy," said Bradley, by way of hello.

"Stacy," I said, same.

"Mr. Bradley, Mr. Goodman," said Stacy, pushing up his glasses and letting us know he'd decide when we could call him by his first name. But, hey, it was the American way with celebrities. Wasn't Frank Frank? Marlon Marlon? And Dustin Dustin?

"*Mr.* Jaeger," I corrected myself. He nodded, gave me a smile. I got the feeling he was a guy liked to give little tests. And I passed number one.

"I was just making us some putti putti oobla dee. Very special favorite of mine."

I looked up, raised an eyebrow.

"Tremendously difficult to get boar's balls in L.A. I have them flown in from Papeete," he said.

"Which must leave a lot of lady boars disappointed," I said back, glad to see he had a sense of humor (and dug music). "Putti putti" being Slam Stewart, and "Oobla dee" Dizzy Gillespie.

"Life isn't always easy," he went on, with that hoarse whisper in the wind. "I hope you favor oobla. The secret's in bamboo for the grill. Intense heat. And promise you won't tell anybody, jest a touch of ooh shoobe." (Ella.)

I kept a straight face, though I'd noticed Bradley go a little pale ever since "boar's balls."

"So, how's it going?" Jaeger asked, holding out his hand. One of the dusky maidens put two round, fuzzy things in it I couldn't imagine what. But looked disgusting enough to pass for pig nuts. These he rolled in a batter of some kind and carried to a pan of crackling oil sizzling on the stove.

"What I'm doing now," he went on with that soft, southern song voice, "goin' sear the boar balls in this boiling puma piss ..." I was beginning to see we were dealing with a man had a really far-out sense of humor.

"Evaporates the remaining semen," he went on, absolute deadpan. "Although some leave it in, since it's reputed to enhance potency." He dumped the contents into the pan, where they sizzled and popped dramatically, as he went through a lot of flashy Benihana moves—flipping and turning the stuff.

"While that's frying we make a bed of peacock manure patties," he just kept on, turning to god knows what on a butcher-block island and kneading the mixture. "Best use a little rice to hold it together. I favor Uncle Ben for that."

I was really having trouble not breaking up by now. Bradley, on the other hand, to my surprise, was buying it, turning a nice shade of green around the gills. Stacy could see he had a pigeon, so just turned it up a notch.

"What goes good with that, a little filet of mole. But be sure you don't get the deep brown, they're a little tough. The light brown."

"Light brown mole, got it," I said. "You eat that separate, or together with the peacock manure and the boar's balls in boiling puma piss?"

By which time came the dawn for Bradley.

"You guys!" he said, his color returning as we all three burst out laughing.

Jaeger let go with a couple enormous whoops. I was right with him. And the two of us were holding our stomachs, all but rolling on the floor. Bradley, too, but a touch less, still a bit embarrassed. It went on for a minute or two, faded, came back, quieted down.

"So," said Jaeger, wiping his hands on a towel, then taking off his glasses to dry his eyes. "We can either have my specialty—Jaeger's Ground Groin Goodies, or"—and here he went to the huge double fridge and opened it, taking out a covered dish—"Hsien-kan-pei-yao-hua, which of course is Chinese."

"Oh, right," said Bradley, a little leery by this time. "And hsien-kan whatever is what?"

"It's actually stir-fried sea scallops and pork kidneys."

"Yeah, sure," said Bradley.

"No, it really is. Excellent."

He could see it didn't sound all that appetizing to Bradley—plus, I'm sure, he was wary getting suckered a second time.

"Or you could join me in this cold lobster salad I fixed earlier, because Oliver wants me to lose a hundred pounds afore the start of production. As if fat people didn't exist in this life. The late Aga Khan used to get his weight in gold each year on his birthday. Don't imagine *he* dieted too seriously.

At any rate, it's an artistic compromise circumstances have forced me to accept."

Maybe they just wanted to keep him alive till they finished the picture, was my thought.

We opted for the salad.

"I thought lobster wasn't all that low-cal," said Bradley.

"It's really supposed to be tuna," said Jaeger. "But there are limits."

Then he said something to the girls in some language I didn't understand—which is everything but English—and yelled out, "Rex-foahd!"

Clearly Gilbert kept himself in hollering distance, 'cause he popped right in.

"Yes, Stace?"

"We'll eat out on the patio. No calls."

"No problem," said Gilbert, in that cliché way people do even when there *is* no problem—as if they solved one.

We followed Jaeger through the door to an outside deck that went around three sides of the house and to the patio. There, on a lounge, was his girlfriend, Soheila, sunning herself in a string tonga so tiny it made a regular bikini seem like the Salvation Army. There was a lot *to* Soheila, all good, just now glistening from a mixture of coconut oil and sunblock. Which must have given very mixed signals to her body. But no mixed signals to me. I loved the hell out of it.

"You fellows know Soheila Morris," said Stacy, wheezing from the walk, as he collapsed into a very sturdy piece of patio furniture.

"Of course," said Bradley. "Good to see you again."

She smiled. Great teeth.

"Really good to see you," I said, just a touch of Groucho eyebrow leer, being a past master of the single entendre.

"Boys," she said, somehow making it clear she noticed we were a different sex.

"Sweetheart," she then said to Stacy, picking up the coconut oil and the sunblock and holding it out. "Would you mind?"

"My hands are all smelly from the fish," he said, holding them apart, palms front, DeNiro style.

"Would you mind, Mark?" she said, offering the gunk to him and turning over to feature an ass technically covered by something the width of dental floss.

But before he was out of his chair, and as I got the feeling she expected, I jumped up and took the tubes. "I'll get that, Bradley." Then mostly to her, but interesting that Stacy was around, I added, "I do the heavy lifting in this outfit."

And I started rubbing the oily stuff into what had to be world-class skin. When common decency—and a desire to go on living—got me to stop at her waist line, she reached around back and pushed my hand lower.

"I don't want to get burned," she said.

"I don't, either," I said, but allowed myself to smooth a little more gunk on her globular protrudences. Which were maximus. As she gave off an appreciative hum.

"Uhm, Stacy, er, Mr. Jaeger," Bradley said, half tongue-tied by the thick sexual tension, "have you, uh, done any work with the tapes Dick Penny suggested?"

"No, I haven't," said Jaeger, looking away from the skin games Soheila and I were playing. The part of me able to detach wondering what the actual game was. As the part of me not able to detach watched her groan and bare it. Interesting.

"That ought to do," I said, having covered just about her entire back with the oils and creams. And the outer limits of allowable conduct.

At which point she turned over and sat half upright, a towel held to her chest. She looked me right in the eyes, wet her lips with her tongue, and said, "You can't be going to quit with the job only half done?" And dropped the towel. No top.

I damn *was* going to quit. But I didn't get to say it because Stacy, with the kind of move you'd never think possible, sprang up out of the chair, crossed the deck, and socked her smack on the jaw.

22

Mark Bradley

I was still rocking and reeling through various levels of shock and confusion—all internal and numbing—when Goodman had already leaped out of the recliner, grabbed Jaeger's shoulder, turned him around, and delivered a hamfisted punch that dropped him like a stone. A rock. A boulder. A falling safe.

The old man still had a lot of good moves. I was only afraid he might have killed the guy.

Definitely no moving picture, with Jaeger immobile on the floor, Soheila frozen on the chaise, Goodman bent over the felled actor, still anger-fisted, and I, glued to my chair—critic and audience. It seemed an eternity before the tension broke when Jaeger took a huge breath and his eyes settled back into focus. He was apparently OK. Or as OK as one is apt to be when two-hundred-plus pounds of puncher finds the old "button" and nails you to the floor.

"If you have a problem about this," said Goodman, once he was confident of a hearing, "and I could see how you might, I think *I'm* the one you should be hitting."

"Much good that would have done me," said Stacy, remarkably recovered. "As you've clearly demonstrated," he added, rubbing his jaw, resetting his glasses, and rearranging himself into a cross-legged, yogalike position on the floor, with that incredible flexibility and limberness fat people so often display.

By which time the ever hovering Gilbert made an appearance, accompanied by a frightening hulk it took no great discernment to decide was a bodyguard, who I judged to be Samoan. If not Martian.

"What's going on here?" asked Gilbert, anticlimactically.

"Artistic differences," said Jaeger, his good humor evidently restored—for what reason I couldn't imagine.

"It's all right," he continued reassuringly to the Samoan, who seemed to be registering a kind of simianlike concern. As the latter lifted Jaeger effortlessly to his feet, the actor added something in what was probably his native tongue. The man nodded, a gesture suggestive of a mountain tilting, took a long look at Goodman, as if memorizing his features—perhaps as a prelude to rearrangement, I couldn't help thinking—and left the room with a pace, grace, and agility not unreminiscent of the late lead-footed Godzilla.

"Stace? Mr. Jaeger ... ?" said Gilbert, evidently unsatisfied.

"Just a touch of temper," added Jaeger reassuringly. "Mine. You know I do have a temper."

At which point Soheila, who hadn't said a word during all this—one couldn't but feel a good choice in the circumstances—rose, hastily covered herself with a robe, and said, "I'll go to my room."

"I make that a good idea," said Jaeger. And as she gathered her gear, added, "You might also apologize to Mr. Goodman."

"I'm sorry," she said dutifully.

Jaeger crossed to her side, kissed her cheek, and gave her a little pat on the lower lumbars. "There's a good girl," he added, with an obvious disregard for the truth. (Unless the truth was she was supposed to do all this?)

And in a flurry of silk and a flash of leg she departed.

"Really sorry about that," Jaeger said as we all watched her go, a provocative sight even as she feigned modesty. "No excuse, of course. Very uncivilized of me. I sometimes forget Soheila's a force of nature in her own right. Or wrong, as the case may be. Afraid I may have spoiled her a bit."

Which he'd energetically tried to rectify.

"Not all that rare with gorgeous women," said Goodman,

whose spontaneous gallantry nonetheless had impressed me. It was just plain: hit a woman, get a punch. Bam, bam.

But what exactly had happened? It couldn't have been staged. And what impelled Goodman to go along with the provocation? He had to know you don't make time with someone else's girl in front of the someone else.

"As I'd be the first to admit," continued Jaeger, "this was not entirely unmotivated by the young lady. And, of course, directed more at me than you."

"Then we're into bygones being bygones?" I suggested with very little confidence.

"I don't think Mr. Jaeger's going to want to work with me anymore," said Goodman. "Which I understand, even if he did have it coming, hitting a girl like that. Whatever the reason."

Tennis match, we both turned to look at Jaeger. "I'll want to think about it," he said.

"Right," said Goodman, I guess mentally kissing the deal goodbye. "Another day, another million."

"That's why I want to think about it," admitted Jaeger, rocking his jaw back and forth to see if it was still hinged.

"Then I guess that's a wrap, gents," said Gilbert, some high sign evidently having been exchanged, and body-language herding us toward the door.

"Do you mind if I make a call before I go?" I asked, resisting the move. "I want to check the office."

They didn't mind, which stopped the procession. I crossed to the other side of the room, leaving Goodman to cope with the awkward-silence department.

I could have waited to call from my car, but I'd spotted a button lighting up on the phone, and, given Jaeger and Gilbert both in attendance, the likelihood favored Soheila being the user. To report these weird carryings-on, I imagined.

I stood in front of the phone, obscuring their view of it, and gently depressed the button—to see who she was talking to.

Right idea, wrong pronoun. Not so much who as what. The beautiful and sexually impulsive Miss Morris *was* on the phone. I don't know who with, since the other party never got a word in edgewise. It was the *what* I found most intriguing—she was talking in a foreign language. And one I not only didn't speak, I didn't even recognize. Which didn't preclude recognizing the air of urgency to her tone. A clear impression this wasn't simply girlfriends exchanging gossipy chitchat.

I listened harder, the way one does when confronting an incomprehensible language, as if greater attention might penetrate its mystery. But I couldn't catch a single word. Nada. Rien. Nichts.

It definitely wasn't a Romance language. Hungarian? Finnish? Not a clue. But just as I was about to punch another button for a dial tone, the fog lifted for a moment, and the words "Goodman" and "Bradley" were maddeningly clear, before she returned to whatever (Arabic? Farsi?) the gibberish was.

However, on tone and inflection alone, there was no escaping a sense of threat. I continued monitoring in the hope of at least learning who was on the other end, but a pudgy arm suddenly reached around me, at the end of which was a pudgy hand, not unexpectedly connected to a pudgy finger, which depressed another button on the phone.

"I think you'll find," said Jaeger, "it's a mite easier to make a call on an open line."

We drove in silence for about five minutes. Goodman and I weren't too thrilled with each other. He went first.

"You were so damn obvious," he said. "You want to listen in, listen in a little. You can't stand there for half an hour and not dial or talk."

"While you, the master of subtlety, only tried to break the man's jaw. That really made us a lot of friends."

"What was I supposed to do? The guy was hitting a girl."

"A girl whose ass you were fondling at great length and with a lot of enthusiasm."

"It was a great ass."

"We were totally manipulated. I don't know why, but we

were definitely not in control of the situation. She can't really have been coming on to you."

"I have my following," he said with some defensiveness. "I may not be *your* type . . ." at which he decided to drop that line of argument.

"I didn't mean she couldn't—or wouldn't be interested in you. I simply meant that you don't act on it in front of your lover."

"Well, maybe he's not her lover. There's that possibility."

"Yes. But even so, if they have an arrangement, it's for appearances. So, then, the ground rules are you don't compromise that appearance. But whatever possessed you?"

"Love of life. Curiosity."

"Come on."

"It was too weird. I couldn't help wanting to see where it would go."

"Where *could* it go, to the bedroom?! With Jaeger there?"

"It *is* Hollywood."

"You're right about one thing, it was weird."

"A lot of violence in that guy," said Goodman.

Right. That much couldn't have been staged. The punch was real. He'd lost his temper, and pow! Which meant, of course, he was capable of massively losing his temper. With all that implied vis-à-vis Wesley Crewe, his daughter's abusive boyfriend.

I drove on in silence for a bit. But nothing really broke. We kept finding out more and more things, only there didn't seem to be any cohesion between them and no narrowing of focus. The general picture seemed as fuzzy as ever.

"OK, so she talks a foreign language," said Goodman, evidently of a similar mind. "What's that give us?"

"That she's a foreigner?"

"Not necessarily. Lots of people know another language."

"Yes, but stressed? That's when second nature kicks in, you go to your roots. No, she's definitely foreign."

"OK," said Goodman. "I like that line of reasoning. I'd like it better if we knew who she was talking to."

"Especially since our names got mentioned. That's why I kept trying to hang in. For which you put me down excessively."

"Well, it didn't work, did it?" he replied. Quite redundantly, I felt.

"So the question is, what now?" he continued. "Back to the book?"

"No, not today any more. I've got cocktails in an hour and a half with Gilbert."

"You have a date?"

"I have a date."

This surprised him. "When did you ... fellows even have a change to arrange it?"

"We have secret ways to communicate," I said mysteriously.

"I don't doubt that for a minute," said Goodman.

Actually, Gilbert had slipped me a note suggesting the Beverly Wilshire for tea. I had nodded. Secret ways.

"My only question is," said Goodman, "and I'm not sure I even want to know the answer—is this business or pleasure?"

"Well," I replied, "I'm hoping for both."

"Yeah, maybe you can get unlucky," he said, arrow to the heart. Albeit I felt basically with good intent. And not something I didn't worry a whole lot about.

We drove on in silence for a bit. Letting the subject fade.

"Just keep your wits about you," he said finally. "It's getting a tad weird out there."

"OK."

"And don't talk to any strange Samoans."

"Like the one following us in the gray Volvo?" I said, showing how much I was on the ball.

"Especially," he answered, knowing all along.

It worked out well. I had about forty-five minutes or so to kill, which'd be perfect to shower and change. I had to go back to my place anyway because Goodman's car was parked in my garage.

There were two messages on my answer phone. From long-distance Operators 23 and 17 inquiring if "anyone there" would accept a collect call from a Mr. Brian Alexander in

Atlanta, Georgia. Both belatedly realized they were talking to an answer machine and so informed Brian, who said he would try again later to tell "anyone there" he didn't appreciate their hostile attitude and unfair withhol—by which time Operator 17, wise in the ways of deadbeat customers trying to communicate without payment, terminated my part of the connection. I guess Brian had gotten the word the credit cards were cancelled. How could *he* be sore? Though of course he was a champ at vested self-interest.

And everybody's got a reason why they're right.

Bradley's maxim number twenty-two: no man's a villain unto himself.

I shaved, showered, and changed into a deep blue broadcloth shirt, rust knit tie, my camel's hair blazer, medium gray slacks, and brown suede Ferragamo loafers. After which, picture-perfect and button-cute, it was time to go.

To my surprise, the large, dusky gentleman in the dusty gray Volvo who had followed us from Malibu was still parked down the block. Which had to mean I was the principal target rather than Goodman, since the latter had long since openly departed. So be it.

I actually kind of liked the importance it afforded me. I also liked even more the intuitive hunch that'd seen me pack my Beretta 9mm into the Gucci tote.

(Technically, it was probably against the law. But the laws were so weird. You didn't need a license to own a gun. But you did to carry it. You could have it at home. Or in the car, if it wasn't loaded. You couldn't *take* it to the car concealed. It was legal to carry it openly. Except if you did that four neighbors and twenty-two cops would probably take a shot at you. "The guy's got a gun!" Fortunately, the laws didn't specifically mention Gucci totes. Attsa some slim loophole.)

My tail let two cars come between us when I pulled into the alley between the old Beverly Wilshire and the new wing, where one left one's car with the attendant. But I managed to dally at the entry to the old wing long enough to see him leave his own vehicle to be parked and commence an ostentatious amble toward the entrance to the new. There, presumably, he'd lounge casually (or as casually as a huge Samoan could—although he seemed a mite shorter than I'd remembered, from this distance) and wait for me to finish my tea with Gilbert. Whatever evil designs he had toward me surely wouldn't be implemented this publicly.

The tearoom was to the right, if you entered from Wilshire Boulevard; stage left, if you came from show business—or the parking area. It was lovely and new and not quite all that English—since it was lovely and new. There was a while, in the Sixties, I guess, when everything was young and new in England. Then that passed ("I can't imagine what came over us!") and they went back to being old and conventional. Which of course was their role.

Anyway and either way, it was perfect for those who liked tea—or *a* tea, including the sandwiches and pastries. And the nice thing about tea rooms, American style, you could still drink liquor instead, if such was your bent.

And speaking of bent, Gilbert had gotten there before me and selected a table close enough to the piano to monitor the show-tune lyrics yet far enough to allow for conversation. He rose to greet me and we shook hands just as if we were a regular couple of business guys grabbing a bite before making a slick deal—which maybe we were.

He, too, had changed his clothes. From gold to platinum.

It was pretty obvious he'd come into beaucoup de bucks. But one wanted to know why and how.

So after the teas had been ordered, the costly vestments complimented, and the piano player compared negatively to Bobby Short, I got to it.

"Gilbert, before we get into mutual friends we have known, and how, and submit our health cards, it would seem to me nice to know if we're on the same side."

"I think so. What side are you on?" he countered, peering over a cup of Fortnum and Mason Royal Blend through extraordinarily blue eyes and very white whites, framed by the lightest possible to be believable shade of blond eyebrows.

"Truth, justice, and commerce," I replied. "For example, I

noticed you testified in a way that might be considered counter to the interests of the Jaeger family."

"You mean by placing all the interested parties in the interested places."

"Leaving, it would seem, only Carey Jaeger alone able to have helped Wesley Crewe lay down his earthly burdens."

"That's right."

"I mean, no ambiguity, no this person might have been there, I don't know where that person was, you put everybody someplace and Carey at X marks the spot."

"Uh-huh."

"For which, judging from your wardrobe and sundry accoutrements, the Rolex looks new, you seem to've been strangely rewarded. Why is that?"

"Because the family line is, since Carey did it, and since he's going to be convicted of doing it, there's no point in prolonging the agony."

"That being the case, why not plead guilty?"

"He was supposed to. But he backed out."

"Maybe it suddenly occurred to him he was being set up for a fall."

"How could it suddenly?" he countered, rightfully. It wasn't as if there was new news. But there was pressure after he recanted. There was the bomb thing, and Goodman's conviction it had been intended to intimidate Carey.

"What about the bomb thing?" I asked straight out.

"What about some more of these sandwiches?" he responded evasively.

And then what happened, we started to get personal. Which is to say, we, or I, explored the possibility of seeing each other. Which resulted in what, under other circumstances, might have been a blow to my ego. I was more or less rebuffed, which is considerably worse than buffed.

"I'm seeing someone else," he said, ingesting an entire cucumber sandwich, sans crusts, in one attractive bite, displaying, as it did, really perfect teeth.

Which suggested to me that I had been led up the garden path. Prompting the further question, why the fuck why?

So when Gilbert excused himself to request the piano artiste perform a medley of Cole Porter witties, this Miss Otis took the opportunity to get to a phone. I only reached Goodman's answering machine, which didn't tell me much one way or another.

But a hasty check on the alley between the hotel's two wings told me a lot. The Samoan was nowhere to be seen. It suddenly seemed pretty clear that I hadn't been the object at all. That not only hadn't my irresistible charm been the impetus for Gilbert's invitation to tea, but that my irresistible stupidity had played right into their hands. I was to be decoyed out of the picture in order for the ominous Samoan to have a clear, unobstructed shot at the primary target—Rayford Goodman.

23

Rayford Goodman

My Caddy classic still wasn't ready, so I was still driving the Jap loaner. I think it was the Bataan Death March model. I loved it a lot.

When I left Bradley's pad in Boystown, I noticed the Samoan tail we'd picked up leaving Jaeger's place didn't follow me. So I guess his assignment was Bradley.

I headed up King's Road, hung a left on Santa Monica, to La Cienega, and turned north up the hill toward Sunset. Just shy of the top, with the clunker choking and threatening to quit, I opted for a quick left into the North Beach Leather lot. From where I could walk through to the next block and the Playboy Building lot. Where we had our office.

That served two purposes. It kept me from crapping out on a real steep hill you couldn't back down without a major traffic snarl. And I could go check if anything was happening at Pendragon. Well, three—I could also see was Francie there.

She was asleep on her office floor. Boss Penny didn't believe in couches. While it obviously didn't stop napping, it did cut down on sexual harassment among the older, less hardy management folks.

My baby didn't look so hot. There was a telltale white rim around her nostrils, swollen lids, and labored breathing. If the truth was nobody stops anything till they have to, I think we were getting close to "have to."

I had just about decided to let her sleep it off and turned to go when Penny popped in.

"OK, what's this?" said Penny, as if he'd caught us doing something weird, like telepathic sex.

"I get the idea, Francie," I said, fairly loud, nudging her foot with my toe. "That's the way they found the body."

She gave a startled snort, opened her eyes, and popped to a sitting position. "Wha'?" she said, not exactly latching onto the game.

"OK, that's it, I can't put up with this," said Penny.

"Before you say anything else," I interrupted, "let's just— out in the hall?"

"There's nothing more to say."

"There's a little more to listen."

He shrugged, turned, and left the room. I put on a pissed-off face, which was a lot like my regular one, and motioned her to get up. Then followed Penny out to the hall.

"Don't start with me," he started with me. "It's not like I'm some naive nerd who doesn't know what's going on. I'm not going to just keep turning my back. She's out."

"Well, yeah, sure, now, I understand. And I don't say you're wrong. You can't have that in the workplace."

"I don't give a damn what she does on her own time. Well, I do, really. I'm not a total shit," he said, as if admitting some weakness. "That's just my work style," he added confidentially.

"To get employee loyalty," I couldn't help mentioning. "Point is, Dickie, you can't fire her."

"Watch."

"I mean, it's not like the old days. This might be 'on the job related.' Ever think of that?"

"Getting stoned?"

"The pressures, the stress. You might have to pay disability, rehab—maybe damages."

"The fucking lawyers!"

"The fucking lawyers," I agreed. "Look, I'm with you. Not often. But this time. We'll do something, give us a little more slack."

"I can't have it."

"Hey, it's not as if she doesn't really do the job. Just a little more time. You don't want to get involved in lawsuits and government crap."

"Well, you know me, I'm a sucker for a sob story," he actually said. "One week." And he headed on down the hall, peeking in doorways, looking for other malingerers or malfeasers. I went back in.

Francie was at her desk, sipping coffee, bloodshot eyes a color match with her nose, both on the moist side.

"And what is it again, Miss America? You want world peace, universal love, and free aerobics for the underprivileged?" I said.

"No fucking crap from you," she warned.

I showed my palms in surrender.

"Why I'm really here, I wanted to know did you make any progress on the Appleton file," I managed to come up with. Then, since I was into it, "All those funny charities, the loser investments?"

She decided to go along. "I've been on the case, contrary to popular belief around here. I do get my work done."

Enough for now. I dropped it. "They can't all be loser investments," I went on.

"Actually, I discovered one that's a heavy winner."

"Yeah?"

"Appleton, and presumably the whole group—I could get details on the structure later—own something called National Standard."

"Yeah?"

"Which is a company that manufactures flags."

"OK."

"And the flag they manufacture most is the Israeli flag. Overwhelming, no contest, their most popular item—Israeli flags."

"So?"

"So the kicker is, their best customer's not Israel."

Maybe I missed something. "They manufacture Israeli flags?"

"Which they sell in huge numbers," she said.

"Only not to Israel?" I said. "OK, I'll bite. Who to?"

"Arab countries."

I hunched my shoulders in an Israeli shrug. "And Arab countries buy them why?"

"To burn! At demonstrations and riots," she finally explained.

I couldn't totally decide whether she was putting me on, there being a kind of a weird logic (they did have to get them somewhere). So I flat-out changed the subject.

"I thought maybe if you weren't doing anything we might have a little din-din or something," I shot from mid-court.

"I don't know why you never seem to notice we don't go together anymore," she answered—air ball.

"I notice. I just don't respect it." Bobby Bruce—Burns?—the Scottish spider guy, don't give up. "What do you say?"

"Well, I say thank you, nice of you to ask. But I have a date."

"Mickey Mouse?"

"It's none of your business, really," she said, not too nasty, though.

"Listen, if I just minded my own business, I'd be *out* of business. What're you going to do?"

"He got tickets to the Hollywood Bowl. Concert."

"One of those rock groups—Blood Clot, Urban Blight?"

"Classical."

"Ah, one of the Itzhaks."

"As a matter of fact, yes. Together with Yo Yo Ma. So, if there's nothing else, I'll resume my meditations."

There was a lot else. But not much I could do about it at the moment. Maybe Bradley was right, and we'd have to organize something. Since I knew the minute I was out the door the meditations would be medi*ca*tions.

The spider didn't want to let go. I took a breath.

"Good-*bye,* Rayford," she said pointedly, squashing it.

"So long, Francie," I replied. "Give my regards to the Itzhaks. And yo' mama."

Not too snappy. Along the lines of the rest of my day. Actually, head and shoulders over the rest of my day.

After climbing through the parking lot, across the street, to the other parking lot, my battery was totally dead. I climbed out, through the lot, across the street, to the other lot, and back up to the building, and into the lobby. There I asked the security guy at the desk if I could use his phone. The security guy said the line had to be kept open for security reasons. He pointed to a pay phone at the far end of the lobby which he told me was available to the public.

The phone available to the public was out of order.

I told the security guy the phone was out of order. He said he knew that. While I considered killing him, he told me to have a nice day. I didn't think I could have a nice day *unless* I killed him.

I went back up to the office. It was empty. I called the auto club. No, I didn't know the license plate number. No, I didn't know the exact make of the car. They could find it because there would be a purple-faced fellow standing next to it, having a stroke. They said they'd come in thirty to forty-five minutes.

They didn't. In thirty. *Or* forty-five.

Since I was burning anyway, and hadn't replaced my ace-in-the-hole cigarette, I bummed one off a total stranger who seemed happy to find anybody else still smoked in California. But before we could make permanent plans and pick a pattern, the AAA finally did come and jump-start me. I promised to keep in touch.

I went back out the La Cienega exit, forgot, and turned left to go up to Sunset. It wouldn't make the hill. I had to roll back on over to the left side of the road—since by now there were other cars behind me on the right—and coast on down, backwards all the way to the bottom of the hill and the gas station at Holloway. There I backed in, turned around, cut through, and headed out Holloway, and from there back to Sunset on the western end of the street. I turned right, went back to Sunset Plaza, and finally, not at all pleased with life in general, my place in it, and Japan's most especially, headed home.

Since I'd left my garage-door clicker in the Caddy, when I

pulled up to the house I just parked the Coupe de Corregidor at the curb.

I picked up the mail, headed up the driveway and through the people door of the garage.

Which was when the old instincts kicked in. Firstly, the alarm light was yellow instead of red. Might could be I'd forgot to set it, but more—there was a presence in the garage, and it wasn't the Phantom. With all the junk I kept stashed there, the crates and crap, there were lots of places to hide.

I didn't feel like facing whoever down under those circumstances, it being too easy to sandbag me. It was an easy, automatic choice and I didn't waste a second, just about-faced and backpedaled.

I leaped the bird of paradises lining the side of the driveway (lopping off a beak or two—my leap being a touch less springy since I last tried one), onto the stairs and up to the front door. I had my key out, quickly unlocked the door, and popped it open.

As expected, since there was a short there I hadn't gotten around to having fixed, that set off the alarm. I knew it would bug the hell out of the Phantom, but hoped it would do the same to whoever. Avoiding is better than confronting.

But I stayed at the door in case the whoever decided to exit from the front of the garage instead of the back I could get a glimpse of him.

The trouble with that, the phone started ringing. It would be Westec, responding to the alarm. I ignored it for a good two minutes, but when I still didn't see the guy, I figured he'd opted for escape through the rear. And I knew if I didn't answer the phone the Westec folks were going to send a squad of rent-a-cops and I'd have to deal with the possibility *I* might look like the interloper.

"Hi, yeah," I said into the phone. "I accidentally set it off."

"What's your code?" said the Westec lady, which you had to say to let them know you really didn't want them to come with their armed response and weren't just saying that because somebody had a switchblade at your throat (though that might be a good time not to have anybody come storming in, either).

"The code is 'Hooray for Hollywood,' " I said. And she said OK and hung up.

I put my alarm key in the slot (it was an old system) and shut the clanging off.

By now Mr. Whoever was surely gone, and I'd find a spooked Phantom hiding behind the firewood and needing a little reassurance.

I went out the front door again, leaped over the bird of paradises—making it this time (it was downhill)—and through the garage door.

"Phantom? Hey, Phantom, where are you, guy?" I called. But I couldn't see him anywhere. What I did see, not too happy, the back door to the kitchen was cracked. I immediately opened it and stepped through.

I knew the guy was long gone and wouldn't be in the house.

My instincts totally deserted me.

Likewise consciousness.

24

Mark Bradley

I hadn't even gone back to tell Gilbert off, just sent for my car—and I was quickly in and fighting my way through the Beverly Hills Wilshire traffic, all the while trying unsuccessfully to get Goodman on the phone at his home.

Goodman's loaner was in front of his house, and I could see, parked in front of the next house up, the gray Volvo that'd trailed us from Malibu.

I pulled up just past the garage and eased out of the car, careful not to slam the door.

I hugged the side of the building and sidled to the open entry to the garage, took a quick look in. Nobody. But the kitchen door was open. I tiptoed through that and peeked around the corner toward the dining room.

Goodman was on the floor, facedown, the back of his head bleeding profusely.

Standing over him—still unaware of my presence—was the guy who'd been tailing us. I could see now he wasn't the one who'd been at Jaeger's house, but some other South Pacific person, slightly smaller—only about six-foot-four and possibly less than three hundred pounds.

But his size, strength, and personal fiercesomeness were all academic, because it didn't look to me that his intentions were to beat Goodman up.

The reason I thought that was the large, I would judge .45-caliber (I was getting increasingly familiar with such things)

Army Colt he had in hand. And the next thing I knew, he had cocked the weapon and aimed it at Goodman's skull.

I can't say the moment was frozen in time because there was an actual void during which there were no thoughts or awareness at all. Just an incredibly loud gunshot explosion, smoke, and the smell of cordite, followed by the deepest silence I'd ever known.

As I lowered the Beretta in my hand and it began to dawn on me that I'd just killed a human being.

I realized, even in the profound shock in which I seemed to find myself, that there were serious ramifications here. That a simple plea of self-defense was not exactly simple. That there were powerful interests involved, hidden agendas, obscure motives—heavy shit.

Which is why I didn't immediately dial 911 and start confronting the bureaucratic hassles that were certain to ensue.

Besides, the felon fellow was clearly dead, so I wasn't placing him at any added risk by procrastination. Not that I cared much about what happened to him, anyhow, given his murderous bent.

Goodman was struggling back to consciousness, and I was struggling with myriad feelings too complex to immediately confront—or even identify.

How had I progressed/retrogressed from writing fluff biographical pieces about minor Hollywood semi-celebrities to such a violent confrontation that I actually, and I'm shocked to say without a moment's hesitation, whipped out a gun (which, by the way, who would have thought I'd even own, much less be carrying eighteen months ago?) and calmly wiped someone from the face of the earth?!

Well, calmly is perhaps not the most accurate word, I realized as my knees started shaking and my gorge started rising and I had a lot of third-eye concentrating to do to stop both.

I went into the master bathroom, got a towel, soaked it in cold water, and returned to Goodman, who by this time was partially sitting up, leaning against a wall, holding the back of his head.

I gently took his hand away and looked to mop the wound.

"Not that towel, that's one of my good towels!" he said, inadvertently reassuring me he was no more brain-damaged than before.

"You've been coshed over the head, the guy was drawing a bead on you, one second away from being murdered, and you're worrying about a fucking towel?!"

"Oh, yeah!" he said, remembering. "The guy—what a dumbo I am. I knew someone had been in the house, I just didn't think he'd still be there after the alarm. What?! He was going to kill me?!"

"It sure looked like it."

"And you just—blew him away? You should pardon the expression?"

I could see Goodman was back to his charming, customarily bigoted self.

"Yeah, well, he had this gun, pointing at your head, cocked, leaning in to make sure he didn't miss—it seemed the thing to do," I concluded.

"Whew!"

"And by the way, it's not the same guy we saw at Jaeger's."

Goodman took a brief look at the ruined head and said, "I'll have to take your word for that." With which he got to his feet, holding the towel to his head, rocking for a moment. I reached for him as he appeared to become dizzy.

"You all right?"

"Uh, yeah, yeah." And he seemed to steady himself. "I'm not exactly thrilled. Look at this place—fucking mess!"

I guess he had a problem dealing with gratitude. I was more concerned with the immediate problem.

"The thing is, what do we do now?" I said.

"You mean the body?"

"Among other things."

"The body *I* could take care of" came a new voice, that of Armand Cifelli, who'd evidently entered behind me.

"Why would you want to do that, Mr. C?" asked Goodman.

"Well, I feel a little responsible."

Which beat the hell out of me.

"Although it's entirely possible, if you'd taken my suggestion and not set out to win the Pulitzer prize, these untoward developments might not have occurred."

"You know, Mr. Cifelli," I said, "you may be right. But I don't know what the fuck you're talking about!"

"I don't think it's necessary to take that tone," said Cifelli.

"Yeah, what's that tone?" said Goodman.

"I just god damn fucking killed a guy!" I reminded them.

"Exactly why I'd like to help you out," said Cifelli. "It wasn't supposed to be like this."

"What was supposed to be like what!?" I yelled.

"Shh," said Cifelli, which did, somehow, calm me. "You were supposed to be part of the team. You were supposed to write your book, we were supposed to generate a good bit of money for our little group, and when Carey got convicted, hopefully with a moderate sentence, things were supposed to quiet down and we would all go about our business."

"Sounds like a plan—ooh," said Goodman, not as quick to rebound as he thought.

"But," Cifelli continued, "you have that tendency to keep digging and digging and finding and finding."

"We do make a good team," said Goodman, since Cifelli had been addressing his remarks to me.

"You do," Cifelli allowed. "But now things are in turmoil, people are being killed, plans are afoot which I am not aware of or a party to."

"You mean you don't know, either?" said Goodman.

"I may know more than you, but I certainly am no part of this. And I sincerely doubt if Stacy Jaeger is, either."

"I'm not so sure about him," I put in. "Now that I see this guy."

"But you said he's not the one was at Stacy's," said Goodman.

"No, but he followed us from *around* there."

"At any rate," said Cifelli, "let me see what I can do about this ... disposal problem of yours."

"Oh, we can handle that," said what turned out to be Lieutenant Ellard, the Beverly Hills chief of detectives, who apparently had also let himself in.

"Well, I guess I'll be running along," said Cifelli.

"Hold it right there," said Ellard.

"I got to beef up my security," added Goodman.

"Could I ask how either or both of you gentlemen knew what was happening here?" I put in. "The reason being that if you knew and could have arrived in a more timely fashion, a lot of this unpleasantness needn't have transpired."

"I, uh, got a tip there was something of interest might be going down here," said Cifelli noncommittally. Which might even have been the truth.

"And I got a call from someone declaring himself a spokesman for the J.F.I. telling me more or less the same," said Ellard. "And to answer your next question, according to the *federales,* J.F.I. is a new group and they think the letters stand for Justice for Iraq, or Jihad or J-something for Iraq."

"I think we can rule out Jews," I offered.

"Mr. Cifelli," said Ellard, "are you involved with any Arab group?"

"Not on purpose," said Cifelli.

Which prompted Ellard to continue, "Then would you mind explaining—"

"Yeah, in a way," said Cifelli. "Instinct and experience. If you have any questions, Ron Silverman's my attorney. But try to keep it down, it costs me five hundred dollars a question. Free to go?"

Ellard nodded. "The expression is, 'Don't leave town.' "

"Why would I leave town? I like it here," said Cifelli. He nodded to Goodman and me and exited out the front door, just as an ambulance and a cop car pulled up.

"Now, then," said Ellard to us both. "Would you care to give me a statement?"

I ran through the limited sequence of events that preceded my discovery of Goodman all a-sea in dire straits. I included that I was having tea with Gilbert Rexford, but left out my conclusion that it'd been a setup. I mentioned we'd noticed we were trailed from Malibu, but excluded the assumption it was somehow at the instigation of the Jaeger group. In other words, I mentioned whatever was immediately checkable (and might have been overheard) and omitted whatever was a conclusion that tended to implicate us any deeper or suggest we might have any motives other than reportage. Which was basically true, if you excluded the motive to stay alive. And the one Ellard added.

"This doesn't exactly help matters getting your ticket back," he said to Goodman, referring to the threatened suspension of his P.I. license as a result of violating his jury duties.

"I don't see what being a victim of random violence has to do with any of that," said Goodman.

"Random?" said Ellard. "With both Armand Cifelli and me being tipped off, you think it's random?" And then he turned to me. "Of course, there'll be an investigation."

"Clearly self-defense."

"Well, not exactly clearly. You weren't attacked, and he wasn't even facing you. You shot the man in the back of the head. I don't think it's unreasonable we might want to look into it a little."

"Look into it all the fuck you want," said Goodman, losing patience. "Just get the body the hell out of here. And look at this mess. Who's supposed to clean it up? Does the city have somebody does that?"

"I don't think so," said Ellard. "I don't recall any Neatening Up Department."

"How about paying? Does the city at least cover my out-of-pocket expenses?"

"I don't think the city does anything, Mr. Goodman. Well, maybe you won't be charged for the ambulance."

"You pay your taxes, and this is the way they treat you," said Goodman, clearly recovering what passed for his senses. "To say nothing of protection. Some protection."

"Well, evidently your partner's pretty good at that," he continued. Then, to me, "You do have a permit for the gun?"

"Nobody has a permit for a gun, practically."

"It was in the house. He left the gun in my house," Goodman put in quickly.

I could see how much Ellard believed that. But he gave it lip service. "Then I can't really see any reason why you should be detained, as long as you're available for any subsequent investigation."

"I guess you'll want to take the gun," I said.

"Not really."

"No?"

"But I imagine whoever conducts the investigation will want to. Like this gentleman," he said, as detective Lieutenant Frank Chow entered through the open front door.

"You're not going to handle the case?" said Goodman.

"Hell, no," said Ellard. "It's not Beverly Hills, out of my jurisdiction."

"Then what was all this?" I demanded angrily.

"I just dropped by for a chat," said Ellard. "You know—to see how my friends were getting on." And he smiled, nodded to Chow, an old chum of Goodman's whom I'd met when the bomb went off downtown, and left.

And we had to go through the whole damn thing all over again.

And finally we'd re-answered all the questions, the paramedic had slapped a bandage over Goodman's skull (with the admonition he ought to go to the hospital and get X-rayed, MRI'd, and Cat-scanned).

"And two-thousand-dollar pickpocketed?" said Goodman. "Thanks, I been there."

"Don't you have insurance and workman's comp and all that?" asked the attendant.

"No. I work for myself."

"You ought to have it, this stuff wouldn't cost you," said the attendant helpfully.

"Hey, I don't *make* as much as the insurance costs," he said.

"Actually, you'd probably be covered by Pendragon," I suggested. "Aren't you technically an employee?"

"No, Penny said I'd do better being an independent consultant. I could save on the deductions."

"And *he* could save on the deductions."

And the paramedic left. And the coroner's guys left (taking the body and substituting a chalk outline). And the forensic guys were at it.

"You know," I suggested, "you might be more comfortable at my place."

"Yeah, all right," said Goodman. "Let me just put something in the bowl for the Phantom and we'll get the hell out of here."

He wrote down my number, handed it to Lieutenant Chow. "Here," he said. "Call me when you're ready to go. Give me enough time to get back and check my belongings before your guys leave."

"Don't aggravate me, Goodman," said Chow.

On the way to my car I said, "I think you insulted him pretty badly."

"What do you mean?"

"Suggesting he or his officers might steal something."

"You kidding? Cops steal more stuff than crooks."

"I can't believe that."

"Yeah? Ask some next of kin someday there was anything found in the victim's pocket. Or a watch. Or a heck of a lot of gold in their teeth."

I could see he was feeling better and there'd been no permanent personality changes.

25

Rayford Goodman

Well, one thing was clear, whoever'd thought they were co-opting Bradley and me had given up on the idea. And decided taking us out—or at least me—was, to put it Yuppie style, a more cost-effective method of damage control.

I couldn't help being pissed at my carelessness. But I had to think it wasn't for the car hanging me up and Francie driving me crazy and all that distraction I'd of been more on guard. Definitely have to watch my fundamentals I was going to stay alive.

Meanwhile, my house was crawling with cops and technicians and photographers and forensic folks, clearly going to be unlivable at least a day or two. So I decided to take Bradley up on his offer to bunk in with him a spell. Which surprised even me, who would of figured it for enemy territory not all that long ago.

I threw a change of clothes and toilet articles into a carryall, replaced my ace-in-the-hole cigarette and match, and gave Bradley's number to Frank Chow.

"And I hold you personally responsible for my belongings," I told him.

"Who the hell would want your belongings?" said Chow. "You're talking like your spare underwear? What?"

"Whatever," I said. "I happen to have a valuable vodka collection, for one thing. Just keep your eye on these bozos, Chow, or I'm gonna sue the shit out of the city."

"Right, the city's all a-tremble," he answered. He knew I was mostly kidding. And I knew he'd look out for me.

"Can we go now?" said Bradley.

"Yeah, OK. The only reason I'm hesitating, I don't know what to do about the Phantom."

"I can't say I wouldn't rather you didn't take him with us," admitted Bradley.

"Doesn't much matter," I explained. "I couldn't catch him anyway."

"Well, maybe your friends here would feed him."

I didn't think much of that idea. Homicide dicks generally being less candidates for any Doris Day trophies than, say, the Daryl Gates Choke Hold and Baton Bopping Award.

"I think I'll just put out a bunch of food now, and come back if need be from time to time."

So I got a big bowl, dumped in a bunch of critter cookies, and put it by the back door of the garage. A cranky yowl let me know the Phantom was hiding out near the woodpile. So I guess that would be OK. (I couldn't believe here I was worrying about some cat. Which all it did was complain all day.)

We took separate cars back to Bradley's place. Him in the BMW and me in the Tojo Sport Four. Not too bad—downhill.

He waited for me in his underground parking lot and we headed up to his place together. Which went smooth enough except for a snippily snide number got on at the ground floor, looked us over, and asked Bradley, "New daddy?"

I guess Bradley knew I was close to rearranging the smart-ass's features because he slipped an arm through mine and said, "Same dear dad. They threw away the mold when they made this old sweetheart."

And the smile on his face showed me he was more confident of my sense of humor than I was, so I patted his hand and joined the fun. "You're only as old as you feel," I said as the elevator stopped and the peppy person got out. "Which come to think of it is pretty bad news," I added. "Since I feel about a hundred and twelve."

We got out at his floor and headed down the corridor.

"Listen, that was a nasty crack on your head. If you didn't feel something, I'd be even more worried."

And he made another pitch I ought to see a doctor. I explained I wasn't up to it. One of the reasons my doctor bills were relatively light, every time I got really sick or banged up and the doctor wanted me to come to the office, I didn't feel well enough to go. And by the time I did, there wasn't any need. Also, as a P.I. I'd had as many concussions as your average NFL quarterback and was about as used to playing with pain.

But once we were inside I did allow as an ice pack might be a good idea. Especially in a glass surrounded by vodka.

He went into the kitchen to make me the drink.

"Where should I put my stuff?" I called in. Then, old habits (and maybe prejudices) dying hard (even though I knew he didn't mean "old sweetheart"), "Where's the *spare room*? Your office?"

"Yeah, the *couch* opens up," he called back, I thought with a smile in his voice.

I went to the rear of the condo, where he had his office, and dropped my bag, took off my jacket, and hung it up. Which is more than I would of done my own place. But a guest ought to be neat.

Other old habits dying hard, I took a quick peek at the papers on his desk next to the word processor. On top was a page of questions.

1. Who got to Sylvia to sandbag Goodman?
2. Why would Appleton use own gun if killed Crewe? (Though it was dumped in ocean.)
3. Who killed Courtney? Why? Did she hide Iris?
4. Who beat up Stacy, Jr.? Why?
5. What's Cifelli connection?
6. Curry? Soheila?
7. If Carey not guilty, why family frame?

I could see my partner was giving a lot of thought to the

case. I didn't know it was a plus or not he didn't have any more answers than me.

I went back to the living room, but Bradley wasn't back yet with the drinks. I didn't hear them being made, either.

"Bradley?" I called, edging into the kitchen.

He was standing at the sink, shoulders heaving—I guess crying.

"What? What's up, buddy?" I said. "You sick or something?"

"I killed that guy!" he said. "The man's dead."

"Yeah," I said.

"A human being," he said between small sobs.

"Who was about to kill me," I reminded him. "*I* would of been dead. Old human being me."

"I know," he said, getting it together. "It's just ... shock, it's ... hard to believe."

"Listen, you wouldn't be much of a person it didn't affect you. Come on, make me my drink. You have one, too." Which is what happened. We took them into the living room, sat down, and kept quiet for a bit. It would take time. And never quite go 'way. (I didn't tell him that part.)

After a while we both took another long pull, and he flipped on the TV, using a remote looked like it could fire up a moon shot. (I did notice he had more contraptions and electronic toys than I'd ever seen in one place. I personally sort of dropped out after Pong.)

"You want me to send out for something? Pizza?" he said.

"It's early yet," I answered. "I'm not even hungry, let's wait." At least till my head stopped aching.

And not for the first time I wondered I wasn't getting a little old for the physical end of this game. But I might not have to make any decisions about that, we didn't solve the thing. If not, there was more than an off chance this time the authorities would permanently deep-six my license.

The difference was, this time I wasn't totally sure I cared. No way they were really going to put me in jail on the jury thing. Make that slim chance. Judge Steinberg being half Yuppie, half Old Testament, there was I suppose a possibility. But the P.I. part? Who needed it?

Which even I recognized as post-traumatic syndrome of my own. After being beat over the head's not the best time to work out your future.

The news was on TV. Terry Anderson, the last of the American hostages in the Middle East, had been released, and it looked like that particular ugliness was over.

But we had one of our own to face. "Francine," I said to Bradley.

"Yeah?"

"We've got to do something. Penny walked in on her flaked out, and he knows about her doping."

"Of course he knows, everybody knows."

"But he's had it. He wants to fire her. I promised him we'd do something he just gave us a little more time."

Bradley sighed.

"You said something about an intervention. How does that work?"

"Well," he explained, "you start with a professional, a psychologist, who sort of orchestrates things. Then, what you do, you get whoever you can of the family—"

"In her case, no family I know of."

"No. Then, her friends, associates, anybody willing to make the effort, and you plan it so you'll all be together some place."

"Like a surprise party."

"Exactly. Surprise, we're going to pack you off to rehab. And everybody says how she's not fooling anybody."

"Well, she doesn't pretend that," I reminded him.

"Well, right. *And,* how we're all, one by one, convinced she's killing herself and it's obvious she's going to hell in a handbag. Handbag? That can't be the expression."

"And?"

"And, presumably, the weight of all this loving caring pressure induces her to agree to therapy and rehab."

"Do you think it'll work?"

"I think we have to do it. If only for ourselves. We can't

just sit by and watch her self-destruct without giving it our best shot."

"OK, let's go for it," I said.

Meanwhile, we'd been sort of keeping one eye on the news, which went from showing Terry Anderson arriving in Germany and being greeted by his girlfriend and their kid (the wife and *their* kid out of sight in Japan, the world doth change). And now it cut to local news.

This featured a bunch of angry-fisted "Palestinians" (including a surprising number of clearly American blacks—an interesting development since I hadn't seen many before showing up for causes weren't their own), plus a couple actors I seemed to remember who didn't do much work anyway. In the other corner, what looked to be counter-demonstrating William Morris agents, but which the anchor voice identified as Jewish Defense League. I half expected to see if the blacks went Arab, some Koreans going Jewish.

All this in front of the building housing the Israeli consulate.

The purpose seemed to be to show that even if the hostage bit was over, the war went on. To prove this, one guy wearing the basic PLO gear suddenly broke through the ragged police line, holding a flaming bottle, no doubt a Molotov cocktail. And before the cops could stop him, threw it up against the stone side of the building.

People unclear on the subject, this did absolutely no damage—maybe singed a couple plants—before burning itself out. What was most interesting when the cops closed in on the guy and introduced him to gang tackling, it wasn't that he was black, or that the kaffiyeh got ripped off got my attention. It was the Raiders cap which the TV camera zoomed in on laying on the ground.

That was when I said, "Hey, we know that guy."

And Bradley, getting up and moving right to the set, peering in, said back, "Yeah, yeah, yeah—where, wait a minute."

"On the roof of the animal hospital on Robertson."

"Right, he was one of the gang chased us from Stacy, Jr.'s."

"Shooting."

"But missing," reminded Bradley.

"Well, he missed burning down the Israeli consulate, too," I noted.

"Maybe he's in the wrong line of work," said Bradley.

"And maybe he's not the varsity, either," I couldn't help worrying.

26

Mark Bradley

I hadn't been this nervous since my mother dropped in unexpectedly, went to the bathroom, and found His and His towels. However, since Mother and reality were never on the best of terms, it didn't turn out to be that hard to convince her it was really a "bachelor" joke—like, they were both mine. (Just a passing note on that. I know it seems incredible in this day and age that anybody could still be in the closet. But it wasn't that I lacked the courage of my convictions—with anybody else. It was simply an acceptance of where Mother was coming from—heaven, via the stork. Politically, if you started with David Duke and kept moving right you wouldn't reach Mother for two days. And on matters reproductive, as far as she was concerned the jury was still out on *hetero*sexuality. So I was understandably a little loath to get into "Funny, he never married.")

All beside the point, and merely for emphasis. What was making me nervous at *this* particular moment was taking Francine to the dinner I'd insisted on—ostensibly to discuss personal matters about which I needed her friendly input. (Given her condition, she would never have consented to meet to discuss *her* problems, hence the fiction we were to work on mine.)

Since this was not a night that was going to give her a lot of pleasure ultimately, I'd decided to splurge, taking her to Jimmy's, on Moreno Drive, just south of Little Santa Monica—

an elegant enclave at a tactical remove from the offices of
Century City to the west and the Beverly Hills homeless on
Skid Drive to the east. (Actually, the one homeless misan-
thrope who used to hang around Canon, heaping gratuitous
abuse on the affluent, either eventually died or had his contract forcibly renegotiated.)

Jimmy's is a sumptuous, Versailles-like restaurant where
the more staid members of the Establishment go when of a
mood to disregard current cardiac dietary discipline. As we
entered its sumptuous confines, Jimmy Murphy himself, the
canny Irish proprietor who'd parlayed being maître d' at the
Bistro (Sixties and Seventies in-spot) into this—figure *those*
tips—greeted me warmly by name. Since I'd never been a
major customer and hadn't visited his emporium in a good
three years, that'll give you an idea how smart he is. Another
clue is he manages to get surprising numbers of Beverly Hills
Jews to actually march in his St. Patrick's Day parade each
year. He oughta be in pictures.

At any rate, Jimmy then instructed his envoy to settle us in
what turned out to be a right nice spot. (Actually, the restaurant is beautifully designed and doesn't really have bad tables—if we're not talking about the "other room.")

Further, the maître d' (clearly on instructions from le boss,
himself) inquired if I would care for my "usual" cracked crab.
I think we could do worse than Jimmy for president.

It was my misfortune to have this demonstration of my
importance and the esteem in which the community held me
wasted on Francine, whose interest could best be categorized
as "Don't give a shit."

At any rate, this was all a stall, while the elements of her
impending "surprise party" were being assembled back at my
condo, where I was to deliver her damaged body and imper-
iled soul an hour and a half hence. (We had settled on my
condo, as opposed to the office belonging to the psychologist
handling the intervention, on my insistence that friendly surroundings would be less threatening to her. I had a lot of
reservations about the psychologist, a Diane Grotheim by
name, knowing Francine's attitude in general about psychiatry.

But since I had a lot of reservations about the chances for success of the entire enterprise, I had opted to put a professional scapegoat between her and myself as insurance against a permanent loss of her friendship. There's something to be said for *smart* cowardice.)

So, there we were, nibbling crisp veggies at Jimmy's, with my assignment to keep her occupied and diverted before deliverance home to face the ministrations of therapists, friends, and assorted interested parties.

Appropriately, here at least there would be drinks beforehand. Which now arrived with sparkling alacrity, in impressive crystal. (I looked about at the affluent clientele and wondered how many were in danger of lead poisoning from all the years of good glasses and first-rate decanters. How fortunate were the poor!)

When nervous, I ramble. As I said, among other things, we had drinks, and I was gratified to find her going to the ladies' room only at the outset and returning with her makeup retouched, and, to all other outward appearances, the same general personality she left with.

"So what's all this?" she said crabbily, confirming the above. "What are you doing with a twat at this elegant boîte?"

It was clearly time to get on with the stall. "I've heard from Brian," I assayed for openers. "Sort of indirectly."

"What's indirectly?"

"He's been charging thousands of dollars to my credit cards."

"And you view that as what, a subtle attempt at reconciliation?"

"Only very obliquely."

"A plea for help perhaps?"

I had to laugh. "No, really more plain and simple evidence of betrayal."

"Plain and simple sounds familiar. What you ever saw in *that* cat, I'll never know."

"Look who's talking. Aging private detectives and youthful animal transvestites?"

"Norbert is an actor, not a transvestite," she replied in

defense of her friend in the dog suit at Disneyland. "He does not portray *female* animals."

"I stand corrected."

"So Brian's off on a spending spree. You cut off your cards, I'm sure."

"Yes, but I'll cover what he charged to date."

"You're only responsible for fifty dollars on each one."

"Well, technically. But actually, I did give him the cards. If I neglected to get them back, why should the banks get stuck?"

"You are, if nothing else, a moral son of a bitch," she remarked. For some reason I didn't want to inquire what the other "elses" were.

The appetizers came.

"Cracked crab for monsieur; saumon fumé pour madame."

"Saumon fumé," I mimicked for Francine when the waiter was gone.

"Only because I didn't know the French for gefilte fish."

Which we both attacked with a semblance of gusto, relieved we could concentrate on eating. I was finding it hard to pretend the basis for this get-together was my personal life. And she seemed to sense something else was afoot. That neither of us wanted to deal with. God, I hated this.

When we finished, in the lull between courses, she, whether instinctually or not, set about her defense.

"I haven't been exactly goofing off, you know."

"I know."

"I never was a nine-to-fiver, no one could say that."

"Absolutely."

Which seemed a good time for both of us to do up another roll and butter. Since we weren't having soups or salads.

"I had a hunch," she said, evidently and surprisingly being more ill at ease over the silence than I.

"Yeah?"

"When you and Rayford described Iris doing all that mumbling, at Stacy, Jr.'s?"

"Yeah—the moaning and groaning?"

"Right. You know how I always tape those discussions.

Since I never know whether you're just passing the time of day or plotting the book."

"Yeah, so . . . ?"

"What somehow got to me, besides of course the description of Junior's condition and so forth, you were both so definite about how she sounded—the la la la's?"

"I remember that."

"And I don't know why, it just struck me that it wasn't entirely random. It wasn't what someone would say. Even crazy. I mean, except for maybe Jerry Lewis."

"The la la la?"

"Right, so check this out. I punched the 'words' in my computer, because I had a feeling it was a verbalization of something, if not an actual spelling at least phonetically. And it was . . ." She took out some notes and read: " 'la ila la ila la' the first time—which didn't make any particular sense, which you weren't intending to. It wasn't like you were repeating what someone *said,* just the sounds someone made. Then later 'la la la, *uhl* la la la' and again *'ulu* la la la' and so forth. I kept thinking maybe she *was* trying to tell you something. The la la's didn't suggest much, but there were the 'uhl' and the 'ulu,' which seemed like maybe something. So I respaced it, ran the letters together, rearranged them, and then on a hunch, asked the computer for some help. That got me to—you'll never guess."

"I won't even try."

"An electronic bulletin board at U.C.L.A., where I posed the question and got the advice to look into the *Shahādah.*"

"Wild guess, lyrics to an old Sha Na Na number?"

"Gee, you guessed." And here she took out some notes. "No, what it is is Arabic. To wit: *'ashahadu anna la ilāha illa 'l-Lāh'* and the rest goes *'wa anna Muhammadan rasūlu 'l-Lāh'.*"

"Catchy."

"The mere pronunciation of which, by the way, makes you a Muslim."

"The daily prayer?"

"Right. And a sort of mantra for the monomaniacal."

"And the guy who was beating up on Stacy, Jr., was saying this?"

"My guess. On a mission. For the faithful. For the cause. Allah."

"And Iris was just repeating that! Wow, France, the things you find out!"

"Well, when you don't have to sleep nights, you have a lot of time on your hands."

Gulp.

"There have, of course, been all sorts of Arab influences in the case—the stuff at the trial, with the bomb. The girl working at Appleton's, what was her name, Malouf? Curry, who turns out to be Khoury; Stacy's girlfriend, *Soheila*—it definitely could be Iris was trying to tell us something, consciously or unconsciously."

"That was my first guess," she went on. "The second was it could as easily mean it was Iris herself praying—assuming she might be a Muslim, too."

"Oh?"

"In which case it suggests she might not be as *non compos* as everyone thinks, *cappezio*?"

"Fantastic. You are so good at this."

"I do have my moments," she allowed.

How incredibly inventive of Francine to come up with that. She sure was uniquely talented. Certainly transcending mere traditional research.

But my pleasure in her accomplishment was short-lived. The minute I let a silence settle in. First I could see her growing agitation, nonspecific, since I hadn't confronted her in any way. Still, after she'd collected her notes and replaced them in her bag, she started fidgeting, tapping her fingers rapidly, and noisily enough for people to notice.

"Come on, what is this shit? What're we doing here?"

Intuition and sensitivity were definitely two-edged.

"We're eating. We're talking. The entree'll be here in a minute," I said, hoping to sidetrack her. "Called having a good time." It just set her off.

"Yeah, like we're really out doing the town playing Beverly

Hills Monopoly," she said with a strange, barely contained fury, rising.

"Come on, sit down. Be nice," I said softly, trying not to blow the setup.

She threw her napkin on the table, knocking over a glass.

"Please," I whispered.

"Please, my ass!" she shot back, pushing her chair back.

"You don't really have to go to the bathroom," I said, last vague, not-a-hope shot.

"I'll be the judge of that," she said, stomping off.

I smiled at the small audience we had picked up. Decided against a PMS sexist joke (though it crossed my mind), self-consciously passed the napkin across my mouth, and sat back down.

With the intuition for which great waiters are known, mine brought me a refill in an instant. I gulped it down and in very short order (too short order) Francine returned.

I avoided her eyes and kept my mouth shut. You could cut the tension with a silver art nouveau *couteau*.

And, no doubt our semi-prescient server having urged the chef to speed in the interest of restoring tranquility, the entree arrived and was placed with a flourish before us.

I gave him a sickly smile in gratitude.

But it came as no great surprise that Francine had lost her appetite.

27

Rayford Goodman

Naturally Bradley had given me the key to his place. So I was there good and early. Or just early. Hoping for good. He'd wanted to order cold cuts from Greenblatt's and put out drinks and all, but the shrink told him the purpose was confrontation, not socialization. Or more simply, no. I, of course, knew where Bradley kept the booze. In the kitchen. Which was a little middle-class for someone his style, I thought. So I had a pretty good one, or more accurately two, by the time the shrink person got there.

She was an unexpectedly good-looking entry about five-six, soft blond, business cut; one-fifteenish, early forties, good cheekbones, no visible scars, by the name of Diane Grotheim. In the normal course of things I would have hit on her except I didn't need to hear it wasn't really sex I wanted, it was revenge on my father. Or my mechanic, more likely. See, if a guy's car represents his manhood, as somewhere I'd read, naturally the guy who's keeping his manhood from him by changing the pistons—talk about phallic symbols!—well, you get the drift. I hadn't been to all those Hollywood cocktail parties without picking up one or two Freudian titbits.

Still, flat-bellied, pouty-butted, this Diane lady was really a number.

And I started thinking, look at me falling into that trap with the stereotypes and all. Putting the lady down without even giving her a chance. She could turn out the party girl of all time, and there I'm closing it out without a shot. So I looked into her lovely blue eyes and took a chance. What life's all about.

"Are you currently involved with a significant other?" I opened, with my most non-threatening smile, least pushy tone, and most sincere eyes.

Her return look clued me on how the microscope must look to a slimy slide. "I can't believe a creep like you has the balls to even suggest a lady of my class could remotely be interested" is what it seemed like.

What it *actually* was, "I don't think this is the appropriate forum for questions of that sort."

Which made me wonder. Since I knew it was a mistake to come on, why didn't I listen to me? ("Why do *you* think you don't listen to you?")

"You're sure you don't want a drink?" I said, to get me back in a civil mood.

"This is not a party," she answered, perfectly comfortable with things being uncivil.

"If I only drank when there was a party, I'd never get any work done," I answered. And by her look I got the feeling she was considering an open date for an intervention of my own.

Someone buzzed from downstairs. I buzzed back. The back buzzer being in the kitchen, I took the opportunity to refresh my drink. She stood in the dining area, arms folded underneath her nice chest, sort of framing them, watching me. Or checking symptoms.

"So how do we work this?" I asked, adding a drop of soda to my vodka rocks.

"You needn't plan," she answered. "Shouldn't. I will guide the discussion. There are no set rules. It's necessary to improvise, depending on the subject's reactions."

"The subject is going to be pissed all to hell."

"You mean drunk?"

"No, I mean angry."

"Well, that wouldn't surprise me."

"She's not going to want to go along with this," I couldn't help but caution.

"I realize that. If she were willing, she'd be in therapy and/or rehab on her own."

"I don't think you can force her."

"Not technically. But the whole purpose of intervention is to more or less dramatically insist a person confront his or her condition. And hopefully, given that the people airing their concerns are friends and family—"

"No family here."

"So I understand. I was speaking in general. Given that the psychological coercion is done in good faith by caring people, the capitulative increments are fairly substantial."

"Fairly?"

"Often enough."

"And the results?"

"Vary."

"How vary?"

"In truth, the rate of recidivism is a bit discouraging. But in consequence of the alternative—destruction of mind and body, eventual death—one has to try."

"In the words of the late Fats Waller, 'One do.' "

"Was he a psychologist, too?"

"More a healer."

The bell rang and I opened the door for Dick Penny and Armand Cifelli, who'd arrived together.

"Good, guys, thanks for coming."

"I'm just keeping my end of the bargain," said Penny, who insisted on being a shit in case I was starting to think otherwise.

"I just hope we can help," said Cifelli, who I thought was really nice to come along.

Actually, what happened when Bradley and I started to organize this thing, we first realized how few people there were in Francie's life. So, in effect, we had to really stretch to keep from there just being the two of us.

I introduced them both to Dr. Grotheim, who explained that they were to let her guide the proceedings and merely reinforce the premise—that Francie needed help—by truthfully attesting to what they knew about her when and if the time came.

Bradley had insisted on including Norbert, her current boyfriend from Disneyland. Which didn't sit all that well with me. Not that I was jealous, really—how could you be jealous of a guy wore a dog suit for a living?

When I opened the door and saw old Norb, I was ready to answer my own question. You could be jealous when the guy was about two inches taller, fifty pounds lighter, and thirty years younger. With Tom Cruise teeth and Chippendale arms you had to feel it was real rough getting acting jobs these days. Still, with the tune to "Small World After All" humming in my ears, I figured I could be big about it.

"Nice of you to come, Norb. I'm Ray, this is Dr. Diane, Mr. Cifelli, Mr. Penny."

He mumbled a hi and I quick got the feeling he was going to be mostly an extra body. Atmosphere animal.

The last three people were even more of a stretch.

Brian had flown in from Atlanta because Bradley had paid for it (and I suspected wanted to see him again in spite of what Francie had told me about their breakup). And to be honest, since I never was the biggest fan of Brian's, who I felt was a freeloader and advantage-taker, I got the idea Brian would of gone anywhere free.

Luana, my ax-wife, I had nothing to do with being there. Bradley sprung that on me after the fact. I thought it offered nothing but aggravation for me, but he felt since Francie had her new boyfriend there, I ought to have at least my old wife. To balance things out. How that made sense, me being balanced out by having two ladies who dumped me present, was beyond me. And I had a feeling involved some kind of hormonal logic I wasn't in on.

And lastly, my surprise guest—Beverly Hills detective Lewis Ellard. His being there I felt served two purposes. One, it showed him I trusted him (which I almost did) and paid back for him trusting me by telling me he knew about Francie and wasn't busting her. And two, would show Francie this was serious business here. We weren't just talking choice, we were talking possible legal hassles, too.

And besides, I got a kick out of seeing Ellard and Cifelli in the same room. Also taking chances.

"You do like to live dangerously," said Cifelli when he got me to one side.

"This isn't about you or Ellard, it's Francie."

"Right," said Cifelli. "But I can't help wondering is it that you just have this weird sense of humor or some kind of death wish?"

"I'm sure the lady shrink would say the second thing."

Then Luana came over. I introduced them. They said the things you say when you don't want to say anything to each other, and Cifelli excused himself.

"Well, Rayford," Luana began—as always calling me Rayford both to annoy me and because full names kept you at a distance. And keeping a distance was something she was real good at—at least with me. "I can't say I'm thrilled to have been included in this little soirée, but Mark suggested it would be appropriate for me to lend support while you tried to help your little dope-addict girlfriend."

Which shows you how dumb old Mark could be.

"Thanks for coming, Luana," I said, trying not to snarl.

Dr. Grotheim had meanwhile briefed the latecomers and we were all edgily waiting for Bradley and Francie.

Ellard and Cifelli, to my surprise, seemed to be talking shop over in the corner, I guess having more in common with each other than anyone else.

Brian and Luana sort of settled together, which wasn't that weird, either, both having in common an expertise at bad mouthing.

That left Norbert the hunk chatting with Dr. Diane the brain, which should have surprised me, but I found didn't, life being the slider on the outside corner that it was.

And the key was in the door, the door was open, Bradley and Francie were in, and the show was on the road.

Dr. Diane immediately took charge.

"Welcome, Francine," she said. "My name is Dr. Diane

Grotheim, and I've been asked here tonight by your friends and associates to help guide them and you through a process called intervention. Each and every one of them, in one way or another, has been an observer of your addictive behavior and in his or her way has come to the conclusion that you are at great peril and in need of help."

"Hoo hoo hoo—whoa!" said Francie.

"Please, let me continue," said Dr. Diane forcefully. "It's perfectly natural and proper for you to feel resentment and even a sense of betrayal at first blush—"

"Hey, hey, stop this!"

"But," the doctor continued still more insistently, "we are not going to let your natural reluctance and resistance stand in the way of collectively coming to your rescue and helping you put your life back in order."

"Will you, for Chri—"

"We're here to help," said Luana, injecting a needless note of insincerity into the process by adding, "because we care." (And it's our job that "we" get paid for?)

"I don't even *know* you, lady. Who the hell are you to think you can butt in—"

"Francie," I cut in, not wanting things to get sidetracked, "the main thing, babe—you're a doper."

That seemed to put things on a less lofty plane. At least stopped the proceedings for a moment.

"Exactly," said Dr. Diane.

"Exactly what? Exactly who the fuck's business is it?" said Francie.

"For one thing, mine," said Ellard.

"You remember Lieutenant Ellard?" I prompted.

"This is one of my friends?" said Francie, not unreasonably.

"More than you figured," he answered. "I've seen you high in public. I've seen you high where I work. I've had enough legal cause to lower the boom on you."

"Yeah, well, then why didn't you?" she asked.

"All right," he said. "Good enough question. You're right, I'm not your friend. Strictly speaking. What I am, is hip to the problem. Close enough, with an ex-wife who went the same route, to hope butting in *now* could help some way. Since I just let it happen last time, letting my 'duty' get in the way of love and caring. My credentials, beside the point. I know going to jail wouldn't make your problems any easier. I *hope* going some place to kick the habit *will*."

"Thank you, Lieutenant," said the doctor. "Next?"

Bradley stepped forward. "Francine, we love you."

"I'm never going to talk to any of you sons of bitches ever again," said Francie, not exactly responsive.

"Now, it's natural enough for you to feel a sense of resentment, even betrayal," said Dr. Diane.

"Lady, shut up," said Francie, leaving little doubt about the resentment part. "Who gave any of you the right to butt into my life? You can all go fuck yourselves."

"She's right," said Bradley. "How dare we try to save her."

"Don't get cute," said Francie snidely.

"Cute is the last thing I want to be."

"Good, 'cause you sure ain't. Now listen to me—"

"No!" I said. "You listen to us. While you may have been open about your dope thing with Bradley and me—"

"And didn't exactly go to any great lengths to hide it from me, either," said Penny, half ruining what I was trying to say.

"Which is not the main point," I cut in. "The thing is, one of the reasons we're here, if you think you're going about your business with nobody but us insiders any wiser, you're wrong. Everybody here *knows*. You're not hiding it. You're not getting away with it."

"What I do is my business!"

"Not quite," said Ellard. "There is the law, which I'm not threatening—inside these walls—but which one day can and probably will come down on you and add a shithouse full of problems you don't even begin to imagine."

"Plus there's your job," Penny cut in. "Which you're this close to losing."

"Don't I do my job?"

"Yes and no. You do the job probably better than anybody else I could get for it. But I'm not convinced you do it as well as *you* could."

"Maybe I do it better because of dope."

"I'm sure you *think* so," said the doctor. "That's part of the delusional symptomology of drug taking, the impression of enhanced perception, magical insight."

"Forget that crap. Your health, babe," I said.

"*You're* talking health? You, who drink yourself into a coma every night, who still smoke and don't exercise and—"

"Two wrongs don't make a right," said Brian, of all people, to my surprise. "And what you're doing is not only wrong health-wise, it's wrong morally."

Morally?!

"Are you by any chance going to quote the Bible on me?"

"Well, I could," Brian said.

"Yeah, from a copy bought with the credit cards you stole from Mark?"

"You told her that?" asked Brian, turning to Bradley. "That I *stole* the cards you *freely* gave me, as a gift of love?!"

"Let's not get sidetracked here," said the doctor.

And these were a couple of experts at sidetracking.

"Just a word, if I may," suddenly said Cifelli. Then, to Francie: "I've known you now a couple years. I respect you. I like you. I know you do this drug thing. I don't like that. I guess maybe you have a problem with it. We're here, all of us, to see if we can't maybe help."

I could tell Francie was unexpectedly touched by Cifelli.

"No one expects you to do it alone," put in the doctor, sensing a potential payoff. "There are any number of qualified rehabilitation centers where you can detoxify and get psychological counseling."

"Oh, boy," said Francie.

"In the end," said Bradley, "nothing's going to work if you don't want it to. You're not even going to go if you don't want to—and nobody wants to force you."

"The sole purpose," said the doctor, "was for us to come together, to focus on the problem, to let you know both that you weren't getting away with it, and that your friends and co-workers not only know, but care. If *you* don't care that they care, that's another matter."

"I really hate this," said Francie, but a bit less strong.

"Go for it, babe," said Norbert Perfection.

Which for some reason, maybe just to annoy me, seemed to do the trick.

"OK," she said. Because this asshole tipped the scales?!

"Dr. Grotheim has drawn up a list of places," said Bradley, pulling a folded sheet of paper from his inside breast pocket. "Where they offer varying programs to suit whatever you'd feel most comfortable with."

"And you'll be happy to know," added Penny, "that Pendragon will be picking up the tab."

"Get out of here!" said Francie, astonished.

"*Pendragon's* going to pay?!" said Bradley.

"Of course," said Penny, acting insulted. Then, not quite so loud, "Turns out our insurance covers it."

And there were thank-you's to Luana and Cifelli and Ellard and Norbert and they all left. (Not before Luana advised me how much better I might do if I sought a social life with people more my own age. Luckily quiet enough only I heard it. I thanked her for the advice.) Brian went inside to unpack.

That left Bradley, Francie, Dr. Grotheim, and me to plan the next step.

"You're doing the right thing," said Dr. Diane, taking out her own copy of the accredited facilities. "Now the question is where?"

Which was when the thought occurred to me Francie wasn't so sick she couldn't still help. So I pointed to the most familiar name on the list.

"How about," I said, "Marsden's Meadow?"

28

Mark Bradley

After everybody left, and we were pretty much drained of emotion, I suddenly realized I was stuck with The Situation. The Situation was that Brian was "visiting" from Atlanta and automatically presumed, and *I* automatically presumed, he would stay over. And Goodman, his house still taped off as a crime scene, was also a guest. Sort of the odd triple.

Apparently realizing it at the same time and not without a semblance of sensitivity (which I'd be the last to admit), Goodman said, "Listen, no reason I have to bunk in here—I can go to a hotel."

"No, *I* can," said Brian, twisting the knife. "I imagine you have new credit cards?"

"Nobody's going anywhere," I answered peevishly. "Goodman'll sleep on the convertible in my office—"

"Would that make *him* convertible?" said Brian archly, far too archly for my tastes. (I'd have to remember that.)

"... and *you* can sleep on the couch."

"I wouldn't have it any other way," said Brian, ever loath to let me have the last word.

"But first, I think we should all have a cup of teaaaaa ..." and suddenly, there I was again, fighting tears.

"What's going on—what is it?" said Brian.

I just waved a hand, getting a grip.

"Francine'll be all right," he went blithely on. "It's just rehab, for chrissake, not the end of the world."

"OK," said Goodman, crossing to me and awkwardly patting my arm, understanding I was suddenly flashing back to the Samoan, the shot, the mess, the incredibly explosive violence. "You got to expect this," he went on. "Takes a while."

"What're you guys talking about? *What* takes a while?"

Goodman looked at me, I shook my head. Brian was not a person I wanted to talk to about this.

"What?" asked Brian. "You're both acting very weird."

"Doesn't concern you," I said.

"Well, excuuuse me!" he said petulantly, crossing to a corner of the couch and sulking.

Goodman followed me into the kitchen.

"Just to remind you, this is natural."

"I know."

"Not exactly my thing, but a lot of police departments, after a shooting they have a little therapy."

"I appreciate it. But I don't think so. It's just . . . very fresh. And a lot of shock."

"Exactly."

By which time Brian's patience for a peevish show of detachment had exhausted itself, and he got up and stomped into the kitchen after us.

"Are we quite done exchanging our little confidences?"

When neither of us rose to the bait, he was left a little high and dry, sort of like taking that top step in the dark that isn't there. "So," he continued, the noticeable outsider, "we going to have tea or what?"

Once he satisfied himself I had a grip on myself (heh-heh), Goodman begged off on the tea.

"What I'd really like is a little nightcap and to excuse myself. I'm sure you boys have things you want to talk over. And I'm sure I don't want to hear them."

So he filled half a tumbler with vodka, added a few cubes of ice, and with a little wave, shuffled off to the rear of the apartment and my office/guest room.

Once alone, Brian reverted to the cuter him he always carefully hid from the rest of the world. I don't know why he did that, it was positively perverse. Or maybe it takes more talent to be perverse *and* positive. But it was true, in public he was aggressively gay and camp, traits I hated. But on the other hand, in private, he could be as cozy and *gemütlich* as a fur-lined mukluk.

Which would merely suggest there was a slight personality problem, probably amenable to constructive correction. That was the view to which I subscribed when not overtly exposed to his shortcomings. (If I've noted there is nothing so perfect as a departed lover, now was the time to add: nor so disappointing as his return.) Because the flaw in my thinking, absent contact, was that the true character existed in his private persona and the false in his public. Whereas an objective view of how he had taken such advantage of me, and so selfishly looked only to his own advantage, suggested when he was being nice it was only to gain an edge. Since he knew that's how I wanted it.

All of this came to be considered when he badly miscalculated my momentary lapse in inviting him (he hadn't *really* been necessary to support our effort for Francine) and decided to negotiate a return as if dealing from strength.

"I've decided I'm willing to come back," he said. "*But* I'm going to be seeing other people; I'm going to be having other friends."

"And having other sources of income?" I couldn't help interjecting.

"If you think you can *buy* me . . . !"

"You're absolutely right. The fact that I supported you isn't the main consideration."

"I'd have done the same if the positions were reversed." (A line I decided to leave alone, given the cast of characters.)

"I'm sure you believe that," I said neutrally. (I've also noticed it's always the takers who are saying that to the givers. Yet somehow they are always takers, so one never gets a chance to see if it's true.)

But if that was getting too uncomfortably close to home, or merely just boring, I couldn't say. I do know he stopped "negotiating" and, smiling his boyish smile, opted for a less confrontational approach.

"We did have a lot of fun," he said.

"Yes, we did," I allowed.

"And we could again. Tell you the truth, I wasn't too crazy about Atlanta. Well, Kevin, actually. I guess Atlanta's OK."

"Kevin? I thought you left with Michael."

"I left with Michael, and then I *left* Michael," he said with that cute lopsided grin. Look at old irrepressible me.

"You don't have the luxury of those choices anymore, Brian."

"What?"

"It's—San Francisco roulette."

"Oh, come on, don't overdramatize." Then again, that boyish grin that sometimes made you forget it was late to be a boy and time to be a man. "C'mere," he said, holding out his hand.

Misread my smile.

"I wouldn't touch you with a ten-foot pole," I said.

"Doesn't he play for the Lakers?" he said without missing a beat—nothing if not quick on his feet. Or off. "I don't want to talk about those things. I was just trying to be honest with you. I'd like to come back, but it has to be on my terms. I have my own life." The kid wasn't all that swift.

"Well, Brian, I'd be the last one to stand in your way. You do have your own life. I just hope it's a long one."

"What is that?"

"That's good night, have a good night's sleep. And if I don't see you before you leave tomorrow, have a nice flight back to Atlanta."

"But I can't go back to Atlanta. I left Kevin. Where am I supposed to go?"

It's not every day they hand you a straight line like that. "Frankly, my dear—I don't give a rat fuck."

In the morning, Brian wanted to sleep later and leave later—once he made "arrangements." I wanted to stand firm, insist he get out this minute. But I couldn't. I let Goodman go on ahead to the office, since we were going in separate cars anyway.

"OK, Brian," I said once we were alone. "You can make your calls. Your ticket's on the counter here. You want to exchange it for someplace else, fine. You want to cash it in, fine. But I want you out of here when I get back."

With which I headed for the door.

"And oh, by the way," I thought it prudent to add, "if you steal anything I'm going to report it to the police."

He looked at me with narrowed eyes, sighed. "I suppose this means we're off for New Year's Eve," he said.

Humor counts for something. Just not enough.

When I got to the office parking lot, Goodman was still sitting in his car.

"I thought I'd just wait for you and we'd go in together," he said, clearly not wanting to confront Francine alone.

To the best of my knowledge, Dr. Diane was to have made the arrangements and they were to leave for Marsden's Meadow together this morning. Goodman and I had both volunteered to take her, but it wasn't a really sincere offer (I think I can speak for him, too) but a duty one, and I'm sure he was as relieved as I when Dr. Diane said it was important she take this step on her own. That is, figuratively on her own. The good doctor wasn't so naive or inexperienced she would simply trust a junkie to just show up at rehab, but by going with the healer instead of one or both of the "enablers" she was opting for health.

Frankly, I thought this was in large measure bullshit, since Francine was fully aware how much I disapproved of her doping and Goodman outright hated it. So if we were "enabling" it was only because we'd been powerless to stop her. But a part of therapy always seems to be shifting guilt to someone else. We could live with it.

At any rate, Francine wanted to clear out her desk and hopefully wind up a few loose ends before taking off with Grotheim about eleven. (Did they have check-in times at rehabs? "Sorry, you're late, you'll have to do another day of doping before checking in.")

And we were in the elevator heading up.

"I don't mind telling you," Goodman told me, "I'm not looking forward to this."

"It'll be all right. Last night was the hardest part. At least for us."

"I hope you're right," he said. "I can't help wondering, if after she cleans up her act, she might not change her mind about me. You know, and we could get together again."

"I always thought you were part of her delusion," I couldn't help saying. But he looked so stricken, I immediately added, "I'm kidding. It might well be. After all, you were a relative island of normality in a sea of weirdicity. I'm *still* kidding. But not totally. You did, I think, represent some kind of normality, stability, a suggestion of family—"

"Father figure."

"Maybe."

"But then she had to go have the abortion."

"You know she had to do that. The chances of a healthy baby were pretty remote."

By this time we were at our floor and heading down the corridor toward my office.

"Good afternoon, gentlemen," said Penny, who was always lurking wherever you were, especially if you were a touch late—or late by his reckoning.

"One of these days you're going to catch on, Dickie, that we're not salaried employees, hence not obligated to keep company hours."

"You keep a company office. Hey, I'm just trying to help. I know how much writers like to keep from writing. It's always been my theory if they worked from nine to five, they'd get twice as much done as doing it their own way, which they *think* is twenty-four hours a day, but is actually, by my reckoning, about an hour and a half—at the typewriter." (Penny still used quaint expressions like typewriter when he meant word processor.)

"Anyhow, I want to thank you for coming by last night."

He nodded modestly. "She's inside. Your office. I guess waiting to say good-bye."

"Well, thanks. But keep her job open; she's coming back."

"Fine with me. I'm liberal," he said, then, spotting some other miscreant sneaking in, dashed after the malefactor. "Hey, you there, stop right where you are!" Simon Legree lives.

My office door was closed, and I guess it was instinct that caused both of us to take a breath before opening it and entering.

If we felt like the priests entering the *Exorcist* girl's bedroom our instincts weren't far off. She was ripped.

"Good morning, gentlemen," she said with artificial cheer, or cheer artificially induced. Her red-rimmed eyes and red, runny nose gave ample evidence she hadn't decided to flush her stash but, true to her ilk, use it first. But, for that matter, who ever quit smoking with a full carton left, either?

"We're off to a great start," said Goodman sarcastically.

I shook my head, trying to warn him off. In her condition, any remote justification might just seem like a license to abandon the effort entirely.

"I apologize," he said, getting my drift.

"Accepted," she said. "It is true that I have not yet enlisted in the army of the mundane, but I have not entirely wasted my dissipation on recreational pursuits. I've been at my computer, laboring on behalf of our mutual project." A nice little speech, somewhat qualified when she had to shlurp her nose at the end.

"And you have news for us, I have no doubt," I responded, playing my part.

"Indeedy deedy," she said. "Ely Appleton, alias Elias, once Elias X, of the dreaded Black Muslims of yesteryear."

"Yes?"

"Now, having renounced Islam and returned to the Christian fold and the pursuit of moola ..."

"Yeah?" said Goodman, also playing his part.

"Not so."

"Not so what?" I said.

"I was taken by first all the Arab stuff, as we've talked about

ad nauseam, but also not a little intrigued by the appearance
of so many blacks at the anti-Israel rally or demonstration, or
attempted demolition or whatever."

This time we both merely nodded.

"A new wrinkle. True, there've been some notable turns
toward anti-Semitism by the odd black demagogue of late, but
a yoking of hatreds between blacks and Arabs is a new twist."

"And proves our evolutionary development," I added.

"So, the thing is, I've managed to find a paper trail combin-
ing assets of Arabs for Democratic Action—which you'll recall
was the group took responsibility for bombing Judge Steinberg's
court, and the guy who offed himself?—and the AAPAA, which,
you'll be enlightened to learn, stands for the Afro American
Pan Arabic Association, and the BATS (Black Athletic Teen Society) a quasi-athletic, semi-military group practicing 'survival'
techniques. For which you could read, bad bombings (à la the
Israeli consulate)."

"Very interesting," said Goodman. "And the connecting
thread?"

"Elias X heads the BATS, and is chairman of the executive
committee of the AAPAA."

"All really fascinating in its way, but I don't get what you're
driving at."

"All apparently funded in very large part by Stacy Jaeger,
Incorporated—oh, down through layers and layers, but I could
prove it if I had to." With which she dumped a ream or so of
computer printout on my desk.

"Excuse me, I'll get the rest."

And she started out, I very well knew where.

"That's OK," I said.

"I insist," she repeated, and kept on marching.

At Goodman's angry look, I couldn't help defending a little.
"This is really good stuff, you have to admit."

"I admit."

"We could be very close to finding the exact connection
between all this and Carey Jaeger being framed for murder.
At least they all seem to be in bed with each other."

Goodman nodded, fingered the printout. My phone rang

and reception told me Dr. Diane Grotheim was here. I said to show her in.

Francine returned, her eyes ablaze, almost like a cartoon character's when they spin in concentric circles—on the ceiling. But empty-handed.

"So, what was it again you went to get?" Goodman couldn't resist.

"High," she answered, at least honestly.

Which was when Dr. Diane showed up at the door and entered smilingly.

"Ah," said Francine, "the Dragon Lady, come to lead me."

"That's right, Francine," she said evenly. "To the promised land," she added with a smile.

"And where's that again," said Francine. "Stepford?"

I sure hoped "attitude" wasn't as important as I've been led to believe.

29

Rayford Goodman

So after Francie got off, we did a lot of walking around and drinking coffee and trying not to think about it. Finally, Bradley said enough was enough, life goes on. I didn't argue.

Then he said he wanted to work on the book. I said fine, let's work on the book.

He said, no, he wanted to be alone, it was time for some *real* writing. This to me, his co-writer! The nerve of the guy.

But then I figured hell, he was just upset about Francie and all (maybe Brian, too, for that matter, he hadn't mentioned him), and not to make a big deal of it. So I said sure, I had work to do myself, *detective* work, which of course wasn't exactly his forte Apache.

We decided out of mutual respect and emotional exhaustion not to have a fight.

I called B.J. to check was my car ready.

"It's almost. But you don't pick it up here. You go to Lateef Transmission."

"How come—you farmed it out?"

"Yeah."

"This Lateef guy good?"

"Yes, good. He's just down the block. Be ready after two."

"Well, why don't you pick it up and I'll get it at your place?"

"No, you go there."

He sounded a little weird. Too many fumes.

"You OK?"

"Yes. Go there, after two."

"OK. Keep those doors open."

We hung up. Two would be fine because I had a late breakfast date I could stretch. With Lieutenant Lewis Ellard.

I'd wanted to take him to the Polo Lounge, to show my appreciation his pitching in to help with Francie. But he said there were two reasons he'd rather not. One was anybody who knew him and saw him eating in such an expensive place would figure he was on the take, and the other was the rest of the people seeing a black man at the Polo Lounge would likely ask for more butter.

So, somewhere between the Polo Lounge and Winchell's Donut, we settled on Mirabelle's, on Sunset.

There was really nothing French about Mirabelle's except the name. It was one of those basic any- and no-style restaurants that got by on not being pushy (plain tables and chairs and full-wall mirrors). And for California its main feature as far as I was concerned it didn't look like a naugahyde Spanish bunkhouse.

I got there early and settled at the bar for a vodka and tomato juice, hold the spices—a little delicate this morning. Also it was a very hot day, and it sounded refreshing. Like I needed excuses.

It was a small, couple-of-seat bar at the back. Mirabelle's wasn't a place you went to drink, and they didn't need a lot of room to park folks waiting to get in. It had a little TV on the wall in a corner which just now was featuring the Willie Smith trial in Florida.

My own recent jury duty gave me a little more than usual interest in that sort of thing, plus, like everybody else, I was drawn to it by the pure and simple filth. I'd originally figured the kid would have to do at least token time so everybody would feel better about Uncle Ted's getting away with so much. But the minute I saw the jury, I knew he'd walk.

I couldn't believe the prosecution was so dumb they'd allow a bunch of Catholics over sixty, none with more than a high-school education, to sit on a date-rape case. Unbelievable.

First of all, they wouldn't know from date rape. They *would* know nice girls didn't have either abortions (guilty) or children out of wedlock (guilty). Ask any over-sixty Catholic.

And if, heathen devil spawn, she did all that and God punished her with a sick child, you certainly didn't *leave* that sick child and go bar-hopping. Plus, *then* go home in the middle of the night with a guy you just met. Pretty sure the words "She asked for it" came up once or twice.

And finally, if you did all that, you didn't insult people's intelligence in this day and age suddenly dressing up in off-duty nun duds (Peter Pan collar and single strand of beads).

And the capper, say she wasn't interested in sex, just wanted his medical opinion for her poor sick child.

They'd of had a better chance she said they were both drunk out of their gourds and she thought she wanted to fuck him but lost the spark when neither could remember the other's name—*and changed her mind.* Anyway, that's what I thought. Of course, the conspiracy freaks would see it that the D.A. wanted to *look* like he was for equal justice and still not alienate the Kennedys by actually winning.

Ellard showed up, escorted by the pretty mâitress d', and I joined him at one of the tables against the wall. Me facing out, him back to the room, casing things through the mirror.

"Ms. Rizetti get off OK?" he asked once we got settled.

"Yeah, the psychologist lady took her into custody about an hour ago."

"I'll keep my fingers crossed."

"Does it ever really work?" I couldn't help thinking about all the celebrities and athletes with everything to lose still kept backsliding.

"Oh, sure. It's not an automatic, and, to be honest, less so if someone's dragged against their will, but—the only game in town."

"There's that. Anyway, thanks again. I don't mind telling you I was surprised."

"Well, as I mentioned—that shit's cost me a lot of grief."

"Your wife."

"Yep. Broke up my home, my marriage, and everything I

held dear." I could see him suffering at the mere mention. Then, surprisingly, on our short acquaintance, confided even more. And real down home. "My wife actually swapped pussy for dope."

"All the more thanks your being so ... tolerant about Francie."

"Well, I've been there. I know how it locks on. Especially freebase. Some free. My wife threw away everything back of that shit and yet I know, really, she was a good person. It just grabbed hold of her and she couldn't shake loose."

"You tried therapy and rehab and all that stuff."

He nodded. Then, not to discourage me, "Some do make it."

Nice man.

"Would you like a drink?"

"Yeah," he said. "But I won't. Mostly because somebody might see."

"Well, I will, for the same reason. We both have a reputation to maintain."

So I did, and he got a diet 7.

We talked about the Smith trial (he agreed, the kid walks), and got our drinks and settled on the lunch and ordered.

"I was wondering how you were doing on the Courtney Blalock case. Any leads?" I led off.

He took a moment, and a breath. "No, we're going to go a different way. This time we're going to start by your telling me things you know. And then, if I figure you earned some payback, I tell you. We've been down this road before and so far the give-and-take's been my give and your take."

"Fair enough," I said. "And, truth be known, I do have some stuff for you." And the further truth was, I really was grateful for him going out on a limb for Francie. I mean, he was not only *there,* he was actually looking the other way on a felony user, putting himself on the line. Least I could do was try to help him. "It's all mixed up between the Carey Jaeger case and the bombings and Courtney Blalock, and I don't know for sure what the connections are," I said. "But here goes."

And I told him some of the things we'd found out. And some I'd figured out. Starting with the Arafat guy at the trial, there'd been a running connection between the Arab interests and the Jaeger case. While I figured the Arafat guy *thought* he was striking a blow for the PLO, he was manipulated and actually sent to scare Carey into going along with the party line. Which was to take the rap for the murder of his sister's lover. He stopped me right there.

"Why would anybody want that?"

"I'm building a theory. And the theory is first the movers and shakers behind Jaeger—Appleton, Curry, maybe the girls, Soheila Morris and, before she was killed, Courtney, Stacy, Jr., could be even Iris—all wanted first of all for Stacy to go back to work."

"The golden goose."

"Right. When he worked, everybody got paid. When he didn't, everybody still ate, but it wasn't caviar. And certainly not enough to back any terrorist organization."

"You think Stacy Jaeger's part of that?"

"I don't know. I know he's a source, whether as they say wittingly or not, another story."

"Gut feeling?"

"Gut feeling—a sympathizer, not a terrorist."

"Based on?"

"Well, you know, an actor? *That* self-sacrificing?"

"OK, holding that for a minute. Where does the book come in, the one you and Bradley are doing?"

"If my guess is right—and we were doing it anyway—the organization decided to authorize it. Both to add to the cash flow—you got to know Jaeger gets a whole lot of money—and to co-opt our investigation. Figuring they could control whatever we discovered."

"Clearly not the smartest move they made." But he mulled over what I'd said. Then, "All right, hold on that. The other thing you're saying Carey's not guilty."

"My reading."

"Why would they want him to take the rap?"

"That I'm still not sure of. Two theories."

"Simplicity's not exactly your middle name," Ellard put in.

"Can't help it with this one. Anyhow, one way to go—say Stacy, Senior, did it. They can't have *him* sitting in jail or definitely no money. Need a stand-in."

"And if not him, and I must say I don't favor the thought of America's most prominent actor in that part either, who else?"

"Person or persons still unknown, but someone well enough placed to convince Carey to go along with it—at first, anyhow, the false confession. And slick enough to convince the rest Carey really did do it."

"What could convince Carey?"

"If he thought the old man did it. Or, say, his sister."

"Oh, boy, wheels within wheels. And one of the things you're saying is the bombing in court was to tell Carey, who'd possibly lost his nerve, to stop fighting and take the rap or they could get to him?"

"Right. Because ever since, he's practically rolled over and played dead."

Then I told him about the Ely Appleton/Elias X axis, where the former Black Muslim was actually still active in PLO causes and bringing about a merger of black and Arab interests.

"So you're saying the name change back to Ely Appleton's a cover."

"Right."

"And this connects back to Jaeger because why?"

"Because he's the funnel and the source for funding all these outfits." And I gave him the gist of what Francie had found out about the various fronts and money-losing corporations in Jaeger's portfolio.

"Getting back to the Wesley Crewe murder again, you really think it might have been Iris?"

"Possibility. At least one witness places her at the scene, and they've certainly been keeping her unavailable, moving her all over the place, dodging interrogation. For sure, muddying the waters where she was after."

"Where was she?"

"Well, for one thing, not in Bali when they said; she was

up at Marsden's Meadow. Well, no—she was *alleged* to be there, but an actress from Curry's studio pretended to be her."

"Getting weird," said Ellard.

"Is weird. But I know she was at both Courtney's and Stacy, Junior's. Courtney's the night of her murder, Junior's shortly thereafter." (I wanna be around, to pick up the pizzas.) "And Courtney told us there was someone who could prove or knew it wasn't Carey killed Wesley, and we think that someone was Iris."

"And Junior? Who beat him up?"

"Don't know, but it wasn't the Arab guys who chased Bradley and me, they arrived *after* us. My bet it was the same Samoan guy Bradley shot."

"Who followed you from Stacy's. Sent by Stacy?"

"Well, that we don't know, since it wasn't the same Samoan who was there. But it's suspicious—or a hell of a coincidence. Still, no lock."

"So what you're saying, person or persons allied to the Arab cause is or are using Stacy with or without his knowledge and/or consent for the furtherance of their Middle East cause? And possibly Black Muslims?"

"I guess. Put that way it does sound awful farfetched, but so far it's the only way all the pieces seem to come together."

"You know," he said after a bit. "I think I liked it better when you *didn't* tell me everything you found out."

"It is a mess."

"But I suppose the next step would be to investigate Appleton and Curry."

"Right."

"Definitely Appleton."

"Total agreement. So, what do you think, could you do that?" I asked.

"I think you're absolutely right, it should be investigated," he said.

"Good."

"And you're just the man to do it."

"Me?"

"Because I know fucking well if I laid all this far-out crap on my boss, he'd have my black ass out on the street writing jaywalking tickets for Zsa Zsa Gabor inside ten minutes."

"So it's up to me."

"I'll do what I can. Which is not going to include putting any of this on paper."

I couldn't exactly blame him. We both thought about it for a long moment. Then he had another idea.

"I notice there's one thing you haven't mentioned in all this," he said. "And that's the Cifelli connection. Where does he fit in?"

Which is when our main courses came. Fortunately.

"I think we have enough on our plate for the time being," I said, quickly stuffing stuff in my mouth before I said anything I'd be sorry for.

OK, I could tell Ellard wasn't dismissing my theory out of hand. The plus. The downside was he wouldn't be officially doing anything to help prove it. So it would still be all up to me.

Which I guess was fair, in a way, since I had the most at stake. If someone didn't come up with the real killer there was no way I wasn't going to lose my license over the jury boo-boo. (Go try be a good citizen!)

So, I quick popped on up the hill to check out the house. The fuzz were gone, the body was gone—the mess lived on. I called one of those Korean cleaning services, got a guy didn't speak English too good, was terrific at math. Being there was blood and miscellaneous body traces, I didn't feel in the strongest position to haggle. They'd bring a crew tomorrow, first thing, no credit card, no check—cash. Plenty cash.

The Phantom was really pissed at all this change in routine, what with the cops having been all over, strange people marching through the garage, doors left open, and meals missed. I got a lot of snarling and hissing and yowling and general crankiness. But hunger seemed the main thing. So when I put down a big, clean bowl of cat food and fresh water, he came over, took a swipe at my arm to reestablish dominance, and once I'd backed off, settled to it.

Since it was still too early to pick up my car, I checked all the locks, reset the alarm, got back in the tin-can loaner, and headed for Century City.

It was a pure and not so simple fishing expedition. I had my suspicions, and a snatch of proof here and there. But nothing I could take to the bank. Or the grand jury.

No question Ely Appleton and company—which definitely included Curry, might include Soheila Morris, likely included Kiji Malouf, possibly Stacy, Gilbert Rexford, Stacy, Jr., and maybe probably likely Carey Jaeger too—were tied up directly and indirectly to all this Arab/Islam/PLO/Black Muslim stuff. The more important question was, how did that come to include the murders of Wesley Crewe and Courtney Blalock? And who was it did that?

At 2020 Avenue of the Stars, I took the now familiar elevator up to Jaeger's business office—or Curry's, or Appleton's, depending how you interpreted Crescent Enterprises.

As I went down the corridor I could hear music. Dixie. Trombone. Trummy Young. Louie, Barney Bigard—South Rampart Street Parade. Not your usual elevator music.

Because it wasn't coming from the elevator. It was coming from the suspiciously partly open door to Crescent Enterprises.

Which I knew enough to push wide open very carefully.

Kiji Malouf, the beauteous brunette secretary/receptionist would not be taking any more dictation. Or recepting.

Knife again. Shades of Courtney Blalock. Awful.

Not that murder's ever not awful. Just sometimes more so.

She was slumped in her chair behind her desk, head back, throat cut ear to ear. Which meant whoever did it was pretty surely someone she knew, who she was comfortable with letting get behind her. Since she was still in the chair, and even a cup of coffee on her desk hadn't spilled. Your basic friendly fire.

Satchmo finished his chorus, there was an ensemble bit, it ended, and the tape ran out with a click. As they say, the silence was deafening.

Now, the thing was—where was everybody? Assuming, too, the killer was gone.

I poked my head sort of tentatively into Curry's office. Nothing there.

I crossed over to Appleton's—the door was locked. I knocked.

"Appleton? You in there? Anybody?" Nobody.

I didn't want to touch anything in the reception area, so I went back to Curry's office. I reached across and picked up the phone on his desk, called Ellard. He'd just checked in. I told him what I'd found—the Malouf girl dead in the outer office, Appleton's office locked and looked like empty, and nobody in Curry's—when I noticed the window back of his desk was cracked about six inches, letting all the air conditioning out. As I continued filling Ellard in, I walked around the desk to close it.

Which is when I saw the second body. Curry, on the floor.

The good news was, no knife wound, and—by the faint beat of the carotid—alive, just unconscious.

I filled Ellard in on this development.

"Don't touch anything," he said.

"You mean on my way out?"

"No, man—you be there."

I sighed. He was right.

"You going to call the paramedics?" I asked.

"I'll take care of it all."

"Suits me."

"Just hold tight."

I'd be satisfied I could hold on to my lunch.

30

Mark Bradley

I was getting remarkably little work done, fretting over Francine, stewing about Brian. I couldn't help thinking it might be sort of wonderful to have the kind of job you could just walk through some days. Try just putting in your time writing and you were left with two problems—doing it over again, and figuring which were the *parts* you had to do over again.

At any rate, I had wanted to get rid of Goodman because while we each had an interest in Francine's welfare, we didn't share in the nature of the interest. His was ex-lover and mine was best friend. And when it came to Brian, though I had to confess Goodman'd been a lot less overtly homophobic of late, it wasn't something I wanted to share with him. So, the excuse that I had writing to do seemed the best white lie I could think of. And, of course, I did have writing to do. It was simply that I wasn't going to get any of it done at the moment.

And not that I needed a diversion (I was quite capable of producing my own), it was then the phone rang.

Goodman.

At Appleton's.

Finding Malouf dead. And Curry unconscious. And Appleton conspicuously elsewhere.

"So I was thinking," he went on, "(A) you should know, and (B) maybe Penny ought to put the company lawyer on standby."

"You don't think you're going to be charged?" I asked.

"I sure would of, Chief Broward was still on the job."

"But Chief Broward isn't. He's in leisurely retirement in Nassau, or the Seychelles—one of those places crooks and crooked cops go to compare numbered accounts."

"Still, here I am, on the spot—and Ellard knows I'm here and told me stay put."

"You called him?"

"Yeah. I have good vibes about him, and it couldn't hurt to have a friend at court."

"Especially if you interpret 'court' literally."

"Anyhow, I figured somebody should know, in case I disappear for any length of time."

"Well, what do you want me to do?"

"Just keep track of me. I don't expect any tricks from Ellard. But I believed Nixon, too."

"You didn't, really?"

"No."

But I bet the sucker voted for him. I decided I didn't want to know.

"All right. Check in with me from time to time. And if it gets vague, I'll contact Ellard."

We said our good-byes. One good thing, anyway. It was obvious I couldn't be expected to get any work done, considering these new developments.

This was the third case we'd worked on together. And Goodman's modus operandi was in total opposition to that of the past. Heretofore, he'd always played his cards close to the vest, not only hoarding knowledge, often deliberately misleading. Yet this time, clearly not.

So, taking a figurative page from my (ugh) co-writer, I decided to pursue a hunch of my own. I invited Armand (The Dancer) Cifelli to lunch.

I don't know why—you wouldn't take a Chinese guest to a Chinese restaurant—but somehow with Cifelli, it was pretty obviously going to be Italian. Since he was sure to know the difference between Madeo's and Matteo's, I'd invited him to the former, and he'd accepted.

Once I arrived (first) it was clear though I might be the host, I wasn't to be the one most honored by the house.

Yes, of course they had Mr. Cifelli's reservation.

"Mr. Bradley's," I gently corrected. If it registered, I couldn't tell, as I was led to:

"Mr. Cifelli's table."

After an on-again, off-again start a few years back, Madeo's had settled into becoming a really first-rate place, with authentic dishes (and a menu so uncompromising you needed a rudimentary knowledge of Italian to decipher it—or even understand the waiter's heavily accented translations) and a mix of chic and homey.

The waiter asked if I wanted something to drink while waiting, and I opted for a San Pellegrino.

Madeo's has a very European feeling. It's actually semi-basement in the ICM building (which always struck me as a suitably militant set of initials for a talent agency, lacking only a "B" for ballistic to get the total feeling) with nice woods and marble and beveled glass. Abetting the feeling is the constant chatter in Italian of the waiters, who I always get the impression are illegal aliens smoothly slipped into the country hidden in a shipment of olive oil. All very charming and relaxing.

I'd barely settled in and had a sip when a perceptible rise in excitement and a general mass fawning of employees gave indication that Mr. Cifelli had arrived. (Sort of like Rocky entering the arena.)

His limited entourage—the basic minimum bodyguard and chauffeur–bodyguard—took up conspicuous positions at the long bar, one at a vantage point surveying the entry, the other midway, to intercept any interloper who loped past the point man. And a beaming maître d' escorted, very close to doubled over in subservient delight, the illustrious Mr. C. to my table. Or *his* table, in the popular view.

"Ah, Mr. Bradley," Cifelli said on approach, arms minimally open, but in what for him could be perceived as a warm welcome. "How good of you to ask me."

"My pleasure, sir," I replied, shaking his hand, which was properly warm, medium to neutrally strong, and absolutely free of perspiration. (One got the feeling Mr. Cifelli had few occasions to sweat.) And I gestured for him to sit, a purely superficial invitation, of course. It seemed to me three people held his chair, though that must have been an illusion.

In accordance with custom and manners, we asked after each other's family, his wife and children, my "housemates, companions" whatever, gotten over fairly easily, knowing with his conditioning I hadn't any right to expect any great liberal leaning. But then again, he was a man who had certainly been exposed to wider vistas and transcended traditionally narrow origins. For one thing, he was eating with me. A higher, more intimate level of "meet" than mere coffee or a drink.

There were, accordingly, certain procedures and protocol to be adhered to. One didn't, without preamble, discuss business. First there was a leisurely discussion of what the day's offerings might be. Then a consultation with a captain, the maître, and in Cifelli's case, the chef himself as to what constituted a consensus of preference on his behalf. (I was accorded a peripheral semi-respect due to my proximity more than anything else.) Choices were proffered, elections proceeded, votes tallied, winners elected. In his case, *salsiccie alla griglia di spinaci*.

For me, since "I'll have the same" seemed too cavalier in the face of a multiplicity of offerings, I was persuaded to sample the *carre di agnello alla crema di scalogno*.

In lieu of an appetizer, Cifelli challenged the maître to himself select and serve whatever *insalata* his creativity was up to this fine day.

Until the *insalata* was served, I contented myself with subjects of general interest (for which read "neutral"). It was surprising how difficult they were to arrive at. For example, I started to discuss the current Oliver Stone film, *JFK*—suddenly realized there were Mafia allusions. Bad form. Dangerous form.

Politics. Whether Mario Cuomo might—wait, New York, Gotti and company.

World events—the dissolution of the Soviet empire. Potential changes inherent for Cuba. Wait, gambling interests if Havana could again ...

A lot of fitful starts and stops. Till Cifelli himself, with genial tolerance and gentle humor, suggested *he* choose a topic of general interest, prior to discussing our *real* purpose.

"For example?" I prompted.

"For example, how do you suppose a story like that concerning Richard Gere gains such a wide circulation? Ah, but look at me, it is *I* who now intrude upon your area of expertise."

So much for gentle humor.

"I can't imagine why you're looking to place me at a defensive disadvantage," I couldn't help saying.

"You are absolutely correct, and I apologize. If it is any comfort to you, it simply illustrates my point that offense can be given without any intent at all."

I would settle. There weren't all that many people who'd gotten apologies from this old war horse.

The busboy brought a small preparing table. The waiter brought bowls and mixing implements. Another waiter brought the makings. The captain gave some sort of invisible command resulting in these lower-echelon soldiers retreating a few steps and forming a protective phalanx. The captain examined the tools and the order in which each item had been placed, nodded with satisfaction, and himself retreated two steps, coming to attention just in front of the others. The maître d' now came forward, picked up the baton, gave the downbeat, and conducted the symphony that was to become our *insalata di Madeo* (radicchio, arugula, and artfully sliced endive, *con aceto*). Il Duce couldn't have done it with greater extraversion.

We both sat back, watched, and admired the maestro at work as he mixed, tossed, sprinkled, seasoned, dressinged, lemoned—and played the bongos. There was, actually, a scattering of applause as neighboring tables, drawn by the drama, signaled their approval. The maître d' allowed an anchovy smile to suggest itself in the area of his lipless mouth.

It was pretty good. Cifelli nodded slightly to an almost audible relief as the assembled workers retreated into the background to afford us (more principally, Cifelli) the privacy his practice required.

We ate the salad in silence. Finished.

"Very good," I said, deliberately underplaying the theatrics. I wasn't to be upstaged any more than absolutely necessary (next time I definitely would *not* choose an Italian restaurant).

"I appreciate your joining me today," I opened. "There're a lot of things happening, and they're pretty troubling."

"You refer to the events of this morning," he replied, obviously already informed. "Yes, that's disturbing. And I don't understand why, which is even more disturbing."

"Well, we've come up with some information that could shed a little light, and I thought it might be mutually beneficial to share it with you."

That obviously perked him up.

"I wish you would. I don't mind telling you candidly I don't understand this business. If, as seems to be the case, there's been an interdepartmental falling out, I can't for the life of me see what it is over."

"Well, power ..." I suggested. "Influence on Stacy."

"But Jaeger hasn't even been working."

"Maybe that was the issue. Now all of a sudden there's the book, a new movie."

"True."

"We know that you share an interest in these ventures." I put my cards face up. "Information innocently generated by our routine research—an interest, by the way, that seemed pretty generous for the amount of activity going on."

"Also true. We negotiated my ... remuneration, in the expectation of a greater utilization of my influence."

"Unions, picture making, financing," I put in, nothing new between us. We'd been there before.

"As you know. But things are relatively inactive at the moment, what with the trial of Stacy's boy and all the other hassles. So, you think the power struggle's simply over that, to get him to make more movies?"

"For money. But money for other power as well," I said.

"Power over what, I'm not following you."

"Power over the Movement."

"What movement, be more specific."

So he genuinely didn't know. A rarity for Cifelli.

And I told him the works about the Arab/Black Muslim/ PLO terrorist cabal. I went through the whole litany of events, from the bombings in court, through the murder of Courtney Blalock, to the beating of Stacy, Jr., to the attempted bombing of the Israeli consulate, and on to the murder of Kiji Malouf and the whatever (not yet determined) of Curry.

"Well, look at this," he said when I'd stopped for breath. "I can't believe I didn't put this together myself."

I shrugged.

"You've done me a service. There are things that need to be reevaluated here. I knew, of course, that in all likelihood Carey was innocent. I simply supposed he'd been nominated to take the rap to spare the breadwinner—a not unheard-of expedient in my own line of work. But I'm absolutely astounded by the Arab, PLO thing. That is not what I bought into."

And he looked extremely disturbed. It occurred to me there were somehow hidden emotions to be exploited here.

"The anti-Israeli thing might be even stronger. We're not totally sure the bombing of Judge Steinberg's court was just to scare Carey. The ADA took responsibility—blaming Steinberg for an earlier case—and the Arab who shot himself *was* part of that."

He seemed to deepen in color before my very eyes, rapidly approaching aubergine—or *melanzana,* in the current surroundings. The man was plain eggplant-angry.

"Where's Goodman now?" he asked finally.

"I'm not sure. If he hasn't been brought in for questioning, which I think I'd have heard by now, I would say he's en route to pick up his car. It's been in for some heavy mechanical restoration."

"Yeah," he said, distracted, his interest waning.

"At Orma Garage, place he goes on Pico."

He merely shook his head, thoughts elsewhere.

"No, wait, when he called this morning, they told him

there'd been a last-minute switch and to pick it up at Lateef Transmission."

Which is when the procession emerged from the kitchen, bearing our entrees as if they were crown jewels. Again the busboy with the serving table; again the waiter with the implements; the other waiter with the food; the captain to serve; the maître d' to officiate.

For the first time I started to worry in terms of what appropriate tips might be. It was a little nerve-wracking.

"Lateef?" said Cifelli suddenly, a very delayed reaction, with what looked like serious concern. "Is that the Ali Lateef—Lateef's Transmission on Pico?"

"I guess. How many could there be?"

"You better stop him. Sounds like a trap."

"What are you talking about?"

"If it's the same Lateef I know, the guy's major bad news."

"What constitutes major?"

"Drug dealer, chop-shop operator, the odd murder contract—very closely tied to Appleton."

I was up and pushing back the table just as the maître d' put our plates before us.

"*Now* he goes to wash his hands?" he said, deeply offended.

And I started for the phone, with the maître d's feelings a very low priority.

31

Rayford Goodman

I stood to one side, watching the forensic people do their thing. First, pictures of everything from every angle. And the good chance one of the angles would be a way to sell some to the *Enquirer*. Since the Jaeger connection guaranteed lots of scandal coverage. And actually, a lot of legit to boot.

Kiji Malouf's hands had been wrapped in plastic baggies, to preserve whatever she might have touched of the killer. Given how she'd been murdered, I didn't think there'd be much in that area. Once your throat got slit, I had a feeling your main concern centered around trying to hold it together. Yich.

They couldn't do the chalk thing, since she'd been sitting up in a chair. Though they did mark where the legs (rollers, actually) of the chair were.

Ellard, dictating into one of those tiny tape machines, described the scene. I caught the words *lividity* (how gravity pools the blood when it stops circulating)—and *rictus,* used to establish stuff that sets time of death. Really coroner shtick.

In this case, anyway, it wasn't likely she'd been dead half an hour before I got there. First, there would have been foot traffic; then, phone calls not going through would have alerted someone. Any longer struck me out of the question.

He described everything on the desk, called the photo cop over to take another shot. Opened the tape deck on the hi-fi behind her desk, looked at the tape (I remembered that—

Louie). Made another note. Then signaled two cops (one female, one regular) he was through and they were on.

The lady cop, tough, competent, large frame—for sure a
strong stomach—did most of the lifting as they worked the
corpse into a body bag, zipped it up, and slung it onto a
gurney. Good-bye, sweetheart.

Another guy then came over and vacuumed the immediate
area. I was in charge, I'd of had him do that first. By this time
a lot of folks had passed by.

"They should've done that right away," said Ellard, thinking
the same.

The corpse movers rolled the body out, and various cops
and detectives started getting back their color. Slit throats
weren't something even pros ever got real casual about.

Then one of the paramedics who'd been working on Curry
inside his office came out, looked around, spotted me turning
the page in an appointment book with a pencil eraser.

"You Lieutenant Ellard?" he said.

"No," said Ellard, frowning as he spotted what I was up
to. "He's just acting the part. I'm Lieutenant Ellard."

"The guy inside's coming around."

Ellard started in, me on his heels. He stopped. "You wait
here."

"Come on, Lieutenant—give and take?"

Started in. Reconsidered. Without looking back waved me
follow.

Ken Curry was sitting on his beautiful elkskin couch, tie
open, hair mussed, sweaty. But conscious.

His jacket was off, the sleeve on his custom-made shirt had
been unbuttoned and ripped up the seam to his shoulder. I
guess to give him some kind of shot to bring him around.
There was also an IV of some sort through a vein in the back
of his hand, the needle taped down.

"What's the story?" Ellard asked the medic.

"No blunt trauma, no bleeding, no bruises I can see right
off. Needle mark in his arm."

"Say anything?"

"No, and we didn't ask. Clear chain. We follow the book."

"Good. He OK to answer questions?"

"I think so."

"You know what the shot was?"

"Not offhand. We got a blood, though. Easy enough once we get to a lab. Some sort of, you know, IV val, morphine, one of those."

"Does he need hospitalization?"

"Not apparently. Though I'd suggest it."

"Thank you. Would you wait a minute outside?"

He gestured to his para-partner, another female with what they used to call generous hips. She picked up their heavy equipment—there were jobs where a big butt was an asset—and the two of them left the room.

"Mr. Curry, how you feeling?" said Ellard.

"Woozy."

"Can you tell me what happened?"

"Oh, yeah, wait." And he seemed to be having a little trouble getting himself together. "Drink?"

Ellard looked toward the door, but the paramedics had already gone outside. "I guess it's OK. Goodman?"

I started for the water carafe on his desk.

"Cognac," Curry corrected, pointing me to the trick bar in the antique camera.

I looked at Ellard. He shrugged. I put a couple fingers of something looked real expensive into a crystal glass you could light a premiere with and brought it over. Curry gulped it down.

"Oh, boy—needed that."

"Looked like," said Ellard. "The paramedics suggested you ought to go to the hospital and get yourself checked out."

"Well, I'll call my personal physician and see what he says. I don't think I'll have to."

"OK, but I just wanted you to know, that's what the official advice is," said Ellard, no doubt department-advised to watch out potential lawsuits. We were sure living in a disclaimer-loaded world. Warning: we are not responsible for your cleaning in the event of World War III.

"Now then, you're OK?" Ellard asked again.

"Seem to be," said Curry. Then, I guess having met a lawyer or two himself, added, "To the best of my knowledge. At this point in time."

"Can you tell us what happened?"

"Yes. I was sitting at my desk. I needed my secretary for something. I buzzed her. But she didn't come." He looked up. Then added, "She all right, by the way?"

"In a minute," said Ellard. "Go on, please."

"So I got up to see if she was at her desk. But before I could get around my own desk, the door opened, and two men in ski masks burst in."

"Yeah?"

"Big men. One pulled my jacket down from the shoulders to about my forearms." And here he turned to his jacket on the couch next to him, showed the front, button ripped out. "And tore up my shirt."

"Go on."

"I didn't expect that. I thought I might get hit, or have a gun pointed at me, but no, just the one holding my arms at my side. Then the other one came at me."

"Did anybody say anything during all this?"

"Not till then."

"What'd he say then? Which one?"

"The second guy. He said, 'Better not move, or you can really get fucked up.' And I saw what he meant. He had a hypodermic needle and he was going to give me a shot right into a vein."

"Which he did?"

"Which he did."

Ellard took a moment to digest this. "Why do you suppose he did that?" he asked finally.

"I suppose he wanted me out of the way while he did whatever, I guess rob, right?"

"Is there anything worth robbing here?"

"Artwork," he said, pointing to the undisturbed walls. "We have some cash and valuables in the safe."

"Which is?" asked Ellard.

Curry got up wobbily and crossed to a large customized

stereo unit half a mile wide. He opened the front of a large speaker, which turned out to be false. Back of which was a safe. Still locked.

"I guess they didn't get to it," said Curry.

Ellard and I exchanged glances. I knew what he was thinking. Same as me. Why would the crooks knock somebody out before getting the combination?

"Or maybe that wasn't the motive," added Curry, taking and lighting a cigarette. "What does Ms. Malouf have to say?"

And Ellard broke the news.

And I watched.

And it certainly seemed the man was in shock. Nobody would doubt for a minute he hadn't the least notion she was dead.

Which meant one of two things. It was either the truth, or he wasn't called the greatest acting coach of his time for nothing.

I poured Curry another shot of cognac while Ellard called his doctor for him.

"I hate to press you at a time like this," said Ellard gently. "But the more we know the earlier, the better chance we have of catching the perps. Can you give us any more of a description? You say they wore ski masks and they were big. What do you mean, big—fat, like bikers?"

"No, more tall. Muscular for sure."

"Clothes?"

"It happened pretty fast. Sweatshirts? Levis maybe. Reebok kind of shoes."

"All pretty vague," said Ellard with a sigh. "Nothing else, I suppose?"

"Black."

"Say what?"

"They were black men."

Ellard paused a moment. "I thought they wore ski masks."

"The hands," said Curry.

"I presume you're talking the *outside* of the hands," said Ellard, a touch more defensive than I'd of expected.

"Listen, that ought to make them easier to spot in Beverly Hills," I said to bring him back around.

He gave me a small smile.

"OK," he said to Curry. "Why don't you just lie down and wait for your doctor? We'll be right outside."

Curry nodded and, stubbing his cigarette out in a thick crystal ashtray, carefully took off his loafers and stretched out on the elkskin couch.

Ellard and I went back out to the reception area.

There were a lot less technicians and uniforms around. The gore groupies with no clear-cut business had left, and the others were doing whatever it was each of them did.

One of the uniforms came over to say they'd got the key to Appleton's office and scoped it out. Didn't seem anything special there, but nobody home. He'd thought to bring Appleton's appointment book where under today's date was "Check locations for film."

Again Ellard gave me a look. Another thing for him to verify. Was Appleton actually looking at locations? If so, was he doing the looking alone, or together with an alibi? And even alone, inconclusive. But didn't rule him out. Since this could be, looked to be, inside stuff. And he was tall. And black.

Then again, if it was a falling-out between partners, why kill the secretary? Why not the partner?

"Well," I said after a beat, "at least I'm sure that lets me out as a suspect."

"Nah," said Ellard. "I'm not *that* different from Broward. You're still a suspect."

"Even though nothing connects me here and none of the descriptions fit. And there's no motive."

"That's why you're not a *hot* suspect. You can go."

I was down the parking lot and already in my loaner when I remembered I hadn't called Bradley to let him know I was OK.

I considered getting back out and using one of the phones I'd seen by the escalator, but somebody'd already pulled into my parking spot and I didn't see another one any place near. So I decided I'd do it next chance I got.

Which should be B.J.'s—at Orma Garage. Then I remembered, B.J.'d subcontracted the transmission or something or other, to someplace, Lateef's Transmission. I reached in my pocket for the address I'd written on the edge of a newspaper. It should be just a block or two past B.J.'s.

I took the Pico exit and headed due east. About time, too. I was really looking forward to getting the old '64 Eldorado convertible back. My sacred wheels.

I caught a red at Pico and Hauser. Waited. Drummed a few bars of "Sing, Sing, Sing" on the steering wheel. Car pulled up behind. Large black dude in one of those X's or Z's. Eardrum-busting music from one of those stations only black guys' radios get. Threw me off mid-solo.

The light changed, I checked left for no cross traffic, spotted B.J. at the northwest corner, across the street, looking up Hauser. I'd normally of come down that way, if I hadn't come from Century City. He was peering up the street, hopping around, looking real antsy. The thought crossed my mind he could be waiting for me. But before I could roll down the window and call him, the guy behind pumped a horn louder than his stereo. I was holding up traffic. Anyway, no reason I could think of whatever it was couldn't wait till I dropped by to settle up. After I picked up my car at this Lateef guy's.

And sure enough, a block and a half farther east I could see what a limey friend of mine once called the "Splendid Equippage"—my '64 Cadillac Eldorado convertible—all shiny and showy parked out front of Lateef Transmission.

I pulled the midget clunker up to the work bay, where it gave a final gassy cough as I cut the ignition for the last time. (Let B.J. worry about picking it up.) And good riddance.

I must say, it was a little strange nobody seemed to be working, the place looked empty. But the key wasn't in the Caddy, so I'd need to find someone.

Through the bay was a door connecting to the back had to be an office. I went through, opened the door.

Where two big guys with ski masks just happened to be.

Since I knew this wasn't their maiden effort, it didn't surprise me they were well back out of range of any defensive move I might consider.

"OK, relax, bro," said the one with the gun pointing real steady at my head, "and we won't have to mix your brains with the axle grease."

That sounded like a good idea to me. Not a great line, but a good idea.

"Just take off your jacket," he went on. Why was it I didn't have the idea he was going to steal my clothes?

"Not necessary. I'll do what you want," I said, not too hopeful.

"Jacket off," he said, waving the piece.

Jacket off.

"Roll up your sleeve."

Oh, boy.

"Look, I'm telling you, it's not necessary. I'm a pussycat."

He waved the gun, then centered on the middle my forehead. I rolled up my sleeve.

"Hey, my man," said the second guy, closing in with a hypo. "They's guys pay good money for this shit."

Which is really hard to understand. First, how anybody can on purpose put a needle in themselves. And second, what's the fun of going totally and immediately splat unconscious?

32

Mark Bradley

Last I'd heard from Goodman, he was at the murder scene in Century City. Accordingly, I tried to catch him there. Whoever answered the phone immediately shunted me to Lieutenant Ellard, who no doubt hoped I was someone able to shed light on his problems rather than add further complications.

"Oh, Lieutenant Ellard. Mark Bradley here. Could I speak to Goodman?"

"I let him go."

"Oh. He didn't say where?"

"Not that I . . . wait, something about his car."

"Ah, Jesus."

"Anything I can do for you?" said Ellard, evidently sensitive to the note of apprehension in my voice.

I had to fight the notion of sharing the Lateef info, but given Cifelli's understandable penchant for secrecy, I knew better than to involve him. So I simply said no, I just had some business with Goodman, and thanks anyway.

"If it's anything to do with this case, I'd like to know," he persisted.

"Lieutenant, when I know something you ought to know, you'll know," I replied, technically responsive. But leaving neither of us satisfied.

Next, I looked up the number for Lateef's Transmission and tried that—although I wasn't sure what I was going to say. ("I hear you're a major bad guy into mayhem and psychotic violence, and I was wondering if we might get together with an eye toward exploring alternatives to hurting my friend" didn't promise to strike a responsive chord.)

Turned out I didn't get to say anything. When the answer phone informed me in an accent not difficult to associate with a Lateef, "We no here—maybe later," I didn't feel encouraged to leave a message.

Orma Garage wasn't far from Lateef's Transmission, Yellow Page-wise, so I found that number and gave it a try.

B.J. was all upset. He'd been recently leaned on by a couple of bent noses to throw his transmission business to Lateef, pointedly starting with Goodman's Cad. But since the guy did professional work, and by the look of them, so did the bent noses, he figured it was an arrangement he could live with. Or at least had a better chance to.

Only he'd begun to worry about why they'd specifically mentioned Goodman's Caddy.

"Then why didn't you at least warn the man?" I asked.

"I tried to. I waited on the corner, but I guess I missed him."

"Right away. Why didn't you warn him right away?"

"Because I wasn't worried right away. It was only today when the same guys came around and warned me *not* to warn him that I thought I better warn him."

Figured.

"Well, maybe you ought to drop by this Lateef person and check it out," I suggested.

"I did. Nobody home."

"Then maybe it's OK," I ventured.

"No, not OK. The loaner's still there."

That could be all right. Goodman could have figured B.J. would pick up the loaner.

"And so's the Cadillac."

Not all right.

I thanked B.J. and returned to the table.

I settled back into my chair, knew not to say anything to Cifelli while the waiter and captain were about.

"You back," the mâitre d' noted.

"I'm back."

With which he emitted an eye-rolling sigh that clearly registered his opinion of anyone so crass as to disrupt the timing of his performance.

But, ever the pro, he pulled his act back together. And with a magician's flourish, produced my entree by whisking away a silver warmer that resembled nothing so much as a Valkyrie breastplate.

"I try to keep this warm for you, signore," he said with lingering resentment. "Is suppose to eat *warm*."

The man had no idea how little appetite I'd retained.

We left it that Cifelli would nose around a bit and test the waters and whatever other mixed metaphors seemed appropriate.

He'd made no attempt to grab the check, which was proper inasmuch as it'd been my invitation, and I was, I thought, suitably extravagant with my tips. Nevertheless, I did happen to catch Cifelli surreptitiously spreading a little lagniappe of his own on the way out. Image.

Cifelli's car was waiting and only about seven guys held the door. He gave a final wave and was off.

Ma voiture, on the other hand, seemed inordinately tardy in arriving. A fact I was on the verge of seriously sounding off about when it finally made a belated appearance.

Only a single flunky held the door for me (and that only long enough to snatch my tip). But even had there been repeated the showy display which attended Cifelli's departure, I doubt my interest could have been seriously diverted from the biliously banana yellow envelope which lay on the passenger seat. I knew very well I had left no such object. And even if I had, I would certainly not have self-addressed it with letters cut from newspapers and magazines.

I pulled in at the first available parking spot. Which turned out to be the lot in back of the Writers Guild Building at 8955 Beverly Boulevard. And opened the envelope.

"You R been watch," it commenced, in disregard of both the customary salutation and English usage. "Go 2 office. Get all work, nots (notes?), material, taps (tapes?) 4 book. No copy.

No xerex (antifreeze? Xerox?). 5 minute out. Take to Hollywood Vine. Wait car. Or good man dye."

By which I concluded the book deal was souring. To say
the least.

Had Goodman been abducted as a hostage (as all signs
seemed to point) to prevent publication of the book? That was
weird. And considering how everyone connected with whatever this was seemed to in some way profit from Jaeger's
participation in the book, why? A better logic suggested the
interested parties wanted the book to go forward but without
Goodman's and my participation.

That made sense, really. We were certainly closing in on
some monstrous conspiracy and would shortly have evidence
to back it all up. Plus, of course, the expectation that with
those revelations, the solution to the murders would in all
probability ensue. (Though there still remained an outside
chance conspiracy and murders were separate and distinct.)

At any rate, I was in no position to negotiate. Also, given
the timetable, I'd have no chance to make dupes. But they had
no way to account for whatever Francine would already have
put into the computer, or what remained in our memory. One
would assume, given the quality of the note and the level of
organization to date, we weren't dealing with rocket scientists.

But I didn't entirely dismiss the notion that a superior
intelligence might opt for projecting such an image as a means
of cover. (Investigative reporting and detecting made cynics of
us all.)

Be that as it may, I went forthwith to the office (discerning
no one in particular following me, but somehow believing
someone was) and began gathering the requested materials.
The more I examined what I was bringing to the party, the
less I felt confident it was the materials alone in which they
were interested. The appropriation could very likely include
me.

At which inopportune time, Penny stuck his head in.

"Hello, half day here?" he said, characteristically.

"Taking my work home," I replied. There wasn't a chance
I'd confide in Penny. He'd undoubtedly see in Goodman's

abduction a chance for great promotional exploitation for the book and do everything he could to prolong it—including banning me from taking these company materials from the premises.

"I don't know why you'd want to do that, when I'm paying for electricity and supplies right here," he said, perhaps instinctively smelling a kinfolk.

"Hey, you know how weird we writers are. Humor me," I replied.

"Well, if you're going to do it, just do it," he said, substituting crabbiness for satisfying his instinct. "Let's not waste all the daylight hours discussing it," he concluded, surrendering.

And he watched a moment as I dumped the stuff into a carton, probably monitoring for pilferage. Then, spotting someone else doing something of which he disapproved (a wide range), he called, "Hey, you there!" and left in hot pursuit.

I grabbed the carton, schlepped it down to the parking lot, hopped in the car, and drove to Hollywood and Vine.

I couldn't imagine why they'd chosen such a public spot to either take possession of the materials or possession of the materials and me.

First of all, you can't stop. Well, you can. And I did. But the moment I did I was importuned by all manner of sexual salesmen and women, offering myriad services and sicknesses. You had to fight them off with a stick.

Ditto the dopefolk.

But the neighborhood ambience of Hollywood and Vine has been too well documented to merit further exposition. The extent and breadth of its depravity and pure funk nevertheless still retained the ability to shock. It was the sort of spot that gave sleaze a bad name.

But with the liberty and license went a lot of bizarre costumes as well. So it wasn't a particular attention grabber that the car pulling up alongside me contained two men in ski masks. And that one of them exhibited a gun (which was practically decent exposure in that neighborhood) and indicated a desire for me to follow. I followed.

I followed farther as we backtracked, went over the Hollywood Freeway to the Valley, then twisted and turned, and
twisted once again. (Hey, Chubby Checker.)

They doubled back, down side streets, up avenues—all of
which was ridiculous. First place, to me everywhere in the
Valley looked the same. People from our side of the hill don't
know the Valley. It could be Van Nuys, it could be Reseda. It
could be Tarzana. Or Jane. It was the Valley.

Second, I didn't believe they intended to take me to headquarters, or even hindquarters—so, what?

And perhaps the what was to be answered at last as we
pulled into a kitchy Fifties-ish gas station featuring some off
brand I'd never heard of. (Could there be stolen gas?) At any
rate, the exchange appeared imminent. I started out of my car.

Immediately one of the ski-masked terrorists (I wondered,
did they have ski masks in summerweight material? Had to be
hot in there) waved me back into the car, using a fearsome
submachine gun for a pointer. I got back in.

He motioned me to roll down the window. I rolled down
the window.

"You stay, bro."

"Someone's meeting me here?"

"No, man—we outta gas."

With which he turned and retreated back to his vehicle.
Jesus Christ, I was really dealing with some deep planners
here.

They filled up the tank. The attendant having weathered
his confusion on being waved away from a Full Serve tank as
they pumped it themselves.

On completion, he approached them.

"Twenty-six seventy-nine," he said.

"Take credit cards?" asked the ski-masked driver.

"Visa and MasterCard," said the attendant.

"How 'bout Kalishnikov?" said the driver, pointing the gun.

"In a minute!" said the attendant, hands up, backing off.

With which we were off once again. (They didn't appear
to need a tax receipt.)

Twisting, turning, in and out, doubling back—I had an

impression we'd reached something called Chatsworth, a name invoking an image of England—but a countryside disputing it. Maybe it was San Chatsworth, for all I knew.

More twists and turns, more countryside, then suddenly we came to a remote instant city. It was a middle-class development with dozens of identical houses on dozens of identical blocks, each curved and cul de sac-ed.

By some sign beyond my comprehension they found the one they intended (did the residents have homing beacons?), and pulled into a driveway and stopped beneath a porte cochere which, typically, the Californians had reinvented and carefully stripped of elegance by renaming *carport*. I followed and parked behind them.

Again I opened my door. Again I was motioned back inside.

The two occupants got out of their car and entered the house. I sat in my sweltering car for twenty-five minutes.

That was when a white Porsche roared into the street, zoomed up to the house, and screeched to a stop about seven inches from my rear bumper.

The driver of the Porsche got out, slipped sidewise between our two cars, and came around to the passenger side of mine.

I reached over and opened the door.

For her.

It was Stacy Jaeger's girlfriend, Soheila.

33

Rayford Goodman

I was alive. That part was good.

My head hurt. Different. Weird. Slow. Underwater. Itch.

Can't seem to scratch. Why fizzit? Huh?

Tied. Hands tied. Around post.

Dark.

No, no, no—blindfold.

All right, all right, shape up here! Feel. Ouch! Splinter. Hands tied around *wood* post. Good. So? Older building. Using the old beam. Bean.

Concrete floor. Grimy. Loose chunks what? Pebbles, dirt? Dirty, crumbly concrete floor. Feels big. Whistle. Echo.

Large, empty, dirty, concrete floor, wood post, high ceiling room.

Smell. Spice? Saffron?

Empty old food warehouse.

Something else. Metallic? Oil, grease?

Very hot.

Quiet. No traffic. No planes.

"The body of Hollywood P.I. Rayford Goodman was discovered today in an abandoned grocery and auto-parts warehouse in ..." Tustin? Barstow? Death Valley? "... downtown Gobi Desert."

I felt sharp, in a vague way. I felt I could think through a lot of things, just—I couldn't seem to remember at the end of the thought what it was I'd started in the beginning of the—what?

And why was my shirt all bunched up under my jacket sleeve? Ah-hah—the shot! They'd given me a shot. Not so much given, in the sense of—hm?

Not too bad. Hooo. Sort of high, really.

Something to be said for drugs.

But I couldn't put my finger what it was.

So went back to sleep.

When I woke I hurt. My head was fairly clear now. And I clearly hurt. Stiff and achey. Back pain. Dull headache. Didn't seem right hangover for a party I slept through. Life's not fair. Or necessarily ongoing, I seemed to remember.

I was still sitting on the concrete floor. Hands still tied around the post. It was still dark. Well, blindfold. *Felt* dark. Later? Rubbed my chin against my shoulder. Scratch. Beard growth. Time passed. Night?

At the end of a long soundtrack, big scary echo, lock turned, large door opened. Screech, *heavy* door. Major movie SFX. Death coming to a theater near you. Big, nasty sounds. None friendly. Rapid heart rate. Large fear.

This is not my bag. This is not Hollywood. It's very uncomfortably real. Pay attention!

Steps. Echo through mostly empty warehouse, two sets of boots, creaking leather, clanking stuff. Guns, knives, gear? Dialogue.

"Harruba harruba. Batcha baka." Farsi, Arabic, Turkish, who the fuck knows?

Heavy-footed, clomping over, synchronized spitting. Really alternate spitting. Ptui, ptui. Clank clank, ptui. Squeak. Awareness 101.

And close near, stop. Ptui number one, ptui number two.

"Well," I said, breaking the ice, "what's this—finals of the Don Zimmer/Mike Ditka spit-off?"

Pow, first ptui busts me in the chops.

"You guys never been real big on a sense of humor."

Pow, number two. I *knew* they weren't, why'd I have to

prove it? Speak when spoken to. Right, Mom. (Number one hits way harder than number two.)

Number one leaned down, gave me a whiff of breath like a Calcutta landfill. Grabbed my jacket, tore it off my shoulder and stripped my shirtsleeve down to the wrist. Not a promising start.

It got even less when number two closed in, slapped the vein inside my elbow, and I knew what was coming. The thought crossed my mind whatever was in the not-too-likely sterile needle was the least of my worries. Do the words hydrophobia, leprosy, and AIDS strike a familiar note?

But you don't struggle while someone's giving you a shot because who knows how much worse it might be they missed the vein.

And in the middle of all that, I got a whiff of a different smell from number two. Female. Definitely female. Very definitely female. Not too big on hygiene. (And a song in my mind, "What a difference bidet makes.") Equal-opportunity terrorists.

At any rate, she pushed the juice on home and I was committed. (I didn't think it likely one of the women I'd met on the case before—unless she was a master of disguise, ex- and *in*ternal.)

And that seemed to be that.

As their footsteps echoed on the empty concrete, it got very lonely. I didn't have a feeling I'd be going home soon. Or necessarily. I had a sudden worry nobody'd remember to feed the Phantom. While I was gone. And/or if. Poor cat wouldn't understand. (Are there dope crying jags?)

And the bang, bang, clomp clomp, creak creak, clang going away. And your wanting them to stay, even them—don't leave me alone . . .

And they were at that big old heavy door, and knock knock knock. Sounded like the monster wants Frankenstein open up.

Then the big lock noise again, the door creaking open, and outside another bunch of "harruba, harruba, batcha baka," and then a real big *"Harruba!"* From at least four to six voices, really more like a big cheer.

And the bad juice vibrating through my veins. Wondered

upper-downer? Started counting backward from a hundred. Ninety-nine, ninety-eight, ninety-seven, ninety-six, ninety-seven, twertig.

Any questions?

I was being shaken awake. My chin rubbed against my now bare shoulder. No more beard than before. Not much time gone by. So sleepy. Far away, from the door at the end, music. Branford Marsalis. Rather sleep. (Not big on soprano sax.)

The one doing the shaking smelled familiar. I gagged.

"Goo'man, Goo'man—you wake now," said the voice through a plague of plaque.

There was another burst of Branford (whiny, whiny), then the door slammed shut, music off. And a new set of boots coming closer.

"Goodman, up!" came a new voice from close but high away. But I didn't feel like.

"You up now!" said number two, disguising her voice but not her sex. Not me, up. Just wanted to sleep. Wild whores couldn't get me up.

"Harruba baka harruba," new voice said, real mad. Harruba harruba your own self. I was just finding this somehow very quietly amusing when they switched tactics and moods with a bucket of cold water dumped over my head. Splutter, wake, blach. Blindfold snatched off.

"Got my attention," I said, opening my eyes. Taking a min-ute to focus. Not finding much focus. Dope and dark. In the dim light I could see Riff and Raff. Two guys (guy and a half) in layered Annie Hall look. Rag heads. Somebody in back of me. "Whoozat?" I said, starting to twist around.

Whack, from Riff.

"No turn!" he hissed, flashing a mouth a Beverly Hills den-tist could put his kids through college on.

"If I may have your attention," said the voice from in back and up high. And familiar. "OK?"

"'m atcher serv'ce," I think I said. Then almost fainted. "What *is* this stuff?"

"Scopalomine, I believe. Or maybe sodium pentathol. Not

in the recreational family. I really don't know. Good Muslims don't use the devil's dope. The white devil's dope. Jewish–Italian white devil's dope. OK?!"

"Jus' asking."

And then got a big rambling conspiracy thing—all a plot to keep the black race subjugated. Since old whitey *loved* having a big potential market with no money to buy its products or pay its taxes. I didn't mention that part.

"Affid," I said instead. "Dalmmm!" And pulled against my ropes, frustrated.

"But fuck philosophy," said Mr. X—*probably* Mr. X. "Not why we're here, OK?" And as I struggled furiously, he put a hand on my shoulder, easily holding me still. "We're gonna have us a little interrogation. So, as they say, relax, man—rape is inevitable."

"I hope you mean that femiteemly," I said. Not exactly what I had in mind.

"I can see we better get on with this pretty quick," said Mr. Interlocutor. "And I meant rap, not rape."

"Flakkit," I replied.

"Idiot," said old X, I don't think to me. "You fucking OD'd him!"

I didn't hear the next batch. I was napping. But somehow the nap went away, and I woke real rested. Real, in fact damn near great!

"All right, now, Goodman. We just gave you a little mild meth, so we can chat, OK?"

Chatting sounded good to me. Sounded really worthwhile. After all, if one had nothing better to do and no place to go, why not—great old pastime.

"You said it. Shoot, old buddy," I replied.

"Good. Now, what we have to know is exactly, and in complete detail, what you and your partner have found out, what's down on paper, what's in any computers, and who else knows."

I may have been drugged, but I wasn't stupid. "I don't see any point in telling you any of that," I said.

"How about if we threaten to kill you?"

"Doubly so."

"And the difference is good death–bad death."

"Actually, *any* death hits me on the negative side."

"Well, we are going to kill you, Mr. Goodman."

"If you were going to kill me, you wouldn't be hiding your face."

I wouldn't say it was the best moment of my life when he came around from behind and stepped right in front of me.

Oh, shit.

"Now," he said. "Would you like to answer my questions?"

"Tell you what," I said with that now very clear mind immediately recognizing the value of the old stall. "You answer some of mine, I'll answer some of yours. For example, here you are with all this dope and giving people shots; how're you going to explain you didn't give Curry a shot so you could kill that Malouf girl, who, I guess, found out too much?"

"Well, see, this is what they mean by a little knowledge. It happens I didn't kill Kiji Malouf, I wasn't even there."

"And you have an alibi."

"Not one I can use. At the time I happened to be leading a little terrorist action over in Beverly Hills, OK?"

"Oh?"

"Just came over the news. You heard our little cheer?"

I'd heard.

"They just reported the bombing."

Oh, Christ.

"We're going to make those Beverly Hills Jews understand if they keep supporting the Israeli expansionist butchers they gonna have to pay the price."

"Jesus, what'd you do?"

"We're fighting a war, OK? And in war, there's casualties."

"What'd you *do*?"

He looked me square in the eye and said, "Took out the kitchen at the Carnegie Delicatessen."

"Boy, that's getting them where they live." On second thought: "And there were casualties?"

"Actually, two Mexican dishwashers. But you can't make an omelet without breaking some eggs."

"Or a knish without potatoes."

He gave me a shot in the face. "Don't mock me. A bombing is still a bombing. They'll get the idea nobody's safe, OK? If we can hit them here, it's a whole new ball game."

Not without some truth, I guess. But, god, a delicatessen! These folks weren't just bad at war, they had no understanding of public relations. Leno and Letterman were going to tear 'em to ribbons.

All the same, it did, possibly, get him off the hook for Malouf–Curry. But the jury was still out on Courtney. And it was his gun killed Wesley Crewe.

"But now I answered your question, you'll answer mine."

"I don't think so," I said.

"You don't think we have the guts to kill you?"

"Yeah, I think you might."

"Then make it easy on yourself."

"But that's the point. Your killing me kind of takes away all my incentive to cooperate."

"There are other ways."

"Yeah, well, I'm sure you think so. I guess it's your old test of wills."

"Let me show you—before we get on with the really nasty stuff—just how much will we have." With which he snapped his finger at the girl gorilla. "Hurruba hurruba chaboogabog," or something.

The girl gorilla took off her jacket and rolled up her sleeve. She had more arm hair than Robin Williams. Than Bonzo.

Appleton snapped his finger again. She stuck her arm out. He took out a Bic lighter, lit it, and put the flame under her arm.

"Not necessary," I said. "I get the idea."

He held the flame. It began to smell like chicken feathers burning. She didn't say a thing.

"Got it," I said. "Got the message."

And, very leisurely, he took the lighter away.

"Morhumgha!" he said.

"Morhumgha," she answered.

"Short break," he said. "Think about it. Testicles have hair, too. OK?"

Oi, what a picture.

"We have some bombs to make. They're having a little get-together at Beverly Hills High. Or maybe a get-apart."

His laugh fell a little short of the basic movie madman. But it would do till the fake thing came along.

They put the blindfold back on, marched on down the corridor, opened the door. The music had changed. I got a bit of Grover Washington, "Inside Moves." Better.

The door closed. It got dark again. Quiet. I was alone.

Wide awake.

No place to go.

But a big urge to go *some*where.

34

Mark Bradley

This was a very different, businesslike Soheila. For one thing, she was covered neck to toe in shapeless cotton garments, totally obscuring her excellent body. (But in a chic, Laise Adzer kind of way.) Gone, however, the previous lowcut blouses with their clear view of the Silicon Valley. She carried a shoulder bag that looked suspiciously like an old horse feed-bag, of ecru canvas, with a very nice leather trim—I couldn't help looking for designer initials—from which she now extracted—and the expression is leveled—a very attractive inlaid nacre-handled, chrome-plated handgun I, in my newfound expertise, would estimate to be of a .32 caliber.

"Drive," she said.

"And drive he did," I replied, always one to keep it light, with some difficulty backing out around her car into the street and heading in the general direction of whence.

"You brought all your tapes, notes, disks?"

"I've assembled the whole kit and caboodle. Which I will be absolutely ecstatic to deliver on receipt of my partner, hopefully in robust health."

"Doesn't work that way," she said. "I'll take the data and once it's authenticated by my superiors, then we release Goodman."

"Uh-uh," I said. "I *have* it, but I wasn't foolish enough to bring it with me. We'll have to arrange a swap. You want to tell me where?"

"Just keep going, I've got to think," she said, waving the gun at my crotch, not a big confidence builder. I pulled over to the curb.

"Let's *not* keep going, let's talk," I said, turning off the ignition.

We were still in a residential, almost deserted area. Through the rearview window I could see we were not alone. It was the same car containing the same ski-masked twosome (must be getting itchy in there) who'd led me into the Valley in the first place. They parked about fifty feet behind me.

"OK," I went on, in an effort to get some control over events. "I'm not going to give you the stuff just like that, without knowing Goodman's OK, or, for that matter, getting some kind of assurance you don't intend to kill us both."

"We are not trying to kill anybody."

"Other than the occasional Mexican busboy, according to the news. What's going on, anyway?"

And she went off on a rambling discourse on the history of the Middle East, the plight of the Palestinians, the betrayals authored by various jackal Arab functions in league with the American Jewish media and motion-picture Mafia, and the unmitigated, unqualified, unequal evil of the oppressive Israeli empire. (Personally, I'd always thought they should have just bought Florida outright and forgot about the Middle East.)

"Yeah, yeah, I know all that," I said, not willing to get dragged into a political argument, even though I did favor a negotiated, reasonable settlement. "And I understand you've got a little local terrorist cell going here to do whatever— make war with Mexico."

Here the hand holding the gun stiffened, and I raised mine in protest, with a just-kidding motion.

"Don't make a mockery," she warned. There was a Jewish joke in there somewhere, but my WASP sense of survival overcame the impulse.

"Let's just relax here a minute. Tell me something. First of all, who all's involved here? Is Stacy himself? Curry? Appleton?"

"I'm not going to answer your questions." (Actually, I took

that as a good sign that there was some chance they weren't planning to kill me.)

"How about the Malouf girl? Was she?"

"I told you, I am not going to reply."

"Stacy's kids?"

"Now stop it!" And her knuckles got all white around the gun. Clearly, that wasn't a tack that would produce results.

"All right, whatever you say. Though you can't blame me for being a little curious." She shrugged, figuratively disarmed. At least circulation returned to her fingers.

"Let me ask you something else. I take it, you represent yourself as a good Muslim woman?"

"I certainly do."

"Well, then how come out at Stacy's place you were wearing a wisp of a bikini with your *pipik* hanging out?"

"Pipik?"

"Belly button. In Yiddish."

"You are Jewish?"

"No, but I know a *pipik* when I see one."

"Sometimes to be a good Muslim woman is to obey orders, however distasteful they may be—in service to the one God."

There were enormous numbers of girls in Hollywood serving God, now that I thought of it. "And those orders," I continued, exploiting the opening, "to get close to Goodman? Pump him, as it were, since we were getting too close to all this conspiracy?"

She merely shrugged, but it was a shrug that didn't deny much.

"Let me tell you how I see it," I said. "Stacy I would judge to be a fellow-traveler, in on sympathy, out on the specifics. The reason I see it that way is that when you came on to Goodman in that definitely un-Muslim way, he got very angry. And maybe started wondering if your affection for him was entirely genuine, too, or whether that mightn't be also in service to 'the one God' or at least, 'the cause,' which he finances, right?"

Again she shrugged, then seemed to recognize her conditioned passivity was letting her get lulled into a discussion she wasn't supposed to be having. "This is not why we are here!" she said angrily. "We are here to arrange for you to give me your materials!"

"In exchange for Goodman's release," I added. "What about the Malouf girl? I noticed she was very Muslim-obedient to Appleton, independent to Curry."

"You must stop this! You must attend to the business we have. You are not in a position to be asking questions."

I knew that.

"A person can't help being curious."

At which she poked me in the groin with the gun.

"A person could," I amended, groin gouging being a gesture that engaged my caution.

"So, how are we going to arrange this?" she asked, somewhat lost with no one to give her instructions.

"Easy," I said. "You just—"

Which is when my door was jerked open, and one of the two masked guys took the rest of the line. "You just get on out the fuckin' car, and do it now. What is the matter with you, girl?"

Since this dusky gentleman was waving the Kalishnikov at me, and since rescue appeared to be nowhere at hand, I decided to comply.

"All right, the trunk. Open the trunk, honky. Now!"

I quickly decided reciprocal banter along the lines of "the jig is up" wouldn't play and instead moved to the back of the car, where I opened the trunk and had my bluff called on the materials in the carton I'd stupidly put there.

He pointed the weapon and his co-worker took the box, Soheila retrieving the odds and ends which spilled out of the overflowing container.

"Now what?" I said. "When do I get Goodman?"

"Now we check everything is here and if it serves our purpose we let Goodman go," said the leader.

"That doesn't seem fair," I replied to this representative of a notably fair group. "I thought you took him to get this stuff and get us off the book."

"I don't give a shit what you thought," he said.

"Watch your language," admonished the other guy, holding the box and indicating the "ladies present."

"OK, both you," the exasperated chief of mission said to the box boy and Soheila, "in the car." And they headed back to the other vehicle.

"And?" I said.

"And," said the terrorist, "you have a nice day now."

I had a little trouble dealing with that.

It was damn hard to get a reading. Since they hadn't taken me hostage I had to assume they had an interest in my continued liberty—perhaps as a contact. Or maybe they *were* going to let Goodman go, now they had what they wanted. The trouble being, sooner or later someone was going to realize there was no stopping us by merely possessing the material. It was too easily reconstituted.

And why had they used Soheila at all? Why didn't the masked marauders just do the job themselves?

To show me the depth of the conspiracy? A hint how powerful the cabal was?

I'd, of course, been warned not to bring the cops into it. From the start. And while I felt I could rely on Ellard personally, once he enlisted the apparatus it'd be apparent to anybody I'd broken the contract.

I couldn't trust Cifelli to act contrary to his interests.

And Penny was out of the question.

So I was on my own. I hadn't a clue where Goodman might be, or where to start to find out. So, instead, I decided to take a break from the nunt and drive on up to visit Francine at Marsden's Meadow.

I figured by now she'd have been somewhat detoxified and might be receptive to a show of support. Also, she might have an idea or two. Or an opinion on mine, one of which was that Soheila's apparent amateurism could be a great cover for someone actually the mastermind.

But first I stopped off at Goodman's and fed the Phantom. He was a lot like Brian—took the food and tried to bite my hand.

*   *   *

The drive out to Santa Barbara was uneventful but allowed me a chance to recharge my batteries somewhat and stop berating myself for having been so inept. There really hadn't been anything more I could do for Goodman at the time. I'd had to turn over the "ransom"—our notes and basic intelligence on their operation—per their demands. But the truth was, I knew that they had to be aware we retained much in our memories plus an unspecified amount of backup material on hard disk, so the odds of working a straight trade had always been slim. It was your basic first, go-through-the-motions, unproductive step.

I turned into the long drive that led to Marsden's Meadow, parked in the retro-chic elegant gravel car park, and rang the bell.

The same semi–Addams Family keeper of the keys opened the door, unhesitatingly let me in, and delivered me to Mrs. Wagner (whom, thanks to Goodman's observation, I would forevermore think of as Angela Lansbury).

"You should have called to make an appointment," she said when I apprised her of my desire to see Francine.

"I know, and I apologize," I said.

"It's not a question of protocol," she replied, "so much as the prescribed regimen for detoxification and therapy. We don't permit visits the first week."

"Well, that's really the reason I didn't call. I was afraid you might not permit it, and thought I'd do better pleading my case in person."

"And what is your case?" asked Angela. "A little more paranoia vis-à-vis this institution?"

I decided there was nothing to be gained by pointing out we'd discovered her deception on the previous occasion when a stand-in performed the role of Iris.

"All I can say is it's tremendously important, and it doesn't impact or reflect on this institution at all. Actually, my partner and I recommended Marsden's for Ms. Rizetti."

"Yes. I found that a little odd."

"We wanted to show we appreciated your help last time"

(too thick?) "and I hope you'll bend the rules a little again for me. You know I'm Francine's best friend, and I'd never do anything to harm her."

"Well, she has been having a difficult time of it, and hasn't been in the best of moods—"

"I'll just bet."

"I'll give you ten minutes." She pressed a button on her desk. Lurch knocked and entered. "Show Mr. Bradley to the Oleander Room and I'll have Ms. Rizetti brought down."

And he did and she was.

The room was beautifully and tastefully furnished. Elegant English country-home fashion. Some, perhaps antiques—though, I'm sure not without design, nothing of a fragile nature— and blooming oleanders (you were expecting maybe mums?) through the large multi-paned windows, beautifully backlit by the afternoon sun.

A lot of oak and chintz, heavy art-glass lamps, a blend of Stickley and English of the period. Old money, secure in its taste, no one'd seen any reason to redecorate in fifty years, I felt sure. And they were right (though my personal tastes ran more to chrome and leather and high-tech doodads of the remote-control variety).

And speaking of remote control, the door opened and Francine was gently prodded in.

"Visitor," said Lurch.

"Visitor," said I, indicating myself.

"Patient," replied Francine. "Or, more brain-washedly, 're-covering addict.' "

She didn't rush into my arms. But she didn't throw anything, either. I gave her a hug. "Tough?" I asked.

"God-fucking-awful," she said.

"Gonna work?"

"Better. I don't want to go through this again. It's, on top of everything else, ridiculous. They've got me making beds and cleaning johns—well, I've cleaned a few Johns in my time."

"Me, too," I allowed, certain of at least two entendres. "I think the idea is to humble you."

"I think the idea is to save on housekeepers."

"So, do they give you anything to ease the pain?"

"Bromides. Every Cloud Has a Silver Lining. This is the First Day of the Rest of Your Life. And each day *feels* like the rest of your life."

"Give yourself up to a Higher Power?"

"Right, I *gave* myself up—my connection was definitely higher."

"You seem in good spirits. You're going to make it."

"I don't really know, Mark. I mean, I'm dealing with a society here that counts boredom as a virtue. Well, hoist by my own leotard."

She really looked terrible, of course, but that was to be expected. The physical withdrawal wasn't over, wouldn't be for a long time.

"Just a minute," she said, crossed to the closed door, opened it, and said something to the attendant (guard?) just outside. He took out a pack of cigarettes, proffered them, she took one. He took out a disposable lighter, lit it for her. She nodded, he closed the door, and she crossed back to me.

We sat on a pair of matching oak-framed, chintz-cushioned lounge chairs, and she took a deep drag of the cigarette.

"What's that? You're smoking now?"

"Of course. All the CA's and the AA's get you heavy into tobacco and coffee. The lesser of twelve evils."

"But why start another bad habit?"

"It's just what they do. I suppose the idea that life isn't devoid of pleasures. Or maybe to get customers for some future different rehab. Anyway, what's going on?" And she coughed, evidently not that far along in her new addiction.

I told her that the terrorist thing we'd been relatively sure of was definite, and that Goodman had been taken hostage, and that I'd delivered our tapes and notes and disks as "ransom."

"Well, hell, I've got backup on most of that stuff," she said.

I was sure she would. And that someone would figure that out before too long.

"So what're you going to do about him?"

"I don't know. I was hoping maybe you'd have some ideas."

And she suddenly doubled over, stubbed out her cigarette in a large ceramic ashtray with a look of occupational therapy about it.

"Oh, Jesus."

"What, what? Shall I call somebody?"

"No, no—it's the regular bends. My system is outraged by all this clean living and has to scream every now and then."

"I can't get over them not giving you *some* medication."

"The prevailing theory is it builds character. Ooh."

"What should I do?"

"Nothing you can do. This one's not that bad. I didn't throw up or anything."

And after a few moments she straightened up and started breathing normally. Took out a handkerchief and mopped her face.

"That's so awful. I'm sorry, Fran."

"Yeah. Hey, I'll get through it." And she took several very deep breaths. Then, "All right, now, what are we going to do about Rayford?"

"You do care."

"I care about the whales and the spotted owls, too. The snail darter I'm not too sure of. Of course I care."

"I'm not exactly sure we should do anything. They might just let him go."

"They're not big on that. In case he'd have future value. And if they really want to stop the book, he's the only lever they have."

"Well, they didn't take me."

"Maybe because they need you on the outside to be their advocate. Penny'd certainly put somebody else on if you guys just simply copped out. He'll need handling, and maybe they figure you're the logical one to do it."

"It sounds a little complex for the kind of mental power they've shown up till now."

"No, convolution's their thing. Oh, god!" And she gripped her stomach again and rolled onto the floor in pain.

I kneeled alongside and put my arms around her. "That's cruel, not to do *anything* for the pain."

"They do, they remind you you have nobody to blame but yourself."

"That would snap *me* out of it, just by wanting to kill them."

And that spasm passed.

"So what else happens?" I continued as we both got back into chairs. "You have physical therapy?"

"Of a sort, yeah."

"And group, psychological counseling?"

"Right. It's, you know, the only game. It works for some. Maybe me. I just take it"—she paused for pseudo-dramatic effect—"one endlessly boring day at a time."

And of course only in part to give her a little relief from the subject: "Have you been able to find out if Iris is here?"

"Yes. She's locked up on three—real loony tunes."

"So there's no way you could get to her?"

"Well, actually, I sort of lucked out and connected with her during 'Nature Walk' (it's my nature *not* to walk) when they got a little casual and let us semi-crazies mix with the heavy-duty ones."

"Learn anything?"

"Well, the truth is, she's pretty much out of it—and fading faster than the Lambada."

"But did you get anything?"

"My reading is she thinks her father did it."

" 'Thinks' her father? Doesn't she know? Or she wasn't there?"

"She says no. Who can be sure? She says she thinks she was someplace else, maybe Courtney. Then again, she remembers being with Junior—but that was later, right? My take on the whole thing is she thinks her father did it and they're letting Carey take the blame."

"Not the most farfetched scenario."

"Then again, she says there are moments when she's not so sure she didn't do it herself."

"Oh boy."

"Or at least been a bad girl—whatever that means. Typical abuse-victim stuff."

"And great witness material."

"Right. Oh, then we met a second time and she said she'd been thinking about it, and thinks maybe she wasn't there but at the warehouse."

"What warehouse?"

"The only one I know anything about is the one Appleton and Carey were supposed to have someplace in the Valley, for their videotape operation. Remember?"

"Crescent Videos?"

"Yes."

Why was I getting a slight feeling in the pit of my stomach?

"You wouldn't happen to know where it is?"

"I doubt there'd be anything actually there. My reading of the whole operation was it was a scam, not a real company."

"But they might have real assets. Where?"

"I couldn't possibly remember."

"Well, maybe it's listed."

"As I recall, not."

"Shit."

The old tease held it for another minute.

"But of course, I've got it in my computer."

35

Rayford Goodman

Some hours, days, weeks, years later somebody came in the room. I still had my blindfold on, so I couldn't see who. But I could tell. It was the anti–Summer's Eve lady.

"So, what's new, sit down, let's have a chat—come here often? What's a nice girl like you doing in a terrorist dump like this? What's your sign?"

She punched me on top of my head.

"Not big on chitchat, I can tell. Listen, there's an easier way to get rid of unwanted bodily hair—called electrolysis."

She punched me on top of my head.

Then she took some foul cloth from I don't even begin to want to know where and stuffed it in my mouth, which she then taped shut.

There were easier ways to get me stop talking.

After that I could hear several more. Two? Two dragging a third? A bunch of muffled grunts (which might have been talk). Some fussing around fairly near—five, six feet?

Some more business. Several people left. Maybe all. Footsteps down the echoing hall. Door creaking open. Banging shut. Quiet.

But not exactly. Someone else?

"Ermm?" I mumbled through my gag.

"Ernglk" came back. Somebody else.

So there were at least two of us. Hostages. To be killed. (Because why should they kill me and not him, whoever him

was?) Although, truthfully, that wasn't my biggest concern.
Him. Whoever.

But I was bound, blindfolded, and gagged, with not too
long to live.

What would MacGiver do?

MacGiver would turn to his six writers and say, "What
would I do?"

But I wasn't really quite that scared. Because?

Because I was still doped up, that's why. I wasn't being
rational. I wasn't facing reality. Reality was I was god damn
going to be god damn murdered! There, that's better. Now
I'm terrified. Scared to death, but facing reality. Wonderful.

Then the door at the far end quietly opened, just a tiny
squeak. And I heard light footsteps trotting toward me. And
then—ah, the lady Eve—loosening one end of the tape that
held my gag. I could still smell the burn on her arm. Obviously she felt a little resentment over them doing that. Not
too unreasonable. She moved off, then stopped a moment at
the whoever nearby. Some kind of fussing. Then lightly running back down the corridor, door quietly clicking shut.

It took the better part of, I don't know, eight minutes?
(Whatever the better part is.) And I was able to spit the gag
out.

Of course I had no idea who might be the other person
being held. But the chances were pretty good we'd be on the
same side.

"Hello?" I said tentatively.

"Goodman?" said the other party, the one I'd been counting on to rescue me.

"Holy shit—Bradley?"

"Hi! How ya doing?"

"Never better. What happened?"

And he told me about the ransom, being driven to the
Valley, being met by Soheila, having all our records and tapes
taken—in a swap for my freedom. Go deal with these people.
And then going to see Francie, and how she'd reached Iris
and gotten some clue to the whole crazy scheme.

"I thought it was an amazing bit of good fortune," he went

on, "that she'd be the one person, outside the network, with an insight as to where you might be."

True.

"So I went back to the office," Bradley went on, "booted up Francine's computer, turned to the files she told me, and found the location of this warehouse—which is supposed to be the central shipping point for Crescent Video."

"Up to there I like it," I said.

"Well, it's a pretty fair-size building, in a remote part of town—or, really, outside of town. I don't know what it was used for originally, but there's a railroad spur with a lot of grass overgrowth, so it hasn't been used in a very long time. A loading dock half-rotting. And every indication of a very inactive business."

"Thank you for that enlightening travelogue. So what happened?"

"Well, since I didn't have any proof you were actually being held here, I couldn't go to the local authorities. And since all our contacts were pretty remote and whatever legal ones outside their jurisdiction, I couldn't go to Ellard, either."

"Never mind you couldn't do. What could you do?"

"I thought the first thing was to ascertain if you were in fact being held here."

"And how did you do that?"

"Well, I didn't actually do that. I mean, *now* I know."

"They caught you."

"That's about the long and short of it. But it wasn't as dumb as you might think. My options were limited."

"Your options to be caught?"

"To approaching the building. It's also on some sort of a lake and canal arrangement. Maybe whatever they originally manufactured used water, or shipped out on water."

"You mean the building's like on piles?"

"Right. Anyhow, there was no approach on three sides, so I had to try sneaking in on the one."

"Which, let me guess, didn't work."

"Hey, listen, a little appreciation here. I took that chance for you. And I'm in this spot because of you."

"You're right. I'm sorry. Took a lot of guts."

"These guys are serious. They blew up a delicatessen."

"I know. And they plan on blowing up Beverly Hills High next, can you believe that? They're making the bombs now. Here."

"Which I think kind of lessens the chance of their letting us go."

"They are fucking going to kill us, man," I said.

"Yeah. And the worst part is, damn it, I don't think they even intended to take me," he went on. "I was supposed to be the conduit."

"You are a conduit! Whyn't you at least get Cifelli, you weren't sure of Ellard?"

"Who's any more sure of Cifelli? He has his own interests, don't forget."

Meanwhile, I'd been yanking and pulling at my bonds, and I'd begun to feel a little give. Not in the ropes, in the post I was tied to.

"Listen, how are you situated? Can you see the pole behind me?"

"I'm blindfolded," he answered. "I was gagged, too, but somebody came and loosened it enough for me to work it out."

"Me, too. It's a lady terrorist."

"They're usually the worst kind," said Bradley—I thought a little sexist.

"Well, they burned *her* arm to teach *me* a lesson. Gives you a clue the kinds of minds we're working with. I got a feeling she might have resented it. So what's your situation? You tied to a post, too?"

"Yes."

I'd kept pulling and there was a definite give to the post.

"Well, my pole seems like rotted. I'm going to give it a big yank. This old place, half the ceiling's liable to fall in if I did knock it over."

"But given the alternative ..."

"Right."

"You really think they plan to kill us?"

"Bradley, they *really* plan to kill us."

"I hate that. And they have some nerve. After all, it isn't as if we were doing anything really to merit this unwarranted show of hostility. There *are,* any reasonable person would allow, many merits to their contention. The Palestinian people *have* legitimate grievances which *should* be addressed in a fair and timely manner, and though of course their methods of bringing these matters to the attention of the world lack subtlety and reasoned presentation—"

Which is, of course, when I realized.

"Hey, hey, hey!"

"Yes?"

"You been given a shot?"

"Shot?"

"Drugs. Injection."

"Well, yes, as a matter of fact, now that you mention it. Of course, that must be why there is a relative absence of *real* apprehension and only a semblance of intellectual appreciation of the potential damages to self and substance."

"OK, OK. I think we can safely say it's an upper. Like me."

"I guess we can."

"So this is drugs."

"Yup."

"And you used to take them?"

"Yup."

I was feeling pretty damn good myself, and real unreasonably optimistic.

"Whatever made you stop?"

There was a pause while he thought it over.

"Oh, yeah," he said. "Fear of death."

Meanwhile, I'd kept pulling and yanking, and now the post was definitely showing a lot of give. The cement at the base was crumbling, too. I might not be able to actually break the pole, but it looked like I could break the edges of the hole holding it.

"Well, here goes," I said, and gave it an all-my-might shot. There was a serious noise overhead, and a shower of whatever, cement, roof stuff, who knew.

"Uh-oh," said Bradley. "Pretty loud."

I stopped, and we both held our breath. After a beat the door opened at the far end. Music again. Coltrane. (This guy sure liked saxophone.) Took a few steps in. Stopped. I didn't dare breathe. Then, finally, after six years, whoever it was took a few steps back and closed the door again. "Whoever" not bothering to take the long walk to check us out. ("For want of a nail ...")

"OK?" Bradley whispered.

"I think," I said. "I'm gonna try again. Feels like it'll go." And I gave a real big tug, the ceiling threatened—but somehow less noisy—and I pulled the pole toward me and out of its mooring. I was free!

Well, still tied hand and foot. But free to crawl.

I inched my way over to Bradley.

"OK, I'm right here." I could feel his body next to mine.

"I'm going to put my face next to yours."

"My prayers, answered at last."

"Bradley!"

"Go, man."

"Try to get your teeth into my blindfold, let's start with that."

Not that easy. Tried, nothing. Tried, nothing.

"Goodman. In my side pocket, there's a little tube ..."

"Yeah?"

"Binaca."

"I'm going to punch you out."

But this time he managed to close his teeth around one of the sides, unfortunately including some hair.

"Got a good grip?" I said.

"Um," he answered.

I pulled my head steadily back, then, feeling the blindfold absolutely taut, lowered my head and slipped down. It came off the top of my head, and my head fell onto Bradley's lap.

It was the first time in our relationship either of us passed up a straight line like that.

Our hands were tied with that kind of ratty twine that's like a rope with splinters. Made it hard to work our way out.

Bradley worked for what must have been at least half an hour, back to back, trying to untie my hands.

"I've got to stop," he said finally. "I'm cramping. My fingers just won't work. Amphetamines will do that, too—they cause cramping. Which is only a physical manifestation. They tell the story of the Bowery bum, totally wiped out, a speed freak hitting absolute rock bottom getting the weepers and deciding to confess. Reaches into his pocket, finds a scrap of paper, a nub of a pencil, begins writing his parents, 'Dear folks, Just forget me, write me off as a total loss. I'm no good. I've wasted my life, ruined my health, betrayed my family and friends, and squandered every opportunity I've ever had and any right to love or respect ...' and he reaches into another pocket for a handkerchief, instead finds an overlooked pill, quickly swallows it, resumes his missive, '... so if there's ever anything I can do for you, please don't hesitate to call on me as nothing would give me greater pleasure than to place my entire resources at your disposal ...'"

"Let me try you," I said, since sticking to the subject at hand struck me a better idea.

It was a better choice, whether because I had a superior digital dexterity or a smaller dose of dexedrine—who knew?

I sprung him, my fingers bleeding and cut—but he was free. He first untied my hands, then we each did our own feet.

Standing up was hard—for him, leg cramps; for me, my back was killing me.

Again the door opened—we were standing up, no place to hide! All that work, and they were still going to kill us!

There were a lot of voices all excited and talking at once, most in, I guess Arab. But some English.

"Shut up, cool it. OK!?" which could only be Appleton. "We are doing this according to the plan. You two, go in and take them out. You guys, get the equipment."

Then there was some more mumble mumble, while we both stood there, frozen—no options, really, except to see if we could take someone with us, hopefully Appleton.

"Wait. What?" Appleton again. "All right, back there. I got to take this call. Final instructions."

And the scuffling feet, the noisy creaks unbelievably moved back outside the door, which slammed shut again!

"I would say we have five minutes, tops," I said to Bradley.

"And I would say the variables are reasonably predictable and a curve of likely consequence—"

"Shh! Shut up, Bradley."

"Right."

"OK, quick, we got a break. They left the light on. So you take the left, look for any possible door, window, vent, whatever. Go!"

And go he went.

I circled right. The place was real big, bad news. Mostly empty, good news. Whatever there was we'd either find or know there wasn't.

I did find the explosives, a mixed batch of Semtex and TNT and other shit I didn't know much about. But no doors, windows, vents.

I circled back to rendezvous with Bradley.

"Trapdoor," he said. "Grille. Water underneath. But locked."

"Nothing on my side. Except the bomb stuff."

I looked to see if we could come up with anything to pry open the grille. *Nada.*

"Bradley, did you see *any*thing we could use as a wedge?"

"Nothing. How about the explosives? No, but I guess we'd need a match."

Which is as close to kissing him as I was apt to come. I *had* a match. One. To go with the one cigarette I always carried in case I bumped into Luana or other major aggravation.

"We'll need something for a fuse. I didn't see any there. The twine—the rope they tied us with!"

I loosely braided the bits of twine together and laid it out toward the cache of explosives. I lit the match, which flickered and almost went out with my heart, teasing me a minute before burning, lit my cigarette, handed it to Bradley.

"No thanks, I don't smoke."

"Cute. Hold it to this end, make sure the rope stays lit."

"Shouldn't you first put the *other* end ..."

"No time. Do as I say."

And I carried the loose, unlit end over and to the mixed pile of stuff, half unwrapped, and stuck it under the pallet on which it'd all been dumped. I covering the end of the twine with bits of the excelsior packing. I was hoping there'd be a battery and primer for the Semtex, but if there was, I didn't find it. So I just took a stick of dynamite and rushed back to Bradley.

"Fuse still lit?"

"Still lit."

"OK, take me to the trapdoor," I said. He dropped the lit cigarette. And stepped on it!

"No!" I croaked, and before he could grind it underfoot, lowered my shoulder and blocked him off it. "We need the light, dummy!"

I bent down, picked up the cigarette. No, it couldn't be out! It looked dead. I blew on it gently. Nothing. Oh, god! Blew again, it flickered. I put it in my mouth, sucked, not yet—sucked harder—and it came back!

"OK, now quick!" I said to Bradley, who'd picked himself up and started rubbing his bicep where I'd blocked him.

"I think you could have communicated your feelings in something of a more civilized manner," he began. I made a fist, and a face to go with it.

"Follow me!" I hissed at him.

Then the door opened again, and the gang started to return. Whatever had delayed them was covered. We were totally out of time. No two ways about it now, they were coming for us!

We scooted to the trapdoor, I lit the stick of dynamite, stuck it under the lock, grabbed Bradley, and the two of us started running away from the area.

We were spotted. The group (a fast look made it five plus the obvious taller figure of Appleton) started after us.

"Don't panic," said Appleton. "They can't get away. Spread out."

But one or two shots were winged our way.

"He said don't panic!" I called out, to remind them.

Which is when the grille blew.

"Now!" I said to Bradley and we both raced toward the trapdoor.

The gang was momentarily stunned by the explosion, and there was a good bit of dust and smoke as a result. Plus some falling roof and lathe and plaster and whatever.

"Over there, they're over there!" I heard Appleton shout.

Which, unfortunately, we were. But, fortunately, we'd succeeded in blowing a good-size hole in the floor, and—you had to take some things on faith—Bradley *said* the building was over water—we just plain jumped!

36

Mark Bradley

One good thing, the water was fairly warm, as you might expect of the area. One bad thing, it was filthy—oily and smelly and full of things that go yich in the night.

There might have been a shot or two fired as we jumped— I seem to have an aftertaste, back-of-the-mind sense of it. But it hardly mattered, since obviously we hadn't been hit. Or at least, I hadn't.

I struggled back to the surface, happy in the circumstances that we were pumped full of amphetamines and full of strength. Goodman broke the water close beside me, and immediately put both hands on top of my head and pushed me back under! I thought it a most inappropriate time for aquatic games.

We wrestled like that for what seemed like eons and must have been about ten or fifteen seconds when a resounding, ear-splitting, water-magnified explosion rocked us both, and sent the waters roiling.

And then Goodman let go and we both broke the surface to find various flotsam and jetsam all about us, most either still afire or smoldering. Above, there was an intense wave of heat pressing down on us as beams and bits and chunks of this and that continued to fall and there was no doubt the entire building was ablaze and we'd been saved from being crushed only by having been immersed at the time of the explosion. Score one for the wit and reflexive action of Goodman.

As we swam off to a side and distanced ourselves enough to be able to stop and gasp for breath, I said, "Well, it certainly looks like your makeshift bomb went well."

Goodman, who seemed less in control of his respiratory functions, seemed barely able to nod, and I could see in the flickering light of the flames that he was experiencing some distress. Given his cardiac history, plus the added stress of the drugs, I was fearful all this action might prove a little too much.

"Why don't you lie back, float, and let me pull you to shore?" I suggested.

"Not on your life," he said. And passed out.

I got a grip under his chin with my left hand, lay on my back, and was able to paddle with my right and negotiate the few yards to shore. Only it wasn't exactly shore, it turned out to be a pier, the top of which was beyond my reach. And to make matters worse, I soon discovered there were, in fact, no hand grips or even an irregularity in the wooden piles to afford purchase for a grip merely to maintain my position. Meanwhile, behind me a series of further explosions rocked what was left of the building, which crumbled and collapsed entirely into the lake in a loud hiss of steam and billows of smoke.

We'd escaped, but now I could see no ladder or way up to the street level. And was quickly expending my remaining energy merely to keep us both afloat.

Shit, had we come through this whole thing only to die now, drowning one foot away from safety? I couldn't believe it!

And evidently, neither could the fates, as out of the blue—well, out of the smoky black, really—a looped rope hit me on the shoulder.

Never one to look a gift rope in the noose, I slipped it under Goodman's arms and watched as a shadowy pair of figures hauled him up out of the water, and out of sight at the top.

A few moments later, the rope was lowered again. But this time, as I fastened it under my armpits, no one pulled up. I flicked it, to signal I was ready, but received no response. However, when I tugged against it, I did find, fortunately, that it was secured to something above me, and using what felt very nearly my last ounce of energy, managed to pull myself up.

As I cleared the wall, got first one leg, then the other onto solid ground, I could see Goodman sitting up groggily, apparently OK. And no one else—only the taillights of what, if I were called to testify, I would have to say was the rear of a Mercedes limousine, receding into the inky gloom.

As far as I could see, there were no survivors but us—though one body had made it to the street. There was certainly no building left.

I didn't know how or why Cifelli'd been on the scene (by design or following the trail Goodman and I'd left), but he must have got there just as the warehouse exploded, and in the firelight seen us in the water. Co-conspirator or good Samaritan, I was grateful.

And by the time the first sirens could be heard doppling their way to this remote spot, Goodman had recovered sufficiently that we were already in my car and heading back toward our own, hopefully more ordered, world.

I suspected things were back to more traditional values when the dripping, begrimed, torn, and bloodied Goodman's first post-trauma words were, "Sorry about your upholstery."

Back at Goodman's house, having accepted his offer to crash, we'd both showered and soaked our weary muscles, donned comfy terry cloth robes that bore the crests of the chic hotels from which they'd been pilfered, and were sharing a cup of tea before retiring, he, "for medicinal purposes," having laced his with rum. He was big on "medicine."

It was about four-thirty in the morning and the radio was on. There'd been a five-minute summary of the news, but no mention of the little to-do in the Valley, and the announcer returned to their regular programming which was "Steve Sommer in the Morning"—the show I'd heard about.

"Back again on KHIP," said Steve in one of those bass voices that rattle the windows. "And again to our E to E feature—Edison to Elvis, where you challenge us to find any American jazz record from the earliest days, give us thirty minutes, and if we can't come up with it, or make a phone connection with someone who can, you get one thousand dollars. Here we go, on callback to Mr. Dudley Harrison of Compton. You there, Dudley?"

"I'm here, Steve."

"And once again, the side you wanted?"

"Billie Holliday, and the name of the tune was 'Carelessly.' "

"Right, Dud, so it was, but too, too easy. You folks out there, you're not challenging us! For Dudley Harrison, at four-thirty-seven in the a.m., here's Billie Holliday, with Teddy Wilson and his orchestra, on the 1937 Brunswick recording of 'Carelessly.' "

And the music played, with the vocal in that plaintive, pain-filled voice of Billie Holliday that was so unique even I could recognize it.

"Cootie Williams on trumpet," said Goodman absently. "Johnny Hodges, alto . . ." And he yawned hugely and nodded off.

I wondered if I'd done the right thing letting him talk me out of going to a hospital to be checked over. Though I really didn't have a whole lot of choice.

I shook him gently. "Why don't I help you inside—you'll be more comfortable." He didn't answer, just sort of scrunched down deeper in the chair. I took the cup out of his hand, grabbed him under the shoulders, and lifted.

"Come on," I said. "You'll sleep better in your own bed." And we headed out of the room, as Billie Holliday continued to suffer and wail the woes of mistreated women from time immemorial—or at least since they started making records.

I'd made myself comfortable on the couch. Steve Sommer had saved the owners of KHIP another thousand by coming up with Duke Ellington's "Diga Diga Doo" on Okeh Records, recorded July 10, 1928, for a Spencer someone from Calistoga, and my eyelids were getting heavy.

Till now I'd been tired and wired—exhausted but still too tense from the wild activity to try to sleep. But it was finally getting to me, and the last thing I remembered before nodding off was thinking about a program that used to be on television with David Janssen called "The Fugitive," where he was falsely accused of a murder that'd actually been done by a one-armed man, and remembering when they'd had the climactic confrontation between the Fugitive and the One-Armed Man and missed a great setup to have Janssen say, "All right, put up your duke."

But for the life of me, I didn't know why that came into my mind.

The next morning was the afternoon. We both slept the sleep of exhaustion and didn't wake till after twelve. Though Goodman was already up when I woke, and I heard him talking to his cat in the garage.

"Listen, don't get mad at me. *I* didn't want to be away. Wasn't *my* idea you miss meals. Ow! You got some nerve. Bad dog! Bad dog!" And the door slamming and a very disheveled-looking partner peeking into the living room.

"Damn cat bit me! Sorry if I woke you."

"No, no, I was up. Time anyway. Did you listen to the news?"

"Yeah, they had it on. Fire of unknown origin destroyed the Crescent Video warehouse. Preliminary speculation the extreme heat and intensity might be due to the highly flammable nature of the tapes, etcetera. But suspicion of arson isn't being ruled out. 'Round up the usual suspects!' "

By which time I was up and getting into the sweater and jeans Goodman lent me in place of my own ruined clothes.

"Was there any mention of bodies?" I asked, wondering what to do with the extra eight inches of waist.

"Yeah. Six altogether. One unidentified woman and five men, one who appeared to be exceptionally tall."

"Any traces of a basketball?"

"Didn't say. I guess that's the end of the threat," said Good-man. "I suppose you think we ought to report all this."

"Well, I don't think we're supposed to keep it secret," I replied, slipping into a pair of too-large running shoes.

"You don't, eh?"

"No, I think it will make some very interesting reading—in our book."

"Ah," said Goodman, liking that a lot better.

At breakfast, at Mirabelle's—everybody else's lunch—we began planning the rest of our lives.

"So," I said, "I think it's safe to say the threat's ended."

"Right. The delicatessens of the Western World are safe again—if you don't count calories."

He was certainly in a good mood. "So, we agree Appleton was the main momser?"

"Sure looks that way."

"And that Wesley Crewe was killed to frame Carey Jaeger so Stacy would need big bunches of money to defend him and go back to work."

"Which would mean plenty of money for everybody and everything, including the terrorist stuff.

"And," I continued, "how would we go about proving all that? Which we'd have to do, even if just for the book."

"Uh-huh," said Goodman (instead of "there's the rub"). "We can't. We don't really have any proof."

"On the other hand, once we lay it out in the book, who's to sue us? Of course, Stacy, who I can't help feeling was just a dupe in all this. Maybe first we just wait and see how the verdict turns out. If they find Carey not guilty, maybe we don't have to do anything, about that part of it, anyway. The murders. And the terrorist things we can decide later," I heard myself saying, wondering what had happened to my character to *be* saying that.

"Not that simple," said Goodman. "We've got to prove the whole conspiracy shit or I'll still wind up losing my license for jury malpractice, or whatever it is when you break the rules."

"So what do you suggest?"

"To paraphrase an old joke—eat first, think later."

"OK, what're you going to have?"

"The hot cakes with the bacon and the butter and the syrup and the egg."

"Ah, clever. That way, given your cardiac condition, you may not have to deal with a 'later.' "

"Or, the eggs Benedict."

I kept still. Some people don't take criticism well.

We still hadn't decided how to go about things—and which things—by the time breakfast ended. I didn't doubt the terrorist threat had ended with the death of the conspirators in the warehouse fire. Not that there didn't remain loose ends. Soheila, for one. Lateef, for another. But surely the heart of the cabal (there's a title) had perished. Although, to make our roles credible, and even be able to tell it, we were going to have to be able to prove our assertions.

The part that was going to be most difficult would be solving the murders. The police already knew it was Appleton's gun that'd killed Wesley Crewe. That they hadn't acted on it told me they didn't like the neatness of finding it virtually at the scene of the crime. Plus, of course, Carey's initial confession.

Also, it was possible Carey had access to Appleton's gun, being his partner in the video business. But the police didn't know Appleton's involvement in all that other stuff that we did. It made the case for him being the killer much more compelling.

At any rate, our next step was to zip down to Pico and Lateef's Transmission. For two reasons. To confront Lateef on his part in Goodman's abduction, and to get back Goodman's Cadillac (which I felt fairly certain loomed equally large in his mind).

It came as no great surprise that Mr. Ali Lateef (or "Al," as Goodman referred to him) wasn't standing by his door with a smile on his face, waiting for us.

In fact, not only was no one standing by the door, the door was locked. A crudely lettered sign read: "CLOSE. DEAD IN FAMLY."

So, it began to look as if Mr. Lateef might not prove a loose end, after all.

We went a block and a half down to B.J.'s, where Goodman was delighted to find his refurbished Cadillac awaited.

"So, what happened to Lateef?" asked Goodman innocently.

"He was in that fire last night at that warehouse. You hear about that?"

"Yes, I think so," said Goodman. "He died, huh?"

"Yeah, it was on TV," said B.J.

"Then we won't have to pay for the transmission, right?" said Goodman.

"No, I already laid it out," B.J. replied worriedly, and in fact, looking very much like someone mounting a scaffold, gingerly handed Goodman the bill for his car.

As I watched my partner take slow breaths, trying to avoid hyperventilation, B.J. mentioned to me conversationally, "You know, they say Lateef didn't die from the fire—the guy was shot."

37

Rayford Goodman

I'm sure Francie would have said it was the leftovers from the uppers they'd shot us with when we were hostages, but we did get awful smart in an awful hurry and it all came together for us. In theory.

To prove it, Bradley had gone off to the radio station to pick up the tape, as I went to the local Mama Bell to flash my charms on a contact I had over there.

We both hit paydirt. Though I still owed a dinner and no doubt a share of my favors to a certain Martina Gonsalves, longtime supervisor of operators and coveter of cops—a category she loosely included me in, accent "loosely."

With closing arguments over and the jury charged and out for deliberations (there but for the grace of the law went I), we'd approached Stacy Jaeger to host a get-together to clear the air, and possibly hear some new ideas might be useful in the expected appeal. (It always floored me discovery of new evidence wasn't grounds for an appeal, but you had to instead find some mistake in procedure. Which they always could. Another thing always drove me crazy, when you challenged a judge for any reason and the judge who ruled on the judge was the same judge you were challenging. Not too big a surprise he almost always found himself to be the fairest, most impartial person this side of Solomon.)

Anyway, Stacy turned us down because he wanted to stay close to L.A. in case the jury came back with a verdict.

So, instead, we asked Ken Curry if he'd mind holding it in his office, which he didn't and that's where we'd gone, I'm happy to say in my newly restored classic Caddy, which drove like a dream. Whatever Lateef's other little faults, rebuilding transmissions wasn't one of them.

Fixing the car cost more than the car did new, but I couldn't see replacing it with one of the crappy ones they put out now. And it was still way under half as much to boot. (B.J. did knock ten percent off for aggravation, which I still thought was light, but what're you gonna do?)

We pulled into the subterranean garage under 2020 Avenue of the Stars, and I drove around till I found two empty spots together I could straddle so nobody could open a door into me.

"They could cite you for this," said Bradley.

"Yeah, and you think I wouldn't rather pay whatever, twenty-eight bucks, than a new dent?"

"Got a point," he admitted, getting out on his side, toting his purse, or whatever the hell it was over his shoulder. "OK, let's go get 'em, tiger," he added with a bit more perk than I was comfortable with. But I was a little more concerned with the odds on us tigers entering the lion's den.

A sheepish Soheila, not meeting anybody's eyes, for good reason, met us at the door and led us into Curry's roomy office. Stacy, Stacy, Jr. (who I guess was either back from Bali or hadn't gone), Gilbert, and Curry were already there. So was Attorney J. Wadsworth Nichols, in case legal shit happened. Wise move.

Stacy grunted a greeting as he surrounded a plate of appetizers he was compulsively stowing away. When he finished one plate, Soheila brought another. He seemed pretty depressed—a long way from the funster making all the jokes last time I'd seen him. Pass on the boar's balls.

Stacy, Jr., still bruised and scabby, sat sulking in a corner and didn't answer our hello. (*We* didn't do it.)

Gilbert, on the other hand, immediately crossed to Bradley and tried to mend fences (or who knows what else), talking fast and intense while Bradley kept his game face on.

Curry fixed me a drink and one for himself.

"Terrible thing, out at the warehouse," he said, breaking the ice—and dropping some in my glass.

"Terrible," I agreed.

"You know, Appleton and I weren't on the warmest of terms, but my god, to die like that—"

"Oh, they identified the body?" I asked innocently.

"Didn't you hear?"

I just shrugged. I hadn't needed to hear.

"Uh, why don't we keep to neutral conversation till we have some indication where all this palaver is going?" said the lawyer, Nichols.

"Gee, counselor, I thought that *was* neutral," I said.

He gave me a smile looked like a banker foreclosing the farm. I gave him one back. "Freed any good shnooks lately?" I said.

"Very funny," said Nichols.

"I thought it was funny," said Stacy. "Not riotous, mind you, but mildly amusin'," slicking back his blond hair.

What *I* found mildly amusing was Stacy, maybe the world's greatest actor, who'd played parts with every possible accent, still pretending he had his original southern one underneath it all.

At any rate, that was when Lieutenant Lewis Ellard arrived, to interrupt all this hilarity, which seemed to surprise the others.

"We invited Lieutenant Ellard," I explained. "He has your basic vested interest in all this."

"All what?" said Stacy.

"Mr. Jaeger, please?" warned Nichols, I guess on general principles.

"Any news on the jury?" Stacy asked Ellard, with a look at Nichols. "I can ask that, can't I?"

"They've stopped deliberations for the day," Ellard explained.

"I told you that," said Nichols.

"You said sometimes they keep going."

"If they're close to a decision," added Nichols in a somewhat gentler tone.

Stacy adjusted his glasses, sighed heavily, and since his mouth was open anyway, stuck in a rolled rumaki.

Gilbert went to get some white wine for Bradley, and Lieutenant Ellard allowed himself to say yes to an Amstel.

"By which I gather," said the ever alert Nichols, "you're not here in an official capacity."

"Far as I know, I'm just a guest," said Ellard, accepting the beer. The smile on his light brown face could be taken for cat-and-canary or just plain looking forward to good lager. I did like that man.

"So, what's all this here?" said Jaeger. "Are we ready to start whatever?"

"Not quite yet," I said. "We're waiting for another associate of yours—Mr. Armand Cifelli."

Ellard rolled his eyes at this news, turned to me, and whispered, "Do the words 'highly irregular' strike a familiar note?"

"Wait," I whispered back as he slowly shook his head, wondering what he'd been talked into.

At which point Soheila let in the aforementioned Mr. Armand (The Dancer) Cifelli, accompanied by his bodyguard.

"Why don't you wait out there with Augie?" Cifelli suggested. The guy took a quick look at the potential for trouble, hesitated. "It's all right," Cifelli added reassuringly, and gave him a little push.

Gilbert offered Cifelli a drink, which he turned down with a shake of the head.

"Now, then," said Nichols, opening an attaché case and removing a tape recorder. "Since we have no idea why this meeting has been called, and in the interests of accuracy and to avoid any potential misunderstandings, I trust all you gentlemen will have no objection to my recording this?"

"Why, Mr. Nichols," said Bradley. "You sound nervous."

"I am not nervous; I am merely cautious."

"We don't have any objection at all," I added. "In fact, my partner has a tape of his own he'll be playing by and by." And

Bradley opened his tote bag and took out his own machine, putting it on the desk.

"So what's this all about?" said Stacy.

"Well, part of it is the book, and our mutual interest in it," Bradley began. "By the way of a report, some things we've learned and which we'll be including in the writing."

"You got us all together for a special hurry-up meeting at night to talk about the book?!" said Curry.

"Well, you're right," I said. "That's a stretch, isn't it?"

"Though, of course, it all *will* be in the book," Bradley repeated.

"Not necessarily," said Nichols. "Contractually, the final say redounds to the principal, Mr. Jaeger, under certain specified circumstances."

"Not exactly a given," said Bradley. "Even authorized."

"Gentlemen," said Cifelli. "May I suggest we stop this bantering about the book? We're not here to talk about the book; let's talk about what we're here to talk about."

"As always, Mr. Cifelli is on the nose," I said. Then, looking at his big Roman schnoz, "Which is what they call, I think, a figure of speech."

Cifelli smiled. Sort of. Best keep going.

"We all know—I'm sure Lieutenant Ellard, too—about this whole terrorism thing, and you people's involvement in it."

"Wait, wait, wait," said Nichols. "There is no prior stipulation—"

"Let the man talk," said Jaeger. "There's no point in having a meeting if every time someone starts to talk, you stop them. We do have an interest in the book. Though I got to say right here, I got *no* connection with any terrorism."

"Thank you, Mr. Jaeger," I said. "OK. Here's what. The terrorist things, this office's involvement, whatever, that's all stuff I leave to Lieutenant Ellard. Pretty much. I mean, we were taken hostage and threatened and all that. But the actual *doers* it looks like died in the fire. Whether that includes all the planners and the people behind the people, that's another thing."

"I'm a little at a loss," said Ellard. "I was under the impression you had something to tell me about that conspiracy."

"Well, yes, we do," interrupted Bradley. "But it's part of a larger mosaic."

"You see," I went on, "even once the whole PLO whatever thing came to the fore, even those of us didn't believe Carey murdered Wesley Crewe, and Courtney and the Malouf girl, assumed the murders were part of the Arab thing."

"And not so?" said Ellard.

"Not so," I went on. "Not that they—or at least the first one—wasn't *used* by the conspiracy—"

"To get financing," Bradley finished for me. "The insiders, for starters, let's just say, Ely Appleton, knew that once Crewe'd been murdered and once Carey Jaeger had been charged, the Great Provider, Stacy Jaeger—"

"The money cow," I interrupted, god knows why. "Oops," I started to apologize. "Put my foot in my mouth that time."

"Good thing you didn't put it in *my* mouth," said Jaeger good-naturedly.

"It was no secret he was overextended," Bradley went on. "Investments had failed. Money was tight. But once his son was indicted, Mr. Jaeger would have to go back to work, if only to finance his defense."

"And once he went back to work, with the kind of salaries and fees he gets, there'd be money for the 'cause,' too."

"Which I *do* support; I do feel the Palestinians have a right to a homeland of their own."

"Which we won't go into here," said Bradley. "That's not our point. Our point is the murder, once committed, coincidentally benefited the cause, and whatever else it financed."

"*But,*" I took over, "once it occurred to us the murder might not have been done by Carey *or* by the terrorists—just capitalized on by them—that opened up a whole other can of beans. Or worms."

"Beans, if it's all the same," said Gilbert.

"I think we should stop right here," said Stacy suddenly.

"As you wish," seconded Nichols.

"Don't touch that dial!" I said, trying to lighten things up.

"You don't want to hear what comes next," I said to Stacy. "Which leaves the impression it's maybe because you don't want to hear who did it."

"You can think what you want," said Jaeger.

"As long as we are here," said Ellard, "why don't we listen to what they have to say? It's not a court of law. And they could say the same thing in my office. But if it involves any of you, wouldn't you be better off facing your accusers?"

"I don't think so," said Nichols.

"Let me put it this way," I went on, ignoring Nichols and addressing myself to Jaeger. "You don't want to hear any more because you believe we're about to accuse your daughter of murdering her boyfriend."

"Cut," said Jaeger. "Just cut. Stop the tape."

"We're *not* . . . going to accuse Iris," I got in before Nichols could stop the tape. "Iris is innocent. She may not even have been there at all."

Jaeger put his hand on Nichols's arm, stopping him from turning off the tape. It was obviously what he thought *had* been the case. "All right, I take it back," he said. "Go on."

"We think she was with Courtney, since she'd had a fight with Crewe and left."

"Physical fight, you're talking physical," said Stacy.

"Whatever," I said evasively. "Clear she was no stranger to abuse." (To whom it may concern.)

"But Courtney's dead," reminded Ellard. "Which is a tough witness situation."

"Yes, but we later independently established Iris was with Courtney—actually on the night Courtney was killed—the pizza thing."

"Doesn't do a lot for proving her innocent," said Ellard.

"Well, in a way. Operating on the theory one killer fits all, we have reason to believe she wasn't at the compound at the time. Ditto Courtney's—she'd been taken away, I think Stacy, Junior, will confirm, *before* Courtney's murder."

"Again, family vouching for family," said Ellard.

"Right. OK," I continued. "Let's start with Carey didn't do it. And so, if not Carey, who?"

"Appleton!" said Soheila suddenly. "It's clear—it has to be Appleton."

"Good candidate," agreed Bradley. "Certainly right up there in the top two or three."

"And conveniently dead," reminded Ellard.

"Yes. The unfortunate fire," said Cifelli, real droll, like he didn't know who caused the fire.

"Well, we'll leave that open," I went on. "Let's go back to the premise we started: it wasn't Carey, it wasn't Iris—take my word for the moment. Who does that leave? It wasn't Kiji Malouf, she's dead. We know it wasn't Courtney, ditto. Stacy, Junior, the security man placed in the basement editing room. Scratch Stacy, Junior. Gilbert?"

"Hey!" said Gilbert.

"Very long shot. What possible motive? Serve the interests of his boss, Stacy, upset his daughter was being abused? But would Stacy be dumb enough to open himself to blackmail? And she'd always stayed with people who abused her. They both knew that.

"Well, it was true we'd noticed Gilbert started to dress awful nice, lots of pocket money—but that could easy be for going along with framing Carey, the family decision. And it was the family decision—Carey takes the rap. I think mostly because Stacy thought—or was led to think, or wanted others to think he thought—Iris had done it. And Iris was his favorite. And the weakest. Iris had to be protected. If Carey 'confessed' he could serve the family interests and had the strength and backing to do it.

"So, Gilbert went along with that—which took care of where his new bucks were coming from. And the security guard also placed him in the screening room at the time of the crime. All in all, scratch Gilbert."

I took time out, my throat going dry. "Just let me freshen my drink."

"That left," continued Bradley, picking right up, "very few people. Appleton, of course; Stacy himself; Soheila; and Curry. But it couldn't be Appleton—we happen to know that personally."

"And it couldn't be Curry," I cut back in. "Because the day

Kiji Malouf was killed, he himself was attacked and drugged and left unconscious."

"Nichols, the lawyer?" suggested Bradley.

"I'd be very careful if I were you," said Nichols.

"We're merely hypothesizing here," Bradley reminded him.

"No," I put in. "You're in the cast of characters, but there's absolutely no outside connection. You do business; you make money; you're on retainer. But you do all that for the same kind of money for other celebrities and wealthy people. You're excused, counselor."

"So, let me see if I'm following you, here," said Stacy. "That leaves merely Soheila and—me?"

"So it would seem," said Bradley.

"Well, Soheila," said Stacy, "I guess I must have grievously underestimated you."

"Oh, no, you don't," said Soheila.

38

Mark Bradley

Y ou're not going to pin it on me," Soheila continued. "Oh, no."

"You're certainly not going to deny your part in the hostage business," I pressed.

"What—what did I do, exactly? I met you and took possession of some papers and tapes. And not even me, technically— the people I was with. But murder, no way."

"Well, surely you can't for a minute think I . . . ?" said Stacy. "You yourself said money was the motive—to get money for the cause. And to do that, to get me back to work. Well, if I wanted to get back to work, why would I need all this elaborate conspiracy? I certainly wouldn't need a way to convince my own self!"

"That's, of course, a good point," Goodman agreed. "So, in effect, if Soheila's telling the truth and Jaeger's telling the truth, then what's happened—we ran out of suspects."

"I still don't understand about Appleton," Gilbert said. "Why couldn't he have been the killer?"

"I admit," agreed Goodman, "he certainly looked good there for the part. Except one thing."

And here he took a long, leisurely sip of his drink.

"Which you're going to tell us in your own good time," said Ellard.

"Hey, this is the fun stuff," said Goodman. "The being a

hostage and attacked and almost killed and all that shit wasn't a walk through the park. So don't begrudge us this."

"Go on," agreed Ellard.

"The reason it couldn't be Appleton was, under the one killer fits all theory, he couldn't have done Malouf."

"Why?" said Curry. "He was gone from the office at the time, supposedly looking at locations. Who can prove that?"

"No, actually," Goodman continued, "he wasn't looking at locations—he was bombing delicatessens. Or delicatessen singular. Which he couldn't exactly use as an alibi."

"But which," I broke in, "moved us back to square one. Any of the suspects involved in the terrorist cell, even peripherally, would *know* that. So they would also know he'd have no alibi."

"But you're out of suspects," reminded Nichols.

"Right you are," said Goodman. "Which means we cleared somebody wasn't really in the clear."

"We were tricked somehow," I continued.

"There was a moment there, we thought maybe Curry. When we found out his name wasn't Curry but actually Khouri, originally Lebanese. He had easy access to Appleton's gun. And could possibly be squeezed into the Muslim conspiracy mold, except—"

"Except for Ms. Malouf's attitudes around him. While she was Muslim maiden proper around Appleton," I continued, "she was women's lib, don't take any shit around Khouri, or Curry."

"Added to which, he drinks, smokes, and makes sex jokes—not your working Muslim."

"To say nothing of having airtight alibis for at least two of the murders," added Curry himself.

"Right," said Goodman. "And you were very slick about the first one, too. So cool you actually didn't even offer an alibi. You knew someone else would bring it up. And they did—you were home at the time. Not only home, but with proof. So heavy into jazz—everybody knew that—what could be more natural than you'd challenge Steve Sommer at KHIP to find an old early side and maybe pick yourself up the thousand-dollar prize."

"That's right," said Curry, a touch smugly. "What could be more natural?"

"Which you 'naturally' figured we'd find out—Wingy Manone, right?" Goodman said. "The one-armed trumpet player."

"Which *I* remembered," I added, "when for some reason I thought of 'The Fugitive' the other night, that program with David Janssen and the one-armed guy. Association."

"So, associate the fact that the night Crewe was killed I was home, being *called* by the friendly folks at KHIP," said Curry smugly.

"Yep," agreed Goodman. "That sure seemed to be that."

"To say nothing of the fact when Kiji Malouf was killed, I, too, was attacked—knocked out with an injection, in fact."

"That, too," admitted Goodman.

"So where is this conversation going?" said Nichols, whose interest we had at last apparently piqued.

"Why don't we start with playing the tape?" said Goodman.

I took the tape I'd gotten from the station out of my tote bag, popped it into the machine I'd put on the table earlier, and pushed "play."

I'd cued it to Steve Sommer, saying, "And that was, for Jack Smith in Glendale—I presume *the* Jack Smith, the too-easy Benny Goodman recording of 'Zaggin' With Zig,' featuring Ziggy Elman on Columbia records, recorded in 1939. Coming up on three-twenty-five a.m. And who do we have now, Rick?"

In response to which another voice, presumably the engineer, came on. "Steve, we have Ken Curry, of Beverly Hills, on callback."

"Right, hello, have we reached Ken Curry?"

"Yes, you have, this is Ken," said the voice which *was* Ken Curry. "Do I get to win the thousand?"

"You get *bupkes,* Ken," said the sonorous voice of Steve Sommer.

"I don't know about *bupkes,*" said Curry, his voice fading. Then, something something ". . . atch you . . . is one."

"No, no, my man," said the announcer. "You asked for Wingy Manone and 'Tar Paper Stomp.' "

". . . ight."

"OK, it's on the Champion label, recorded in 1929. Here, at three-twenty-six in the morning, for Ken Curry, is Wingy Manone and 'Tar Paper Stomp.' " And so it went. Goodman signaled me to turn the machine off, and I did.

"Well, I don't know exactly what that does for you," said Curry, "but it certainly places me in my condo, called *by* the station near enough to the time of the murder that I couldn't possibly have gotten out to Malibu."

"So it would seem," I said. "And very neat."

"This is where one of you guys say, 'Too neat'?" asked Nichols. "There are alibis which are valid."

"Right," said Goodman. "And then again, there are alibis which are—"

". . . contrived," I segued smoothly, starting to notice we were finishing each other's sentences. Good god!

"Yes, Curry or Khouri talked to the disc jockey at around three-thirty. Yes, it's on tape. Yes, they called him, not vice versa," said Goodman.

"But you will also notice his voice fades in and out," I continued, "which, of course, suggests not a line phone but a cellular, like in a car cellular."

"They called *me*," insisted Curry. "Check with them what number."

"We did," I went on. "And you're right. They called you at your condo."

"And a Miss Martina Gonsalves of Pacific Bell," said Goodman, "will also testify that you have call-forwarding."

"Call-forwarding doesn't provide any records," put in Nichols, perhaps beginning to assemble his case.

"No," said Goodman, "but cellulars do, because there's a charge on cellulars, not only for outgoing calls but incoming, too. Direct or forwarded. Which, frankly, I think is a little gouging, but that's why I don't have one."

There was a moment while those in attendance digested this fact. Then Curry mounted his counterattack.

"So that proves what? That I might not have been in my condo? That I might have been in my car going, say, for a pack of cigarettes or a six-pack of beer?"

"It proves you could of very well been in Malibu the night Wesley Crewe got killed," said Goodman. "And all the trying to reach you, which you could easily have had also call-forwarded—provable again—would have let you set up a time schedule for the murder, retreat, and hang around for the mop-up call you knew would be coming."

At which Stacy Jaeger rose, like a prehistoric behemoth, eyes flashing. Ellard and Goodman quickly restrained him.

"You—you, who I trusted like my own family, who I shared everything with ..." he raged, seeming to put on bulk in his fury.

"Wait, wait, wait, don't fall for this!" shouted Curry. "Plot, all a plot. Listen, hold it—hear it all out!"

"That's right," said Goodman. "Hear it all out."

"Pass for the moment whether I might have been in my car and not my condo, which doesn't make me a killer," Curry went on, a speck of spittle forming at the corner of his mouth, strangely compelling one's attention. "Why would I do it? What do I have to gain? You admit I'm not part of the Palestinian thing."

"Money, for one—you are part of the good-living thing," said Goodman, indicating the luxurious furnishings, the lavish setting.

"Nah, that goes on whether Stacy works or not. More or less. Get back to the one killer kills all, your own theory," insisted Curry. "Why would I kill, say, Courtney?"

"Because she knew—she told us—Carey wasn't even at the compound till you roused him and got him back. Another reason you had to keep driving around and keep unavailable till almost five. What a shock that must have been for your patsy to have taken a hike and be out of range for the pie in the face. Because, too, in spite of Nichols and everybody telling her to cool it, to go with the family decision for him to take the rap, she *wasn't* cooling it."

"She'd gotten Carey to recant his confession," I found myself stepping in again. "Which prompted the second so-called terrorist attack, allegedly on Judge Steinberg, but actually intended for Carey. Well, she wasn't about to sit still for that. That was definitely way over the line. She'd come to us."

"Just to dot the *i*'s and cross the *t*'s," Goodman added, "she'd also hidden Iris once she got out of Marsden's, and Iris was a loose cannon if the wrong person put a bug in her ear."

"OK," said Curry, noticeably perspiring now. "All terrific theory, great supposition. Adding up to nothing. Forget motive, forget opportunity, forget profit, even—if I *could* have killed Wesley Crewe, if I *could* have killed Courtney, you still have no case because I could *not* have killed Kiji Malouf. I was unconscious. I'd been given an injection, and you've got medical evidence to prove it."

"In spite of the fact your shirt was torn *up* from the cuff, yet your jacket pulled *down* to your forearms, meaning the jacket was *off* when you got the shot," said Goodman.

"Oh, give me a break!" said Curry sarcastically. "Now you're going to say I gave *myself* the injection? Aren't you forgetting one thing?"

"The hypodermic needle. No, I'm not forgetting. You're sweating, I notice."

"It's hot, I'm under pressure."

"Uh-huh. Well, the day you discovered Malouf, who I suggest *was* part of the conspiracy, which was to cover up that Iris was supposed to have killed Crewe, for the sake of the cause, started catching on it was *you* likely killed Crewe and Courtney, her fate was sealed. Whether she let on to you or threatened to tell Appleton, I don't know. But you had to get rid of her."

"The needle!" insisted Curry.

"Getting there," said Goodman. "Heat affects you. You just told us that. We can see it in your sweat. Yet the day your secretary was murdered and you were found unconscious in your office—a very *hot* day, by the way—the air conditioning was working just fine. But you had the window part open behind your desk, letting the cool air out."

"I like, uh—"

"No, no. You tore your shirt and gave yourself a shot. Then you tossed the needle out the window, where it would fall twenty-six stories and break into a zillion pieces, put your jacket back on around your wrists, tearing the button, and calmly passed out on the floor."

"Nev-er, nev-er prove it," said Curry, mopping his brow.

"But it is probably time for you to stop making any further statements," said Nichols.

This time, when the raging, infuriated animal that was Stacy Jaeger in full frenzy exploded from his seat and lunged for Curry, neither Ellard nor Goodman even tried to stop him.

"No, no," screamed the actor, "you are going to say it with your own lips, you are going to confess, you are goin' admit it!"

And he grabbed him in a huge bear hug and began to squeeze.

"Stop it, get him off me, stop it!"

But no one was stopping it. Cifelli, because it wasn't his style to be so intimately involved physically—or his immediate business; Ellard because he hoped there *would* be a confession; Gilbert because why would he?; and Nichols, because this might be the basis for a police brutality defense.

"All right, all right!" hissed Curry, red-faced and wind-deprived.

"It won't stand up," said Nichols.

"Uhm," said Cifelli, very, very quietly—I may have been the only one who overheard it—"keep your mouth shut, counselor."

Advice which Nichols evidently saw fit to heed, as he opened it once, thought better of it, and stopped.

"Just ... fucking ... tell me why," whispered that great, familiar voice, gaining an incredible intensity by its very softness. "I'm a Muslim my own self," he continued, to our surprise. "I worked for the cause. I did. Though I never for a minute thought it was for terrorism. But you—why?"

"Not for the cause, you don't for a minute think *I* was into the noble cause? What, because I'm from the Middle East? Oh, they were—Appleton, Soheila, Malouf ... Lateef, the whole group. But me? Never. What the hell did I care?"

"Why? Why?" It was a wail now, a feral pain. "Why would you let me think my daughter killed a man, set me up to let my son take the blame? Why would you *do* that to me? You were *family*!"

"Yes, I was family," said Curry with scathing sarcasm. "Family when there was dirty work to be done; family when there was no one else to pick up the pieces, to clean up the shit. Family for everything but *being* part. And god damn it, the man *was* scum," he went on. "He beat your daughter, the daughter you would go to such lengths to protect, oh yeah. OK, with Crewe dead, everybody jumped on the chance to get you back to work. You'd have to, to pay for the defense of the designated dumbo, Carey. And, incidentally, of course, finance their real agenda. *I* did it to get you back to work, for the *work*!"

"For the work?" said Jaeger, so softly, so woundedly southern again.

"Yes. Because of who I am, don't you get it? All right, I'm not family. But I am the man who 'discovered' Stacy Jaeger. I am the man who coached Stacy Jaeger. I made you! I took that young, unformed, raw talent. I saw the spark. I fanned the flame, I brought it to a blaze! I created an ac-tor! And when Stacy Jaeger acts, *I*, really, act. When you are somebody, I am somebody!

"And when you—slothfully, irresponsibly, lazily—give it up to just ... hang around and dissipate your gifts, throw away your beauty, get monstrously out of shape, and turn into, become this ... waste of one of the greatest talents the world's ever seen ... Well! I wouldn't have it! How could I allow it? No, no, no!"

And he fell sobbing into a chair (not exactly breaking ground theatrically).

"So, the thing is," said Goodman, "he did it for show business."

*   *   *

And we could have left it like that. We'd seriously discussed doing just that—to make it easier on Stacy, who'd had such a rotten run.

But making it easier on Stacy made it easier on Curry, too—and that, justice, some kind of belief in accountability, we couldn't allow.

"It's possible you even think that," said Goodman with a sigh, "that your motive was for art. *I* sure didn't want to believe the real one."

At which everyone in the room sort of froze. It was as if the audience had watched the curtain fall, and suddenly, on the way out, discovered the play was still unfolding.

"It was just a bunch of little things," I continued. "Iris, in the classic form, calling herself a 'bad girl,' your fury at her mistreatment by Crewe, which somehow came off less as concern than jealousy. Your own slightly off phrasing, the 'poor darling.' The *way* you said 'darling.' "

"Stacy, Junior's hints at some sort of—we first thought— incestuous abuse," said Goodman. "Which Courtney seemed to be saying, too." (Nobody dared look at Senior.) "Till we rethought it."

"Appleton's mention that the Malouf girl was too old for you, you liked them even younger."

"One by one, a piece here, a piece there ..."

"... and it started to take shape," I went on. "It's true, my partner was a little more reluctant to accept the idea."

"It at least seemed like people didn't do things like that when I was a kid," explained Goodman. "I know people say they just hid it better. But it's hard for me to believe. It's *still* hard."

"But eventually it became very clear," I continued as Goodman was angering perceptibly, "once we figured out the mechanics, what the real motive was."

"What?" whispered Stacy. "What are you saying? You can't be saying what I think you're saying!"

"I'm afraid so."

And it was terribly hard. To tell this great man how much he had failed to protect his daughter.

"Good old Uncle Ken—just one of the family. Better, not even actually a blood relation. More than mentor, more than a life devoted."

"No," said Stacy.

"Has to be said. Curry was, is, has been, in love all these years with Iris. Since she was a child. *Especially* when she was a child."

"Oh, god," said Stacy, terribly softly.

"And poor Iris, the classic victim, emotionally destroyed by confusing feelings and repulsion and violation from kindly, good, sweet, devoted ... Uncle Kenny."

It was the most awful silence I ever heard in my life.

39

Rayford Goodman

Because life had to go on, Jaeger sort of collapsed. Really like the air went out of him.

Nichols stayed cool. The world's ugliness was no news to him.

Cifelli you never could read—but I knew how he had to be feeling, we had enough in common. (Curry was lucky it wasn't Cifelli he'd have to face.)

And Gilbert and Soheila, my take was they just wondered how it all would affect them.

So what happened next, Ellard took over and life started to go on. He cuffed Curry to the arm of his expensive desk chair and phoned in for the army of uniforms, detectives, or whatever that would make it all official. I don't recall the words "I'm booking you for murder one." Maybe when they did the mini-series.

Gilbert was pretty much in the clear. Certainly nothing you could or would want to get him for. Soheila was another story. Since she was part of the post-murder conspiracy to blame Carey (thinking Iris had done it), and, of course, the hostage thing, I wasn't too thrilled to see her walk.

But I knew Stacy was going to give her a rough time, and I had to admire what was I guess his deciding the show had to go on. With, I thought, a lot of class, and no shortage of guts, he reached back for his sense of humor to pronounce the sentence. "We'll start off by giving her a hundred hours of community service at the B'nai B'rith—after which we'll see if Cedars-Sinai can't use a bedpan volunteer. I may support a Palestinian homeland, but that don't include terrorism and blowing up folks' delicatessens." (I had the feeling that was where they'd made their fatal mistake.)

Nichols was conferring with his new client, Curry, while Bradley found himself a word processor and was furiously making lots of notes.

I, on the other hand, by one of those freaks of acoustics, was surprised to overhear a whispered conversation across the room between Lieutenant Ellard and Armand Cifelli. Went like so:

"Of all the bodies at the warehouse," Ellard was saying, "only Lateef's had bullets in it."

"Unlucky guy," said Cifelli.

"In addition to being a terrorist hit man, I've got some unofficial information he was the creep who undid my woman."

"He was a dope peddler and a pimp," agreed Cifelli.

Which I guess indicated Ellard knew something about Cifelli's action out at the warehouse, because he added, "And now I owe you." Something he clearly found painful. "A policeman *can't* owe . . ."

He was definitely looking for some kind of nice way to say it.

"An entrepreneur?" suggested Cifelli, helping him out.

"Yeah."

Cifelli took a moment—these guys really played big with silences. Thought about it.

"I guess that would be up to you to decide," he said finally.

Then they each kind of examined their nails, the ceiling, their shoes. Nothing much more was going to be spelled out. But Ellard couldn't help asking, "I don't suppose you have any idea where she might be?"

"The wife?"

Ellard nodded. Cifelli took a moment.

"I don't think you'd like to know," he said.

*   *   *

It was Saturday night. The notes were long since noted. The new charges filed, Carey released, and the "twelve men tried and true" discharged—including the women. Officially, my jury duty was/would have been over.

The three of us automatically looked right as we passed the Jaeger compound on Pacific Coast Highway. We knew there wasn't anything to see. The house was way back out of sight of the highway.

But we had a feeling old Stace would be in the kitchen, fixing something scrumptious for the boys, Junior and Carey; daughter Iris; and just possibly Soheila, too—if she finished her duties as the *shabbas shiksa* in time. Solomon would have loved it.

I was at the wheel of the smoothly humming Caddy, top down, hair blowing in the wind. On the far side, my partner, Bradley—and between us, our stellar researcher and reformed doper lady, Francine Rizetti, we'd just picked up from doing her time at Marsden's Meadow.

And now we were heading for our traditional wrap party at Chasen's, which would be extra-special for having Francie back.

I had a nice Sinatra tape going ("Come Fly With Me"), the evening was balmy, and you had to feel life was getting better.

Once in the city, we approached from the west, meaning we were on the Hughes Market side of the street, where I could park for nothing. But I thought the occasion being so special and all, I'd compromise my principles and pop for the Chasen's valet robbers.

That meant a U-turn in the middle of Beverly Boulevard, which would have been no trouble if the fucking shmuck hadn't zoomed out of the parking lot full speed without so much as giving a look across the street. (He said later he thought looking right and left was enough. Like ahead would of been too much to ask?)

But I wasn't going to let a dented right front fender on a car that was only like family to me and I'd just spent a small fortune on restoring ruin the evening.

Besides, there was a good chance the restaurant would

pop for it. They had insurance for those things. (And I was actually right—if you didn't count making a U-turn across a double line.)

Anyway, I put a good face on it. I've learned to take life's little shafts in stride, and I pride myself on not letting things upset me unduly. It was only money, not really pain and agony, and aggravation, and wondering why why why me, god, what have I done to deserve this?—the way some people might have.

Julius met us at the door and told us "our table" was ready. Which, having the above total under control, felt pretty good since we weren't exactly regulars and only ate there to celebrate solving a case or winning the lottery.

We passed through the front room, where Cifelli was seated (I think he inherited George Raft's table) and got up to greet us. That really was something.

"Evening, Mr. Cifelli," said Bradley.

"Mark. Ray. And a very special welcome to you, Miss Rizetti," he said, taking Francie's hand and kissing it.

"Thank you, Mr. C., it's nice to be back."

"Among the living," he prompted.

"If you call this living."

"Yeah, I do," he said, smiling.

"Please, sit down," she answered, also smiling. (But he didn't.)

"Whenever you're ready, Mr. Goodman," said Julius.

"Yeah, let's go. Nice to see you," I said to Armando with a little finger wave. Then he did sit back down, and we followed Julius into the tap room and our preferred booth, right away joined by a captain.

"Enjoy your dinner," said Julius and split.

"Would you care for something from the bar?" asked the captain, a line I seemed to have heard before.

I ordered vodka rocks with an onion. My young greyhound ordered vodka and grapefruit juice. And we both held our breath.

"And for madame?" asked the captain.

"I'll have a Drew Barrymore," said Francie.

The captain raised his eyebrows, and she explained, "It's a Shirley Temple with heroin."

After she got our reaction, she laughed and changed it to "Kidding. Make that Perrier, or any of them, doesn't really make all that much difference."

We put on brave smiles. The truth of the matter is she did have that haunted, wounded look people who've given up whoopee seem to have. Like something's been amputated.

"We could pass on the drinks, if it'll make you more comfortable," said Bradley. It wouldn't make *me* more comfortable.

"No," said Francie. "I've got to get used to it. And I doubt anything's going to really make me comfortable."

"Bad up there?"

"Walk in the park," she said. "Central Park. Actually, about what you'd expect. Though they're pretty skilled at it, and the amenities aren't bad. But the chef's not exactly world-class—since who's hungry anyway except for a sugar rush—and most of the upkeep's out front where you can see it. The rooms leave a lot to be desired, plus the plumbing's about a hundred years behind state-of-the-art. The good news is the water's so hard it makes for very entertaining douches."

We'd told her a lot about the case on the drive down, but there was still a good bit of detail left.

"Tell me again about that pizza business," she asked while we were waiting for drinks and no drink.

"We established it was Iris's choice, the pepperoni—which was common knowledge," said Bradley.

"She was practically addicted," I added. "Oops, sorry."

She laughed.

"Curry, after killing Courtney, and finding evidence Iris had been staying with her—didn't know she'd been picked up by Junior—figured he'd throw up a smoke screen that could implicate her," Bradley went on.

"What we figure is he went elsewhere to try establishing an alibi, *then* called in to have the pizza delivered to the already dead Courtney's, with the knowledge the thirty-minute delivery time frame would at the minimum muddy the waters, obscure the trail, and mix the metaphors," he wound up.

"OK," said Francie as the drinks came. "OK pertaining to the exposition, not the refreshment. And while you were hostages?"

"They kept us doped up. Me especially," I said. "First some downer to get me to tell the truth, then some upper, so they could understand what I was saying."

"Poor darling," she said with I got a feeling something less than total sincerity.

"Oh, it was horrible," I lied.

"Youth is wasted on the young," she said. "And dope is wasted on the old," she added.

"It really was uncomfortable," I kept on.

"I wish I could have done it for you," she said.

Then, rather than do a whole big thing about the drinks and order another round, I called for the menus (which I then pantomimed to the guy he should do me again by pointing to my glass on the sly).

"We have the deviled beef bones tonight, if you like, Mr. Goodman," said the captain.

"That sounds wicked to me," said Francie, meaning she'd try it. And being a good sport.

I went for a steak and salad, not too original, but awful good.

And Bradley went off on a seafood medley of some sort.

"So, Cifelli really was keeping an eye on you guys, it turns out," she went on. "At the warehouse."

"Yes," said Bradley. "I don't know that he would have intervened in any event. I like to think he would. But it definitely seems he broke with the group when he found they were into Palestinian terrorism."

"Well, he's a businessman," I added.

"But breaking with them would *cost* him money," said Bradley. "He was in on the take."

"It wasn't money," said Francie.

"Oh?"

"He wouldn't want to be involved with financing any PLO kind of stuff."

"Because of business, because in the end it would *cost* money," I suggested.

"Because," said Francie, "of who he is."

"Who he is," repeated Bradley. "The Mafia has a policy?"

"No, dummy, *Cifelli* would have a policy."

We just stared at her.

"Being half Jewish," she finally explained.

"Cifelli!? Sicilian Cifelli?"

"According to the Xerox of his birth certificate, on file at the INS and available under the Freedom of Information Act— and my general curiosity and competence—his father was Guillermo Alfonso Cifelli, and his mother, one Isabella Levi, not all that uncommon in Italy."

It took a moment.

"I hadn't thought of it," I admitted, "but I guess there are Jewish Italians."

"There are Jewish everythings," said Francie. "There are *Chinese* Jews."

"Now, *that's* scary," said Bradley. "The food alone ..."

Which was when our appetizers began arriving (plus my drink), and we pretty much concentrated on that for a while.

The food was like you'd expect. And the company good. One of those nights you remember. Here we were the three of us, admittedly not the same as when Francie and I were hot and heavy, but just the same a real good warm feeling. On a real good night.

We'd just solved a complicated, terrific case, Francie was on the road to recovery. And maybe, as my mother used to say, in the fullness of time she'd come around again and we could—you never knew.

Which was one of the better things about life, really. (After two drinks I tend to get philosophical.) I mean, it wouldn't be any fun if there was no suspense in it, you knew how everything worked out. I'd say there was a good chance she'd come around. We'd had some great times together. It had meant a lot. It was sort of almost like love, you might say.

"One other thing I don't get," said Francie, interrupting this pleasant train of thought. "Who beat up Junior? It wasn't the group that chased you, they'd just arrived, or been sent for. So who was it?"

Bradley gave me a look. "You're on," I said.

"Can't be totally sure, but my guess is it was Stacy, Senior. Convinced Iris had killed Crewe, the family position being to get her out of the picture up at Marsden's and allow Carey to take the blame, here he had a rebellious son throwing a monkey wrench into things, rescuing her from Marsden's, picking her up at Courtney's, in essence *defying* his father's will."

"The la ilahs?"

"He's a Muslim. A son defies the wish of the father, who's only carrying out the greater wish of the greater Father? A father, by the way, who we've seen has a hell of a temper. He says his prayer to Allah and brings the son back in line."

"That's meshugga," said Francie.

"Hey, he's an actor," I reminded her.

And it was nice, and it was warm, and when the bill came we charged the whole thing to Dick Penny and Pendragon Press.

I dropped Bradley off at the Venus de Penis Arms, or whatever—though the poor guy was living alone and hurting.

Thought for a moment Francie might be agreeable to spending a little R&R at my place, but she smiled in that way that said I know you're playing a long shot and I know you know there's no chance whatsoever so I'll just make believe you're kidding.

So I dropped her off, and didn't even press to carry her bag up, but watched her safely to the door.

And went home.

It was quiet.

It was empty.

I noticed the garbage was getting a little out of hand in the kitchen. So I took it out to the can in the garage, spotting a flash of gray fur dodging under the car.

I put the garbage into the can and headed back inside. I decided I'd get rid of the newspapers that'd been piling up in the living room, so I left the door open and went to get them.

But I was starting to feel a little blue. So I went to the bar and fixed myself a drink.

I took it over to the ugly easy chair I'd bought after the divorce now that things didn't have to be pretty and could be comfortable. I sat down and had a long pull on the drink.

I thought of turning on the TV, but somehow I didn't want to.

I didn't seem to want to do anything. Just sat.

Then after a while there was a quiet little squeak and the Phantom came in and climbed on my lap.

You never knew.